THE ALL FATHER PARADOX

IAN STUART SHARPE

VIKINGVERSE: The All Father Paradox

Outland Entertainment | www.outlandentertainment.com

Founder/Creative Director: Jeremy D. Mohler

Editor-in-Chief: Alana Joli Abbott

Publisher: Melanie R. Meadors

Senior Editor: Gwendolyn Nix

Published by Outland Entertainment

5601 NW 25th Street

Topeka KS, 66618

ISBN: 978-1-947659-52-0

Worldwide Rights

Created in the United States of America

Editor: Shannon Page

Cover Illustration: Jeremy D. Mohler

Cover Design and Interior Layout: STK•Kreations

For my wife, who has Thiassi's Eyes

*Detail
Area
Below*

Gosforth
and Environs

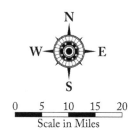

N
W E
S

0   5   10   15   20
Scale in Miles

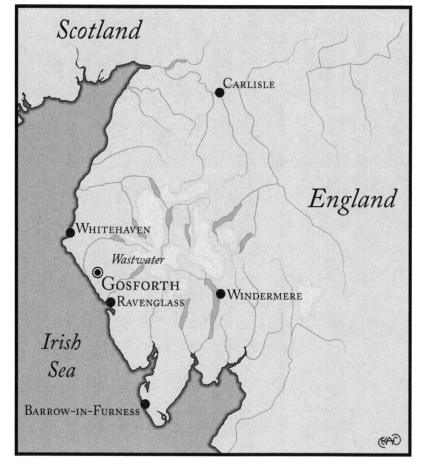

Scotland

CARLISLE

England

WHITEHAVEN

Wastwater

◉ GOSFORTH
● RAVENGLASS

● WINDERMERE

*Irish
Sea*

BARROW-IN-FURNESS

EXEGESIS I

WELL, YOU TOOK YOUR TIME!"

The roaring complaint was so unexpected that Churchwarden Michaels dropped his freshly printed parish circulars. The gale swept them up and chased them across the churchyard, pink sheets flapping between the moss-bound tombstones, like confetti at a giant's wedding.

"Jesus!" Michaels scrabbled on the worn slate floor, preferring to salvage his photocopies over his dignity. There was little hope of either. The coastal winds were merciless in winter and howled at the churchwarden in derision. He gave up and watched the last of his newsletters wing their way across the countryside to roost in far-distant hedgerows.

"I hope you don't keep your God waiting this long." The voice that had startled him was clear above the wind.

The churchwarden swallowed his irritation and peered out of the gabled porch. An old man stood by the Viking cross, unmoving in the storm, wrapped in a plain grey cloak. He was tall, burly even, but still the cross towered over him, a slender scratch against the bruising sky.

The churchwarden grimaced, summoning the courage to brave the weather.

"I'm sorry," he called out, "did you have an appointment?"

"What is the date today?"

Michaels was amazed at the lungs on the old chap. He could really project.

"November eighth. Have you got the wrong day? Happens to the best of us." The churchwarden practically bellowed, shrugging to emphasise his point in case it got lost in the bedlam.

"No, I am exactly on time," the visitor said.

It was commonplace for visitors to appear in the churchyard at all hours. The Viking cross seemed to defy time as stalwartly as it withstood the elements. Even the name was stubborn—he'd long since given up trying to explain that calling all the Northern tribes víkingar was like saying all Englishmen were pirates. No, Vikings were in vogue. All kinds of people paid their respects—although nowadays it was generally hikers on their way to Scafell Pike or sightseers checking off historic sites from Visit Cumbria guidebooks. Only academics made appointments, and the vicar's wife hadn't mentioned anything about special guests today. Besides, other than his long beard, the old man didn't seem especially professorial.

Michaels sighed deeply. He had no choice in the matter. He'd have to conduct an impromptu tour. He was custodian of a grade-one listed building, and that came with responsibilities, or so the reverend had said, not just to God, but to the fabric of society. You only had to glance at the newspapers to know that the world was becoming a little frayed around the edges. Community, shared heritage, those were the only things that could mend it.

A stitch, in time, saves nine. Armed with that thought, the church-warden begrudgingly left the safety of the porch and huffed and puffed towards the visitor as fast as he could. He took a deep breath.

"Reverend Riley normally invites guests from the university to meet him at the rectory—" he shouted, struggling to be heard, "—for a nice cup of tea and a chat first." He let the thought trail into the wind, realising mid-sentence it was a forlorn hope.

He ought to preserve a modicum of respect. This was hallowed ground, after all, and he didn't want to wake the dead. Most of the tombstones dated back centuries, to when St. Mary's was reconstructed in 1789, and he supposed if he made enough of a ruckus, he might disturb the two ancient chieftains entombed below the church itself.

Tea, he reflected, would be especially welcome on a day like today. Michaels had always thought it a shame to leave the cross standing out in the British weather. One thousand years of this, it was a miracle that it had survived at all, but there it was: a wealth of detail carved into fifteen feet of red sandstone, round at the base, rising to a square top with a cross head, each of the four sides carrying images of a horseman, dragons, serpents, and all kinds of gorgeous, interlaced patterns.

The old man didn't respond. He walked around the column, examining all sides. Close up, he looked like stone-made-flesh, weathered certainly, but also uniquely carved, with withered tattoos intricately woven over his face and arms.

Michaels kept a discreet distance. He didn't mind heathens. Ásatrú or Forn Sed, they called themselves, the worshippers of the Old Ways. Neopagans, the newspapers said. Either way, they went with the territory. Admittedly, it was a little odd to find them venerating their long-dead deities on parish soil, but Reverend Riley always reminded the laity that the Church of England was a tolerant church. St. Mary's must strive even harder, he insisted, in this day and age, especially after the referendum. If the drugs or the drinking got out of hand, a quick call to the Cumbria constabulary was all that was needed to move them along.

This man though… there was something belligerent about him. Something wild. He looked like a contestant on *Neo-Nazi's Got Talent*, , arms emblazoned with the symbols of the progenitor race. That was the other sort Michaels had to deal with. Soldiers of Odin they called themselves; mean streaks, full of piss and vinegar, telling anyone who would listen that they'd turn back the tide of immigrants, send everyone back where they came from. In fairness, Mrs. Jones had said much the same thing at the Parish Council last month. It had fallen to Reverend Riley to point out that her beloved Vikings were immigrants to these parts themselves.

Michaels decided to try his own voice of reason.

"Beautiful, isn't it, the cross? I have a pamphlet inside the chapel if you'd like to know more."

If he could get the man out of the storm, so much the better. He might be able to hear himself think. There was still no reply. Instead the man continued to prowl around the pillar.

"Are you from the museum? The V&A?" Michaels probed.

"Jorvik," the old bear grunted at last.

"Ah, Jorvik! The Viking Centre! Have things recovered after the flood? I went to York Minster and saw one of the temporary exhibits."

The churchwarden was delighted to have placed the visitor. The York Archaeological Trust did all kinds of work in the community, even sending actors on tour. That would explain the booming voice. Authenticity, that was the key, even if things went a little askew when looking down the long lens of history.

"In that case," Michaels continued, "*Heill ok sæll*, be happy and healthy, Mr.… I'm sorry, I didn't catch your name."

The old bear offered a sly smile.

"You speak the Northern tongue, do you?"

"Well, churchwardens in the Anglican Communion are legally

responsible for all the property belonging to a parish church. I like to think I have a duty under ecclesiastical law to keep up to date on everything to do with the cross and the people who made it." He was starting to go hoarse. "As the Bard said, 'How far that little candle throws his beams! So shines a good deed in a weary world.'"

"The eighth of November," the man said. "There is a saint whose feast day it is?"

"Well, we don't really go in for all that business at St. Mary's, but you are right. One of yours as it happens. St. Willehad of Bremen. Well, he was the first Bishop of Bremen, but he was an Englishman. Local chap, born in York. Placed in charge of converting the Saxons, sometime... well, before this cross was carved. Escaped a big rebellion, if I remember correctly."

"Very good, Churchwarden. That is quite right." He seemed lost in thought.

Old age comes to us all, thought Michaels, and he was about to prompt the man further when he emerged from his reverie and spoke.

"My name is... Chandler."

Michaels brightened, then felt compelled to explain. "One of my favourite authors, Chandler. In fact, I'm currently rereading *The Long Goodbye* for the eighth or ninth time. Terrific stuff, that."

Michaels was brimming with enthusiasm, so much so that he barely noticed the wind drop from an anguished howl to a conspiratorial whisper.

The visitor held him with a steely gaze.

"You like detective stories, Churchwarden?" Chandler said. "Well, as it so happens, I'm embroiled in one myself. I am looking for those who murdered me. In fact, I've sent someone to bring them to justice."

BOOK ONE: FATE

NORTHERN SAXONY

ANNO DOMINI 782

In principio creavit Deus caelum et terram.
[In the beginning, God created Heaven and Earth.]

FOLKWARD SMILED, WATCHING THE INK bite into the parchment. A new copy of the Holy Writ, a fundament waiting to be filled with wonder.

The old monk looked up from the manuscript and exchanged glances with Hemming, his genial companion, who was eagerly smoothing parchment with his broad hands. Folkward blew softly on his forefinger, and the novice dutifully stretched across the table to pass a fresh candle. Simple signs for the simple life engendered by vows of silence.

Folkward's smile rarely wavered these days. As the candle flickered into life, he carefully slid his goose quill into the phial and bent his head back to his task. It was the precision that he relished—two columns to a page, a continuous flow, letter on letter, word on word, until he reached the neatly ruled margins. He scratched large, clear, beautiful letters, each one a joyful spark of creation. There were frequent pauses, dabs of fresh ink, time to stand back and savour. Time to enjoy the intimacy, the sense of surrender that came with inking His word.

If pressed, he would confess to a modicum of pride in his work. His eyesight was undimmed, his fingers still nimble—and his penmanship was renowned, or so he was told. Kings and potentates across Christendom asked for Folkward by name; and for these talents, he was grateful. They were worth a touch of backache. He did worry a little about how his shoulders hunched—he seemed to slouch even when standing tall or singing full-throated at Mass—but considered the matter a trifle in the bigger scheme of things. He was a vessel for the divine; such was the price of allowing His Word to direct his quill.

Hemming busied himself arranging the manuscript's pages into gatherings of eight and pricking the pages with a small knife to mark the highest numbered page, shaping each folio. The silence was amiable, each monk content in the halo of his candles. Folkward glided across the page as the spirit of God moved over the waters.

Terra autem erat inanis et vacua et tenebrae super faciem abyssi et spiritus Dei ferebatur super aquas.

At the edge of his hearing, there was a stirring toot of a hunting horn, although the Saxon boar-chasers with their long spears and sallow dogs often simply herded the slowest and most wobbly old sow in sight. The hogs were certainly at their fattest now.

Folkward's stomach growled in anticipation. In just a few weeks, sides of delicious bacon would be hung in the rafters, making a virtue of the smoke that thickened the air. The first crop of onions, leeks, and celery would soon be hauled from the garden. Next year, there would be fruit from the orchard. Better still, bees had settled in the thatch, which would mean all the riches of honey and an end to the pungent aroma of tallow candles—burnt mutton fat and fresh pigshit made an unholy, cloying alliance. The September harvest would soon be matched by the woodland bounty of beechnuts, acorns, chestnuts, and other fruits of the forest. No wonder his belly seemed rounder with every passing year.

The forests were the most bounteous portion of the Saxon lands, showing the sheer detail of His creation. Folkward found it fascinating. Take the oak tree, for instance. It was like a Book of Genesis unto itself, providing the ink the monks curled across the page in such intricate fashion. A wasp had once gnawed into the wood to lay its eggs, and then, in self-defence, the tree formed a gall around this rude intrusion, circular and hard-skinned, bulbous like a crab apple. It was Hemming's job to crush the oak galls in vinegar, thicken them with gum arabic, then add iron salts to colour the acid and get the mixture ready for the labour ahead. You couldn't help but wonder at the majesty of creation, revealed and replicated even in nature's minutiae. It was sobering to think that the Lord provided everything, even the means to copy Sacred Scripture. Folkward pondered for a moment, then realized that the Lord had even provided Hemming. He chuckled at the thought and arched his back, feeling his spine and shoulder blades crack.

He looked back to Hemming, now rustling around the book chests. The novice was an ungainly fellow, not quite comfortable in his own skin, but Folkward loved him all the more dearly for it. Hemming wore the ground-length tunic of undyed wool given to every novice, belted, but still so loose and ranging he was prone to sweeping every room he entered. His sleeves, three quarter length on most monks, hung all the way to his wrist. A Dane by birth, Hemming bathed at the well every Saturday, as was the custom with his people. Folkward had named him Hemming the Heaven-Scent when he first arrived although, of course, he never uttered the phrase aloud.

The Dane went barefoot, in penance for whatever mischief brought him to the abbey five years before. Folkward heard from some huntsmen that Hemming had stolen fruit as a young man, but he hadn't pried; his vows required him to avoid unnecessary speech and gossiping about a man's past transgressions fell squarely in that category. Even in his habit, the young man would smile at every Saxon woman that passed, but in all other matters, he was a model convert, a quick learner, and a fond favourite of all the monks. Folkward trusted the Lord would forgive the flirtation as a foible.

Dixitque Deus: Fiat lux. Et facta est lux. Et vidit Deus lucem quod esset bona: et divisit lucem a tenebras.

Hemming hovered nearby until Folkward finished the verse, then delivered some welcome refreshment: a wooden cup, brimful of mead. The blessed bees—God's cattle indeed! It was probably time to take a short break. His stomach could use the exercise. Folkward made the sign of the cross, nodded his head in thanks, and then beckoned his companion outside, down the short corridor to the courtyard. He stretched a little and then sat down next to the well, surveying their own parcel of creation, brimming with life and dappled by the evening sun. By the grace of King Karolus, Folkward and his fellow missionaries had brought light where there once was only pagan darkness. That was why they were here, after all, at the very edges of the kingdom. A Royal Commission, to bring the Saxons before God now that the Saxon War had brought them to heel. He peered into the trees past the stables but couldn't see any sign of the hunters. They were lazier than the swine.

My cup runneth over. He grinned as he sipped his drink, trying not to let it spill. The old monk had come a long way from his days as an earnest young scholar in York. This place was a delight, especially when it was quiet. When the brethren fell into silent prayer, the bees buzzed, the wood pigeons cooed, and you could take pleasure in all its subtle variety.

The monks were never idle. *Ora et labora*—to pray and work. That was the life of a monk. Benjamin, Artrebanus, and Genoald would educate the young while Folkward and Hemming copied manuscripts, illuminated the missal, and transcribed the gospels. Others cultivated the soil, guided the plough, planted vines, bound iron supports to the oak shaft of the watermill. Genoald was soon to fire glass for the chapel in his charcoal furnace.

They had built the monastery with a practiced eye—seeking out the proper site for their new monastic home, making sure that it stood close to the Saxon tribes and that it had fertile soil and the benefit of a coursing stream. And then, with a prayer, trees had been felled, a well was dug, and buildings began. They blanketed the sturdy beams and planks with willow branches and then daubed the walls with clay, straw, and dung. Through their toil, they heralded the Kingdom of Christ, whose holiness redeemed the bodies as well as the souls of His creatures. The monk's songs of praise, echoing into the ancient glades, had tamed the ancient Saxon forest. His song, from Matins to Compline, was the channel by which they spoke to God, its rhythmic beauty an act of homage. The monks were practicing for the glorious day when they would stand in His presence.

The monastery was visible proof that progress had been made, and not just at the point of the king's swords. Over five years of holy toil and perhaps heaven-sent good luck, the brethren had built churches, ordained priests, and made so many converts that, after two years, hardly an idolater could be found in all the lands between the

Weser and the Elbe. If the king's favour was true, there would soon be a new bishop in the nearby town of Bremen, the first diocese in this part of the world. Brother Willehad's cathedral already had the first beams in place.

The horn blasted again, closer this time, although still lost in the trees. Birds startled into the sky, shrieking in caustic reply to the martial sound. Folkward drained his cup hurriedly and set it down on the grass. He paced back, round through the chapel and library then back to his desk. Perhaps it wasn't hunters after all. Perhaps it was the king's outriders, attending to their safety. That was not a welcome thought. Folkward found himself easily irritated when his peace and quiet was disturbed. That was the problem with an abundance of contemplation, it made the mind restless. He reached over to the Master Bible, his source, and traced his finger down the second column, searching almost to the end of the leaf, until he came to the words:

Produxitque Dominus Deus de humo omne lignum pulchrum visu, et ad vescendum suave lignum etiam vitae in medio paradise, lignumque scientiae boni et mali

The Tree of Knowledge of Good and Evil… of course, the tree and its fruits were not themselves evil, because everything that God created was good. It was disobedience of Adam and Eve that caused the disorder in Creation, that saw mankind thrown out of Paradise. Just like the disobedience of the Saxons threatened disorder now, threatened to upset this little patch of perfection, his home now as much as theirs. He frowned, his face flushing with annoyance.

Folkward dearly hoped the king's army had no cause to ride out. The monks had been forced to flee west before, more than once. But after the last uprising, he had been convinced the troubles were over, especially as the rebel leader had escaped north. A warrior called Widukind or Widuking, or some such, although it was clearly a nom de guerre. The Saxons told him it meant *child of the wood*. Willehad said he was just a story to frighten Frankish children.

The surrounding woodland suddenly felt more ominous, and it flashed through the monk's mind—and not for the first time—that *he* was the intruding wasp. Karolus was a great king, fourteen years on the throne of the Franks, and most of those at war with his Saxon neighbours. He was already proclaimed a new Constantine, equal in might and magnificence to the old Emperors of Rome. But he was a stubborn king too. He preached with a tongue of iron that grew more severe with each rebellion. Folkward had debated the campaign often with Willehad.

If you used evil means to achieve the peace of God, were you a good man? Faith required free will, not compulsion by fear and bloodshed. And thus the cycle was doomed to repeat itself. He knew that old Eahlwine, the new master of the palace school, thought the persecution of the tribes was too harsh. They had studied together at York and still exchanged letters. Eahlwine reasoned that, if the king trusted Northumbrians to establish his church in foreign lands, perhaps together they could persuade him to practice leniency, to gladden hearts and minds rather than alienate them. Folkward didn't reply. Karolus might ask for his books, but he certainly didn't ask for his counsel.

Nor was the old monk under the illusion that the heathens were impressed by him—either his age or supposed wisdom, or the fact that he had the gall to enlighten their ignorance with his sermons. The Saxons had their own sly learning; nothing like the lessons of Plato, Aristotle, and Augustine of course, but their own sources of cunning and revelation all the same. Their chief idol, the archfiend Woden, was an elusive figure, lurking at the fringes of the forest, wandering widely in its shadows.

To a pagan, the idea that there was only one True God was baffling. Folkward had made it a point to understand their thinking—you couldn't hope for conversions without a little insight and understanding—and found it simplistic but practical. When famine or disease was rife, why bet on just one God when you can gamble on the intervention of any number of them? The crucial thing he'd realized was that the Saxons had lots of these demons. There was probably a god of pigs out there, rooting around for sacred acorns. Folkward knew most of them, by name at least, all the better to affect their abjuration. That was the *real* battle, for the newly baptised tribes would just add Christ to the list of spirits and elves to be appeased each day then think no more of it. Folkward knew how they thought—baptise now, take the Frankish linens and jewels, and carry on as before. Greedy creatures. Perhaps he should write to Eahlwine with his thoughts. The distraction might help calm his nerves.

He opened the wattle shutters and scanned the treetops from the window. There was no smoke. In his experience, rebellions always began with smoke. Perhaps it was just the huntsman's horn after all, rather than anything more disturbing. Nothing more worrisome than that. There had been two years of peace after all. Folkward tried to smile and told himself he worried easily in his old age, that the ache in his back shortened his temper. He was certain that God guided and protected their efforts, that He ensured no harm would come to the brethren. There were plenty of proofs. Willehad himself had survived a blow from a heathen sword, the blade diverted by a box of relics suspended around his neck at the last moment. And had not Bishop Wynfrith cut down Thunaer's Oak and done so with impunity? At the time, at least. He later found martyrdom in Frisia, so perhaps the heathen gods were just biding their time. Still, if Woden were out there, in the forest, he'd hardly blow a horn to signal his arrival, would he?

There was a commotion somewhere in the courtyard, raised voices out by the refectory. Unusual, so soon after Vespers, when the brethren were mostly at study, but not unheard of. There were plenty of pupils eager to receive wisdom, perhaps even more so now after the harvest had been collected. The words of Benedict himself decreed, "Let all guests who come to the monastery be entertained like Christ himself, because he will say 'I was a stranger and you took me in.'" Folkward thought about attending to the visitors himself but found his legs strangely reluctant to move.

Hemming coughed lightly to attract Folkward's attention from the window, hoping to avoid startling the older monk. Such a kind fellow, Folkward thought, realizing that his sense of panic was all too obvious. The Dane then nodded toward the door, putting two fingers to his head and taking hold of a hank of his tonsured hair, signalling that the abbot was on his way. The abbot! Of course, that would explain everything. The horns were announcing his arrival, clearing the forest paths. Folkward's grin relaxed back across his face. A visit from Bremen would inevitably involve good wine. The noise outside the scriptorium was louder now, an unmistakable flurry of footsteps, punctuated by the heavy thud of the staff of office. The footsteps stopped outside the door and, for a moment, silence returned. Folkward tidied his quills with a stifled sigh and reached to seal the ink, but his hand froze mid-action.

There was a woman in the room.

She stood in the now-open door, silhouetted against the gloaming beyond the candleflame. Her head was partly covered by a hood made of black lambskin, a dark cloud above the swirling storm of the cloak. A large leather pouch hung on her velvet belt, dangling all kinds of mystifying charms. Her feet were covered by hairy calfskin shoes with metal knobs at the toe, her hands covered by white, supple gloves.

Folkward stared at her, stunned by the turn of events.

When she spoke, the woman's voice was sing-song, soothing, a lullaby sung to a restless child.

"Blakkr prestr, hvíta Kristr, rauda Thorr."

She used a Northern tongue, but her words were almost discernable: *Black priest, white Christ, red Thor.* The monk could guess what she meant—the Benedictine habits were black, the linens they gave to the newly baptised were pure and white, which led to Christ's name in the North. Thor was the thunder demon, maverick son of Woden, and a favourite in these parts. Folkward suspected she was a seer, a *völva*, a pagan priestess. In her hands, she held a staff with a knob on top that was covered by brass and more gemstones than adorned any bishop's crozier.

The hunting horn rang out again, this time with three shorts rasps—a call to arms. On the last note, the seer tossed back her hood, shook out her dark, sooty hair, and slid her staff across the threshold, scraping across the beaten earth as if inscribing her own Holy Writ on the floor. Unbidden, she drifted into the room like an unseasonable flurry of snow, a glass bead necklace dancing around her neck, a dark blue cloak glistening with the countless precious gemstones that had been sewn into it.

The scribe tried to gather his wits. Why had that dolt of a Dane signed for the abbot? Who was blasting that awful horn again? And how had this heathen woman found her way to his sanctuary? The scriptorium led off the chapel, which meant she had thumped past a half dozen monks. He was also extremely disconcerted by the way she was gyrating around what looked like a pastoral staff and the fact that she was very clearly as savage as a wolf, despite the richness of her sheep's clothing. Folkward groped for a suitable way to address the woman.

"Dóttir…"

He half-pleaded, half-suggested, hoping that Hemming might come to his rescue with the right phrase, but the word caught in his throat when he realized Hemming wasn't behind him. Folkward turned, bodily, on his heel, startled first by the disappearance and then panicked, more so when his companion was not to be found. It was a small, empty hovel of a room, square, bereft of anything but manuscripts and the cases that held them. Had the Dane stolen away so quickly? And how, with the Norse in the doorway and the wattle on the windows undisturbed? Folkward grew more frantic. Was he being punished for his sins, his foolish pride? The Lord knew his true thoughts; the nickname was in jest! Anxiety and anger seized him as he fought for an explanation. He felt compelled to shout, to shatter the silence, to call for his God and for his countrymen. What devilry was this? The monk paused, breathing methodically, running his aching fingers over his rosary beads, quelling his stricken mind. He held his peace and gave a small prayer for the mercy.

The woman spoke again in the same sing-song voice.

"Tonsured and torn, shaven now shorn."

Folkward turned, slowly and very deliberately, back to the woman. She loomed over his writing stand, tracing the curves of his lettering with one long, wicked fingernail, smiling guilefully at him. *Soft answer turns away wrath*, the monk determined—and hopefully, rhyme too. He had enough riddles for one day.

"I am delighted you speak English, dóttir. My name is Folkward, a humble servant of the one True God and—"

"Frakkar," she said and gave a short winsome sigh. "Grikkir, Serkir, Gyðingar. All the same lies, whispering across deserts, blinding men as surely as sand in the eyes."

Her eyes peered around the chamber, then alighted on the Holy Scripture. She was evidently reading the Latin, and translating, haltingly at first, then with an eerie fluency.

"And the Lord God formed man of the slime of the earth: and breathed into his face the breath of life, and man became a living soul.

"And the Lord God had planted a paradise of pleasure from the beginning: wherein he placed man whom he had formed.

"And the Lord God brought forth of the ground all manner of trees, fair to behold, and pleasant to eat of: the tree of life also in the midst of paradise: and the tree of knowledge of good and evil."

Folkward felt his breathing hasten again. Perhaps it had been unwise to drink the mead so quickly. He wasn't accustomed to loud debate, or heathens who read Latin, and he felt unsteady on his feet.

The woman looked up from the manuscript and grinned.

"You know what the Hebrew word for 'In the beginning' is? *Bereshit.* Bear shit. That's what we say in the North."

She stepped away from the books and walked slowly towards the monk.

"There is an order to a well-told story, I'll grant you, but you are mistaken in your tale here. The trees were here first, and Askr and Embla—or as you call them, Adam and Eve—were fashioned from their great trunks. Only a Kristin would build with slime."

Folkward opened his mouth to reply but found he was gasping for air. He stumbled and fell to his knees. His heart was racing now, his eyesight blurring. The woman's voice droned on, coated with honey and the hum of the hive.

"But in fairness," she said, "there are similarities. Which do you think was written first? Óðinn's Rune Song or the Gospel of Matthew? Perhaps only time will tell. You do know, Folkward, fulltruí of Kristr, that writing things down doesn't render them true? What is written can be *rewritten.*"

His mind skittered through Psalms, snatching at scraps of verse. The plainsong vibrated inside his skull, the same refrains melding into one. He was only dimly aware she scratched at the ground with her staff again, and began to yawn, over and over, her eyes wide and her mouth agape.

"Tanahk, Avesta, Quran, and Bible," she said. "They all repeat the same stories. A Lord of such celestial majesty and terrifying power there is no question in portraying him as a man. And so you use a book instead. Books, old in years, bearing inscriptions in ancient letters and long dead tongues, written by men, copied by men and used to justify your earthly realms. Meanwhile, you fast, sing psalms and avert your eyes from temptations—and the greed of your kings. But as you sow, so shall you reap. Your petty, punishing God has created a world he teaches you to scorn. You commune with your Lord with song, bread, and wine, yet your God replies only to the few. You pray, and you fear, and you seek to be saved. You maim and murder for a reward of everlasting glory and eternal love."

Then she started to sing—hauntingly, beautifully—the beads and gems joining her, a slow procession of stars in the darkness that swallowed him. When her voice returned, it was as cold and deep as a well.

"You should know, my people have been gifted Midgard and are protected here. We laugh, and we love, and we meet our end well. My Gods are here all the time. I celebrate them with every breath, every touch. And they fade and falter as surely as summer turns to autumn or winter turns to spring, but I know they will stand again. Folkward, dear Folkward, did you know I have watched you these three nights from by the river?"

He was somewhere else now. There was Eahlwine, the schoolmaster, in all his court finery, cavorting, naked with his assistants. He saw Willehad, saddling an eight-legged horse and galloping to the sea. First Hemming, now Willehad! Why had his friends forsaken him? He felt a gnawing grief. Someone was dead. And true enough, there was a body, attended by hundreds of concerned and watchful figures, all in black, all in mourning. He felt very distant from God, but surely this place was Bremen Cathedral, somehow completed, already consecrated with great riches and relics. The crowd parted to reveal a mitre atop a skull, then flapped up into the rafters, a flurry of jet black feathers and unkind eyes. They cawed and shrieked as they flew. Folkward flailed his arms to protect his face, only to find he was in the air too, his screams adding to the cacophony. He pecked, once, twice, a third time and his tongue flushed with warm blood. He hopped between three broken bodies, recognizing each in turn—Benjamin, Artrebanus, Genoald. Shrouded by ravens, always pecking, tearing, watching.

Then the black fiends were gone, and only ash, soot, and smoke remained. Folkward flew above the land, beseeching God for mercy, but his penance went unsaid and unheard. Far below, Saxons strode from the forest, their princes now returned from across the Danevirk. He saw the Frankish army ride east, ordered by their king to end this temerity. They were led by the highest of the high, chamberlains and counts, seeking a reckoning but finding only judgment. Saxon knives flashed, and rivers ran with blood. Folkward watched as the skies darkened, as daylight shrank to a thin white line on the horizon. Now came Iron Karolus, the cross in his hand, a wild beast gnawing at his genitals. The river grew darker still, alive with human heads, thousands upon thousands, bobbing like bloodied apples. The Ring of the Fisherman applauded with ancient hands, the Ring of the North thundered, his dog-headed children broken free of their chains. And then the Norse woman was there, her thighs pinning him down. He could feel himself engorge, and he shuddered as she mounted him.

Complevitque Deus die septimo opus suum quod fecerat: et requievit die septimo ab universo opere quod patrarat.

Words tumbled through Folkward's fevered mind. He was worried about his books, all his work going up in flame. He tried to imagine himself, standing at his desk, busily writing. Happily writing. *And on the seventh day God ended his work which he had made: and he rested on the seventh day from all his work which he had done.* Perhaps this was all a dream. The Lord would protect him.

The monk kept his eyes firmly closed and mentally recited the scripture again and again. He grimaced as the Norse shifted her weight. He was still pinned. Folkward tried to struggle, but he was bound too. He strained to see his fetters but saw no rope or chains. In frustration, he started to weep, silent, anxious tears. The seer bent towards him and whispered straight into his ear.

"Henbane, Folkward, from the Vanir. Quite potent when imbibed. And, yes, you are right, it is Sunday. But today, there will be no rest, at least for the wicked. What do you think, priest? Can you hear the oncoming storm?"

THE HORNS CARRIED ON CALLING long into the night. The monastery provided ample wood for fires, and its slaughtered pigs warmed the bellies of the many Saxon warriors who answered. Meat was boiled in large pots, blood splashed with ritual abandon. The tribesmen drank mead, passing drinking horns, one after another, around the circle formed by the steaming cauldrons, swearing oaths to kith and kin. Tomorrow, they would take the hidden paths through the beech trees, up onto the Süntel ridge to wait for the Franks. The riders of Karolus scared no one here, their horses just more sacrificial flesh this side of the ford. Lord Widukind had returned, and with him ran the wolves of Sigurd Hring, newly crowned King of Danes and Swedes, and mortal foe of the Kristin. They would meet the Franks with spear and seax in Woden's name. The camp rang with toasts.

"Til árs ok friðar." *Good health and peace.*

The völva stood alone by the small altar of stones she had made by the monastery well. The sacrificial ceremony, the *blót*, would gain favor with the Gods, maybe it would direct their wrath at the Frakkar. But peace was not what she had seen. Peace would be a long time coming.

The warriors were wary of her divinations and magic, the *seiðr*. To them, she was the path to the hidden, the healer of the sick, the blight on the land, the weaver of destiny. Only the bravest of them even stole a glance in her direction, in case she happened to be staring back and put them under a spell for their insolence. She didn't begrudge them their fear. It was the simply the way of things.

The well was a simple affair, dug by hand, the water table high enough to reflect her torchlight. Not enough of a fall to kill a man, but enough water to drown one. She sung softly to herself, not that any of the Saxons would hear her over their din.

I know that I hung on a windy tree
nine long nights,
wounded with a spear, dedicated to Óðinn,
myself to myself,
on that tree of which no man knows from where its roots run
No bread did they give me nor a drink from a horn,
downwards I peered;
I took up the runes,
screaming I took them,
then I fell back from there

She cut the leather sack and the rope at the top of the well, making it all but impossible to draw water from it quickly. No sense poisoning everyone. The All Father, Óðinn, had gained his wisdom from drinking at Mímir's well, although in exchange for that knowledge, he had been forced to sacrifice an eye. As she turned into the dawn, the völva wondered how she'd be rewarded for the sacrifice of a whole monk.

EXEGESIS II

‹ O S F O R T H ,   E N ‹ L A N Ð

2 0 1 7

M URDERED, MR. CHANDLER? YOU LOOK well enough to me!"
The churchwarden laughed uneasily. If the old man was joking,
he had a gift for deadpan, and if he wasn't, well, it wasn't polite
to chuckle at senility.

"Let's just say I am in recovery, Churchwarden," the old bear
growled. "Feeling better by the moment."

Whoever he was, the visitor had a certain gravitas, an air of quiet
authority, like he was treading the boards, playing The Dane as they say.
He had a presence. Michaels wondered if he'd been in anything he'd seen.
He surely couldn't be just a bit player in one of the Jorvik touring groups.

"So, why the interest in Willehad of Bremen?" Michaels asked.
"Research for a part, is it? If you'd care to come down to the rectory,
I am sure we have a copy of Alban Butler's *Lives of the Saints.* Better
yet, we can do a search of PASE."

Michaels fumbled for his phone, which nearly fell from his pocket.
He caught it just in time, then thumbed in his passcode.

"We had some people here from the University of Cambridge.

All funded by the Arts and Humanities Research Council. They have an amazing database: the Prosopography of Anglo-Saxon England. PASE. It has information on all the recorded inhabitants of England from the late sixth to the late eleventh century. Look, I'll show you." He enjoyed having immediate access to ancient history, and PASE had helped him win several quiz nights at the local pub. The screen hung momentarily, then flashed up an error page:

This site can't be reached

http://www.pase.ac.uk/server DNS address could not be found.

"Oh, it's offline. Must be down for maintenance," Michaels muttered, crestfallen.

The old man was looking at him, seemingly amused by the churchwarden's antics.

"Like you say, Churchwarden. Ancient history. Water under the bridge. Tell me about your cross. Why only one?"

Michaels checked his watch. He had to drive into town to collect some groceries, but he had a little time to devote to his elders and betters. It was only Christian, after all.

"There used to be another. Maybe even a third. You can see one stump just there." The churchwarden pointed to a small fragment just seven feet away. "But I'm afraid they were dismantled some time ago. This has been consecrated land since Anglo-Saxon times, but the church was extensively rebuilt in the eighteenth century. That's when the damage was done. The remaining cross was identified by a Victorian gentleman, an amateur antiquarian called Charles Parker. His colleagues found remnants of the other crosses in the parsonage, used as a sundial, even as a step. The Fishing Stone in the church is thought to be a remnant too, showing the Viking god Thor fishing for the Midgard Serpent. It's an old legend. I can show you if you'd like." He gestured back to St. Mary's. Even though the wind had died, he was keen to get back inside.

"No need." The old man strode purposefully to the second stump.

Michaels wondered where he got his manners. A please or a thank you wouldn't hurt.

"How about the Hogback tombs? Part shrine, part grave, both found under a twelfth century wall, so their origin must have been long forgotten even then. The tombs have very distinct curved ridges, hence the name. Very intricately carved too..."

The churchwarden realised he was staring at Mr. Chandler's own intricate markings. The thought crossed his mind that the old man might have one foot in the grave himself, and that offering tours of the long-deceased might be ill-advised.

His guest glared back, and even before he spoke, it seemed to Michaels that the old man had read his thoughts.

"Never judge a book by its cover, Churchwarden. This leathery old binding, these spindly tattoos, they tell a saga. These marks are the birthright of my people; they bind me to the dead."

Michaels didn't know whether the display was method or madness, but he decided not to antagonise the man further. He wasn't comfortable with confrontation. *Best just to plough ahead...*

"Well, we do have some idea about who made the cross, and the tombs. This land is formerly part of the kingdom of Northumbria, settled by Scandinavians some time in either the ninth or tenth century, after the Great Heathen Army seized the throne. This is before England and Scotland and referendums, of course, when the Northumbrian kingdom straddled the current divide. The cross itself dates to the first half of the tenth century, probably in the last years of Viking rule. Right in the middle of the Dark Ages, meaning the youth of today can conveniently ignore most of what happened and misrepresent everything else in comic books. The national curriculum is sorely wanting. Sorely."

The old man trailed back to the cross, his grey cloak sweeping the grass on the overgrown graves. If he sympathised with the churchwarden, he didn't show any sign of it. He called back over his shoulder, "What makes you the expert?"

Michaels was taken somewhat aback by the question.

"The Church of St. Olaf, down the road in Wasdale," he said collecting himself. "It was dedicated in 1977, the year I was born, and that kind of stuck with me. It's part of the Benefice, if you want to visit it. It's at least a thousand years old. The beams come from a Viking longship."

"Saint Olaf? Is that so?"

The old man seemed calmer now. He stroked his long beard, as if soothing ruffled feathers. He looked even more full of himself, as if enlivened by the spirited debate. His eyes danced with delight.

"Tell me about the cross that remains," he barked.

Michaels checked his watch again.

"Well, all right. But then I must be going, I'm afraid. It's Pies, Peas, and Puds night, and I have to get into town for supplies. The vicar will be happy to reschedule you, I'm sure."

"Time and tide wait for no man, Churchwarden," the old man said, unrelenting.

"Quite so, quite so. Well, Mr. Chandler, if you'll look here. The shaft is full of these remarkable carvings, all of which illustrate a tenth century poem, called the Völuspá or the Prophecy of the Seeress. It tells the story of the creation of the world and its coming end, related to the audience by a seeress or *völva* addressing Odin, the All Father, the chief of the Viking Gods. It is one of the most important primary sources for the study of Norse mythology. You know it, of course?"

"Of course," the old man scowled. "Ragnarok. The twilight of the gods, the long-heralded last battle, where the monstrous Jötnar set about destroying the entire cosmos. Fenrir, the great wolf, consumed the world so swiftly that even the sun was dragged from its zenith and into the beast's stomach."

Michaels was relieved. He was beginning to think the actor hadn't bothered to learn any of his lines. You'd imagine that you'd do a modicum of reading before donning that ridiculous garb and gallivanting around the Lake District.

"Exactly," said Michaels. "And you can see the story brought to life here: the great wolf swallowing the sun; two dragons attacking Heimdal, who wards heaven with his horn and staff; Loki, bound and tortured beneath a snake; Surt, attacking Odin from his ship of Hell. The lower part of the cross represents the ash tree Yggdrasil, which the Norse men believed supported the universe. And here on the east side, you can see Balder, the bright god, on the eve of his resurrection."

Michaels reached as high as he could to point out the key features in the sandstone. It was an odd guided tour, orbiting around one tall column, squinting into the weak winter sun, but the churchwarden could tell the old man was following intensely.

"Fascinating, isn't it? The similarity between Balder and Jesus, I mean. The notion of a dying-and-rising god is common enough I suppose, but I think the Viking Age was really about rebirth. The Old Ways were experiencing their own kind of Ragnarok. So when a Norse colony established itself in Northwest England, it had to find a way for its old traditions to interact with the traditions of the locals, locals that were Christian. It's quite possible that the ambiguity in the images on the cross is intentional. That the pagans were in transition, from the Old Ways to our familiar faith."

The old man snorted so loudly that the churchwarden jumped out of his skin for the second time that afternoon. This time he dropped his phone, which cracked loudly on the base of the column. He bent to retrieve it and came close to swearing a second time. Channelling the vicar, he bit back the impulse.

"Is that what you tell people? When they come to look at the carvings? What nonsense!" the visitor snarled, suddenly not just peremptory, but downright hostile.

Michaels coloured up brighter than his long-lost parish pamphlets. His heartbeat was ringing in his ears. He thrust his phone into his pocket and jangled around for his car keys. That was quite enough of this cantankerous Yorkshireman and his goading comments. He snapped back, flustered.

"What is there to disagree with? I'll have you know even Eric Bloodaxe is rumoured to have converted. This cross, it dates from that time. 954AD. We have pamphlets—"

"And that's what passes for expertise, is it? Pink pamphlets! *Rass-ragr*! You people need a wake-up call," scolded the visitor.

The churchwarden was flabbergasted. This was the problem with modern Britain, he thought: they'd let old men like this have the vote. Stingy old buggers who couldn't be trusted with a civil conversation, let alone a ballot box. Michaels felt that, Reverend Riley or no Reverend Riley, it was his God-given duty to try and talk some sense into him.

"Go and look at the replica in the Victoria & Albert Museum," he said. "All modern scholars agree. Every image has a Christian counterpart. Heimdal as the Archangel Michael, blowing his trumpet. Loki, the fiend of Northern legend, is a version of Satan. Balder himself is Christ standing with his arms spread wide, while below him are Mary Magdalene and Longinus with his spear."

The old man chuckled.

"You are seeing what you want to see."

Michaels was incensed. If only he had one of his pamphlets handy, or one of the newsletters that blew away, they had some quotes from the Old Norse poems that he'd recited to such telling effect at the Scout Hall last week. He tried to scrabble together something articulate.

"You are ignoring the evidence of your own eyes," the churchwarden said. "The carving is self-evidently the Crucifixion. Not to mention the Norse poem. Go read the Völuspá, why don't you? This was the world of Harald Hardrada, Olaf the Holy, Canute the Great,

Haakon the Good. All Christian Viking Kings!"

It came to him, then, the line he wanted, purloined from an old Victorian scholar.

"Simply put, the cross is a translation of the Gospel story into Northern thought."

The old man grinned like a row of runestones.

"Oh no, Churchwarden. Northern thoughts are never set in stone. And your memory is a fugitive from fact. Botulfr the Black is the only Viking prince worth his name. I am afraid you need a history lesson."

Botulfr's
Journey

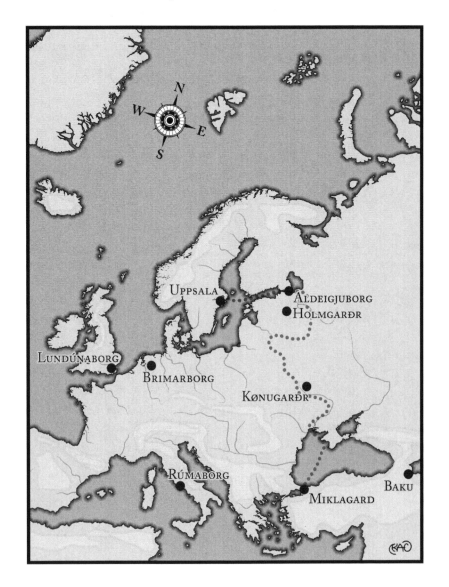

BLAKKR SAGA

KUNTA... FUKJA... DRIT!"

From somewhere above him, a torrent of abuse was hurled at a grey sky, but if the gulls or the gods were startled, they made no reply.

In the hold of a ship he did not know, Botulfr groaned. He instinctively rubbed at the pain in his neck and realised he was no longer bound. His abductors had bundled him in his bedding and carried him to their ship in the middle of the night. Botulfr had struggled, and even managed a muffled shout or two, so they had quickly knocked him unconscious. But now his hands and feet were free. His head, however, was still pounding, so he didn't dwell on why.

Botulfr listened from the shadows of the cargo hold to the men above him. They had stopped rowing and let the striped sail take the burden. Their argument had been swept beneath urgent oars for the past hour but now rolled back around the ship. At first, only the creaking mast groaned, filling the silence that followed the oaths. Then, he heard a second voice.

"We had enough sworn swords when the ale was flowing."

Oars were being drawn up and stowed, each one clattering to the deck. The accented words of a third man came tumbling out impatiently.

"Pine and oak will serve us well until we find more iron. Can you stay quiet so I can think?"

The expletives returned, giving the man his answer. Even below deck, Botulfr could feel the speaker's fury.

"*Ormstunga*, can you speak without riddles? I have no idea what he just said. Did you understand what he just said? Did anyone understand what he just said?"

"Perhaps you understand this, *reðr!*" An unseen gesture in the salt air.

A fourth voice now, calmly ignoring the squabble.

"We should dye his hair blond with lye soap so we are not recognised."

"Gest, he's the only Norseman alive without a beard. I've known women with more hair on their chins. There is no point dyeing his hair."

Footsteps across the deck above.

"The völva said—"

"That *bikkjuna* can piss wine before I care what she says."

"It's not what she says, it's what the runes say. If—"

"Runes, *hundrfretr!*"

"Must every sentence be an insult?"

"Your very breathing is an insult, *rassragr.*"

There was a long silence. Botulfr shrank down into his furs, listening to the waves break and lap around the ship. The gulls filled the air with their cries, wheeling above him and the open cargo hole amidships.

One of the men stepped into view and stared down into the hold, directly at Botulfr. Though older, with perhaps forty winters or more etched across his face, the man's fair hair betrayed no grey and was pulled back in a single braid. There was some red in his beard. He had dark eyes, and around his arm, he wore a plaited silver ring. As soon as he spoke, it was apparent he was one with the heavy accent.

"We'll sail east. I have friends among the Rus. And then we can travel on to Grikkland. The prince looks Grikk. Plain sight will be his disguise, at least until we can get word to his father."

HIS FATHER.

Alhróðigr Fylkir Veðrhallar, Ríkir Jǫfra, Allsráðandi—All-Glorious King of the Storm-Hall, Ruler of Princes and Lord of All. It was a pompous title, bestowed by a court who grew more grandiose and conceited with every victory. Most called his father simply *Fylkir*, the Leader.

His empire, the Himinríki, stretched six weeks' sail in every direction; to the west lay Írland, Skottland, and England; to the north, Nóregr, Danmǫrk, and Finnmǫrk; and far to the east, Garðariki. Across all these conquests, vassal kings ruled in his name. The Fylkir was a man who held counsel with gods; he set down laws and the fates of men at the Well of Urðr; he rode across Bifrost and further still, if you listened to the skalds, into the realms of spirits and gods.

The Lord of All Heavens, and yet, he had let his wife be taken from him. Botulfr hated his father for that.

He hated the way his father endlessly counted coins, sliding bezants, florins, dirhams, and marks into columns on ledgers. The prince wondered when his mother's rivals would be held to similar account. He despised those ostentatious side-whiskers his father wore, a fiery red plumage, once, in his youth, but now grey shrouds of mourning. That this bear of a man, this great chamberlain of the gods, was so reduced, so enfeebled by inaction, caused the prince to burn with hot shame. The edifice of the empire—its storied heroes and unfailing ingenuity, its restless fleets and ceaseless hunger, an empire built around the Always

Victorious King—was a nothing more than a drifting hulk, riddled with worms. His father was much more controlled than controlling. There was no body. There were no questions granted and no answers given. There was no discussion of the funeral feast; no runestone carved for a fresh barrow. Her bond-women and thralls vanished overnight, without so much as a murmur. The only proof that Kera, daughter of Burikhan the Tall, had ever graced the emperor's bed was a fifteen-year-old boy and all his confusion and anger, the fury of the dispossessed.

The whole glistening court at Uppsala melted away whenever Botulfr stalked the halls, infuriating him further. They said his brother Eirik had returned from the west, full of spite and menace. Jarls and godsmen gathered in whispering pools, coldly speculating on his princely fate.

His father would offer no protection. He had already disappeared, back to roaming the passes, the bogs, fens, and forests, ever further from his palace, seeking solace in a fresh hunt or a new bed-slave. In hindsight, that was all he ever did. Escape.

Then, the prince, too, was gone. And the whole inconvenience could be forgotten.

"AHA, THE PRINCE IS AWAKE at last," said the man. "Our apologies, young master, but we all know a boy's will is the will of the wind. We thought it best to keep you quiet, at least until we reached the docks. I had thought a gag would suffice, but Harald here is not one for half measures."

He gestured to the Jötunn-of-a-man looming behind him, who evidently swore the same way other men breathed. Before Botulfr could react, the giant reached down and effortlessly hauled him up through the hatch and onto the deck, where, struggling to find his sea legs, he careened over some leather sacks and clattered down heavily among them. The man who'd plucked him from the hold was a massive barrel-chested creature a full head taller than any of his companions. A blooded warrior in his prime, with a mane of straight blond hair. A long moustache overran a short-cropped beard, and there was a knot of charms inked on his powerful forearms.

Botulfr could see now that it was a cargo ship—a byrding. Its hull wider, deeper, and shorter than a longship, it could be sailed with smaller crews, although never with as few as four. They must have been in a breakneck hurry to put to sea so short-handed.

The two other men sat nearby, watching. The first was clearly learned—below his piercing blue eyes and a frothy crown of golden hair, he had four large copper beads knit into his beard and half a dozen bracelets on each wrist. Symbols of the gods.

The second man was less well groomed, weathered even, with a thick dark beard and long moustache arrayed around a nose that had been broken at least once.

"Introductions!" said the man with the accent. "I am Olaf, and this great brute before you is my brother Harald. Over here we have Askr of Brimarborg," he said, nodding to the man with the bracelets. "And this stale old fart is Gest."

Botulfr searched his captors' faces. He was expecting a twitch of madness, a butcher's snarl, or even the cold, dead eyes of a draugr. What he wasn't expecting was an array of expectant smiles and toothsome grins. No one was carrying weapons, although, with Harald aboard, perhaps they didn't need to.

Gest reached out a hand to shake and offered a greeting.

"Heill ok sæll, my Prince."

Be healthy and happy. The prince took the hand but remained tight-lipped, his silence meant as an admonishment.

"Yes, yes, we owe you an explanation," Gest said, accepting the implication. "And so. Where to begin? No place like the beginning, I suppose. We are all honourable men, I believe. Men of good name and character. We fought for your father in Sikiley and in Spánn against the Grikk Emperor. Sometimes against the Frakkar, too. The emperor in the East is Gregoras. You have heard, of course, of Miklagard, the Great City that the Kristins call Constantinople?"

Askr snorted. "Brawl with a pig and you go away with his stink. That explains Harald's stench." Luckily, Harald wasn't listening, being too busy urinating in a wide arc over the side of the ship.

Olaf sat down on his thwart and tapped the oar impatiently.

"A prince of Himinríki understands the politics and geography of the world, Gest. Man can only rule the world from the city of Constantine. I've heard his father say that a hundred times on campaign. What's more, he will have seen the likeness of Gregoras on bezants. I know that is hard to imagine for a farmhand whose idea of immense wealth is a silver penny."

Gest belched a reply, and the company laughed to a man. Botulfr tried hard to suppress a smile himself. The mariners seemed very comfortable in their own skin. Except for Harald, he thought, who was scratching around inside the great bear pelt clasped around his shoulders. The exposition was clearly annoying him. The rest of the men were dressed in brightly coloured woolen tunics trimmed with silk. If this Gest was a farmhand, he had seen many, many years' good harvest.

Olaf went on.

"What Gest is trying to say is that the Kristin emperors are rich, and they have plenty of lands to plunder. We conquer their coasts, sack their towns, bloody their armies, and burn their priests—but our raids are bee-stings to a bull. A very rich bull, with big golden testicles."

Askr let out a deep, frustrated sigh.

"Have you people no sense of perspective?" He turned back to Botulfr. "We were sorry to hear of your mother's death. These men all take their oaths seriously. They heard plenty of treacherous rumours from the ranks, heard about the empress passing and assumed the worst would happen to her young prince. They are well intentioned, even if the 'rescue' didn't go quite as planned."

He looked back at the other men, with mock accusation in his eyes. Olaf smiled broadly.

"I excuse myself of any impropriety by claiming insobriety instead. It is well known that birds of recklessness flutter o'er ale feasts."

"You oaf," bellowed Harald. "You weren't supposed to drink the ale."

The big man had decided enough was enough and began roaring his impatience at the sky again. Olaf and Gest glanced at each other, grabbed oars and started prodding the great bear. Askr, meanwhile, hurried over to the prince and muttered an embarrassed apology.

"They are sworn swords; we can't expect them to be articulate. Or attentive, it would appear. As odd as all this seems, we do have a plan, my Prince. There are no better men in your father's *hird* and we can trust them with our lives."

THE BYRDING HAD SIX DAYS sailing ahead, across the Eystra Salt, and along the coast to Aldeigjuborg, a lowland village that that had been transformed into a major port by trade from the east. In Uppsala, envious merchants would mutter that it overflowed with dirhams and complain that their Rus rivals had both veins of silver and hearts of bronze. The reality was more prosaic. Aldeigjuborg, like all the towns of Garðariki, was a walled fort, linked by ships plying the Olkoga River at the edge of the empire. Where there was wealth, there was danger. Botulfr hadn't travelled much—no further than his father's broken promises had allowed—and ached with excitement. Nevertheless, he tried to feign an indifference to the men on board. It seemed more princely.

Botulfr had plenty of time to learn about the crew—*his* crew, it seemed. Olaf looked to Botulfr to be the oldest of the group, old enough to have a family of his own, although not as tired as his father. He was a Norse-Gael, an Austman, born in Dyfflin to the west, and he wore the red shaggy cloak of the Imperial Guard with style and swagger. When he spoke, which was often, he was always several octaves above the other warriors. Words tumbled from him either in rapid, excited bursts or forlorn, wistful sighs. At first, Botulfr struggled to understand him, and Olaf would have to patiently repeat himself. Askr had explained that, as the Saxar, Vindr, and Englar came under the Norse yoke, their tongues were twisted together by the waves of invasion, creating a rough pidgin that could be broadly understood across the empire. Two hundred years of dynastic marriage and bloody battle—recounted at length in the sagas—cemented the common tongue further. Askr was happy to borrow words from any source, as long as it added to the beauty of his stories, he said.

In fact, poetic license proved to be the whole basis for the "rescue" and the impromptu journey east. When pressed for answers, Askr would wave the prince away and tell him that all would be revealed in time. Not that Botulfr cared any for explanations. He was revelling in the freedom and had no intention of returning home. Besides, there was nothing to return home to. His questions seemed petty given that the guardsmen were clearly trying to put distance between them and Uppsala as quickly as possible, despite being short-handed.

Big Harald was the son of a wealthy war-chief in the Uplands who had either married Olaf's mother, carried her away in a raid, or both. He boasted that he was known as the Ravaging Tide, claiming it was because he beached his longship and stormed a Frakkar castle single-handedly. His elder sibling countered that it was because he pissed over the side of the boat twenty times a day, but in fairness, they all knew Harald was the only reason the byrding made it anywhere.

He did the work of ten men. He argued like ten men, too, and never spoke when he could swear instead—and *always* swore when he heard Olaf talk for more than five minutes.

Gest was thankfully much quieter, a Dane and one-time candle-man to Olaf before joining the hird himself. In peacetime, these armed companions acted as the lord's officials, forming embassies, exacting tribute, gathering taxes or acting as messengers; in war, they formed the core of his army. Together, the three men had fought the fylkir's wars for the best part of a decade. No wonder the prince hadn't seen them before.

Askr was cut from a different cloth. He was a skald, a court scholar, from Brimarborg in Saxland to the south. Like the other hirdsmenn, he was tall and strong, but Askr was also clearly a devout man, who dripped with charms, arm rings, and beads. From the days when the fabled Bragi Boddason penned *Ragnarsdrápa*, every king and chieftain had commanded skalds to record their feats and ensure their legacy lived on. The skalds had been the first to record the sagas on parchment, to bind them in books and to carry them across the lands of the empire. Over time, they had become clerical workers too, recording laws and happenings of the government, some even being elected to the regional Things, while others worked in temples, recording the lives and miracles of the godsmen.

In the case of Prince Botulfr, the skalds could trace ten generations at least, in a direct line to Ragnar, the first ruler to boast the title fylkir. It was a long list, meticulously recorded. The Norse had always had a rich oral tradition, with a thousand years of sagas honouring mighty heroes and their deeds. The names Ivar Vidfamne, Harald Wartooth, and Sigurd Hring were known to every Norse child—but to Botulfr, they took on an extra significance. They were his ancestors and his guides. Long dead kings were not just an inspiration or a page in a historical saga, but names he could invoke for every aspect of daily life:

a successful day's fishing, a prayer for rain, a swift recovery from illness.

Their spirits had watched over him since he was born. He had fond memories of his early childhood, every feast full of tales. His favourite feast had been Ostara, when the rime and hoar frost began to drip away. He would decorate an egg with oils, ochre, and lapis; this he always did for his mother, to wish her well for the months ahead. She encouraged him with warm smiles, watching him daub his masterpiece with intense pride—although he was often too intent on his work to notice—and every year, she received his gift like it was Midgard itself.

Then he would be summoned to the great temple. His father presided over the larger feasts, rather than the goði, making them much grander occasions. The men all brought ale and began drinking at once, or often, several days *before* they set out from their farmsteads. Cattle and horses were slaughtered, and the blood collected. Then his father would take a blood staff and pace back and forth, dousing the altars and the temple walls in blood, both outside and inside, before he turned to his people and solemnly showered them in gore too. His father would bless the beef and horseflesh, then turn his eyes to the goblets of ale. First, Óðinn's goblet was emptied for victory and power; then toasts were made to other gods for peace and a good season. Then the guests drained their cups to the memory of departed friends, and again, to those they were too drunk to remember.

There were markets too, with all manner of goods from across the world: Serkland slaves, Grikk silks, Frakkar weapons, Groenland ivory. The freemen would gather for the Althing, voices raised to answer the official, the lawspeaker; they'd solve disputes and recommend new laws to be enacted and try not to trade blows as well as words. And finally, his father proclaimed the leidang, levying ships from the provinces and marshalling the fleets for that summer's warfare. When Botulfr was too young to do more than watch from his father's knee, the family skalds would keep him entertained, reciting whatever saga he requested.

There were stories of the triumphs and travails of the gods across the Nine Worlds, and of course, their doom on the plain of Vígríðr. Ragnarok was long foretold as Óðinn's last battle; the chief of the gods swallowed whole by the ravening wolf Fenrir, his son Thórr slain by the serpent Jörmungandr, the worlds consumed by the fires of Surt. Óðinn had seen *how* he met his end, but had not seen *when*, and so gathered the greatest warriors to his side at Valhalla, ready to resist the inevitable. From their gods, the Norse learned that it was foolhardy to struggle against fate, as foolish as sailing into a strong wind. If the outcome was already decided, the only thing that was important was how they stood to meet their end. Óðinn, whose very name meant fury, had chosen to fight and rage.

Botulfr had long resolved to do the same. No one else in his family seemed to care.

At the end of autumn, when the crops had been harvested and the animals had meat on their bones, his mother would organise the Álfablót, or elven sacrifice, just for the family, a private affair in their home, to ask the ancestors for their protection. His father and uncles would lift her gently over a doorframe to help her see into the worlds beyond. Those were the special times; quiet nights, safe in her arms, his uncles boasting of past glories. Then one year, his youngest brother had grown sick. Botulfr had asked the Álfar to help him, but they hadn't listened.

Yule was a time of fear and dread, the coldest, darkest part of the year, when ferocious winds and storms howled over the land. Óðinn led a flurry of spectral horsemen in a hunt through the night sky. The forest fell silent except for the barking of the hounds. Some said that Óðinn hunted with large birds when the dogs got tired, transforming a host of sparrows into an armed brigade. The year his brother died, his mother suggested he leave out hay in his stockings for Sleipnir, Óðinn's eight-legged steed. She always seemed to be finding excuses for him to go and play. Botulfr thought better of it. The idea of the one-eyed, angry god walking into the stables terrified him. He didn't want to be taken like his brother.

There hadn't been much in the way of ceremony after that. Just stolen trips to thieve for attention at the market, sullen feasts with the same tall tales repeated, again, and again, masks to hide the suffering. His ancestors were silent. She was gone now, his mother. There was no one to peer after her into the worlds beyond. No one to ask her to come back.

BOTULFR LOVED THE OPEN WATER. Though at fifteen he was some ten years younger than either Harald or Askr, and not yet a man grown, he enjoyed hefting the oars, as well as the sense of routine that came with rowing. He felt his anger fall away, diminishing with each stroke, with every headland they passed. Of course, he was escaping, just like his father, but he began to understand the attraction of leaving your problems on a fast receding shore. The easterly currents weren't strong, but they were constant, and a breeze would often pick up at noon to provide further respite for the oarsmen.

The men sang as they rowed, or else they swapped stories. When they beached the byrding at night, Olaf would determine the distance run, dead reckoning between two crags or other landmarks. Botulfr oversaw pitching tents while the cooking fire was kindled, and when he was done, he would watch the shadows stretch across the mountains, fleeing the long, low rays of the sun. Gest would strum his harp, playing "The Harping of Gunnar" or the "The Wiles of Guthrun" long into the evening. Old songs, as old as the crags that ranged to the sea, echoes of times beyond memory. The fire would hold the men's gaze and thoughts, and then suddenly all would be darkness, except for Aurvandil's Toe, gleaming above the crescent moon.

The travellers sat to either side of Botulfr every night, chatting conspiratorially. It reminded him of the way his uncles had spoken when his father was out of earshot, full of fond but merciless teasing and long explanations of what was worth fighting for. At first, the conversations dwelt on the practical, such as the best way to skin a bear or the respective merits of each man's homeland. It took until the fourth night for the innocuous to become the insistent. No sooner had Gest began to strum than Askr sighed deeply.

"Those songs were nearly lost," he lamented, kissing one of the amulets that jangled around his neck. The skald pulled down his woolen cap tightly around his ears and stared into the distance.

Botulfr had no idea of how you could lose a song.

"How?" he asked, incredulous.

"Karl, the Butcher of Saxar. He wasn't content with killing our gods, he even tried to murder our music. '*Let them listen to the lector not the lyre, our house is not wide enough to hold both,*' he said. Well, in truth, it was his tutor Alkuin who wrote those words, but Karl did worse. His laws made refusing baptism punishable by death, the soothsayers were all handed over to the church, assembly at the *thing* was banned. You only had to look at a tree to receive a fine."

Askr swayed gently, listening to his friend sing.

Botulfr liked listening to the skald. His father had told him that listening was the scourge of being a prince. Men wanted you to right ancient wrongs and to settle old scores, he'd complained; they wanted you on their side in the battles to come. But Askr seemed different. He simply enjoyed explaining the world and how it came to be. The past was a story to be told—an old ballad composed not just once, but brought to life again and again on the lips of friends and strangers. He spoke with the confidence of familiarity, reciting texts from memory as easily as if he held them in his hands.

"We have had our revenge. '*On the sixth of the ides of June, the havoc of heathen men miserably destroyed God's church on Lindisfarne, through rapine and slaughter.'* That's from the Englar chronicles. Ragnar led the conquests of the isles as a direct retort to Karl and his assault on the Saxar. Were you taught much history, my Prince? Who was it that tutored you? Unni? That bloated fool Oskar? No, they must have died years ago. Adalbert perhaps?"

Botulfr didn't recognise any of the names beyond his famous kinsman Ragnar and shook his head.

"I read the king's sagas and the legendary sagas, of course."

"In the runor? I am just trying to understand what clay we have been handed to mould, so to speak. Do you have any Latin? Have you read the Bible? Any of the great Grikk texts?"

The runic alphabet had been used since time immemorial across the North. It had a practicality to it; if you had a knife and a piece of wood or bone, you could start writing by carving lines. The Latin alphabet was florid by comparison and only suited to parchment, in itself rarely seen outside of temples, so the Roman letters were all but nonexistent.

Still, the question put Botulfr instinctively on his guard. Centuries of enmity between Norse and Kristin were threaded through his core. He'd never spoken to a Kristin and never expected to. All he knew was that they never washed and enjoyed mounting from behind, like a mare in heat. Unsurprisingly, foreign tongues were used strictly by the skalds to prevent corruption, and even then, they were only tolerated for diplomacy or commerce.

"My father is well known for burning all the Kristin teachings."

The skald raised an amused eyebrow.

"Your father doesn't burn *every* Kristin book. The Lindisfarne Gospels, for example: far too valuable for Thormund to turn to ashes. As much as it galls me, the whole empire is built around writing down the sagas. If we hadn't learned the value of books from the Kristin, our gods would be ghosts in the trees."

"You make it sound personal."

"History *is* personal. I was born in the cradle of Saxland, I have suffered Kristin depredations directly. But it is also professional: Latin is a language of learning, Grikk a language of ideas. The runor is for farmers who want to whittle a love note on a stick or mark the days to sowing on a calendar. Besides, what kind of skald would I be if I couldn't tell my prince stories of his enemies as well as his ancestors?"

Botulfr warmed to the thought quickly.

"Will you write my saga, Askr?"

"That, my Prince, depends very much on whether we do anything worth reading, but I will keep it in my thoughts. Let's make sure you can actually read and write first, shall we?"

The skald laughed heartily, placed a reassuring hand on the prince's shoulder and left the thought to dance in the flames of the fire.

THE NEXT MORNING, ASKR THRUST a leather-bound book into his ward's face the moment Botulfr's eyes opened. He was clearly excited.

Botulfr grimaced in the dawn light.

"Askr, the birds aren't even awake," he groaned, only to realise the birds *were* awake and happily chirruping all around: the sun smiled early at this time of year. The hirdsmenn were readying the ship, and he was still rubbing his eyes.

"Copies, of course, although not translated. They are still in the original Latin. Saved from the cathedrals at Jorvik and Kantarabyrgi during the conquest."

Someone crunched past the tent, scattering stones as he headed to the byrding. Olaf, already packed.

"Furore Normannorum libera nos, Domine," Olaf called into the tent. *From the fury of the Northmen, Deliver us, O Lord.* "Or at least, spare us their lazy children. Come now, Askr. Stop worrying the boy. You train yourself in the art of being mysterious to everyone, my friend! What if there were no one who cared about guessing your riddles, what pleasure would you then take in it?"

Askr scoffed at the Austman.

"You thought enough of my story to mount the rescue."

"I still do. Once you are born in this world, you're old enough to die. I agree, something is rotten in the kingdoms of the Danir. He has to be told. But at least let him eat first."

With that the Austman walked down the beach. Botulfr struggled into his tunic and hoisted his trousers, grateful for the reprieve. It seemed the whole mood of the camp had changed overnight, and he wasn't sure he wanted to find out why. Even the birds seemed to fall into an expectant hush. He fretted so much that, unsurprisingly, his tent was the last to be tossed aboard.

Olaf was hauling the byrding off the beach. As he waded alongside Botulfr, he winked, then nodded toward the skald.

"This is important, young Prince. You should listen when an old dog like Askr barks."

Harald gripped the other gunwale. He was more surly than usual; he clearly hadn't had much sleep either.

"And do I have to listen? Something tells me I am going to be stuck listening to his barking for weeks. Look, we fight with the Frakkar and the Grikkir every year. Most of the time, Óðinn is with us, and with axe and spear, we take our inheritance. Sometimes, we are forced back to our ships." With a grunt, and one last push, the byrding was free of the breaking waves and into the open sea. "That's just the way of things."

Askr planted his feet squarely on the deck and gestured to the horizons, as if he had learnt his sense of theatrics from a Grikk rhetorician.

"For two hundred years and more, we have warred with the Kristins. That is our way of life. We sail our fleets every summer to faraway lands, and we bring back fresh plunder, slaves, silks, and silver. We settle new lands, and we farm until it is the next season to fight and the *leidang* is raised. We fight to live, and we live to fight. But how does the cycle end?"

Botulfr stared blankly, feeling sheltered and foolish and focused on his oar. He was thankful it saved him from meeting anyone's gaze.

"A truce?" called over Olaf, guffawing at the thought.

"A truce, he says! My grandfather was murdered by the Frakkar during a so-called truce. Let me ask another way—we know why the Northmen fight. Why do the Kristins fight?" A practiced pause. "They fight until we accept their god, or until we are all dead. Saxland is proof enough of that."

Askr rummaged in a sack at his feet and withdrew a wooden case with parchment inside. He unfurled it and then lowered his voice, speaking with the sadness and solemnity of a funeral oration.

"It's all here. These are the Royal Frakkar Annals. Karl the Butcher's saga, if you will. Parts of them, at least. I have retrieved other manuscripts too, letters from Frakkar scribes, Grikk texts. If you can read the words of your enemy, you can understand him, and if you can understand him, you can defeat him. The raid on Lindisfarne, seen through Kristin eyes, was a divine punishment, and we Northmen were the agents of reprimand. Do you know what that means?"

"They don't like us much," said Gest laconically as he finished with the sail and let the coastal breeze carry them along the shore.

"Worse. Much worse. The Kristins are Polar Night to our Midnight Sun. They believe us an enemy sent by their god to test their faith. They fight to destroy their demons—us. To them, ours is a war between Heaven and Hell."

"*Such* a performance," clucked Harald. "I'd applaud if my hands weren't busy doing all the work. Now tell him the bad part. The reason we so kindly invited the prince on board."

Askr sighed, and paused for a moment, then moved to sit opposite the prince.

"As much as it pains me to say, there was, there *is*, a faction at the palace that planned to have you... go missing. Your mother was born at the ends of Midgard, near the Vargsea, near Persiðaland, yes? Your father found her there, a beaten child, in need of rescue, and took her north?"

"So I was told. They married before he was crowned. My brother Eirik, his mother had died in childbirth and my father remarried quickly."

"And you look like you mother? Her same olive skin, her lustrous black hair?"

"That is plainly true. Your point?"

Botulfr felt very self-conscious. He had clearly been different to most of the fine or fire-haired Norse; he assumed it was because he had royal blood. His mother used to tell him he was as dark and fearsome as thunder; he was coming to realise she had made a virtue out of necessity.

All four men loomed over the prince now, close enough to make him feel uncomfortable. There was nowhere to hide from either the discussion or their inspecting eyes, and he suspected that was why Askr waited until they were at sea: the intimacy demanded honesty.

"You don't look anything like a typical Norse prince, carving your path through the sagas. If anything, if I am being charitable, you look like a Grikk or a Serkir, a hero of Troy perhaps. Pardon my directness."

Botulfr nodded, almost imperceptibly, as he weighed the implications. The skald's face grew graver still.

"The jarls whispered it is because you were conjured by Kristin angels. Some say you were born a *Svartálfr*, a dark elf. Your father's marriage and your birth were called affronts to the gods. A pretense, of course, but heresiarchs are wont to divide opinion."

"This *nonsense* is why my mother was murdered?"

The words burst from the boy, frustration and anger turning to tears. All at once, he was disgusted by the colour of his skin and the weakness it conferred, horrified at all the lies he had swallowed. His face twisted with grief and hatred. Tears welled in his eyes, and he let out a high-pitched moan, then flushed further with embarrassment. His whole life having been exposed as a façade, the prince gave up trying to maintain any further pretense. The men had the good grace to pretend they hadn't heard. Askr didn't even flinch.

"In a word, yes. The great magnates often make the mistake of thinking that a skald exists only to sing their praises. They forget that we have ears as well as mouths. Olaf heard the same plotting. These men believed there were women better suited to sit at your father's side than your mother, women born of the right blood. And they told him so. The fylkir prevaricated, and so they forced his hand."

Olaf too, was still watching the prince intently, with an oddly sombre expression. Perhaps he wasn't well practiced at being serious, or perhaps that was what pity looked like.

"It goes deeper still. You see, my Prince, Kristin coins are behind all this. If they can't defeat the Northmen in battle, the cowards think they can tempt us to turn on each other."

Gest sat alongside him, looking equally earnest. They picked up each other's sentences as easily as they kept the rhythm of the oars.

"This isn't a wild suspicion. There is an old saying: he who sees his friends roasted on a spit soon tells all he knows. Good men, loyal servants, have been turned against your family."

"Why didn't you warn my father?" Botulfr mumbled petulantly, through a mask of mucus and tears. He kept his eyes downcast as he tried to digest the bitter and the bewildering news, further humiliated now at having to be spoon-fed conspiracy, like a babe in arms sputtering out an unpalatable new taste.

Olaf shrugged in reply and started to say something, but it was the skald who interjected.

"Because deceit sleeps with greed. The Emperor of the East has agents *everywhere*. Who knows who is in his pay? These three fine fools turned out to be the only ones I could trust. There were others but... like them, I expect the fylkir will have an 'accident' soon. Perhaps someone more sympathetic to the Kristin cause will assume his place, someone happy to embrace their faith and be baptised by their god. I'm sorry for it."

"Askr, what am I supposed to do?" Botulfr howled. "If you hadn't noticed, I am Thormund's *second* son, with at least three uncles and a half-brother who stand to be elected, by might and by right, before me."

Askr reached over to the boy and pulled him close. His voice was almost a whisper now, murmuring consolation.

"Those very same kith and kin murdered your mother and planned to kill you. Think then of your sagas:

Brothers will fight
and kill each other,
sisters' children
will defile kinship.
It is harsh in the world,
whoredom rife
—an axe age, a sword age
—shields are riven—
a wind age, a wolf age—
before the world goes headlong.
No man will have
mercy on another.

"My Prince, mark my words. The Grikkir seeks to loose the hound of Hel and bring Ragnarok upon us. What *you* must do, Prince Botulfr, is stop them."

Botulfr couldn't move. He suddenly felt like the one-eyed god had found him in the stables after all.

THE PRINCE KEPT HIS EYES on the rolling waves as they approached the shore that night. He was numb. One short exchange had torn the finery of his life into tattered rags, and now he sat exhausted and exposed. At first, his instinct was to cover himself with whatever dignity he could muster, to hold onto the warmth and comfort of memories. But even those fluttered from his grasp. Nothing seemed real; he found himself discounting thoughts almost as soon as they chanced into his mind. His whole courtly life seemed grotesque. He was a parody of a prince, sailing a sea of misfortune. What cruel gods had given him the shape and form of his despised enemy? His mother might have been kinder to smother him at birth.

His hirdsmenn gave him space, clearly understanding that they had pummelled their charge beyond submission and into despair. They weren't to blame: the Norse weren't known for mincing words or pulling punches. Botulfr reasoned that they wouldn't have broken their oaths lightly, for there was a special place in Helheim reserved for murderers and cowards. The story rang true in other ways. Vikings had a long history of extorting tribute; the Kristins had often been happy to see them off with silver rather than suffer their depredations. Ragnar and his sons had refused bribes on principle after the Saxon wars, but those days were long gone. The Northern Empire could and *had* been bought. Asgard knew his uncles loved the counting house as much as the ale house. He couldn't say the same for his elder brother, but then he barely knew him—Eirik was four years older and had been marauding around Spánn since he came of age, and it was openly assumed that he'd be elected fylkir when Thormund died. Botulfr didn't covet the crown or resent his brother the inheritance, although, if there really was a coup, he knew he ought do better than run out of sight with his tail between his legs.

It dawned on him that he hadn't even considered his own future. His mother had been wrong—he wasn't oncoming thunder, he was a shadow, lurking out of sight and out of mind. A half-brother starved on a diet of half-truths. He decided to change that. Perhaps then, he could uncover some certainty for himself.

That evening, he began to read the manuscripts the skald carried with him, some bound in untidy books, some simply leaves of parchment secured in wooden cases. Askr had crammed as much as he could into a leather sack when they fled Uppsala, but he had not snatched randomly; rather he had chosen methodically, his plan unfurling over many months once he caught wind of the conspiracy. He kept listing the names of tutors and scholars, expecting at least one of them to have crossed paths with Botulfr, but he was always disappointed. A Norse nobleman learnt to fight, first and foremost, and then to assize and to write. It wasn't out of ignorance or so-called barbarism, just simple necessity. The runes may have held all their fates, but sword and coin ran the empire. His father had been fond of saying that the fragrance of spices was financed by a debt of dust and blood.

But that life was lost now, a past marooned on a hostile shore. When he faced it again, Botulfr determined it would be on his terms. And so, over weeks and months, in the corners of days, Botulfr would study; his court education, fragments of knowledge puzzled together by a wily skald sailing at the fringes of the world.

OLAF TRUSTED MEN AMONGST THE Rus, the *men who row*—Norsemen still, but ones accustomed to the deep, icy lakes, and slow, rolling rivers that criss-crossed the steppe. Centuries past, the Norse were invited into these lands to reign over the local tribes and bring order. Then, like a beetle, they burrowed deeper and deeper, boring a fiefdom among the endless birch trees. To defend their incursions, they built their distinctive ring forts; circular earthen ramparts with gates opening to the four compass points and a courtyard divided into equal quadrants, each holding a square of large houses interlocking like shields. From the Olkoga to the Nepr, the Rus managed all trade between the Norse and the Grikkir.

The great stronghold Holmgarðr anchored the North, near the lake city of Nýgarðr, the seat of King Valdamarr. One of his father's more distant vassals, Valdamarr protected cargoes of timber, fur, honey, and wax. The real prize though was the trade in amber—so valuable, the traders called the route the Amber Road. Six hundred miles to the south, a second prince ruled, Jarizleif of Kœnugarðr, his great boatyards filled with wine, spices, jewellery, glass, fabrics, and even books that sailed up from Miklagard. Between the rivers were portages, trails used to carry vessels overland until they could navigate south again. In truth, the Rus kings held little sway once more than a day's march from the river, beyond the sedge that formed a border of sorts. Between the endless expanses of grass and sky, the rites of the Norse merged with stranger, local customs of the people who dwelt there. The Erzya tribes claimed Thorr hatched from an egg, and the Moksha believed the world was spat forth by Freyja. Few godsmen were zealous enough to argue in the turgid, fly-blown summers that were the true princes of the lands beyond the reeds, and none were foolish to venture out in the frozen winters.

Even though Olaf judged the risk of being followed to be slim, their rest in Aldeigjuborg was kept brief to be prudent. They stayed overnight in a simple house of turf, sod, and stone, one of the dozens of buildings straggled along the hills above the shore.

Adils, their host, was grey-haired and grizzled, a veteran of many battles who now acted as a warden for the port, extracting the *heregeld* or army tax from traders of behalf of his king. He greeted the hird warmly, as old companions do, happy to find a shared mooring in his past.

The hirdsmenn took their seats around the fire pit in the middle of his hall. Smoke holes dotted the roof of the house but did their job poorly. Botulfr sat on one of the benches, by the wall, not six feet from the fire, and he had difficulty seeing anyone through the haze.

"What news from the west?" Adils asked, as he handed out hunks of bread.

"What do you hear?" Gest replied.

"I heard snow lays on Groenland pastures all year round and that the Snaeland farmers are reduced to eating foxes and ravens."

"The winters have been cruel, but they've brought the worst of the misery on themselves. The lawspeakers are refusing to covenant with the fylkir in return for relief. Grain is in plentiful supply from the Englar ports. Instead, they've made a common cause with Thorkell Leifsson—the passage to Vinland is free of ice."

Botulfr blinked, surprised. "They aren't part of the empire?"

"When there is nothing left to inherit, men seek land outside your father's realm. Or we join his armies…" said Olaf with a flash of smile. "What else? There are more blámenn thralls sold in Dyffin than ever. Old Sigtrygg Silkbeard sees to that, king of the dark and the fair, indeed! Vilhjálm Baesingr was granted the lands around Parisborg. And of course, this one's brother is causing trouble as usual."

Olaf darkened as he pointed out the prince through the smoke.

"Is the east at peace?" asked Gest.

"Who can tell? I've heard King Jarisleifr is building more forts to prevent the Kangar getting close to his Golden Gates. Built with Kangar gold I imagine," said Adils.

"Jarisleifr the Lame is king?!" Harald spluttered.

"These few years past. And married to the fylkir's sister, the boy's aunt, to keep the peace and keep the silver flowing. The sons of Ragnar may have obeyed their father, and chosen one of the royal blood as Overking, but the sons of Rurik dispensed with tradition and murdered their way to the throne."

"Ragnar's law—"

Adils interrupted. "—is honoured more in the breach than in the observance these days. By the time the fylkir sought to end the feud, four princes had their throats cut. Jarisleifr was the last man standing, and the only candidate for the Thing. The lands are drenched with blood and heartsick for it."

"Then the King of the Rus is no friend of ours," said Olaf.

"No, neither Holmgard or Kønugarðr are safe for the whelp. Long gone are the days when a man can sail seeking safe harbour in the east."

Askr wasn't amused. "That's as it should be. We should be strict in observing the law."

"In which case, petty kings and their lapdog jarls should not be allowed to contest the heritage of our forefathers, laying their hands upon kingdoms like they were Kristin baubles and trinkets," said Harald.

"Who doesn't have some great injury to avenge? That used to be the law," Gest said.

"If every Norseman could carve himself a kingdom, there'd be no loyalty to anything but the axe. Better that we keep to our oaths," Askr said, before changing the subject. "And what of the Grikkir?"

"Jarizleifr refused all their ambassadors, saying there was no gladness among them, only sorrow—and a great stench. If you are headed there, you have a long journey ahead. It takes a month or more to reach Nýgarðr," said Adils. "From there, three months more to reach the mouth of the Nepr and Grikk waters. You'll need something warmer than your bare legs for the winter."

Olaf was irritable. His eyes were watering.

"Well, we have plenty of time before the frost comes and the rivers freeze. The problem isn't the season or the distance, it's the cargo. We may be plying the backwaters of the empire, but this passage still starts and ends at court in Uppsala. Who knows what traders, or soldiers, are making the journey. If they recognise the fylkir's son…"

"We could wait till winter, then use sleds," Gest suggested.

"With me as the horse I suppose," Harald growled, cramped, crotchety and half-smoked in the small space. "Tell me when you old women have figured out the plan. I am going to sleep by the ship."

Adils watched him go and then went to his larder.

"All the more for us!" he grinned, producing a stout barrel. "One thing hasn't changed. Drinking is still the joy of all Rus. Anyway, I doubt you can drag the byrding, even on wheels. There are fifty leagues of hauling ahead of you. Most travellers use dug out log canoes downstream."

"I remember. We have to manage the rapids too when we get south of Kœnugarðr," Olaf grumbled.

Botulfr was curious. "Rapids?"

"Seven. All with amusing names," Askr said, without the faintest trace that he found them funny. "Don't Sleep, Roaring, Always Violent, Laughing, things like that. The river turns south and the land falls away steeply. You just carry the ship around them."

Adils passed around ale in simple wooden cups. "Named after the Khagan who rules there, no doubt, or perhaps his daughters, the fifth one is Belching. What is your plan when you reach Miklagard?"

"What we all once did best: plunder and reave," Gest grinned.

"You don't mean to sack the Great City? Even Helgi the Seer didn't manage that with a fleet of two hundred ships." Adils was clearly skeptical.

"Why bother remembering a past that cannot be made into a present? We leave here paupers, but in the east, we'll fight for whoever pays us most and make our fortune. We'll return home as kings. Literally, in the prince's case," Olaf lectured. "Let's face facts, the only way to reclaim his birthright is to change men's minds with silver. But no, not Miklagard itself. The castles around the Grikksalt maybe. The plan is evolving, frankly. This isn't a table game with every move prescribed."

"We can't wait here until the Rus winter freezes our pricks," said Gest. "Momentum is our friend. Stay here and sooner or later, someone sells us out. No one will look for the prince outside the empire, least of all inside the Great City. With Askr's help, he'll speak Grikk by then. We can take our time to consider next steps."

"I feel for our skald, I do." Olaf was wracked with coughing. "I would rather be a swineherd, understood by the swine, than a poet misunderstood by princes. Adils, how do you live with this smoke?"

"It's good for the fish. Provisioning for winter starts early. As Gest said, the Marshall of the Snows is a mighty foe, but he might just be your best ally in the days ahead."

WITH ADIL'S HELP, THE TRAVELLERS planned the journey ahead in meticulous detail.

The cataracts of the Nipr were a hazard. They had proven the perfect place for raiders to launch ambushes against Rus traders, especially at the portages, when there was no choice but to haul boats along six miles of rocky trails to clear water.

Deadliest of all was the crossing at the Ford of Vrar. A bowshot in length, a dozen Torkmen tribes had crossed the great river here over the years, each fleeing a greater, more savage horde. Some had settled and carved new kingdoms of their own, but most had warred with their neighbours and been ground into dust. The oldest of sagas described these great migrations and the heroes who marshalled them. Some even said Óðinn and Frey began their wandering in far off Asaland and crossed over the river there themselves.

In years of peace, the ford was dangerous, but not often deadly; however, no-one could be certain as to the current state of affairs. The present warlord, the Khagan of the Kangar, had been in the pay of the Rus, the Grikkir, and the Bolgarar, often at the same time. His men fought in rippling waves, archers on fleet steppe horses, firing a continuous stream of arrows as they galloped back and forth across the ford. Their wheeling, whinnying circles had been the end of many an expedition in the past two years.

Having heard all this, Olaf decided to make their way as far as Kœnugarðr, then wait for the snows as Gest had suggested, for the Kangar would then ride their horses and wagons to winter pasture, to the south, in the deserts of Bolgaraland. They would then drive horse-drawn sleds onto the frozen river and give a wide berth to the treacherous areas, even if it meant travelling through the ice-bound marshes.

The hird spent one last evening with the old warden before saying their farewells. Instead of forcing the pace, they rowed south leisurely. The summer was a time for roving and reaving through foreign lands, so it was rare to meet other travellers; when they did, Olaf or Gest would share news and greetings while Botulfr busied himself with the cargo or his lessons. Some days they would rest and hunt elk in the pine forests beyond the long sandy banks or waste time hallooing at women drying hay in gaps between the trees. In the wetlands, Harald would amuse them all by wrestling the great pelicans, who clacked and squawked even more than the big Viking.

"From the Ravaging Tide to the Prince of Pelicans! Have you met your match, Harald?" Gest yelled.

"If you fish-bellies want a Rus bride, you only have to ask." Harald enjoyed the sport. "Watch out, this one bites more than the likes of you can handle."

Botulfr sat down next to Gest. "Did he really storm a Frakkar castle on his own?"

Watching him grapple with great birds for fun, nothing seemed implausible. The bear-shirts were possessed by Óðinn in battle, and for that reason, they were the champions of the fylkir's armies. These were men who rushed forwards without armour, slavering like wolves, biting their shields, felling enemies left and right.

Gest delighted at the memory. "Harald is a great fighter, but also owns a wolfish cunning. He's a second son too, incidentally. His brother Halfdan inherited, so Harald took the bear-shirt. The forts he stormed, Frakkar and Serkir—he didn't discriminate—well, let's just say they made him a rich man in his own right. If he didn't take them alone then, certainly, it was against the odds."

"How so?"

"Olaf and I were with him near Jorsalaborg, at a castle that defied the fylkir's siege for weeks. Harald kept proposing this absurd plan. We all thought he was crazy, driven mad by impatience, but he went ahead anyway, cursing us as curs and cowards. What he did was this: he caught some sparrows, set them alight near the walls. Tapers, I think he used. He made them into tiny flying candles. Then he let them go and watched them fly back to their nests in the castle thatch."

"And it worked?"

"He was the first man into the smouldering rubble! He's touched by the Trickster God, that one. Another time, in Kípr, he pretended to be dead, before the siege was even started. He had me parlay and demand a Kristin burial, alleging that he was a recent convert. Well, the Kristins loved that and couldn't open the gates quick enough. As soon as the priests brought him inside their fort, Harald resurrected himself like the Hvíta Kristr himself. He opened the gates from the inside and that was that. I suppose he was the first man over the walls that time too."

The prince laughed. "He's not just teeth and snarls then."

"Olaf is relying on Harald's wiles in the weeks to come. Harald pretends he doesn't understand the Gael part of him, but the truth is, they are a great double act. Ruses, stratagems, and ploys are meat and drink to them. So, we'll raise a warband and maraud our way to riches. We'll hire more men in the Great City. The Grikksalt is full of pirates doing the same, but none can hold a candle to our little crew."

"And you've all sailed to Miklagard before?"

"Not all the way there, no. Close, yes, but always from the west, through the Norvasund. And always with fifty ships or more."

"But you've seen Grikk soldiers, up close?"

"Close enough. Thankfully, they bathe more than the Frakkar."

Botulfr hesitated before venturing his next question. He tried to make himself sound nonchalant, but ended up a muddle of words.

"I look like them, do I? Grikkir, I mean?"

"Listen, my Prince, don't think badly of it. Tork, Grikk, Blamen—they are all slave races as far as the jarls are concerned. But then the jarls are old men, set in their ways. They tell themselves the wolf does not play with the dog, and that is an end of it."

Gest leaned back against his thwart and combed his hair for a few moments.

"Are you concerned?"

"My mother was murdered. I think I should be."

Gest shrugged.

"I've spilt enough blood to know it's all the same colour inside. You've nothing to fear from us. And believe me, I know what problems foolish uncles can cause. I wouldn't be here now if it weren't for family embarrassing me as a child. What doesn't kill you makes you stronger. Take comfort in that."

They lapsed back into companionable silence, watching Harald's latest conquest unfold.

WHEN SUMMER DREW TO A close and the Rus men returned to the fields to harvest the grain, the travellers found a fishing hut a few miles to the north of Kœnugarðr. The three hirdsmenn travelled to the fort to organise the transport and provisions for the winter part of their journey.

Askr and Botulfr had stayed behind, planning on reading and study. But with summer rains behind them, the temperature had dipped sharply, and the priority was to ensure they always had a warm fire. To that end, the skald had showed Botulfr a fungus called touchwood that grew on tree bark. He'd boil it for several days in urine then pound it into something resembling felt. The result would smoulder into a fire even with damp wood.

Botulfr grasped the Latin and Grikk easily and pored over the manuscripts. The hut was dry and roomy, which meant that the skald could unpack his bag fully, something he had been loath to do while on the river, for fear of damaging the contents. Together, they thumbed through the bindings and cases, making a rough inventory.

"Why do you care so much about those old scratchings?" Botulfr asked.

"Have you ever been to Saxland?" the skald asked. He hummed as he worked, as if composing a song.

Botulfr shook his head.

"Those books remind me that I was born a stone's throw from a very different life. From Brimarborg, where I was raised, you can see the Frakkar border forts all along the Veisa and Sax-elfr rivers all the way to Verden. This parchment has a certain smell. Some of them are damp now, but to me, that dusty, oily scent is redolent with betrayal."

"I don't understand. How can you smell betrayal?"

"Perhaps you can't. You are too young to understand. I seem to have a nose for it. Time for some fresh air. If you'll excuse me, my Prince."

Askr grew prickly when the Saxon Wars or its various protagonists came up in conversation. It occurred to Botulfr that the selection Askr had stolen wasn't just for his education. Reading the text was meant to help him understand his enemy, but perhaps it might help him understand his companion more.

He thought better of probing the subject directly, so he fixed on a more oblique approach. He rifled through the manuscripts, looking for one particular scrap of vellum, an old letter, written around the time of Ragnar. The words of this author spoke across the centuries of an enemy he barely recognised, careworn and cultivated, but very human. It was just what he needed.

He followed Askr down the short path to the river. The skald was already busy, cutting wood for the fire, hefting his axe one-handed, presumably for his exercise rather than efficiency.

"I was just looking," said Botulfr, "and we don't have a copy of the Kristin Bible?"

"Too incendiary. We already have the touchwood," Askr laughed.

Botulfr waited for Askr to place a new log. "Well, would you like to hear me read something else?"

"What have you in mind?"

"I have grown quite fond of Alkuin of York. I have one of his letters here, addressed to Bishop Higbald."

The skald stopped swinging the axe and leaned on it instead, obviously tickled.

"And why quite fond, my Prince? Has the spirit of the sage visited you, accompanied by a host of heavenly angels?"

"In a way. We have a lot of his scrolls. I admire him, how he saw himself as a mentor and confessor to all manner of men, dashing off letters to every parish of the realm. He cared about his flock. He was trying to save them."

"No," said Askr. "Treachery and nothing more. Don't get enamoured of them. They are parasites, whatever they profess." The skald punctuated the comment by splitting another log.

"But he has this evident love of books. He talks of them as invaluable treasures and goes to great lengths to collect all the knowledge he can. Is that why you kept so much from that time?"

"I'll grant you," said Askr, "without Alkuin, we'd have lost precious knowledge. For that, we are in his debt. But as a scholar? The man was a plagiarist and a rassragr, whose only real thought was to be buggered by his students. Go back to the Codex of Tertullian, De Superstitione Saeculi perhaps—that was the last time a Kristin did any thinking. By Alkuin's time, it was all Divine Providence and ceremony, with conversion at the point of a sword or else impaled on a monk's prick."

Botulfr had clearly hit a nerve, but he decided to get to the bottom of the matter.

"Imagine what he'd think now. All his demons come home to roost."

Jorvik and the whole of Northumbria, in fact, had been under Norse rule for one hundred years or more, although Alkuin had not lived to see it.

"There is no need to imagine. That letter you have there tells you all you need to know. *'You who survive, stand like men, fight bravely and defend the camp of God.'* He'd have his brethren carry on the struggle from the hedgerows and hills."

"Isn't that how the Saxar defeated Karl the Butcher?"

"Yes, but Thorr didn't demand we stop drinking ale, counting silver, or wearing anything more comfortable than a sack. Why the sudden sympathy for these Frakkar mares?"

"Why the hatred for them?"

Askr's only reply was to shoulder more wood. After a few minutes, the prince tried another approach.

"Where did the Kristin God go?"

"What?" Askr flashed him an irritated look.

"It says here, in Alkuin's letter. *'O Lord, spare thy people and do not give the Gentiles thine inheritance, lest the heathen say, Where is the God of the Christians?"*

"Who says he went anywhere? Who says he isn't right there, in your hands? That's the real power of the Hvíta Kristr. He is inside those pages, in every chapter and verse. Be careful because, from there, he can leap inside your mind. That's how he works."

Botulfr dropped the parchment and eyed it suspiciously. The skald smiled ruefully.

"Ragnar's greatest gift to the North was the idea that the word of god *is* the god, or at least, his commands. What army can survive without a great commander? That is why we burn their priests *and* their Bibles. But it is also why Ragnar kept the Kristin texts he stole, and why we skalds keep them still. To remind us of those who were murdered in the name of the Kristin God. Four generations of my family, since you were wondering, converted or murdered or both."

"I'm sorry. I didn't mean to pry. But are they really such a threat now? Can they really reach all the way to Uppsala?"

"A game never truly ends in stalemate. The borders won't hold forever. And it is your family and future under threat now. You'll come to understand Kristin treachery soon enough, with or without my advice. But their dependence on the *word* is both a strength and a weakness."

"What do you mean?"

"The Kristins seek something more than this world, yes? But their holy book is not so much a guiding light as a gilded cage, with patriarchs and kings squabbling as to who owns the key. Take your precious Alkuin. He spent years arraigning bishops about whether their god was a human who became divine or whether he'd been divine all along. If you claim authority over the divine, you clearly think you stand above your fellow man."

"My father rides with the gods. How is he different? Surely, he stands above us all?"

"Not so. In the North, we are all equal before the gods. We are all Óðinn's sworn swords, even the fylkir. Your father was elected by his people at the Althing, just as you will be elected by your people. If they chose you to serve them, how can you be above them?"

"The Kristins don't elect their rulers?"

"No, they are anointed. Their emperors are chosen by their god and rule by divine right. But there are two of them, each seeking to stand above the other, not to mention the five patriarchs. The West will claim ownership of the gilded cage, the East will scorn his brother as a blasphemer, and all the time, neither will dare to look inside, for fear their god lies dead at the bottom. Imagine if our godsmen debated that nonsense all day long, telling kings how to behave rather than dealing with the harvest or the feasts?"

Botulfr nodded. Worship was a practical matter in the North, designed to put food on the table and beer in the belly. The Norse priests inspired more by deed than by word, leaving religious debate to the skaldic classes, who in turn, traded more in lewd poetry than in fervent piety. Askr of Brimarborg was probably the closest thing to a theologian in the whole empire.

"You asked why I care for those scratchings? When a priest like Alkuin sends you a letter, claiming to speak on behalf of the gods, you would do well to be wary. Puppets always have hidden masters. Go back to their writings and learn their ways. When we reach Miklagard, we might just cut the puppeteer's strings. *That* will make for a good story."

The sermon apparently over, the skald began to stack the wood at his feet. Botulfr started to ask another question but thought better of it. Instead he traipsed back to the shack to find the codex he'd been recommended. The Saxon always hinted at hidden Kristin mysteries, only to dismiss them as base politicking. Perhaps he'd just practice the runes. Askr had shown him how to make his own manuscripts from birch bark and he just—

With nothing but a wild blur between that thought and the next, the prince found himself face down in the wet grass. He hoped the skald was out of sight and hadn't seen him tumble, or he'd never hear the end of it. Askr would write it down for all the ages to snigger at. It would probably merit his very own kenning "Soil-Licker" or some such. He pushed himself up, dusted himself down and realised he wasn't alone in the clearing. Lying close by, inches from where he had tripped, was a young woman; moist with dew, her long, dark hair plastered across her flushed face, her naked body white in the sunbeams. She arched her back, rolled onto one side and smiled up at the prince.

"For fertility," she said and stood up, leaving Botulfr to puzzle out the explanation. She walked up to him until they stood face to face, almost touching, their breath mingling in the morning air, her eyes scouring his face. In the moment of silence, Botulfr began to stir, his heart a drum in his ears.

Then, still smiling, she spun on her heel and strode into the forest.

"The Álfar have gone now," she called back to him. "You scared them when you interrupted us. Tomorrow, please announce yourself first."

EXEGESIS III

A HISTORY LESSON? I NEED NO such thing!"

Michaels burst into nervous laughter again. The thought of a history lesson from this old relic was enough to end any pretence of further politeness. People had come from as far as Ravenglass and Whitehaven to hear his last talk; he was well known as the leading authority on the tribes that had thrived here, in Wordsworth's own country. He fervently wished the old man would follow the poet's example and go wander lonely as a cloud.

"Now, listen to me. I don't know what kind of Yorkshireman *you* are, but don't presume to lecture *me* on history. Have you read any Alcuin of York? Your blessed Willehad was tutored by none other than Archbishop Ecgbert, himself a disciple of no lesser a personage than Venerable Bede. The Venerable Bede! Bastions of the faith, paragons of philosophy, fathers of English history. I have an A-Level in this stuff."

It was something of a bluff. The churchwarden knew the broad strokes of history, but he'd have to consult PASE to really put the old man in his place. If he could only get the database to work. He thought briefly about how he might go and do a quick search from the car then come back full of righteous indignation and furious facts.

Too conspicuous perhaps. Instead, he ducked back into the porch and swiped at his phone settings.

Vikings loved their nicknames. Eystein Foul-Fart could always be relied on to raise a chuckle—and of course, Harald Bluetooth had lent his name to the ubiquitous wireless technology. He'd read it somewhere; the founders were history fans. The first Christian King, he'd united the North just as their technology united just about everything. Not that it was working now, of course, Michaels groaned, stabbing icons on his phone and noting the irony.

But Botolph the Black? That was a new one.

The churchwarden didn't like being outshone. He dimly remembered a Halfdan the Black, and then, of course, there was Olaf the Black, a sea-king who ruled the Isle of Man eight hundred years ago. You could see the island quite clearly from St. Bees Head. Michaels' father had taken him there once, catching the ferry from Heysham. They'd made a day of it at the Manx Museum. His Anglican counterparts there had an embarrass-ment of riches: they had a cross too, Thorwald's Cross it was called, and almost as many runestones as Norway—although, frankly, even thinking about them just made Michaels feel worse about the gaps in his knowl-edge. Perhaps he should give the old coot a ferry timetable? Knowing his luck, they'd be cancelled because of the wind. He glanced back outside.

The visitor hadn't moved, but the wind was threatening again, tearing through the trees on the north side of the churchyard. With the first gust, a small flock of stonechats looped above the church and off into the hills beyond. Chandler watched them go, then picked up the conversation as if no time had passed.

"I didn't *say* I was a Yorkshireman. No use for them. They dis-owned me."

The churchwarden almost blew a gasket.

"You said you were from Jorvik!"

"But I didn't say *when*."

BLAKKR SAGA

T
ELL ME ABOUT YOUR MOTHER."

They had lain together most nights since they'd met, their bodies close as the leaves danced to the ground and twirled into a river swelled with rains. The cliffs of the Nipr valley had an abundance of caves, some used as shelters or storage by travellers, some haunted by the spirits of the land. The girl had found some great labyrinthine tunnels, dug by some long-dead hermit, and made it her home. She spoke sparingly, reluctantly almost, as if unused to conversing. She gave her name as Ellisif and clearly had some Vindr blood in her veins, but didn't go to any great lengths to explain herself. She was escape personified, and he had fallen for her right away. Botulfr imagined they were both outcasts, a pariah prince and a forest-dweller, finding solace as the strangest of bedfellows.

"I can't see her anymore. Her face I mean. I remember places where she was and have memories that she inhabits, but the details change every time I recall them; the words she said or didn't say, a smile I wish she'd smiled. I try to picture her, and she distorts like ripples across a reflection in a deep pond."

The branches outside rustled in answer, whispering of sorrows and secrets. Despite the wind, they were warm and content. Ellisif unclasped her hands from his and closed his eyes with her fingers as she explored his features.

"You are your mother's child? These hands, these eyes?"

"As dark as a gathering storm, my father would say. Proudly, I think. He said he could see the lightning flash in her eyes. She described me the same way sometimes. She'd tell me of her lands, where they worshipped the eternal blue sky and a goose god who made plants grow and lightning flash. Beyond the Grikk lands somewhere, far to the east. My father brought her back from a raid along the Olkoga, no doubt intended for a bed-slave. He had a wife already, although she died in childbirth. She was darker than I am, not like the blámenn, but they called her Queen Hel all the same. Partly because of her skin, as I said, but they also thought she was close to the grave and could conjure draugr. She had other children—Gudmudr died a babe in arms; Oysteinn was a mare, a rassragr, who took his own life. They said my mother's magic was to blame for his perversion. They said the same thing about me."

Over the past weeks, the young, bewildered boy had kept strong by submerging his thoughts beneath the surging rivers of the Rus, beneath Askr's flood of damp parchments and blotted letters. But now the prince began to unfurl his thoughts, trying to marshal them on the field, to show the strength of his command.

"In fact, she was a beautiful, beautiful woman who throbbed with sadness and sorrow from a lifetime of loss. My father was cruel to marry her, foolish to think he could fix her when he was the reason she mourned. Perhaps he really believes he is the Thunderer and that he can command the storms."

Ellisif's eyes were deep, dark wells. "And they killed her?"

"I don't know. I can see her death, smothered with furs, or slashed with knives, or drowned beneath the ice. Every time it is different. She was happier when I saw her last. She always felt freer when my father was campaigning or orchestrating his next hunt. I can't even be sure of that, that she was happy then. I hope she was, for a moment at least. Askr and Olaf tell me my brother and uncles were conspiring. They blame spies in the pay of the Grikkir."

"Shameful enough to touch a woman in anger—"

"What penalty is there for the death of an empress? My father has banished people for tilting a hat, but for his own wife? He didn't even call out his guard. He rode off to hunt bear. As if nothing had happened."

"To hide his grief perhaps?"

"What shame is there in grief? All creation wept for the death of Baldur. The Fylkir of the Himinríki has been unmanned and his son swept out to sea."

"You'll return on the tide?" Her lips murmured around his neck, trailing questions, hastening the young man's plans.

He was a prince now, strapping on his armour, desperate both to impress and to hide the fact he was unaccustomed to the weight.

"Olaf is fond of saying, 'two heads cut off and thrown high into the tree have only the winds with which to scheme.' But not yet. We're not ready yet."

They clung together in silence a while, her midnight tresses shuttering his vision, her gaze engulfing him. She was heat and sweat, filled with purpose and pleasure, ardent yet absent somehow. She seemed, in that moment, to be no more real than the memory of his mother, a tangle of half-thoughts. He wondered if he was even in the cave, by the river, in the lands of the Rus. And then her distant wandering ceased, and she returned, a waif in his arms.

He felt smaller still now, inconsequential, but forced a return to speech to cover his shame.

"My men spoke to me of Miklagard, the city of the world's desire, and home of my enemy. We'll travel there, hiding in plain sight as they say. I want to see where the Kristin god lives."

"The Kristin god no more lives in Miklagard than Thorr lives in the oaks or the fields."

"I don't mean literally. You've been there?"

"I have travelled to many places. But yes, I have seen the brazen domes of their churches, heard the mournful tolling of bells, witnessed the ponderous parades of icons around their endless walls. I followed the Kristins there. I was not tempted."

"So why does it call to men, both in victory and in defeat? Why don't the Kristins yield or succumb? Perhaps the City itself is their god. Perhaps their god is desire or fear, or both, a greed for glory, wealth or the life eternal. Perhaps that is why the Great City is sieged by Serkir, Bolgarar, Khazar and Húnar. I want to see their talismans, their relics, I want to understand how man may build a replica of Heaven."

He surprised himself with the spontaneity, but he spoke earnestly, the words bubbling up from some deep wellspring within him.

"Why?" Ellisif laughed. She was amused now, propped up on one arm, waif become wolf.

"Not for the wealth. Olaf wants his riches and plunder, and he shall have them. We will go to the Grikk lands, and there, I shall nest, just below the surface, burrowing into their vaults, gnawing at their fears. As they have infiltrated my inheritance, I will infest their kingdom and make it my domain."

"I am impressed, Son of Óðinn. Like the Allfather, you have tamed your fury; like the Wolf Foe, you have ridden far and wide; like the Blind God, you seek out knowledge. All of Midgard is your birthright," she said. "It is time to claim it."

Botulfr was elated, enthralled by his own cunning and her ferocious praise. She was slavering over him again, aroused and hungry. It suddenly occurred to him that this slip of a girl had the sight. He'd been blind all right, bound by his own one-eyed god. She could see not just his swarthy skin, his foolish hide, but his very breath, his petty spirit, his lustful mind, his fabrications of fortune.

Fjölkyngi. Magic. This woman snared spirits, haltered fates, and bound them to her will. He opened his mouth and then thought better of it.

"Oh, don't worry, my Prince," she said, as if reading his mind. "You and I have only just begun."

"NOT THAT *BIKKJUNA!*"

Harald slammed his helmet repeatedly against the side of the hut door, as if trying to knock some sense into the world. Gest tried to stay his arm, but the oak had already started to splinter, and the helmet would need a hammer taken to it before anyone could wear it. He was red-faced, and roaring incoherently, his beard flecked with spittle. Most Norse swearing involved animals, copulating with animals, or being sired by animals. Botulfr had begun to realise he had been mollycoddled—he knew most of his kin had foul mouths, and even made sport out of insults, but no one had ever sworn directly at the fylkir's son. As Harald continued to rave, the prince caught a phrase "child born of a long-dead sow," and he bridled, the memory of his mother still raw even after all these weeks. He glanced towards his sword.

"If you cannot bite, never show your teeth, little man," Harald glowered, evidently not so mad that he couldn't spot the slight shift in the prince's stance.

Gest spun the dented helmet around to examine it more carefully. He laughed mirthlessly.

"Harald has a point. Ellisif, is that her name? Well, she is a fine-looking woman, but everyone knows you should never, and I mean *never*, sleep in the arms of a sorceress, lest she lock up your limbs—or worse." Gest trailed off, leaving the unmentionable to their imaginations.

Harald made sure they didn't miss anything. "Why does she need your pathetic cock when she has her own staff to ride? And a dozen spirits fucking her morning, noon, and night? Jarl Hakon slept with a völva and became so itchy he had two of his hird put a rope up his arse and play toga hönk."

Askr started to object, but Harald stared him down. Botulfr had all his answers ready.

"First, I have no money. We have no money. I can't pay the bride-price or afford a morning gift."

His men groaned loudly in unison.

"It is marriage now?! Bad enough to couple with the she-wolf, but a wedding is out of the question."

"She has ensorcelled him already."

"Careful now. A 'no' does not hide anything, but a 'yes' very easily becomes a deception."

Botulfr raised his voice and persevered. "Second, she speaks Grikk and has travelled to Miklagard, and further still."

"Oh, well that changes everything. I often thought of marrying the first person I met who spoke in a funny way. It's a wonder you haven't bedded Olaf."

"Never trust the words of a woman. Their hearts were shaped on a spinning wheel; falsehood is fixed in their breasts."

"I think he is fixing on her breasts."

"Third, I am to be fylkir and King of the Storm Halls. I am a son of Óðinn. Do you not think I can see that my marriage is fated? And she dreamt of me on Midsummer's Eve with seven flowers under her pillow. She has the sight."

Askr sighed. "My Prince, this long summer I have seen you grow brains and brawn although, sadly, not beard. You were nearly a man when we invited you to join us." He said this with no trace of irony. "You will make a fine fylkir for our people one day—if you are elected. But stripping out of your breeches and taking oaths with a Vindr and a seer is—"

"Is no different from Óðinn, Lord of the Aesir, bedding any number of mistresses," said Botulfr. "Your objections are noted."

It wasn't a question of confidence, but he delivered the much-rehearsed line with too much petulance and felt instantly childish. In his mind's eye, he could see himself reduced to trembling and tears again. Defeated, he turned to skulk back to the cave. He was surprised to hear Olaf interject:

"Lucky for you, young Prince, I know just where to get mead enough for your bridal ale."

THE ARGUING CONTINUED ALL THE way to Frigga's Day, but the ceremony went ahead, after a fashion.

When Norse nobility married, the watchwords were invariably opulence and abundance. Arrangements took months of negotiation at the Althing, with nobles vying for consideration with gifts of clothing, jewelry, livestock, and slaves. It was said King Ake gifted his future wife the entire land of Danmørk, although it soon returned to him in the civil war that followed. For the wedding itself, ancient custom demanded that the bride and groom symbolically purify themselves in the steam of the town bathhouse, required that they exchange oath-rings and ancestral swords to protect their sacred vows, and mandated the sacrifice of a living animal to the gods for health and long life.

They came as close as they could. Botulfr and Ellisif were married in a cave after a plunge into an icy river, and they shared borrowed swords and rings of twine. The sacrificial goat escaped and fled into the hills before Askr could catch it again. At least the bridal crown was proper, woven from straw and wheat and garlanded with flowers. Botulfr was in awe that his wife glowed like spring, even as the land around was brown and fading. If he had been impetuous, her beauty was the reason why.

Olaf gladdened everyone's spirits throughout, hurling enough insults at Harald to distract him from all the ill omens. The Austman had procured enough mead for the whole month of the honey moon. Ellisif recited an old verse as the prince drank first, and then he passed the bowl to her and did the same. Then the toasting began, to Óðinn, to Freyja, to kinship. Olaf offered up a toast to "Praise day at dusk, a wife when dead, a weapon when tried, a maid when married, ice when 'tis crossed, and ale when 'tis drunk." Round and round they went, telling stories as old as time.

They were put to bed late, and when the witnesses left, splashing back to the fishing hut in the dead of night, the marriage was complete.

In the morning, she spoke of her dreams. The Norse paid great attention to the dreams of a wedding night; the dreams of a married völva were said to deliver unrivalled prophecy. Ellisif recalled clearly: in her vision, she took a golden brooch from her cloak and hurled it out in front of her. Roots immediately writhed out and took hold in the ground. Branches then shot out from the brooch, and a tree emerged, a tree that grew so tall that she was unable to see over it. The tree's bole was blood-red, its upper trunk green, and its branches snowy white. The branches spread out to cover all of Midgard and then on through the heavens. She saw then three witnesses, each nurturing the tree. The first lay face down in the blood-red roots, the second had climbed high up into the leafy green boughs, and the third had vaulted further still, beyond the rime and frost, touching the stars.

Botulfr was fascinated and quickly shrugged off the blankets to look directly at his new wife and delve deeper. His questions were urgent and insistent.

"What does it mean? Are the witnesses maids or men? We had four witnesses at our wedding. The three Nornir perhaps? The fylkirs consult with them. I am to be crowned, that must be it!"

Ellisif was sleepy still and rolled away, leaving him with the smooth ivory curve of her shoulder. "My Prince, I am certain you will be crowned. Just as I am certain we are to have a long and happy life."

"Because you have the sight? You have seen my destiny?"

She glanced back, her eyes both terrible and tender. "What do you know of the Nornir?"

"I know their names: Urðr, Verðandi, and Skuld. Three wise giant-maids, huge and mighty, that shape the fates of men and tend the roots of the World Tree, Yggdrasil."

"The Nornir only reveal their fateful secrets as a life comes to its end. Not even a fylkir may peer into the future."

"But you can see the future? You just dreamed of it!"

"In my mind's eye, the Nornir are a knot, that which has happened, that which is about to be, and that which ought to be. To tease the threads apart is folly. A Jötunn may appear to be a giant, but that is not their only shape. Do not dress the spirits in the garb of angels, or the Kristins will have devoured us all."

"I don't understand."

"Then let us speak of it another time. Now it is time to enjoy the present." Ellisif clearly had other passions on her mind, but Botulfr gently rebuffed her.

"Call it your wedding gift to me. Ellisif, please."

"You have a lifetime of gifts ahead."

"What do the Álfar say? What do they look like?"

Ellisif propped herself up on her elbow and clasped her hand over her eyes in exasperation.

"Only the Dökkálfar are awake, and they are as black as pitch."

She thought for a while, before speaking again.

"Do you know why a rooster will crow before afternoon rain, or a cat will hiss before an earthquake? Or why dogs will bark when there is no intruder to be seen? It is because they see where men cannot. The gods are always in the skies, the Dvergr are always beneath our feet, and the Álfar are always in the trees. Most folk just don't know how to reach them, and we have all forgotten how to follow them to their homes. But they are all around us, all the time. Now, answer me this: What does a great king look like?"

Botulfr grinned and tried to kiss her. "Broad shoulders, muscular arms, a mighty chest, and a fiery eloquence on his lips."

Ellisif laughed at this, but quickly grew serious again. "A king can be grey-haired and feeble, with the shaggy beard of a priest, and still command armies. True splendour comes from the will to power, the struggle to survive. There will always be forces you cannot control. A true king doesn't fear change, he creates order from chaos. The greatest king of all, Óðinn, bent all things to his will and made the world. Now, answer me this: Why do men follow you? It is important to know because many of them will die doing it."

Botulfr realised he didn't have a good answer, and Ellisif didn't wait for one.

"It isn't because you know where you are going, for you are as blind as they are. It isn't because they can see the doors ahead of you, for you cannot perceive them. It is because they think you can give them something they want. The maids who determine the waxing and waning of men's lives, we call Nornir, but there are many lesser seers. We come to each child that is born to bless the life ahead. Or to curse it. But only a king has the power to lift a man up from the fields and make him a jarl, or to cast him as a thrall. That is why the fylkir are said to consult with the fates. Now, another question: What do your men want of you?"

"Riches, lands, eternal glory. What all men want." He recognised he was only half-joking.

"And what about your woman? Why do I follow you?"

Botulfr sensed a trap and withdrew slightly, mumbling vague thoughts.

"My Prince, the sight doesn't allow me to know the future with certainty. Portents are signs that one must choose to follow or ignore. But I will answer your question, about my vision, if you will give me a morning gift of my choosing."

Botulfr was excited to be back on comfortable territory. All the questions had made him recognise he didn't have many answers. Ellisif, on the other hand, seemed more worldly and regal than he could ever hope to be. She was as severe as she was beautiful, and he couldn't have resisted her if he'd wanted. He nodded, quickly, and she coiled on top of him, caressing his broad shoulders and muscular arms.

"The tree is your reign, your realm, and your dynasty. It will grow strong if you nurture it. If *we* nourish it. I will be all-wise Mímir to your Óðinn. As he hung for nine nights on the windy tree, so shall we. Menglöð has nine maidens to serve her and Ægir had nine daughters, so shall we, for all of the nine worlds we will rule. You and I will glide down from the heavens to deliver the judgement of Kings and Urðr. Together. Grant me this gift, and each of those who follow you will have their wish. All save one, who seeks to shake the tree to its roots."

She clambered over him, kissing him softly. Botulfr decided he was perfectly content to be shaken to his roots.

THEY STOLE THE HORSES AND sledges. Olaf and Gest left one day at dawn and returned before the fire was alight that evening. The horses had grown thick coats for the winter and would keep a brisk trot along the ice, pulling the two sledges in turns. They were not like the compact, bristle-maned farm horses Botulfr knew; these were long, sloping beasts, tall and powerful with a silvery sheen that caught the fading light. Olaf said they were Tork horses that could run for days, stolen from a Kangar raiding party he'd overwhelmed.

Botulfr was duly impressed—until Gest mentioned that the overwhelming had been accomplished by copious skins of ale, dosed with henbane for good measure. What's more, the whole scheme had been devised by Ellisif, who knew the paths the Kangar took through the forest. The prince was mildly annoyed not to have been consulted but realised he had little to add. His wife had quickly shown her worth, and even Harald had stopped grumbling. Besides, Botulfr was given cold jobs now, away from the fire and tents, work worthy of a man and not a boy, which made him feel like he had earned his place too.

The next part of the plan required Gest and Olaf to range ahead of the party, Kangar standards hung on their spears. On clear days, at a distance, the horse and colours were a fine disguise; for the rest, the foul weather kept them concealed. Warbands were scarce and any encampments easily skirted.

Their luck held for the first week, but on the eighth day, Ellisif gave warning that the Nornir demanded blood for safe passage. She led them to shelter by a river bluff, escaping the biting wind. No sooner had they set camp than ten horsemen cantered out of the gale, seeking to share the same spot with fellow tribesmen.

The hirdsmenn kept their backs to the Kangar, ignoring their greetings, while pretending to feed the horses or the fire. Only when the hetman grew angry did they spring up, all sinew and spittle.

Harald ran at the riders with a raised axe, tall enough to strike a mounted man. The first he split at the waist; he then spun around the horse's bridle and jabbed the horn of his axe into a second throat. Askr fought with both hands. He raised one sword with his left hand and struck with the right, lunging at the hetman, taking off one of his legs below the knee. Olaf hurled a spear, and his foe fell backwards, the shaft pinning him in the snowdrift at the foot of the bluff. Gest grasped a rider with one hand on his belt and threw him onto the frozen ground a short distance off, where Ellisif sliced through his skull without a word. The horses screamed in reproach, and the remaining Kangar scattered.

Botulfr hadn't moved a muscle. There simply hadn't been time. Olaf retrieved his spear with a grunt and came back to the fire.

"You've heard it said, 'From his weapons on the open road, no man should step one pace away.' Now you understand it." He stared at the prince from under his hood.

"They died quietly. Without even a curse on their lips. *Seiðmaðr*, the lot of them." Sorcerers. Unmanly. Gest sat down heavily.

"That one is still gurgling," called Harald, steadying the horses, his voiced raised against the wind.

"I'd personally hope for some memorable last words when I die," said Gest. "Something that can be recorded for posterity."

"*Prick!*" bellowed the giant. "Write that down."

"Good idea. I might just do that." Gest got up again and began to search the bodies.

Ellisif crept up to her husband and rested her head on his shoulder, her back against the rock. She began to sing softly, tapping her head against the stone to match the rhythm. It looked ungainly, fitful even, and Botulfr shifted so to look at her face.

Olaf answered his unspoken question.

"The *Vardlokkur*. The warlock song. She sings to protect us from the spirits of these tribes. A Serklander once told me 'When the Norse sing, the growling sound they make reminds me of dogs howling, only the dog is more in tune'. We should be thankful there is some beauty left in the North."

When the wind died, they all climbed to the top of the bluff. Gest thrust a spear deep into the ground and then hefted a horse's head onto the shaft, drained of blood and half-frozen. The hirdsman raised his voice and called to the gods.

"Here is set this *níðstang*, this cursing pole, and my curse on the Kurgan of these lands. This curse I turn also on the guardian-spirits who dwell here, that they may all wander astray, never to find their home till they have driven the Kangar from this land."

Askr cut runes into the shaft to mirror the words, and they turned the head to face the east, completing the ancient ritual.

"Well, I for one am terrified," mocked Harald as they hitched the sledges and continued the journey. Ellisif slept soundly, hearing no more whispers from the fates.

AT THE MOUTH OF THE Nipr, they traded their horses for passage by sea—the Hospitable Sea, the Grikkir called it—the crossroads of commerce for a hundred peoples. The days were cool but sunny, and the freezing rain became a thankfully forgotten memory.

They first spied the Great City on the horizon, distant domes dotted with painted sails of foreign fleets. The company stood near the bow of their ship as she swung across the waves. Towers, palaces and churches grew from salt-soaked blurs and became a city aglow with marble and porphyry, beaten gold and brilliant mosaics. On the landward side, the city was defended by the impregnable walls of Theodosius, twenty yards tall, ramparts that vaulted the heavens, protected by the Virgin Mary herself, as well as the dauntless defenders of the Grikk Empire. The ports teemed with galleys, cogs, and ships of all sizes, including many Norse vessels with shield-hung gunwales, most

Northmen being more accustomed to trading than piracy.

Upon docking, they were poured onto streets awash with activity. A sluice of colonnaded streets, gilded arches, and cypress-strewn gardens spread before them. Liturgies rose and fell in waves as they marched past a procession of churches, through a surge of people pooled in market squares and outside exquisite baths. Bronzesmiths mixed with furriers and horse traders along the Meze, fermented fish and fresh baked bread and horseshit caking the air. Towering above it all, treasures both ancient and modern caught the sun's rays and held them like vows.

It was indeed the City of the World's Desire. It all seemed to rest not on solid masonry, but on a tide of cantors and clerics, as if suspended from heaven; on the head of John the Baptist, the Crown of Thorns, nails from the True Cross. At its heart, the Church of Holy Wisdom, Hagia Sophia, beamed with a magnificent golden halo that humbled all who gazed at it.

"Kunta, fukja, drit." Harald was awestruck. They all were.

Botulfr drifted through the streets, swirling in thoughts. His father's empire was turf and iron, linen sails and wooden beams. The Grikk throne was one of much greater majesty, like marble powdered with stars. He hadn't appreciated that until now, hadn't seen that the true edifice of empire was tangible. Empires were full of buildings cemented by greed, and they drew on a history written in blood.

"Askr," said Botulfr above the tumult of the crowd. "The death of the gods, Ragnarok. Surtr and his fiery sword. Tell me the story."

The skald was walking slowly behind, eyes wide at the spectacle. He glanced at the prince.

"Amid this turmoil, the sky will open, and from it will ride the sons of Muspell. Surtr will ride in front, and both before and behind him there will be burning fire. His sword will be very fine. Light will shine from it more brightly than from the sun." The words were mechanical, delivered by rote.

"Then there is your Surtr, your devourer of worlds." The prince pointed to the golden dome of Hagia Sophia, then widened his gesture to the whole of Miklagard. "You were right, my friend, this place and its god are our doom. I see it clearly."

Botulfr could almost feel the hand of destiny. If he didn't strike at the belly of the beast, his world would be swallowed, and its pages overwritten by the Kristin priests. History was written by the victors, and so his people would be penned as ravagers and despoilers, malicious wolves set on destruction. The Valkyrja and the Nornir would be recast as winged angels, and Óðinn thrown down as a son of Shaitan. His world would be eclipsed as surely as the Garm-hound would swallow the sun.

He could hear his saga in his head and was growing smitten with each chapter. There was a *different* future. This city would one day be his city. His eyes met those of his wife, and he wondered if she could see his thoughts. She might have nodded, or it could have been the bobbing crowds.

The rest of the hird was apprehensive. Gest blanched.

"They have an unearthly fire too, these Grikkir, given to Constantine by their angels. Great flames, smoke, and thunder spill from their ships and burn even on water."

"The dragon Níðhöggr, who feasts on corpses on the Shores of the Dead," said Askr. "Another portent of the end."

Harald snorted derisively. "I thought you were trying to encourage us to fight?"

"Óðinn gifted me the Mead of Poetry to spare you the mundane."

Olaf laughed at that and clasped him on the shoulder, grinning. He was the only one who seemed to be having any fun. Botulfr reached out to Ellisif, drawing her to him through the throng. The völva wore a simple woolen tunic, her hair bunched under a sheepskin cap, so as to seem to be a boy amongst Norse traders. It was a disorienting guise, especially when she spoke in her soft, sparing way.

"Did you see this in your dream? Is the Great Temple the golden brooch? Or is it our doom?"

"This doom or the next. There is seldom a single wave." She shrugged and reached for her wedding ring, unthreading the twine from her finger. "A ring has no beginning, no middle and no end. They are a series of threads that can be coiled… or cut." She snapped the twine taut to demonstrate.

"Draumskrok. *Nonsense.* If it was a proper ring, it would be made of gold," muttered Harald, towering about the seer and half-hoping his voice would be lost in the crowds.

"Everything has threads," she said. "Even if they are invisible to your eye. Even gold. And every disturbance is a ring. Drop a pebble into a river and make a ripple. What is a ripple but a ring of water? What is a wave but a larger ripple?"

"Then we had best introduce ourselves at the palace," said the prince and strode purposefully into the street.

THE IMPERIAL CORTEGE ADVANCED IN steps, pacing towards the throne with infinite patience, the halls echoing with hymns of thanks and praise. At the centre of the procession sat Gregoras Chrysaphes, in Christ, Emperor and Autocrat of the Romans.

He was flanked by men-at-arms, soldiers covered head to toe in mail so brightly polished that it was difficult to see the man they were guarding. The emperor was further obscured by the scarlet flags of his standard bearers and silver rods of the heralds, who in turn were surrounded by the pious crowds gathered in the Great Chamber. Hallelujah, intoned the cantors, time after time, a chorus echoing the soloist. The beauty of their voices was astonishing.

"Bikkju-sonr," Botulfr cursed.

This didn't seem like such a good idea anymore. They had been carefully positioned by the door so as not to distract from the spectacle within. Five hulking Northerners and a slave-boy didn't go unnoticed. Botulfr had tried to explain himself to the palace guard, but his halting Grikk had just resulted in the hasty summoning of the magistros. Askr had gracefully intervened and ensured that they gained entry to the auditorium—although the guards held onto their weapons.

"What did you say to them?" whispered the prince.

"I told the master that we were expected by the Bureau of Barbarians."

"Don't be ridiculous."

"I am being serious. The bureau handles protocol and supervision of visitors. You wanted to be introduced. If you join the dance circle, you must dance. The bureau has spies everywhere. If they weren't aware of our arrival, I'd be surprised."

"Spies? Who knew we'd arrived?" Botulfr scowled at Olaf, who had originated the whole expedition, but he just shrugged.

Askr came to his defense. "In fairness, I only learned of it from the master and improvised from there. He'll have scuttled off to find the logothete, a functionary who will have the ear of the basileus."

"The basileus?"

"The emperor. The Grikkir call themselves the Rhomaoi, even though Constantine had moved the capital from Rome centuries ago, the official language changed from Latin to Grikk sometime after that, after the West had fallen to the Frakkar. With a stroke of a quill, the Imperium Romanum became the Basileia tōn Rhōmaiōn."

"With a stroke of his prick. I could end that old peacock before they could stop me." Harald cracked his knuckles, while the rest of the hird tried hard to keep their composure. Ellisif looked pained and murmured to quiet them.

Botulfr turned back to the hall and tried to relax. He felt oddly suffused in the chant. The cortege continued to step forward across mosaic floors strewn with laurel and ivy, the short journey designed to be as majestic and unhurried as the man on the throne. The intonations ringing all around were arranged for the same reason, a divine endorsement of his rule. The whole chamber was gazing at the emperor in rapt silence: senators, magistrates, monks, soldiers of the city watch, imperial secretaries and notaries.

All except one.

Harald had spotted him first and given the prince a hefty nudge to attract his attention. On the far side of the chamber, nestled in between soaring columns, embroidered curtains, and gleaming silver plates was a tall figure who stood apart from the dignitaries and patricians. Most of the men wore short red woolen capes, pinned at the shoulder, but this man wore a long, loose-fitting robe adorned with green eagles, like a Tork kaftan. Even at this distance, there was hint of something menacing about his eyes. They were as piercing as a hawk's, even under the heavy hoods of his eyelids. The man disappeared for a while, lost in the crowd, then appeared again behind them, close to the huge golden organ that the Grikkir used to serenade the heavens.

The man beckoned them over, away from the procession to a nearby vestibule. He spoke in almost-perfect Norse, in a deep baritone voice.

"Allow me to introduce myself: Gilpractus, Logothete of the Course. We are glad you have come to pay your devotions to the emperor, it is quite delightful if unexpected. However, you must be dressed suitably for the occasion."

Some servants milled around, offering garnet tunics, with roses embroidered across the shoulders and cuffs. The Grikk official watched as they changed, his eyes a calm sea of deepest blue. Gilpractus was so assured and graceful it was impossible to argue, even though Harald clearly wanted to. Once they were in suitable attire, the logothete bowed deep and low in formal greeting, as if seeing them for the first time.

"How is the most magnificent and most noble and distinguished Archon of Thule? How is your father, the fylkir, and his council of jarls? I am sorry the chartulary was unable to receive you in the harbour. Did anything unfortunate or distressing occur on your journey? Leave cheerfully and delighting in the fact that today you dine with our holy emperor."

At first, Botulfr tried to gather a suitable reply, but as the words tumbled towards him regardless, he realised he wasn't required to answer any of the questions and that his host was effortlessly reciting a formula. Protocols had been adhered to, even if they threatened to disrupt the orderly and elegiac proceedings behind them. Having drifted through the address, Gilpractus allowed himself a sigh of what must have been relief.

"Now, please join us and implore the mediation of Our Immaculate Mistress, the Mother of God, both for the cause of God and the life of the emperor."

The hird were steered forward, and for the rest of the interminable ceremony, Gilpractus stood immediately behind them. Botulfr had to keep his head fixed forward for fear of revealing his crushing boredom. The Grikk capacity for tedium was staggering.

Eventually the emperor stepped to the dais, although he still paused for one last prayer. Botulfr found it hard to imagine that this solemn and ponderous ritual occurred before every imperial audience, but it was an impressive display of the empire's supreme power, a reminder that Gregoras was the inheritor of the ineffable glory of God, that he was the viceroy of the Saviour. That he owned the gilded cage.

"O Mother of the God of Love, have mercy and compassion upon me, a sinner and a prodigal. Accept this prayer which is offered to thee from my impure lips; and thou, being gracious and compassionate and tender-hearted, be thou ever present with me in this life as my defender and helper so that I may turn aside the assault of my enemies and guide me into salvation."

The prayer complete, the crowd were then led in cheers and proclamations, which provided enough noise to allow Askr to provide some translation into the prince's ear.

"You who have been chosen by divine election, to the concord and exaltation of the world; you who have been married into the purple by God and so on and on. It is all just hot air."

"Who or what is the Archon of Thule? I have this terrible feeling they have mistaken me for someone else."

Askr laughed. "It's just what they call us. They can't address you as the Prince of the Storm Hall without implicitly acknowledging our gods, so they stick with ancient forms of address. Allows them to keep the heavens in order. A place for all things, and all things in their place."

Botulfr looked towards his wife, who returned his gaze steadily. Her disguise had all but disappeared with the change of dress, but she didn't look concerned. The silence that followed the hymns seemed as unearthly as the chants themselves. He turned back to the stillness of the great hall and looked around. The whole charade was preposterous, but still, with so many complicit courtiers, it made Uppsala seem an empty shell.

The emperor sat, and his priests placed the imperial diadem on his head; a crenelated crown, profusely adorned with pearls and jewels, lappets gleaming from his temples to his cheeks. The logothete ushered the hird forward and urged them to kneel. There really was no other choice. Three others approached first, showing the customary reverence, and so the Northmen tried their best to imitate them. Now cloaked in the imperial purple, Gregoras beamed a welcoming smile straight at his guests.

"Arise, Varangoi! Today is a blessed and auspicious day. I have a feeling we shall be great and fast friends. Now, which of you is Gog, and which is Magog?"

THE BANQUET WAS A LAVISH but confusing affair. Everything was made of gold: the couches and chairs, the tablecloths, even the food was served in golden bowls, so heavy they had to be hoisted onto the table by servants using ropes and pulleys attached to the ceiling. Anything that wasn't gold was either red or purple.

The hirdsmenn had evidently shaken any discomfort they felt earlier and were gorging themselves as if it were the last food and drink they might ever see. Botulfr didn't begrudge them; the journey had been a long one, the meals infrequent and meagre. He was used to eating with his fingers or from a knife, but Botulfr noticed all the emperor's men used long forks and spoons. There was nothing on the tables that was unknown in the North, but foods that were rare delicacies in his father's halls were here in abundance. There were wheels of cheese; piles of figs, walnuts, almonds, chestnuts, and pears; a fat goat stuffed with garlic, onions, and leeks; eggplant and spinach steeped in fish sauce. There were the sweet and strange smells of peppers, cinnamon, vinegar and cumin; copious sweet rice dishes made with milk and sugar; unleavened cakes soaked in honey; free-flowing wines spiced with aniseed or pine resin. They ate until they were fit to burst.

Gilpractus found them huddled in a corner. One of the host of servants bobbing at his heels politely coughed to attract their attention, while his master coolly surveyed the scene.

"Honoured Archon, the great and high emperor who sits on the golden throne will grant you an audience shortly."

Olaf fell mockingly to one knee and offered a hand to Gest.

"What did I tell you, farmboy? Wag your tail and yelp loud enough, and they'll raise you up! These Grikkir have mistaken you for someone who matters!"

Askr also started with theatrics, sweeping into a bow that looked quite dangerous in the ill-fitting Grikk garb. He answered for the group, replying in Grikk, explaining that they would all be honoured.

The logothete immediately shook his head.

"The Emperor of the Romans will see the Archon of Thule alone. Your skald is welcome to join my secretary and peruse the library. The rest of you too, if you wish. Your good lady wife might wish to pray at the Monastery of the Peribleptos?"

Harald was not to be dismissed so lightly a second time. He towered above the crowd, splintered a glass goblet and pointed at the food. "Do you teach your goats to swim in this land? There is enough oil to drown a whale!"

The logothete smiled thinly.

"My apologies if the food is not to your liking. As your arrival was somewhat unexpected, I am told we were not able to provision appropriately. We have improvised as best as possible in the circumstances, given the necessity to... embellish. God clearly wishes to restore the dignity of your family, but, to be clear, since the Year of Calamity, we have received no formal embassies from Thule."

"The only calamity I know is this wine," Olaf sniggered into his cup before draining it. "He means Sikiley. We fought there against the old emperor, Antiochus."

"Meinfretr," cursed Harald. *Stinkfart.* "Why does no-one say what they mean?"

The Grikk was still a model of calm and decorum, despite the antagonism.

"Indeed, Antiochius the Bold was unable to gain the shores of the Catepanate of Italy, and the land was lost to us."

"Unable to gain the shores?" Gest was smirking too now. "The waves were so high it was as if Ægir were pouring out his wrath upon you, showing you from the very start that the Grikkir would not be successful. Never plan an assault when Loki's Torch is rising in the sky. Some of the ships were lost, crews and all; others were dashed on the rocks and broken to pieces. We buried your dead with due rites, and ransomed you back the survivors."

"Thank you for the colour," Gilpractus said, a mote of irritation creeping into his voice. "Regardless, your nation of pirates hasn't treated with us since. Am I to assume you are sent by your father to return the territory?"

This time, Ellisif answered for the prince, addressing the hawkish Grikk directly. "You *know* why we are here. To put an end to your meddling. Did you imagine that because some Northern cur took your bait we could be all so easily bought? My husband is a scion of Óðinn."

This made Gilpractus at least raise an eyebrow.

"I am at a loss for your meaning, daughter. The Emperor of the Romans does not transact with the North. Paying your jarls and generals to leave us in peace only seems to encourage more of your kind. I once hired your kin as mercenaries to help reclaim land stolen by the Saracens, and you assumed the right to move onto it in their place."

Askr was first to respond, more heated than Botulfr had ever seen him. "If not your gold, then your god. If he does not tear down men's homes, he ruins their minds, and then they tear them down themselves. We shall not kneel and pray."

Botulfr looked at the red faces of his hird. Their swaggering was becoming perilously close to swaying. He had the creeping realisation that they were more drunk than godsmen after a sacrifice. They were only going to get more belligerent as the evening wore on.

One of the functionaries joined the fray. "Rest assured, there is no pig whose stink cannot be masked by the scent of holy oil."

Only Gilpractus remained unflappable. "And to think we have only just met! I imagine it must be so cold in the North that, unless you speak quickly, your tongues become frozen. We welcome anyone to renounce their demons and to be baptised in the name of undefiled, unstained, all-chaste and Pure Lady."

He held up his hands to wave away further comment and turned pointedly to Botulfr.

"Honoured Archon. My distinguished predecessors thought it… *inappropriate* to allow vital aspects of the imperial glory to be mutilated, and so they embarked on a plan of impeccable order. We have provided the senatorial body and every subject with a suitable standard of life and conduct, as a result of which they should become better regarded and behaved, as well as beloved by their emperors, respected by each other as well as admired by every nation. A wise precaution, don't you agree? Splendid. Then, if I might suggest you accompany me—alone—and we can discuss affairs of state in a more refined manner."

The logothete bowed and stalked away, replaced by a squall of lesser functionaries and menacing soldiers. Botulfr looked around at the hird, expecting them to look contrite, but if anything, they looked even more like wolves among the sheep.

"Well, that went well," he said as they all collapsed in gales of laughter.

When the amusement subsided, Olaf offered some advice.

"If the emperor offers you a sword on which to swear fealty, refuse the point and ask for the hilt. Tell him that it is our custom to pledge allegiance by touching it. As soon as you clasp hold, drive the blade through him."

The Grikk bureaucrats hadn't a full grasp of the Norse tongue, but clearly understood the gestures the Norse had made. The guards shuffled around, nervously. Who knows what stories they told of the fury of the Norse?

"Then sever his ribs from his flimsy spine and flop the lungs onto his womanly chest. A blood eagle to match his Roman banners." Harald walked slowly to the nearest one, grasped him by the collar and belched in his face.

"The only thing that has kept Miklagard from the same fate as Sikiley is that you have fortifications bigger than those of Asgard. I bet they cost the sun and the moon!" Olaf roared.

The scene threatened to get ugly quickly, but Gest defused the tension by drawing out his harp and starting to sing. It sounded like a caterwaul in comparison to the choir earlier. The prince hoped it was because he was drunk and not because his ears had been corrupted by the Kristin God. Ellisif took his arm.

"Go," she said. "Discretion is the better part of valour. I will watch over the men here. Remember your mother."

She planted a kiss on his cheek, and with that, Botulfr hurried after Gilpractus.

"PEACE AND MERCY, HAPPINESS AND glory from the Aesir be with you, high and mighty Emperor of the Romans. Wealth and health and longevity from the north, peacemaking and good Emperor. May justice and great peace rise in your reign, most peaceful and generous Emperor."

Botulfr had practiced the formal greeting prescribed by Gilpractus, who insisted on the exact words. He'd managed the Grikk as best he could in the short space of time. Diplomatic form appeared to prevail over common sense in the East. Botulfr had refused to scrape and grovel further; there was a limit to the façade he was willing to put up with these days. He wanted to look his enemy in the eyes and understand the type of man he was.

The hall was pierced by light from glorious windows; above the imperial throne was a glass image of Christ enthroned, while another over the entrance depicted the Virgin Mary; in between, the full beauty of the heavenly court, angels, priests, and martyrs was on display. Gregoras was arranged, very deliberately, at the epicentre.

The poets called him Gregoras the Brave, a fitting epithet for a man at the pinnacle of his powers. The basileus was a greying but vigorous man, neatly bearded with near-set eyes, which, as soon as they focused on Botulfr, seemed to sparkle with delight.

"Come, my boy. Let me look at you. Bronzed and strong, a veritable Achilles. Young too, barely any down on your cheeks—Patroclus then! Such harmony of limbs and features; why, not even Apelles could have sculpted something so entrancing. As a newly-shod emperor, I might have done such things but, forgive me. An old cat always hungers for tender mice. I understand you are married?"

He was as effusive as he had been during the ceremony earlier, almost the opposite of the restrained logothete, and had an impressive command of the Norse language. Botulfr barely had time to nod before the emperor gushed on.

"My congratulations. Fiery, Gilpractus tells me. Did you know when the gods gave gifts to Pandora, Hermes gave her lies, seductive words, and a dubious character? Outside a doll, inside the plague. Well, if the wife doesn't behave, there is always the red-hot iron. That would quench the light of those stormy eyes forever! That's why you don't see the empress," he added conspiratorially, "and conversely, why she doesn't see you!"

Botulfr remained stiff and ill at ease. "High and mighty Basileus, I will speak plainly. You greeted me as the best of friends, but I fear you are mistaken. An old enemy can't become a friend."

Gregoras stood and pondered his ornate throne for a few moments, wistful, even remorseful. Botulfr stayed respectfully silent.

"Do you play games, young Prince?"

"Of course, as all gods do in their golden halls and meadows."

Botulfr was proud of the self-assured answer. Gregoras walked over to a table and patted his arm affectionately as he passed. The prince felt himself swell with pride, then immediately felt guilty for it. He was here to honour his mother's memory. If the truth could be found, he would ask for it plainly and directly.

The emperor sat and invited his guest to do the same. He clapped his hands and two liveried servants hurried over with a circular board.

"Zatrikion? The Persians call it shatranj."

"My people call it skáktafl, but we use a square board."

"When you sit at the crossroads of the world, you are obliged to reshape the flotsam and jetsam that wash up on your shores. Fashion it in your own image. Now, the rules are the broadly the same as your version. Shall we? A god will master it in minutes."

Gregoras smiled good-naturedly at the prince. Botulfr studied the pieces and tried to plan his moves around the unfamiliar circle.

Gregoras motioned to the board and explained.

"With the Persian square board, you must try to force the defending king into the corner. Impossible here, there are no corners in which to cower, or to be caught. Most games end in stalemate, but I think that is closer to real war. We play games for inspiration, don't we? To solve intractable problems. But some problems have no solution, and war is generally protracted. With Zatrikion, you may play on in a position which might give the Persians cause for resignation. In one of the endgames, however, my board favours the bold: with king and pawn against king, unless the defender can capture the pawn before it can be promoted or protected, the game is always won."

He pushed a pawn forward and looked steadily at his guest. He lifted the hem of his cloak and held it across the table.

"This purple cloak, you see? The signifier of emperors. Did you know the dye is made from sea snails that live in the Inland Sea?"

"I did not. Not woad? That's what my people would use."

"Ah, the Asp of Jerusalem. If only, but not the right shade. It must be like blood, black, clotted blood. And that means snails, decomposing in the dyers' workshops. The smell is enough to make the angels weep. Imagine that. All those snails, crushed, just to elevate a man to the heavens. What colour will you wear when you are emperor?"

"If I am emperor," Botulfr corrected.

"What? Nonsense! Because your own family seeks to make worm's meat of you? Yes, yes, I have my apparatus, my spies. An emperor must see clearly. Tell me, do you think that blood cannot turn to water?"

"We Northmen keep our oaths."

"And what oaths has your brother sworn to you? None. Let me tell you about these thrones of ours. I am a grandson of the great Antiochus, but to claim the purple, the purple I was born to, I had to march an army to the Charisian Gate. How the people rejoiced to proclaim me Basileus! The whole world longed to see the true pilot of imperial dignity. The army loved me; I had shared their salt, sweated across mountains and plains with them, knew them as a body and as men."

Botulfr was having a hard time following the meandering mind of the emperor, but he was charmed despite himself. Botulfr slid a pawn across the board. The basileus immediately countered with a knight.

"Where was I? Ah, I was telling you about my throne. My own family, the House of Chrysaphes is an old one, and trust me when I say it is as murderous as it is ancient. Antiochus had marched my pawn forward—like so—and bequeathed me his empire. I shouldn't have been surprised when my small-minded cousin Zenon wrested the purple from me. Palace coups were common enough; any fool with a belly full of wine and envy can claim a throne. But I had forgotten the centuries circle each other. I did not learn the lessons of Herodotus or Procopius."

Botulfr took his move, and the emperor continued without looking up.

"I escaped into the country and went north, to my homelands, where I pondered on the game ahead. The solution seemed to me to be the same as before, so I called for my captains, and I marched my army again, like so."

He pushed a second pawn into play. "The jubilation of the crowds was all the sweeter the second time. They opened the gates for me before the first cock-crow."

"And your rival?" Botulfr wasn't very familiar with the game, so he mirrored his opponent's move with the knight, hoping that a frown would mask his inexperience.

"Zenon? He managed to escape capture, just as I had done. He put to sea. You and I could be at full sail in less than ten minutes from now. The prefect's men found him three weeks later, just across the Horn, visited by the bloody flux for his sins. He was shitting out his last with the Devil at his side. He got off lightly. The Arabs do revenge well—one rebel prince was recently gibbeted alive and sewn into a cow's skin, the horns were arranged at ear level to gradually crush the prisoner's head as the carcass dried out. I should have handed Zenon to them, but he stank worse than the snails."

The basileus edged another pawn forward. Botulfr shifted in his seat.

"My people have a punishment called the blood eagle, reserved for very special oath-breakers."

"Yes, I've heard. Never let your own guards get raucous and reckless in the halls of another nation. It puts you at as much a disadvantage as imitating your opponent in a game you have never played. Perhaps your wife had Hermes whisper in your ear too?"

The emperor hadn't stopped smiling, but Botulfr was finding it impossible to keep his resolve from buckling.

Gregoras continued. "Do you know why I adopted a double-headed eagle as my emblem? It is because I claimed the imperial diadem not once, but twice. I am an emperor who sees past and future. I play the long game."

Botulfr had contained himself as long as he could. He picked up his queen and twirled it between his finger and thumb until the emperor paused.

"Why was my mother murdered?"

Gregoras seemed taken aback. "I could not say. Your people do not take oaths lightly, but I give you mine that I had no hand in your mother's death. I have no guilty mind, as God is my witness and judge. I shall pray for her soul. So we all have our demons, and now I know yours. Would you care to know mine?"

The prince nodded. The emperor didn't seem perturbed or offended. Botulfr was relieved and felt a burden lifted from him.

"You might wonder if I have been successful. My empire is resurgent, and the old enemies of my youth have withered and faded away. The wolves of Arabia, the Saracen Caliphs and Emirs, have turned their fangs on each other; the Hashimids, Umayyads, and Rassids who used to banquet here and challenge me to shatranj now war with each other over who is the best custodian of a heap of sand. In Persia, the Red Khurramites rose in revolt against their Muslim masters, fomented by my coin and supported by my armies of course. They are a much more amenable neighbour, content to rule in a stupor. The Turkish tribes have wandered south, down along the Caspian Sea, first into Azerbaijan, the Land of Holy Fire, and then south to the Tigris and Euphrates where they now pitch their yurts and graze their sheep. The Danube forms a natural border to the north, secured with new forts; the Bulgars are beaten and integrated into my armies; the Kurgan of the Pecheneg's paid off, too, until I have time or inclination to catch him. There, I have named my demons, and I have bested them."

"All of them except for my father."

The emperor smiled. "Your father? Your father and his father before him, all your forefathers in fact, are guilty only of plucking thorns from my paw. They are St. Jerome to my lion. They have routed the heirs of Charlemagne and their bastard empire in the West. Around the time you were born, your father's longships sailed up the Tiber and carried off Gelasius, the Bishop of Rome, still clinging to the verdict of Chalcedon. We share no borders and manage a healthy trade. Your father and I have no quarrel, beyond my lands in Sicily perhaps."

"My advisors tell me otherwise."

"An open enemy is better than a false friend. Prince Botulfr, everyone receives advice. Only the wise profit from it. The larger your realm grows, the more voices you will hear. Will you have some wine?"

The servants appeared again with crystal decanters and goblets. Botulfr put down the queen and picked up the king from the board.

"Well, then, as my enemy in plain sight: my wife asked me once, what I thought were the essential qualities for a great king."

"What did you answer?"

"What would *you* answer?"

"I determined early in my reign that, where force of arms failed, Christian meekness might overcome. I have sought to reconcile with your malevolent North. I have sent my spies into the lands of the Rus, into old Britannia and even to that log-pile that passes for a court at Uppsala. Not to preach and proselytize, though; that has only hardened heathen hearts."

"Your minions seem to think all the Norse want is wealth," said Botulfr. "Silks and silver can be as much weapons as swords and spears."

"Gilpractus is my treasurer, a financier. He thinks everyone is as obsessed with gold as he is."

"So kindness is your answer? I was taught a king's son should be thoughtful, thorough, and silent, and brave in battle."

"I am also known as Gregoras the Gregarious; I wouldn't council the same. Industry, rather. I am the rule and the measure for all men. I spend the greater part of each night in singing hymns, yet, even when worn out with continual prayer and want of sleep, I rise at dawn. I find the will to apply myself to state business, deciding about the election of magistrates and the requests of petitioners. How to care for the pawns—because they will win you the game. If your wife were to gauge the art of ruling as a science, then I strive to be the highest of philosophers. Do you hunt?"

"My father does."

"Of course he does. His reputation precedes him. Does he breed his dogs and coursers?"

"Dogs. He has a pack of moosehounds who follow his every move."

"And does he have dogs for herding cattle and sheep?"

"Yes, yes, Vallhunds and all kinds."

"And does he feed even the lame dogs and the mongrels?"

"Yes, scraps from his own table."

"Then your father is a good king. An empire is a hybrid, a mutt born from the conquest of a dozen fathers. In my army, I march with Saracens, Indians, Egyptians, Assyrians, Vandals, Alans, and Armenians. Not just Greek and Roman soldiers. Sooner or later, every empire is a misbegotten mongrel. Did you know I am Bulgarian by birth? Treat your poor and your debased with kindness. They will anoint you with the purple, birthright or no."

"My skald said the same. That I should listen to all manner of men. My father barely notices the poor and debased because he is hunting so much."

"Then I mourn for you, having lost both a mother and father so young."

Botulfr melted at that comment and blushed profusely. There was an intimacy to the conversation that he hadn't expected, that he hadn't experienced with his own father. This great emperor was talking to him, if not as an equal, then as a favoured son. He decided to change the subject.

"I didn't understand your comment earlier. Who are Gog and Magog?"

"A small joke. There is a book called the Apocalypse, written during the Arab invasions, to remind us they were just a sandstorm and that the real end of days, predicted by Christ, was still ahead. The true harbingers of our doom are the unclean nations, led by the giants

I mentioned, Gog and Magog. They will issue from the North and devastate the whole world."

"So, it was a joke at my expense?"

"Yes, but a learned one. I offer my apologies. I am afraid the worst of it is that Gog and Magog were so ugly and so foul that Alexander of Macedon prayed to the Lord to draw mountains together to wall them in. They ate the dead. Decomposing snails, too, in all likelihood. I shudder to think."

"Jötnar then? Not men. They sound like the foes of all men and gods. Askr, my skald, will tell you that the Jötnar have the power of oncoming storms, roaring volcanoes, and the clamorous oceans. I had come to believe you and your Kristins were that self-same doom."

"That I was a giant?"

"A Jötunn can be as huge as a mountain or as beguiling as the changing seasons. This Great City and its churches seem to swallow people whole."

"Beauty is in the eye of the beholder, I suppose," said the emperor. "God does not swallow souls, he saves them. You sound less convinced now? Perhaps your Jötunn and my giants are the same. Our sins returned to haunt us. Christian sins are nightmares that suffocate your sleep, serpents that strangle reason, burning envies that grow into a mighty fire. They are forces we cannot control, the passions that enslave us, and God helps us in that struggle."

"Either that," said Botulfr, "or the North and the East are each the doom of the other, and our gods will meet in battle."

"A pact then! To avert disaster for our people and to show proper respect to Heaven. We need not hasten to our demise. The longer we hold to our oaths, the more righteous our path, the better the world in our charge, is that not so?"

"And that is why you spoke of Væringjar, of faithful companions?"

"Perhaps. Tell me, who do you trust? You are suckled by a she-wolf and you run with a loyal pack, like a latter-day Romulus. Perhaps you are a son of Troy after all. You are blessed with your mother's fierce loyalty, but cursed, like me, with a fickle family. There are many men who think this pretty purple thing would suit them well."

The emperor patted the hem of his cloak, then stopped smiling and abruptly turned solemn.

"Not far from these walls is a harbour, constructed long ago from native stone and marbles. The buildings there, and the harbour itself, are named Boucoleon for the sculptured lion that sits seizing a bull. He clings to the bull's horn, pulling his head back, fixing his teeth in the bull's throat. Return home now, and you will be the bull, brave and resilient but also torn and savaged. In that harbour is also a fleet in need of a commander. Stay with me now, and I will return you home a lion."

"BIKKJU-SONR!" *SON OF A BITCH!*

All of Boucoleon resounded with the curse, the gulls answering with shrieks and cries as they winged their way to safety. Botulfr stayed calm and listened to the waves lap the harbour wall. He was accustomed now to arguing on a rolling deck and kept his feet firmly planted.

The hird were all idling around the Roman ship, except for Gest, who was resting his forehead on the mast, partly for support and partly because he was then out of reach of Harald, who was stomping around the deck.

"Just to be clear, we march into the palace of Surtr the Black, the destroyer of worlds, and you come out with a commission and a fleet?"

"More!" said Botulfr. "A Golden Bull decreeing me the captain of his faithful guard. Look, a seal of three gold coins!"

"I'm not sure what you expected," said Olaf, examining the fore-castle and the *pavesade* where the crew would hang their shields. "The last time we left him alone, he got married."

Gest gently rocked backwards and tapped his head on the mast. "Old button-arse has given us permission to wage his private wars for him? How kind."

Botulfr thought about Gregoras, and how he projected himself. The emperor was always calm, always methodical.

"We will be seizing the emperor's enemies at sea in return for our share. For our part, we lend him our axes and our wits."

Harald turned suddenly, thought for a second, and then slapped Gest hard on the back, which in turn, knocked his head hard against the mast.

"Well, then, my only question is, how big is the share?"

"*Exactly.* We wanted to raise men to raid the coasts and make our fortune. We wanted to hide in plain sight, safe from assassins and treachery. This way, we have everything we need—" Botulfr insisted, spreading his arms wide, "—weapons, dromons, soldiers, *and* a license to plunder."

"What will she carry?" asked Olaf. "One hundred and fifty men? Two decks, two masts—I bet she flies."

Askr had been silent and still throughout. When he spoke, he sounded resigned and weary.

"You've made us thralls to the Kristins. Their god is not to be worshiped but mocked."

"Or just ignored," said Botulfr. "We are still free men, Askr, just sworn to Gregoras. He'll make us rich, and even if we are his puppets, well, the art of being a slave is to rule one's master. You wanted us to cut the strings? At least we hold them in our grasp."

Ellisif was the last to offer her opinion. She was watching Olaf prowl towards the captain's tent and peek inside.

"The Austman looks like the cat who got the cream, while the skald is lost for words. Even if this Gregoras is mulling civil war, like so much communion wine, the path ends with my husband on the throne. The end justifies the means."

She exuded authority as if she were already a queen.

"In the meantime, my husband needs a father. This Gregoras is a man like any other, and he fears us as much as we fear him. I followed him in his hall. Most of all, he fears death and tries to save himself with prayer. It is a foolish man thinks he will live forever if he keeps away from fighting; old age won't grant him a truce, even if the spears do."

Olaf hopped down, and perched beside her. "You followed him? How, with all the guards? That sounds like a trick worth teaching."

"It is a trick that would unman you. Save yourself for whipping the soldiers into shape."

Harald leant against the gunwales and started humming. "Well, that settles it, then, if witch-wife has seen everything. As long as any Grikk soldiers sleep on different ships. I don't want to be buggered in my sleep. Now, is it time for dinner? That last feast was a good one— you missed a lot, Princeling. Olaf turned a fish on his plate and all those rassragr courtiers jumped up and whimpered about how these barbarians were insulting their emperor. A fish! Do you know what the punishment for turning your fish around on a plate is? Death! I want to see what they do to murderers and oath breakers. No sense of proportion, these small people."

Gest guffawed, punched Askr on the arm. "Cheer up, skald. We'll write that saga yet. My Prince, how many ships in our fleet? And what shall we call this ship of ours?"

The tide was turning, Botulfr noted. The hird debated, their prince ruled, and they moved on with his decision. He stared at his wife in admiration, unsure of what she knew or how she knew it, but glad she was always watching. They all started back up the gangplank, the inspection over. Even Askr was smiling now.

"It is Surtr's ship, we should call it Naglfr," the skald offered.

Harald seemed appalled. "Why not just put Loki at the helm

while we are about it?"

Olaf chuckled and offered up a short verse:

With ships the sea was sprinkled far and nigh,
Like stars in heaven, and joyously it showed;
Some lying fast at anchor in the road,
Some veering up and down, one knew not why.

A goodly vessel did I then espy
Come like a giant from a haven broad;
And lustily along the bay she strode,
Her tackling rich, and of apparel high.

The ship was nought to me, nor I to her,
Yet I pursued her with a lover's look;
This ship to all the rest did I prefer:
When will she turn, and whither? She will brook
No tarrying; where she comes the winds must stir:
On went she, and due north her journey took.

Askr almost hooted in surprise. "Who's been drinking the mead of poetry now?"

"Ormstungr," spat Harald. *Snaketongue.* "He is always babbling nonsense. He should have been a skald, or a Kristin, singing Psalms on Sunnudagr."

Botulfr smiled at his wife and helped her onto the dock, the rest of the hird marching off in search of sustenance. It was odd, to be in such a warm place with the Yule feast so close. The sky was reddening, Sol hung low on Midgard's belt. Tomorrow would be a fine day for sailing. He called up to his men.

"Did I mention that the Kristins think the end of the world is coming too?"

Harald bridled and let out a yell. "I'll end your world if you don't shut up." Adding, after a moment's hesitation, an apologetic, "...my Prince."

They all laughed and walked on to their meal.

COELESTINUS IMPERATORIS NUMERUM ANNORUM

THE ᚲELEᛋTIᚾE EMᛈERᛟR: A TALE ᛟF ᛈAᛋT YEARᛋ

AᛋKR ᛟF BRIMARBᛟRᚷ (1066 AD)

T O THE MOST BLESSED BOTULFR, *in Óðinn's name elected Alhróðigr Fylkir Veðrhallar,*

Askr, the greatest of the skalds at your Temple in Uppsala, offers this exquisite token of his devotion. Many years ago, we admitted you to the number of our company, and you asked me write your saga. Since I will soon die on this bed of sickness, old and full of days, I have been anxious to ensure that I acted on your request. In this book, I have written down our old stories, as we lived them: the pedigrees of a young king reckoned up, in the manner of old songs and ballads which our forefathers had for their amusement. You'll excuse the Latin script. I've decided you need the encouragement. Wouldn't all fit on a standing stone, I'll wager.

It is told of Fylkir Thormund that he had the custom of riding out in the uninhabited forest to hunt the wild beasts that are dangerous to man. This Thormund also roved the seas to tame the wolves of Kangar and claim all the silver that flowed from the Vargsea.

One season, among his bounty was a girl of mean birth named Kera, who had been captured in war and, therefore, was called the king's slave-girl. He had her brought to him and took her to his bed. She was a remarkably handsome girl, of high spirits and fierce, and lived then in the court of King Thormund. Kera was a devoted householder, who often went about herself to inspect her corn-rigs and meadowland and paid close attention to the spirits of the land.

That same summer, it was reported that Kera was with child. The girl prepared for her confinement but became so ill that she was nearly dead; and when she was delivered of a man-child, it was some time before they could discover whether the child was in life.

But then the infant drew breath, and the godsmen praised Odin and had water poured on him. He was named Botulfr.

When Botulfr grew up, he was not tall, but middle-sized in height although very thick and of good strength. He had dark brown hair and a broad face that was dusked by the sun. He had particularly fine eyes, which were beautiful and piercing, so that one was afraid to look him in the face when he was angry. He was much beloved by his mother but less so by his father, who would often travel on Viking excursions.

Thormund was much addicted to women and had many wives and many children. Among them was his first son, who was called Eirik, a hardy man-at-arms who was strong and stout beyond most men. The fylkir set him over the Western Isles, in Jorvik, to judge according to the laws of those lands and collect tax upon the account of the emperor. King Eirik was a man of firm resolve; in battle, he exceeded all in bravery, but he was known for his cruelty when he was enraged.

At that time, the Grikkir were ruled by Emperor Gregoras the Brave. He sent men to the Western Isles to King Eirik with the errand that the messengers should present him and his candlemen with silver.

According to the proverb, a rotten branch will be found in every tree. Eirik was a man fond of money and self-interested; and when he saw the heap of money, the fine promises, and the great presents, he was led by covetousness and gave the oaths of friendship to Emperor Gregoras. Soon Eirik was a very rich man and a powerful man, who had many soldiers in his service. In time, King Eirik considered how he might lay all the Northern kingdoms under his rule. It was his intent, as soon as he had set himself fast in the land and had subjected the whole to his power, to introduce Kristin ways. He went to work first by enticing the men who were dearest to him, and many in England, out of friendship, greed, or the old tradition of the land, allowed themselves to be baptised, although they resolved to keep their practice private. Thereupon, Eirik disclosed what had been long concealed in his mind, that his stepmother Kera was a great idolater and very skillful in witchcraft. He called her hel-blue and a shapeshifter and said her hard-twisted songs were enchantments on his father.

Eirik got ready with a dozen ships and came over the Western Sea to Uppsala. He came to the palace in the grey of morning and beset all of the doors and stairs. At dawn, as she was going to the temple, Kera was struck down and her body burned, along with eight other warlocks. And so, she was deprived of life. Thereafter, Eirik was known as Volubrjotr, 'one who breaks the skulls of witches'.

Eirik came then to the hall of Prince Botulfr, who was then fifteen years old; bribed the watchman first; then broke open the door and went in with drawn swords. But it so happened that Harald Sigurðarson came to Uppsala that night, and naught came of their onslaught, for they were afraid of him. Harald and his brother, Olaf the Stout, together with Gest of Groning and a Saxon skald, Askr of Brimarborg, led Botulfr from the palace, and attended him on the way east over the ridge of the land, and they went by all the forest paths they could, avoiding the common road.

Many men took part in the design to seek the patrimony of Eirik with battle-axe and sword; and among them some who rode with the fylkir on his hunts. Thormund wept sorely for his losses and sought distraction from them. One morning early, he rode out with his dogs and falcons and his men around him. When they let slip the falcons, the falcon of the king killed two black-cocks in one flight, and three in another. The dogs ran and brought the birds when they had fallen to the ground. The king ran after them, delighted with his sport. Then the court-men shot off an arrow, which hit the king in the middle of the body. At that moment, the men of Eirik ran against him and assaulted him, some with spears, some with swords, and was his death. Eirik's men took the body

and transported it to Uppsala and took good care of the treason.

Botulfr and his men made themselves ready for a journey without delay. It was said of his hird that they were the finest men of the age.

Olaf was a great warrior, a very merry frolicsome man, and remarkably bold in arms; very handsome he was in countenance, and had beautiful fair hair. He wore generally the Gael dress of short light clothes. The Norse language was difficult for him, and he brought out words which many laughed at.

Harald was a passionate, ungovernable man, and a great man-slayer. He had a short beard, and long mustaches, and he had long yellow hair, as fine as silk, bound about his head with a gold ornament. He could strike and cut equally well with both hands and could cast two spears at once.

Gest was a tall, slender-grown man of a long neck and face, black eyes, and dark hair, a man of low birth, who had swung himself up in the world. He was, besides quick in speech, straightforward, and free in conversation, very exact and knowing in all kinds of musical arts.

Askr had blue open eyes; his hair yellow and curling; his stature not tall but of the middle size. He was wise, intelligent, and acquainted with the laws and history. He had much knowledge of mankind and was quick in counsel and prudent in words.

The Northmen all wept over the grave-mound of Thormund, where his standing stone remains. Thereupon the jarls led Eirik into the Thing and saluted him with the title of fylkir. The whole empire's desire was to make Eirik supreme king and raise again the kingdom which Ragnar had made for himself. Eirik held a Thing in each land and bound them by oath in fealty to him, and hostages were given him. He then returned south to England in great splendour, after having conquered the North with one arrow shot, and he ruled now over all the kingdoms of his people.

He sent a message over all his kingdoms that all the people should be baptised and convert to the true faith and used power and violence where nothing else would do. And when King Eirik thought himself quite firmly seated in his wide empire, he became so unreasonable with the small kings as to take to himself not only all the tax and duties which Ragnar himself had levied, but a great deal more.

Botulfr went east in summer to Gardariki and travelled far and wide in the Eastern land. There he found a girl in a Rus hut, whose equal for beauty he had never seen. The prince wanted that very night to take her to his bed. Ellisif and Botulfr both drank together and spoke a great deal with each other during the evening. The next day, when Botulfr and the hird met, Botulfr spoke of his courtship, and they all approved of it highly and thought it very advisable. The wedding followed soon after. The same day there was a marriage feast.

Ellisif was clever, with much knowledge, and lively; but a very devious person, haughty and harsh in her speech. She understood the art in which the greatest power is lodged and which Kera the mother of Botulfr was said to practise; namely, what is called magic. By means of this she could know beforehand the predestined fate of men; and also bring on the death, ill-luck, or bad health of people, and take the strength or wit from one person and give it to another. But after such witchcraft followed such weakness and anxiety that it was not thought respectable for men to practise it; and therefore, the priestesses only were brought up in this art.

B otulfr sailed south to Grikk lands to avenge the mockery and scorn that had been shown to his family. When he came to Miklagard he presented himself to the emperor and told him for what reason he had come before him; namely, that he could not remain with safety in his own country; and in recompense Gregoras promised to assist him. He was generous, but a strict ruler, for he was a wise man and well understood what was of advantage to his kingdom. Botulfr went on board the galleys manned with troops which went out to the Grikksalt at the behest of the emperor and fought much against his enemies. He had always a fair wind wherever he wished to sail, which came from the arts of witchcraft. He took into his own keeping all the gold he plundered, which made up so vast a treasure that no man in the Northern lands ever saw the like of it. Botulfr soon became stout and strong and, by reason of his black hair and deeds, was called Botulfr the Black.

A t this time, the Patriarch of Rúmaborg argued much with Gregoras about how the Kristin Son differed from the Father. The patriarch had always spies in the army of Gregoras, who entered into conversation with many of his men, offering them presents and favour. Many allowed themselves to be seduced and gave promises of fidelity to be the men of the patriarch, and to reforge the bond between East and West. With his armies, the patriarch strove to put Romanos, who believed in the Trinity and was therefore a true son of the purple, onto the Eastern throne. Old age had chilled Gregoras and made him over-fearful; though in youth he had been very brave, now he only breathed freely as long as he was encircled by the walls. He fled to his stronghold at Baba Vida, known as the Grandmother of Bolgaraland, and there the old man persisted in his practice of drinking his belly full, until he at last suffocated and burst.

On hearing this, Botulfr sailed north along the coast; and when he came to the Golden Horn, he landed, and made a great blood-sacrifice. There came two ravens flying which croaked loudly; and now Odin had released him from his solemn oath to serve his Grikk father.

At that time, in the Lands of the Holy Fire that were called Azerbaijan by the people who lived there, Yetirek had risen to the command of his people, who were called Uzes and Torks. He was the great-grandson of Ilik, the first of his name, who made the kingdom and ruled over it for three score years. Botulfr came along the mountain paths to Baku, the City of Winds, which some say was the land of his mother,

Kera, and of the sons of Tengri. He entreated with Yetirek all through the cold and rough Khazir and mild and gentle Gilavar.

In consequence of this entreaty, Yetirek promised to assist the Northman. He came to the neck of land north of Lake Van, and immediately challenged the newly crowned Romanos to battle. But before the lines came together, Botulfr urged his men to stand down and told them to sheath their swords. The Varangi marched to their ships, leaving the field. Undone, Romanos fled to Miklagard, and Yetirek laid the whole country in subjection to him. And so it was that Botulfr repaid the treachery of the Grikk against his kin.

Botulfr asked his wife to travel to Uppsala in some altered shape and to learn there of his brother's rule: and she set out in the shape of a narwhal. And when she came near to Northern lands, she saw all the mountains and hills full of guardian-spirits, some great, some small, and saw that the realm had not yet submitted fully to the Kristin.

Without delay the prince made himself ready for a journey, took with him ten score men who were chosen from among the Varangi, and who were carefully equipped in all things: clothes, weapons, and horses. Botulfr rode from his ships with his followers who were dressed in purple and rode on gilt saddles, and all were they a trusty band, though Harald, Olaf, and Gest were peerless among them. He had coats of reindeer-skin made for them, with so much witchcraft that no weapon could cut or pierce them any more than if they were armour of ring-mail; and they had Ulfberht iron girt on them, whose blades never dulled, and the grips woven with gold.

Eirik, in the meantime, heard some whisper that, over the Eastern sea, was a man called Svartr, who was looked upon as a king. From the conversation of some people, he fell upon the suspicion that he must be of the royal race. It was, indeed, said that this Svartr in his infancy had gone east to Miklagard and had been brought up by pirates. The fylkir carefully inquired about this man and had his suspicion that he must be his lost brother and a slave-woman's son.

Botulfr advanced to Uppsala where, in summer, there was assembled a numerous Althing. Olaf recommended the cause of Botulfr to the people and proposed him to the bondsmen as Emperor of the Storm Hall, who had returned mighty and rich from Miklagard. Then Botulfr himself stood up and spoke; and the people said to each other as they heard him, "Odin himself is come again, grown and young," for the gods have long protected their descendants even though many now neglected their faith.

Many came unto him and complained of the sorrow and evil his brother Eirik had wrought, who was at this time fylkir. As hatred of Eirik grew more and more, the more liking all men took to Botulfr; and they got more boldness to say what they thought. The Northmen agreed they would not have the kingdoms go out of the old ways of their ancestors.

Thereafter Botulfr set forth this

determination to all the people and his demand on the kingly power. He desired that the jarls should receive him as King of Kings, and desired from them the title of Fylkir and aid and men to reclaim the empire. In return, he promised that he would not only hold by and improve the laws and rights of the country but also to return to the Great City and make it his own and give every man new lands and wealth in the south. Then the jarls rose and spoke, the one after the other, and supported his cause, and the whole public cried and shouted that they would take him to be fylkir. And so it was that the Himinríki took Botulfr, who was then twenty-five years old, for emperor; and he proceeded through the country with great feasting.

Fylkir Botulfr, early in summer, collected a great army at Uppsala and fitted out ships. He also had caused a great drakkar ship to be built and had it fitted out in the most splendid way by master-builders: some to fell wood, some to shape it, some to make nails, some to carry timber; and all that was used was of the best. The ship was both long and broad and high-sided and strongly timbered. The forecastle men were picked men, for they had the banner of the king. Such men only were received into his hird as were remarkable for strength, courage, and all kinds of dexterity; and they alone got place in his ship, for he had a good choice of house-troops from the best men of every jarldom. He also had a great troop of Finnar. They could run so swiftly that neither man nor beast can come near them in speed, and they hit whatever they took aim at. By their witchcraft, they could conjure up a dreadful storm or bad weather on the sea.

Botulfr gathered an innumerable mass of people and sailed against his half-brother at Jorvik. King Eirik assembled a great army from England, Írland, and Skottland. Eirik had a great body of horsemen and still greater of foot people.

Then they advanced against each other, and gave battle at Vatndalar in the fells of England. Both parties had a great force, and it was a great battle. Olaf went forward bravely, and Eirik met him with his troop, and they exchanged blows with each other. Olaf did come up swinging his sword, and made a cut at Eirik, but Eirik thrust his shield so hard against Olaf that he tottered with the shock. Now the king took his sword with both hands, and hewed Olaf through helm and head and clove him down to the shoulders.

Many fell on both sides, but the most by far on Eirik's side, for the Finlanders fought desperately, sharply, and murderously and shot right through the shields. So many arrows were shot against Eirik that his armour was altogether split asunder, and he threw it off. Whereupon, Harald threw a spear at King Eirik, and hit him in the middle of the body, so that it flew through and through him; and Eirik fell down dead. Many people fell around him. The army of Eirik then took flight to their ships and rowed away with the loss of many a man.

So great was the sorrow over the death of Olaf that he was lamented both by friends and enemies; and they said that never again would the North see such a man. His friends removed his body from the field and made a great mound in which they laid Olaf in full armour and in his best clothes, but with no other goods. They spoke over his grave and wished him in Valhal. Harald told that when he wiped the blood from the face of his brother it was very beautiful; and there was red in the cheeks, as if he only slept.

After this Botulfr gathered together a great force and prepared for an expedition to the Kristin lands. He took it much amiss that the Kristins had caused such loss in his dominions. When the fylkir sailed down to Langbardaland, he ordered all the men there to be killed and everything wide around to be delivered to the flames. The patriarch was in Rúmaborg when the Black Fleet sailed across the mouth of the sacred Tiber. He rode to them with all his army assembled in a great body and determined to defend their land and fight. He saw a great battle-array with many banners flapping in the air. Before the army of the North was riding a huge witch-wife upon a wolf and a hill-giant with an iron staff in his hands. He was a head higher than the mountains, and many other giants followed him. The patriarch fled from the ridge down upon the plain to the Aurelian Wall. There he turned himself again, and all his monks and godsmen and many troops of their men assembled there.

Then Fylkir Botulfr stood up and ordered the war trumpets to sound; on which the whole of the army of the king stood up and advanced against the Kristins. There was afterwards the warmest conflict. Harald Sigurðarson ran on before all his men to the army of the enemy and hewed down with both hands, and all who were nearest gave way before him; but Harald fell and many people with him. After that, the battle was not very long, for the Northmen were very fiery, and where they came the Kristins fell thick as tangles heaped up by the waves on the beach. Askr of Brimarborg struck at the patriarch with his axe, and the blow hit his left leg above the knee, then Gest of Groning struck at him with his spear, and the stroke went in under his mail-coat and into his belly, which was his death-wound. The Kristins betook themselves to flight and were hewed down like cattle at a slaughter. Thereupon, Botulfr went west of the Tiber to the papal palace. He lifted up his axe and struck their White Christ so that the body rolled down from its dais. Then the Northmen turned and threw down all the saints from their seats. Whereupon, Fylkir Botulfr took away the golden cross and made payments to worthy men and honoured his pledge at the Althing. From this victory, he became very celebrated.

Ellisif knew where all the Roman silver was concealed under the church of St. Peter and understood the songs by which the earth, the reliquaries, and tombs were opened to her. She bound those spirits who dwell in them by the power of her word and went in and took ornaments and relics as she pleased. Ellisif taught the most of her arts to the priestesses of the sacrifices, and they came nearest to herself in all wisdom and witch-knowledge. Many others, however, occupied themselves much with it; and from that time, witchcraft was at the heart of the empire and spread far and wide, and continued long.

Thereafter, King Botulfr carried war over all the Kristin lands, plundering some, slaying others, taking some prisoners of war, taking ransom from others, and all without opposition. Fylkir Botulfr made this law over all the lands he conquered, that all the Kristin church property should belong to the bondsmen, both great and small. In time, he returned to Miklagard and claimed it as his own.

Botulfr was a wise man, a man of truth and uprightness who made laws, observed them himself, and obliged others to observe them. In the Great City, he was proclaimed Coelestinus, meaning of the heavens and of the sky. He assembled an Almighty Thing that surpassed even that fashioned by the sons of Bor, and a vast multitude of people were assembled there. And when the Reginthing was seated, the fylkir spoke to the people and began his speech with saying that they should all renounce Kristr and should believe freely in all Gods and indulge in all sacrifices and feasts that were holy to them and their conscience. Kristin priests who refused to appear, showing an excess of madness and obstinacy, were burnt alive in their holdings. In his reign, there was no further strife, and the Urdr protected him and his realm against enemies abroad; and his nearest neighbours stood in great awe.

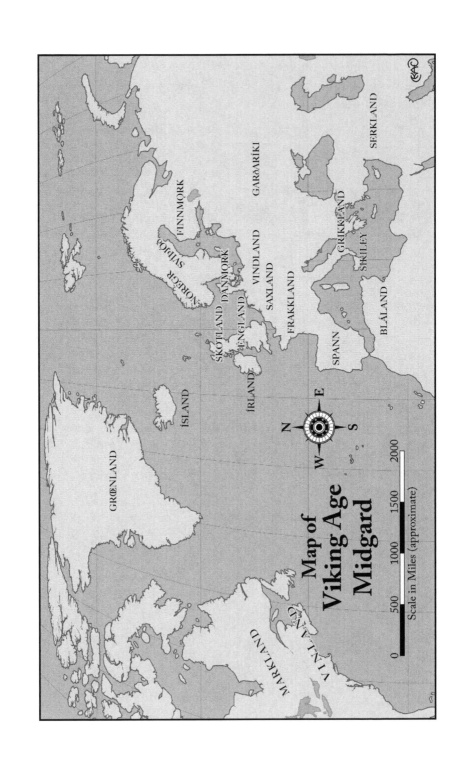

Map of
Viking Age
Midgard

Scale in Miles (approximate)

0   500   1000   1500   2000

GRŒNLAND

ÍSLAND

MARKLAND

VÍNLAND

FINNMORK

NOREGR

SVÍÞJÓÐ

SKOTLAND DANMORK

ÍRLAND

ENGLAND

VINDLAND

SAXLAND

FRAKKLAND

GARÐARÍKI

SPANN

GRIKKLAND

SIKILEY

BLALAND

SERKLAND

N
W   E
S

BOOK TWO: BEGINNINGS
EXEGESIS IV

GOSFORTH, ENGLAND

2017

W HAT ON EARTH ARE YOU talking about?!?"

Michaels decided there and then that enough was enough. He wasn't going to dignify the old man with any further response. He dangled his car keys by way of farewell and marched back to the car.

Chandler called out after him, like an old friend providing reassurance.

"I'm not going anywhere. Turns out I've got all the time in the Nine Worlds."

The churchwarden slammed the door in frustration, turned the key in the ignition, then reversed quickly down the Wasdale Road. *No good deed goes unpunished*, he thought. He glanced back at the old coot in his rear-view mirror, and sure enough, Chandler was still there, glued to the cross. If he wasn't gone by the time Michaels got back from the supermarket, he'd have no choice but to call the police to move him on. He considered that it might be sensible to call social services too.

He turned on the radio. It occurred to him that there might be a news bulletin about an escaped lunatic, but he dismissed the idea as a flight of fancy. There wasn't any news on anyway, and CFM seemed to be broadcasting folk music. *Ah well*, he thought. *That was one for the annals. The Diary of a Country Churchwarden.*

Some wag had changed the road sign so the A595 now went to Hvitrhafn rather than Whitehaven. It seemed an overly erudite joke, well beyond the local Scouts. He must have really impressed them last week.

He checked his watch. He still had plenty of time before he was needed at the Village Hall, but better to be safe than sorry. He nudged the accelerator. Then immediately slammed on the brakes. Not because of anyone on the road—most of the traffic ran up the coast, not into the National Park. But there was an absence.

The rectory was gone.

Michaels opened the car door. He'd driven this road a thousand times. Parish newsletters might get blown away in the wind but not whole buildings.

He sat, bewildered, watching the sun set. Just yesterday, he'd sat right there with his friend and mentor, the Reverend Riley, having a nice cup of tea. They'd talked about lopping off the damaged branch on the old oak at the end of the garden. The tree was still there, and the churchwarden couldn't fathom how that was possible. An act of God? He wracked his brain about the rapture and other revelatory passages in the Bible, but those surely only applied to Christian personages and not their property?

The folksong on the radio stopped. And the voice of the DJ came over the air

"Who is ignoring the evidence of their own eyes now?"

Michaels stopped staring at the treeline and glared, horrified, at the dashboard of his car. *What was that?* If this was a prank by the Scouts, they had really outdone themselves.

"I was giving you a history lesson, Churchwarden, when you so rudely left. I was explaining why I came back to this part of the world. My world, my Jörð. Before she was taken from me…"

There was something else out there, haunting the dusk. The churchwarden couldn't see anything, not directly, but there was something there, in the corner of his eye, at the back of his mind. Something was loose where the rectory had once been.

Adrenaline seized Churchwarden Michaels, his primeval brain responding to a primordial threat. He slammed the door shut and put the car into reverse, the tires squealing louder than the wind. In desperation, he jabbed at the power button, over and over, but the voice on the radio continued.

"Don't worry, this won't be a trip down memory lane. See, you perceive time as a river, flowing from one place to another. For me, it's a great eternal ocean, lapping on all the shores at the same time. You'll feel it soon enough. Like ripples emanating from a single, solitary drop, the waves will roll though history. For a real Viking, the passage of time isn't a corridor. It's a surge across boundless seas…"

The voice belonged to Chandler, of course. But how? A walkie-talkie perhaps, Michaels reasoned. Something to do with Bluetooth, maybe. He rummaged through his pocket, awkwardly twisting in the driver's seat to free his phone. Dead battery.

"Let me tell you a story. In the Year of Your Lord 625, the Northumbrian King asked the members of his court for their views on whether the kingdom should abandon their Old Gods for Christianity. Edwin of York was his name. Eadwine of Eoforwic. You couldn't go around calling yourself Tom, Dick, or Harry in the Dark Ages. Well, okay, Thomas would work, although it's too apostolic for my taste. Rikard and Heimric

are the timeliest versions of the others. Names are old, see? They go way back, and they all mean something. You think that a rose by any other name might smell sweet, but that isn't true. Edwin means rich friend, like there ever was such a thing…"

Michaels turned left, back onto a road that was apparently now called Vatndalrgata, without bothering to indicate. The changing sign was the least of his concerns. He was gripped by this terrible, irrational fear that St. Mary's might have vanished too. He changed gears and drove down the darkening country lane.

"Edwin asks his question, holds his mini-referendum, albeit one where only the richest got to have their say. One noble steps up and delivers a lovely speech comparing the life of man to a sparrow flying through the king's hall on a winter day, 'For a short time, he is safe from the wintry storm, but after a little space he vanishes from your sight, back into the dark winter from which he came.' Isn't that poetic? We Northerners are very partial to some cleverly constructed lines. Don't you think, Churchwarden? 'Of what went before and of what is to follow,' the noble continued, 'we are utterly ignorant. If therefore this new faith can give us some greater certainty, it justly deserves that we should follow it…'"

There was something wrong with the car now. The dashboard lit up like a fruit machine coughing up the jackpot, and the engine choked into silence. St. Mary's was just ahead. Momentum was his friend, as long as the wheels kept turning.

"So, my little sparrow. You are back in my hall. Back in my Midgard. Your Christianity is being ripped from the past like so much rot. You have seen the dark winter outside, the worlds of the Álfar and the Jötnar. The realms of the dead, all joined by the great World Tree. Are you so certain of what went before and what is to follow?"

Michaels rolled the car back into his usual spot and breathed a sigh of relief. He wrenched his keys from the ignition, which finally severed the vocal chords of the broadcaster.

The church was still there. The tombstones were still there. Old Man Chandler was still there.

And so were the crosses—all *three* of them.

Lind
Expedition

Detail Area Below

0   500
Scale in Miles

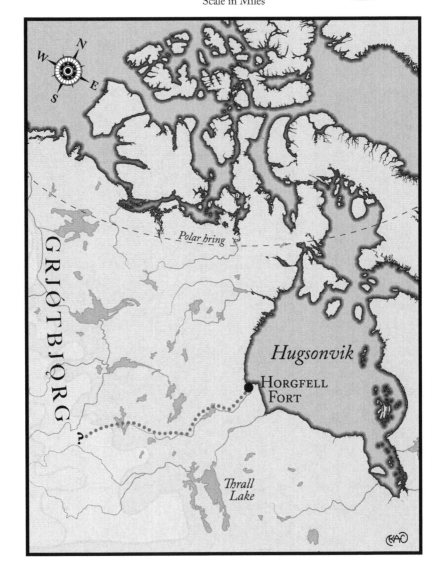

N
W   E
S

Polar hring

GRJÓTBJØRG

Hugsonvik

HORGFELL
FORT

?

Thrall
Lake

MY NÁTTÚRA BÓK—A JOURNAL

ENTRY ONE

HUGSONVIK, MARKLAND,
THE NEW WORLD SKAMMDEGI—
"THE DARK DAYS" OF WINTER 1735

H OGINANAYE-TROLLALAY, GIVE US OF *your white bread and*
none of your gray.

On the first day of this new year my people woke me at the
break of day with the discharge of firearms, the endeavour meant to
wake the hill spirits and help banish the trolls to the sea; a traditional
if startling beginning to my journal. For my part, I treated them with
plenty of my own spirits (rum mostly) and added to their regales. I
am not by nature a man inclined to superstitious thoughts, but at this
great remove from civilization, I will entertain the notion that the
spirit folk are at play on days like these. I should like to engage them
myself should the occasion arise.

From there, we indulged in what remained of the Yule Goat
and idled the days with beer and games of tablut. I had made certain
to bring the game mat from my Finnmørk expedition; fortunately,
the reindeer hide is well suited to travelling, and the embroidery has
held. Herra Kyndillson delights in defending Holmgard against the
Horse Lords, so much so that he has even had carved new pieces from

whalebone. Herra Rothman made a proposal of a fox game instead, whereupon, Herra Rubeck took up a piece and struck him on the cheek bone for his insolence.

This quarrelsome beginning to my journal is to be expected. The guardsmen are a rowdy crew, and with the war having broken out again with the Maharajahs, no doubt they are apprehensive of being obliged to join the fleets.

After the long vicissitudes of winter, we are all eager to be moving on from Horgfell Fort and Hugson's accursed bay on which it sits. The men have taken to calling it Dritvik or Shit Bay, on account of the all too common fog, particularly when the wind is from the east; then it drives against the high barren rocks on the shore by the fort and dissolves in torrents of rain. I am sure Heimríkr Hugson would find it apt. Another barb from the guardsmen: they call it Frey's Own Country (I assume in homage to the god of precipitation) and they refer to themselves as the Imperial Rainguard (which I imagine is a peculiar pun on their duties as vanguards and frontiersmen). As we survey the interior, I suspect we shall be obliged to reclassify many features according to their whims and mood.

MEN OF QUICK TEMPERS SELDOM cherish rancour, but I'll admit that it was my own quarrel that consigned me to these trackless Markland barrens.

Scholars may be compared to the trees of a nursery; often among the young plants are found some which resemble wild shoots, which when properly transplanted at a later period, deliver both a much-changed nature and the promise of delicious fruit. Having undergone so many fatigues in Finnmǫrk, I had assumed such was to be my trajectory, but for now it seems I have instead become tangled in a briar patch. In court, the Urðr labelled me ambitious, superior, irritable, and obstinate and bound me to keep the peace.

I cannot fathom why Róssteinn denounced me to the university. Envy perhaps. I had maintained the society of Finnar warlocks where all others had failed. Either that or he harbours the prejudice against male practitioners of the seið that is so commonplace. I know from his papers that the wretch scorns my methods, but in natural history, errors cannot be defended, nor truths concealed. My appeal I shall save for posterity.

I am, of course, eternally grateful that Speaker Högen wrested my sword from my hand in time to prevent the vengeful blow and thus a more permanent charge; and to a similar degree, am indebted for his interposition with the Urðr. As a reflection of that gratitude, I have determined to make the best of the reprimand I have been given; after all, the fur trade being carried on in these very distant colonies is considered of the first importance to the fylkir.

More importantly, a second appointment from the Commonwealth must be viewed as a mechanism to build on the exigencies of the first in Finnmǫrk, namely, to reinforce man's dominion over the three kingdoms of nature. The speakers have made clear their desire to ascertain how the much-vaunted fourth realm sits alongside the animal, the vegetable, and the mineral. How does a natural philosopher classify Álfar, Dvergar, and Jötnar? Who has ever collected a specimen? Högen believes their hidden secrets will only be revealed through the exploration of hitherto little-known lands.

I also had no great desire for a posting to Dagon, there to prop up some ailing Nawab or, worse, to chase Moro pirates around the Sulu Sea. In case the authorities had a change of heart, I packed in haste—my possessions consist chiefly of those that served me in Finnmǫrk before: a light coat of West Gotland linsey-woolsey cloth, lined with red shalloon; leather breeches; a green leather cap; and a pair of half-boots. I carry a small leather bag, furnished on one side with hooks and eyes, so that it can be opened and shut at pleasure. This bag contains one shirt; an ink stand, pencase and microscope; a gauze cap to protect me occasionally from the gnats; a comb; my journal, and a parcel of paper stitched together for drying plants, both in folio. My pocket-book contains a passport from the Governor of Uppsala and a recommendation from the university, for which I am again indebted to Högen.

And so, a New Year beckons in the New World, and soon a warming sun for my journey. I have ascertained, by various observations, the latitude of this place to be 56° 9' north. On this occasion, I am to the south of the lands of Polar Night, and so while the sun sinks low, it does not vanish entirely. My Finnar hosts were terrified that the sun might not return each year and would send a godsman up to the highest mountain to observe the sky. I have also the tube of my spyglass swung across my shoulder, which is a troublesome addition to my burden, but on balance, better than a priest around my neck.

ENTRY TWO

MARKLAND IS A VEXING PLACE, a labyrinth of tree and lakes, entirely out of the reach of legal restraint. It is now some seven centuries now since Leif the Lucky first sighted these lands, and I can't imagine much has changed. There are no borders—the country seems inexhaustible—and so there is free scope given to any ways or means of attaining advantage. Once Hugson and his heirs penetrated the ice, even more chaos ensued as pioneers and pathfinders began to trek north and west seeking their fortune. What with drinking, carousing, and quarrelling with the Skræling along their routes, and among themselves, it is a wonder that the foresters ever return safely to winter quarters.

Consequently, three great ring-forts have been established at the confluence of the various Great Lakes to provide bastions of order. Horgfell is the furthest outpost, seven weeks sail from Skotland through very dangerous and troublesome waters. By license of the viceroy, several colonists make their abode here, breaking up the soil into corn and pasture lands. They pay a certain tribute to the crown, and each family is still obliged to furnish a soldier for the army or a sailor for the navy. Otherwise, whether it is a time of peace or war is all the same to them, as they are burdened with no taxes. There is no doubt that most of the land will, in time, become colonized and filled with farmers as Vinland was before it. What this means for the Skræling tribes is for the Nornir to tell, but I imagine they have decided it is wise to howl with the wolves one is among.

The Skræling outside the walls are the mildest nation that is to be found on the borders of Hugson's Bay, regardless of affronts or losses, and by being now so frequently engaged with the fylkir's servants, they have acquired several words of Norse. They call themselves the Denésoliné, the "people of the barrens." One evening, we were joined from the Westward by a group, travelling with furs, and other articles for trade. They informed me that they had returned from a hunt at a large lake, which they represented as several hundred miles from Horgfell. They call it the Thrall Lake, deriving its name from that of its original inhabitants, who were made army slaves and transported east to help construct Leifsbúðir, Botulftun, and New Jórvík. The tribes, when they used to maraud against the Marklanders, would come in canoes to that lake, and then leave them there, journeying farther along a beaten deer path all the way to the fork in the Horgfell river (which they call simply Missinipi, the "big waters"). This became their war road. No-one alive remembers those times, of course. They have been engaged in making their snowshoes; the weather has become bitterly cold, and it froze so hard in the night that my watch stopped.

I found that one of the young Skræling had lost the use of his right hand by the bursting of a gun. His companions brought him to me, having heard something of my abilities. His wound was in such an offensive state and emitted such a putrid smell that it required all the resolution I possessed to examine it. His friends had done everything in their power to relieve him, but the wound was in a deplorable state. I was rather alarmed at the difficulty of the case, but as the young man's life was in a state of hazard, I was determined to risk my already damaged reputation. I immediately fashioned a poultice of bark, stripped from the roots of the spruce-fir, which I applied to the wound, having first washed it with the juice of the bark. This proved a very painful dressing, but in a few days, the wound was clean, and the noisome flesh around it destroyed. The salve I applied on the occasion was made of the Vinlander balsam, wax, and tallow dropped from a burning candle into water. In short, I was so successful that my patient soon embarked on a hunting party and brought me the tongue of an elk by way of thanks. A generous gift; I must remember to do the same for Högen!

This episode underlines my irritation when I am told healing is a womanly art. It seems to be the vilest hypocrisy to prevent a man from contributing to the wellsprings of knowledge on the spurious and sanctimonious grounds that medicine is an exclusive female preserve. The Skræling have no such great divide—neither for that matter, do the Finnar, who live on the very doorstep of the empire.

I WILL DIVERT MOMENTARILY TO some observations about my latest hosts. These Denésoliné are excellent hunters, and their pursuits and exercise in that capacity reduce them to very lean appearance. The males eradicate their beards, and the females remove their hair from across their body, except their heads, where it is strong and black and without a curl. In many respects, they remind me of the Finnar: their stature also very diminutive; their faces of the darkest brown, eyes dark and sparkling, pitchy-coloured hair hung loose. One might even imagine they were arranged around a common ancestry, were the distances not insurmountable.

The Skræling religions I have encountered are of a very contracted nature, and I have never witnessed any ceremony of devotion which they had not been taught by Northmen—you will hear our hosts refer to us as Ashmen—with feasts and fasts introduced to them by our people and heartily adopted. In addition, there are many uncommon cultural ties between Northman and savage. The skalds appear to have ranged far, beginning their work in these lands by teaching the Skræling some of their written forms, and leading indigenous minds by degrees to greater understanding of the gods. However advantageous these lessons may be, their interpretation leaves much to be desired.

For instance, from what I have seen, when death overtakes any of them, their property is sacrificed and destroyed as Odin decreed. But whilst it is the practice of these people to burn the bodies of their dead, the larger bones are excepted and are rolled up in bark and suspended from poles. Cremation of this sort was common in the interior of Asia and among the ancient Greeks and Romans, and has also prevailed among the Hindoos up to the present time.

Funeral ale is unknown, but there is no failure of lamentation or mourning on such occasion: those most nearly related to the departed person black their faces and sometimes cut off their hair. They also pierce their arms with knives and arrows. The grief of the females is carried to a still greater excess; they cut their hair and cry and howl, but even so, they oddly refuse to follow their masters into the next world on the pyre.

There are many old men among the Skræling, as they avoid battle for the most part and know nothing of the glory of Odin's halls or the gleaming leaves of Glasir beyond what the skald have repeated. A

Denésoliné tried to explain his age to me, by telling how he remembered the hills and plains on the opposite shore, when they were covered with moss, and without any animals to hunt but reindeer. By degrees, he said, the face of the country changed—now, it is interspersed with groves of poplars, with elk migrating from the east, followed by the buffalo; the reindeer retiring to the high lands above the river. I was reminded of how Uppsala had changed since the days before the university was built.

I took the old Denésoliné with me when I made another observation of Thor and his chariots for the longitude. He wasn't perplexed by the lens, which surprised me, but rather pointed to indicate some geese he had seen, and excitedly told me these birds are always considered as the harbingers of spring. His name is Keskarrah, as best I can gather, but whether it is a given name or an honorific I cannot be sure.

ENTRY THREE

ROM MY FIRST ARRIVAL IN Finnmørk, I noticed that all the inhabitants used a peculiar kind of boot that seemed at first sight very awkward. I soon found, however, that they had many advantages over common shoes, chiefly that they are easier in wearing and impervious to water. Those who wear them may walk in water up to the tops without wetting their feet. They are cut so that not a morsel of leather is wasted. Nature, who no artist has yet to surpass, has provided once again. I instructed the Denésoliné in the required stitches, and they taught me some of their spirit songs in return. A fair trade I thought.

Suitably dressed, I went to great Bare Frost, as was the custom; the weather was calm, clear, and of course, very cold. The wind blew from the southwest, and during the afternoon, it began to thaw. On hearing this, the guardsmen engaged in drinking to the gods: this wind never failed to bring us clear mild weather, whereas, when it blew from the opposite side of Dritvik, it produced snow. The warm winds come off the Peaceful Ocean, which I hope cannot be very far from us; the distance might be so short, that even though the winds pass over mountains covered with snow, there is not time for them to cool. I fear this Continent of Hvítramannaland is much wider than many people imagine, particularly Hugson, who thought that the ocean was but a few days journey from the West coast of his bay, for I have not met with any Skræling, either Northern or Southern, that ever had seen the sea to the Westward.

Not long afterwards, we were visited early by our usual summer companions, the gnats and mosquitoes. On the other side of the lake, which was still covered with ice, the plains were a delight. Trees were budding, and many of the plants were about to bloom. Herra Dahl, the company cook, brought me a bunch of flowers of a pinkish colour, and a yellow whorl, a corolla with six petals of a light purple. We determined to press them and catalogue them in due course. The change in the appearance of nature was as sudden as it was pleasing, for a few days only were passed away since the ground was covered with snow. In just a few days more, the river was cleared of the ice.

ENTRY FOUR

WITH OUR ICY CAGE MELTED away, I was most busily employed in trading with the Skræling bands. I ordered our canoe to be repaired with bark. I retained six of the men from the fort, and they agreed to accompany me on my projected voyage of discovery and examination in return for three silver crowns apiece. I also engaged some hunters and closed my personal business by writing my dispatches to the university, in accordance with the terms of my expedition, and to the viceroy at Leifsbúðir, as required by the court.

I found that my chronometer was one hour forty-six minutes slow to apparent time, a consequence of the freezing no doubt. Having fixed it as best as possible with dabs of fish oil, we embarked at seven in the morning or as close to it as I could practicably measure.

Our canoe was put into the water. It was twenty-five feet long, excluding the curves of stem and stern—at the same time, it was so light, that two men could carry her on a good road three or four miles without resting. In this slender vessel, we shipped provisions, goods for presents, arms, ammunition, and baggage, to the weight of three thousand pounds, and an equipage of ten people. The voyagers: Halsand Kyndillson, Jósepr Laufrey, Karl Ljótsson, Gjafarr Audvard, Anders Dahl, Göran Rothman, and Olof Rubeck. They laughed and swore their oaths to protect me from all things but made a special exception for the rain. I have also contracted with two Denésoliné, as hunters and interpreters—the first, the young Idotliazee, whose injury I treated so ably, who no doubt imagines he is in my debt; the second, Keskarrah, seeming to have need for his own adventure, despite his advanced years.

My winter interpreter, whom I left at the fort, shed tears on the reflection of those dangers which we might encounter in our expedition, while my own people offered up their prayers to Odin that we might return in safety from it.

ENTRY FIVE
NÓTTLEYSA—"NIGHTLESS" SUMMER 1735

W E BEGAN OUR VOYAGE AGAINST a strong current one mile and three quarters, south by southwest one mile. I was aggrieved to discover that the canoe quickly became strained from being very heavily laden. It became so leaky that we were obliged to land, unload, and gum it within hours of having set out. As this circumstance took place about noon, I had an opportunity of taking an altitude.

When the canoe was repaired, we continued our course, steering west by southwest one mile and a half, when I had the misfortune to drop my pocket-compass into the water. This was most vexing, and I let out a loud shout of frustration. I became momentarily understanding of my father's resolve to bind me as apprentice to a shoemaker where I should have caused altogether less harm. Perhaps I might have made my fortune with the Finnar boots rather than trampling around in them.

On this stretch of river, the banks are steep and hilly, and in some parts collapsed by the river. Where the earth has given way, the face of the cliffs reveals numerous strata, consisting of reddish earth and small stones, bitumen, and a greyish earth, below which, near the water's edge, is a red stone. Water issues in bubbling, roiling springs, a veritable Hvergelmir, except the ground on which it spreads is covered with a thin white scurf, or particles of saline. A large and dreary pine forest loomed above, in which the herbaceous plants seemed almost starved in the barren sand.

At half past six in the afternoon the young men landed, killed an elk, and wounded a buffalo, determining that the gods required a blood sacrifice to ease the passage ahead. In this spot, we formed our encampment for the night. In the interlude before sleeping, Herra Audvard advised me that one should not vent one's wrath on animals because, in his estimation, both animals and men have souls. His demeanour was such that I now take him for a Christian. I am not anxious as, for the most part, Christians practice their piety in quiet corners. It is well known that many Vinlanders are Christian, having migrated to colonial shores to enjoy new beginnings. Nevertheless, I think it is unwise to give men freedom of conscience and still expect them to hold their oaths sacred. Sedition is at the very heart of the Codex religions.

ENTRY SIX

AWOKE AT DAWN, AS IF in a dream of distant Alfheim, fairer than the sun to behold. It truly seemed that I had reached the residence of Frey himself. The west side of the river displayed a succession of the most beautiful scenery I had ever witnessed, a magnificent theatre that had all the wonder that the nature could deliver: groves of poplars in every shape and size, vast herds of elks and buffaloes and, no doubt, a myriad of Álfar watching over all. Being spring, the buffalo were surrounded with their young ones, who were frisking about them. The whole country displayed fecund Freyja's blessing; the trees that bear blossoms were thriving and the rosy rind of their branches reflected the beams of the rising sun, the goddess's tears of red and gold, to which none of my expressions can do justice. The east side of the river consisted of a range of high land covered with the white spruce and the soft birch, while the banks abounded with alder and willow, all of which seemed to sing to us of creation. We saw bluejays, yellow birds, and one beautiful hummingbird.

The water continued to rise, and that day, the current being stronger, we made a greater use of setting poles than paddles. We perceived tracks of large bears along the river, some of which were nine inches wide and of a proportionate length. We saw one of their dens in an island, a gaping hollow ten feet deep, five feet high, and six feet wide; but we had not yet seen one of those animals. The Denésoliné entertain great apprehension of this breed of bear, which they hold in almost godlike reverence. Larger and more aggressive than the black bears to the east, they boast grizzled golden-brown fur tipped in grey, and Keskarrah explained they never venture to attack them but in a party of at least three or four. Herra Laufrey maintained he was descended from bear-shirts, who often entered battle naked but for an animal mask and pelts, howling, roaring, and dangling his courage. We dissuaded him from following in his ancestor's footsteps lest he bring wrath down upon us.

A S WE PROGRESSED, THE WIND blew from the north throughout the day, and at times it raged with considerable violence. Our hunters, though they had been much farther than this by land, knew nothing of the river.

The land above our encampment spread into an extensive plain and stretched on to a very high ridge, which, in some parts, presented a face of bare rock, but was generally covered with verdure and enriched with poplar and white birch trees. Not far distant, a huge stone was to be seen. Idotliazee related that it was a remnant from a malignant game of skittles, with the stone hurled by an ancient giant. As a confirmation of this history, he pointed out the evident marks of four huge fingers and a thumb on the upper side of the stone. The country was so crowded with animals as to seem like a Jötunn farmyard, from the trampled state of the ground, and the quantity of dung scattered over it. To add to our sense of foreboding, we saw two of the feared brown bears. Herra Laufrey stayed firmly in his canoe, at which juncture, it was remarked that he ought to change his talisman to the wolf-hide instead.

Further upriver, the land took on a very irregular elevation and appearance, composed in some places of clay, and rocky cliffs, and others exhibiting strata of red, green, and yellow. This beautiful scenery is a pristine paradise for my studies, Finnmork a dreary rehearsal by comparison. The banks of the river are coated with elk and buffalo, which, unmolested by the hunters, feed in great numbers. On an island which we passed, there was a large quantity of white birch, whose bark we employed in the construction of canoes. Keskarrah mentioned that, following a war expedition, his party had returned this way and made their vessels in the general vicinity, an account that reassured me that he had our bearings.

Herra Kyndillson killed two elks and mortally wounded a buffalo, but we only took a part of the flesh of the former. The newer rifles are most deadly at short range. Herra Kyndillson has sailed on many Viking expeditions—he bears a long scar from a Hottentotten spear he received in the Suðurnes to prove it—and he swears by their manufacture. We discussed the merits of gunpowder over the magical arts of vǫlur and the Finnar, which are said to include magical archery. These practices include being unable to miss a target, being able to shoot three arrows simultaneously, and magic arrows which fly back to the bowstring of their own accord and hit whatever they are aimed at. Neither of us had seen such arts first hand, so we agreed saltpeter, sulfur, and charcoal were just as potent as any sorcery.

ENTRY EIGHT

T FROZE VERY HARD DURING the night. When we continued our voyage, we had not proceeded two hundred yards before an accident befell the canoe. The canoe struck on the stump of a tree, and unfortunately it was at a point where the banks were so steep that there was no place to unload. It required two hours to complete the repair, and by the time they were complete, the weather had grown dark and cloudy. A violent thunderstorm was brewing. We persevered along our course half a mile, and only at six in the evening were we compelled by the rain to land for the night. The guardsmen began to openly consider that we might have offended Frey or his Álfar by venturing too far into their realm. Herra Ljótsson remarked how, in Uppsala of old, Frey demanded dark-skinned sacrifices and suggested we see if a

Skræling would serve. I politely ignored his fanciful notions.

Upon exploring the woods, we came to an enclosure, which had been created by the Skræling for setting snares for the elk. In the morning, after we had travelled for some hours through a forest of spruce, birch, and the largest poplars I had ever seen, we sank down again upon the river where the bank was low. We were near the foot of a mountain, the river flowing in a channel of about one hundred yards broad, rushing on between perpendicular rocks.

We then passed with some difficulty along the foot of that rock; fortunately, it was not a hard stone, and we were able to cut steps in it for the distance of twenty feet. We climbed the rocks, creeping on our hands and knees—often slipping back again. Sometimes we caught hold of bushes, sometimes small projecting stones had to suffice. Had either failed us it would likely have meant our lives.

At one juncture, a large mass of rock broke loose from a spot above where I had just passed and struck with such force that it sent up sparks as it went. Shortly afterwards another fragment came tumbling down and so, at the risk of my life, I leaped on a small rock below, where I received those who followed me on my shoulders. In this manner, four of us passed and dragged up the canoe, in which attempt we broke her yet again. Very luckily, a dry tree had fallen from the rock above us, without which we could not have made a fire, as no wood was to be procured within a mile of the place.

When the canoe was repaired, we continued towing it along the rocks of a high island of stone, till we came to a small sandy bay. As we had already damaged the canoe and had every reason to think that we soon would risk even greater injury, it became necessary for us to supply ourselves with bark. Two men were accordingly sent to procure it, who soon returned with the necessary store. I joked that, with all the troubles with canoes, the least Frey might do is lend us Skidbladnir, his Dvergar ship, but they looked at me very darkly in reply.

We now continued our wearisome and perilous progress. As we ventured further, the rapidity of the current increased so that, in the course of two miles, we were obliged to unload four times and carry everything but the canoe. Indeed, in many places, it was with the utmost difficulty that we could prevent it from being dashed to pieces against the rocks by the violence of the eddies. By evening, we had proceeded to where the river was one continuous set of rapids.

Once again, we took everything out of the canoe in order that we might tie the cargo together with a line. The agitation of the water was so great, however, that a wave striking on the bow of the canoe broke the line. We were filled with inexpressible dismay, as it appeared impossible that the vessel could escape being dashed to pieces. Another wave, however, more propitious than the first, drove her out of the tumbling water so that the men could snag her and bring her ashore, and though she had been carried over rocks by these swells, the canoe had received no material injury. The men were in such state of exhaustion that I deemed it imprudent to propose making any further progress that day—particularly as the river ahead was one white sheet of foaming water.

The discouragements, difficulties, and dangers which had assailed us quickly soured the men's taste for adventure. It began to be shouted about, on all sides, that there was no alternative but to return to Horgfell. Herra Rothman and Herra Rubeck reached for their sword-belts. It always amuses me about Norsemen that, in their quarrels with each other, they quickly proceed to blows, wrestling, and drawing of swords. At these times, curses are bred by crossing the name of the most offensive animal to the object of their displeasure and appending the word "ugly," or "mare," or "still-born." I, myself, might have run through Róssteinn after assailing him with the utmost fury had it not been for bystanders interfering.

On this occasion, instead of joining in the quarrel, I charged Herra Rothman and Herra Rubeck to exert themselves in ascending the hill and establishing an encampment there for the night. In the meantime, I set off with Idotliazee, and though I continued my examination of the river almost until there was no light to assist me, I could see no end of the rapids and cascades. I knew that it would be impracticable to proceed any further by water. We returned from this reconnoitring excursion very much fatigued—our Finnar shoes worn out and our feet bleeding. Fortunately, we returned to find that, by felling trees at the foot of the first hill, my people had contrived to ascend it. Give a Viking an axe and he'll give you the world.

ENTRY NINE

T RAINED IN THE MORNING, and the downpour did not cease till about eight. As the men had been very fatigued and disheartened, I suffered them to continue their rest. Such was the state of the river, as I have already observed, that no alternative was left us; we had to devise a passage of the mountain, over which we were to carry the canoe as well as the baggage. As this was a very alarming enterprise, I dispatched Herra Kyndillson with three men and the two Skræling to proceed in a straight course from the top of the mountain, and to keep the line of the river until they found it navigable again.

At sunset, Herra Kyndillson returned with one of the men, and in about two hours he was joined by the others. They had penetrated thick woods, ascended hills, and sunk into valleys until they travelled beyond the rapids. The two parties had returned by different routes, but they both agreed: according to their calculation, this was a distance of three leagues. Unpromising, however, as the account of their expedition appeared, they did not sink into a state of discouragement. Herra Kyndillson is a model companion and very professional soldier.

A kettle of wild rice, sweetened with sugar, which Herra Dahl had prepared for their return, with their usual regale of rum, soon renewed everyone's courage. We went to our rest, with a full determination to overcome the obstacles ahead on the morrow. I sat up, in the hope of getting an observation of Thor and his first companion, but the cloudy weather prevented my obtaining it. Herra Kyndillson informed me that, in passing over the mountains, he observed several chasms in the earth that emitted heat and smoke, and which diffused a strong sulphurous stench. I should certainly have visited this phenomenon—to have offered scientific conjectures or observations thereon—but did not want to be accused of seið-work. There is a fine line between being a scholar and being a magician, and I fear it was crossed even with the thesis on Finnar shamans. Let us hope time can heal such wounds.

ENTRY TEN

THIS MORNING, THE WEATHER WAS clear at six. I joined Herra Ljótsson and the two Skræling in the labour of cutting a road. The ground continued rising gently till noon, when it began to decline—though on such an elevated position, we could see little beyond the snow-covered mountains that ranged far above us in every direction.

Herra Ljótsson worked alongside me and began a conversation with remarks on my extensive tuition. He further suggested that we had been undone by the wrath of malicious Nøkker and that I should find a way to appease these river trolls. He then moved onto discussing the clouds, worrying openly about how they strike the mountains in their passage over the country, carrying off stones, trees, and cattle.

I ventured to suggest that such accidents were rather to be attributed to the force of the wind, for the clouds could not of themselves lift or carry away anything. He laughed at me, saying everyone knew of the Jötunn who takes eagle form and sits at the end of the world, causing the wind to blow when he beats his wings in flight and, furthermore, that the clouds were solid bodies, straight from a Jötnar pipe.

I replied, that whenever the weather is foggy I walk in clouds, and when the fog is condensed, and no longer supported in the air, it immediately rains. To all such reasoning, being above his comprehension, he only returned a sardonic smile. He reinforced his assertion with an oath of Thor, silencing me by his authority, and then laughing at my foolishness. I was judged to be mad and told that too much learning had turned my brain. For my part, I began to despair that men like Ljótsson were entitled to sit in assembly and elect kings.

In the afternoon, the ground became very uneven, alternating between hills and deep defiles. The construction of the Serkland Raða was called to mind—and how it has been sabotaged a dozen times now. I have heard that it will never complete on time and will ruin the early investors like my father. For that reason alone, I do not think it is possible to be near-sighted when discussing the Near East. I resolved to ask Herra Audvard his Christian opinion on the Mawali. I suspect I will find him sympathetic to the Serkir. There is a complicity in all the Abrahamists, even the Gyðingar, who ought to know better.

Though difficult, our progress quickly exceeded my expectations; however, I was in a state of fatigue that may be more readily conceived than expressed. We encamped near a rivulet that flowed from beneath a large mass of ice and snow.

ENTRY ELEVEN

◊UR TOILSOME JOURNEY TODAY I compute at about three miles. For the first mile, the land was heavily wooded, consisting of large trees, encumbered with little underwood, and we proceeded quickly by following a well-beaten elk path. For the two succeeding miles, however, we found the country covered with the trunks of trees, laid low by fire some years ago, among which large copses had sprung up of a close growth intermixed with briars, and passage through them was painful and tedious. The spiders spread their curious mathematical webs over the trees, rendered conspicuous by the moisture with which the fog had besprinkled them. I watched Ljótsson repeatedly poke the air with his sword and grimace.

Having found plenty of wild parsnips, we gathered the tops and boiled them with pemmican for our supper. The soil in the woods is light and of a dusky colour. In the burned areas, it is a mixture of sand and clay with small stones. The trees are spruce, red-pine, cypress, poplar, white birch, willow, alder, arrow-wood, redwood, liard, and a strange plant known in these parts as Loki's Walking Stick. I never saw anything of the sort before. It rises to about nine feet in height, grows in joints without branches, and is tufted at each extremity. The stem is an inch in diameter, and it is covered with noxious and irritating spines—these caught our trousers, and working through them, sometimes found their way to the flesh. On inspection, it may well be that what appears to be several different plants may have all been one plant originally—when a branch touches the ground, it produces adventitious roots, and at later time the connection with the parent is severed and a new plant is produced.

We saw beaver during the afternoon but did not discharge our pieces from the fear of alerting them to our presence. There were also swans in great numbers, with geese and ducks, which we did not disturb for the same reason. We observed also the tracks of moose-deer that had crossed the river, and wild parsnips grew here in abundance, which have been already mentioned as a grateful vegetable.

I enquired of Keskarrah concerning the food of the beaver and was told it was the bark of trees such as birch and fir. I wonder that no naturalist has classed this animal with the mouse tribe, as its broad depressed form at first sight suggested to me that it was of that family.

I confirmed this opinion having examined them further with my lens: the broad naked tail, the short obtuse ears, and the two pair of parallel front teeth, so well formed for cutting.

ENTRY TWELVE

THE RAIN WAS SO VIOLENT throughout the whole of today that we did not venture to proceed. I wagered that we would soon want a beaver construction of our own, but the jest met with silence. Dritvik had given way to Dritland in the eyes of the sodden Rainguard.

As we had almost emptied the whole rum keg, and without any other requirements of active employment, I amused myself with the experiment of enclosing a letter in it and dispatching it down the stream to take its fate. I accordingly introduced a written account of all our hardships, carefully enclosed it in bark, deposited it into the small barrel by the bung-hole, and then I consigned this epistolary cargo to the mercy of the current.

Also, I confess that, from this day to the beginning of the Sun month, the details of my voyage are sometimes omitted, as I lost the book that contained them. I was in the habit of sometimes indulging myself with a short doze in the canoe, and I imagine that the branches of the trees brushed my notes from me, which renders the account of these few days less distinct than usual.

ENTRY THIRTEEN

AT AN EARLY HOUR OF this morning, the men began to cut another road to carry the canoe beyond the rapids, and by seven they were ready. That business was soon completed, and the canoe reloaded to proceed with the current, which ran with great force and speed. In order to lighten her, it was my intention to walk with some of the men, but Herra Rothman and Herra Rubeck insisted that I join them, demanding that I too embark, declaring that if they perished, I should perish with them. They were convinced we were surrounded by Nøkker, creatures that would only be satisfied with a treat of three drops of blood.

I did not then imagine in how short a time their apprehension would be justified. We accordingly pushed off and had proceeded almost nowhere at all when the canoe struck a rock. The violence of the current was so great as to drive her sideways down the river and smash her against the first bar. I jumped into the water, and the men followed my example. Before we could set her straight, or stop her, we came to deeper water and were obliged by the grasping hands of the river trolls to hurriedly climb back aboard. We had barely regained our seats when we drove hard against a rock that shattered the stern of the canoe, leaving the boat held together only by the gunwales. The violence of the impact ricocheted us to the opposite side of the river, where the bow met with the same destructive fate as the stern.

At this moment, Rothman seized on some branches of a small tree in the hope of arresting the canoe, but such was their elasticity that, in a manner not easily described, he was catapulted to the shore in an instant—and with a degree of velocity that suggested the Valkyries would be hard pressed to catch him. We had no time to turn from our own situation to see where, or indeed if, he landed; for in a few moments, we came across another cascade which broke several large holes in the bottom of the canoe.

In hindsight, if this accident had not happened, the vessel would have been irretrievably capsized and lost—as it was, the wreck lay flat and level with the water. We all jumped out a second time while Rothman, who had not recovered from his fright, called out to his companions to save themselves at all costs from the swarms of Nøkker that were inevitably coming to drown us.

I came to my senses first and insisted they all held fast to the wreck instead, to which fortunate resolution we owed our safety, as we should otherwise have been dashed against the rocks by the force of the water or driven over the cascades. In the event, we were forced several hundred yards downriver, every yard on the verge of destruction; but at length, we most thankfully arrived in shallow water. Here, at last, we could stand and rest the weight of the canoe on stones without fear of being swept away.

This alarming scene, with all its terrors and dangers, lasted only a few minutes. We called to the people on shore to come to our assistance, and they immediately obeyed the summons. Herra Rothman was the first with us; he had escaped unhurt from the extraordinary jerk with which he was hurled from the boat. Keskarrah, when he saw our deplorable situation, instead of making the least effort to help us, sat down and gave vent to great gales of laughter.

I remained outside of the canoe until everything was on the shore, albeit in a state of great pain from the extreme cold of the water, and at length, I collapsed from the benumbed state of my limbs. Our losses proved considerable, consisting of our whole stock of balls, and some of our bedding, along with the Tabul pieces—but these considerations were forgotten in the light of our miraculous escape. We had sustained no personal injury of consequence.

All our articles were now spread out to dry. The powder had fortunately received no damage, and all my instruments had escaped. Indeed, when my people began to recover from their alarm, and to enjoy a sense of safety, Ljótsson remarked that he was by no means sorry for our recent misfortune because it must finally put an end to our voyage, particularly as we were without a canoe, and all the bullets sunk in the river. It did not seem possible to them that we could proceed under these circumstances. I listened to the observations made without offering a reply till their panic was dispelled and they had got themselves warm and comfortable—with a hearty meal, and rum enough to raise their spirits and ward off the river trolls for good.

I then addressed them by recommending them all to be thankful for their very narrow escape. I also stated, with peremptory command, that the navigation was not impracticable in itself. I further suggested that our experiences would enable us to continue with greater understanding. I brought to their recollection their oaths and the fact that they were made acquainted with the difficulties and dangers they must expect to encounter before they engaged to accompany me and, finally, that they had been handsomely paid. I also reminded them of the honour of conquering disasters and of the disgrace that would attend them on their return home were we to surrender now. Nor did I fail to mention the courage and resolution which was the eternal boast of the Northmen. I quietened their apprehension as to the loss of the bullets by bringing to their recollection that we still had blades that our forefathers had sharpened for this occasion. At the same time, I acknowledged the difficulty of restoring the wreck of the canoe, but I extolled our skills in building a new and better one. In short, my haranguing produced the desired effect—a general agreement that, if the Nornir had not cut our thread today, then they might not until we were old and white-bearded.

We had an escape this day, which I must add to the many instances of good fortune experienced in this perilous expedition. The powder had been spread out—to the amount of eighty pounds' weight—that it might receive the air. It was thus spread when the dunderhead Ljótsson carelessly and composedly walked across it with a lighted pipe in his mouth. I am confounded and amazed there was no ill consequence resulting from such an act of criminal negligence. I need not add that one spark might have put a period to all my anxiety and ambition in the mortal realm.

ENTRY FOURTEEN

WE TOOK SEVERAL DAYS TO build anew. I observed several trees and plants on the banks of this river, which I had not seen to the north of 52° latitude, such as the cedar, maple, and hemlock. This time the men determined to build sturdier craft, each dug out from an individual cedar tree, quicker to make and more durable on the rocks, but far heavier.

Every night, it rained very hard in the early part of the evening. I now considered myself a fulltruí of Frey, a disciple able to describe every detail of a downpour. I was instructed as a child that Frey bestows peace and pleasure on mortals, not abject misery and damp.

The weather became godlessly clear on the fourth morning, and so we embarked at our usual hour, which is to say, several hours later than I would have liked. The water had risen quickly with the rains. The current was so strong, in fact, that we dragged along the greatest part of the way, by grasping the branches of trees. Our progress, as may be imagined, was very tedious, and involved the most exhausting labour; the guides who went by land were continually obliged to wait for us. Further calamity struck when Herra Laufrey's sword was carried out of the newly-made canoe and lost at a time when we appeared to have very great need of it. For that very moment, two canoes, with sixteen or eighteen Skrælling in each, came down the stream with the rapidity of an elf-shot, whistling and whirring bullroarers about their heads.

I have a notion that Askr and Embla were giants and that mankind, from one generation to another, owing to poverty and other causes, has diminished in size. This tribe was very low in stature, not exceeding five feet six or seven inches; and they were of a very mean and meagre appearance. Their faces were round with high cheek bones; their hair was a dingy black, hanging loose and in disorder over their shoulders, and their complexion was swarthy. Their organs of generation were left uncovered and as proudly displayed as their necklaces of the grizzly bear's claws.

From their general deportment, I was very fearful of a hostile design, and I acknowledged my apprehensions to the men. Herra Kyndillson agreed and advised the others to be very much upon their guard and to be prepared, if any violence was offered, to defend themselves to the last. Each Skræling had bows made of cedar, six feet in length, with a short iron spike at one end, to serve occasionally as a spear, much like the Norse attach their seax to their rifle muzzles. From these, the enemy began to volley arrows, pointed with iron and two feet in length, but at such a great distance, they fell short of our tiny fleet.

Those of us in the canoes landed, found the ruins of a village, and took positions calculated for defence. The place itself was overgrown with weeds, and in the centre of the houses there was a temple fashioned from ancient logs and moss. Herra Dahl kept watch on the riverbank. A dreadful silence then followed and persisted for many hours. Fearing the worst, I now mixed up some vermilion in melted grease and inscribed, in large characters, on the southeast face of the rock next to the temple, this brief memorial:

Karl Lind
Sólmánaður 1735

Towards the dusky part of the evening, we heard several discharges from the fowling pieces of our guides. Then, sometime after it was dark, they arrived fatigued and alarmed. They had been obliged to swim across a channel to get to us as it appeared that we were situated on an island—although we were ignorant of that circumstance until that moment. Keskarrah was positive that he heard the report of firearms above our encampment, and on comparing the number of our shots we heard with their estimations, there appeared to be some foundation for his alarm. He was certain that a war expedition must be in our vicinity, angered that we had entered some sacred grounds. If they were numerous, we would have no reason to expect the least mercy from them.

Though I remained unconvinced of that circumstance—or of the notion that the Skræling could be in possession of firearms—I thought it right we should be prepared. Our seax were readied, and each of us took his station at the foot of a tree. Herra Kyndillson directed the people to keep watch by threes in turn, and I laid myself down on my cloak and spent a restless but uneventful night.

In the morning, as I made to relieve myself, a trio of our enemies approached so closely that one of them contrived to get behind me and grasped me in his arms. I quickly disengaged myself from him—why he did not avail himself of the opportunity which he had of plunging his dagger into me, I cannot conjecture. They might have overpowered me then, and though I should probably have killed one or two of them, I'd almost certainly have fallen.

As it was, however, Herra Laufrey came out of the trees to investigate the commotion. On his appearance, the natives instantly took to flight, and with the utmost speed sought shelter in the forest from whence they had issued. I acted similarly—but in the opposite direction—while Herra Laufrey followed them, cursing them for cowards, the sons of cowards, and generally questioning the valour of their ancestors since time began. He was still raging through the trees when I spotted the trap and called to him. Like crows, the Skræling had scaled every tree in sight and were making ready to assail us from their perches. They had clearly determined it was better to wait and lure us into an ambush than assault our impromptu stockade.

In that instant, I saw Herra Laufrey change his footing. He heaved his buttstock and dealt one of the raiders a hefty blow and then attacked another so furiously that he was driven back along the side of the river. They struggled along the cove until Laufrey's feet found purchase on a slab of stone, whereupon he released his hold on his firearm, took the foe by both shoulders and sprang backwards over the stone. As he did so, Laufrey jerked the Skræling so suddenly that he fell across the stone with a loud crack, proving that if you run from a wolf, you may run into a bear.

Herra Kyndillson came running up next. Hearing the reports of enemy rifles, he acquired the fowling pieces from our guides and thundered into the fray, belching fire from each hand. He marched into the treeline without hesitation. Without lead shot, he resorted to handfuls of gravel and scrap, blasting from the base of a trunk, then moving to the next. Our own hunters struggled after him, crouching with their bows and issuing strikes of their own when opportune.

A few moments later, the rest of the men emerged from the village under the cover of improvisation—the cedar canoes lashed together as a wooden wall. Audvard, Ljótsson, and Dahl hefted this moveable redoubt while Rothman and Rubeck fixed their rifle blades, ready to defend against any charge. Their ingenuity allowed us all to scurry to safety and then retreat to the village in good order.

The Skræling departed from the island shortly thereafter, having lost a tenth of their number. We picked through some of their weapons. Their spears were double edged and of well-polished iron. They were, indeed, furnished with muskets in a manner that I could not have supposed, and plainly proved to me that they have communication with the inhabitants of the sea coast and the means of procuring gunpowder of a more distant origin.

E N T R Y   F I F T E E N

A T FIVE THIS MORNING, WE were again in motion and passing in haste along a different river for fear of crossing paths again with the warband. This stream was not more than knee deep, about thirty yards wide, and with a jagged, stony bottom that we desired would hamper their pursuit, but to which our new and solid canoes were immune. At eleven, however, we unexpectedly came upon yet more Skræling, though thankfully of a very different kind. These received us with great kindness and examined us with the most minute attention. They even presented us with some fish, which they had just taken from the stream, at which Dahl, the faithful cook, appeared to be very much delighted at having encountered them.

I passed the rest of the day in conversing with these people, with Keskarrah assisting as best he could—it is clear there are many and varied languages amongst these tiny nations. They consisted of seven families, containing eighteen men in total. They were clad in leather and handsome beaver-skin blankets and so our guide named them *Tsattine*, "the people who live among the beaver." They had not long arrived in this part of the country, where they proposed to pass the remainder of the summer catching fish for their winter provision.

When we spoke of our encounter with the warband the previous day, they descended into a worried silence, for our attackerswere a malignant race, the *Xaayda,* who lived in large subterranean recesses and, for generations now, had sailed from their island home to enslave their neighbours. They worshipped a cannibal giant with four terrible man-eating birds for companions and a black, bedraggled hag with long, pendulous breasts for his wife. This evil race they described as possessing iron, arms, and utensils, which they procured from people like ourselves, who brought them in great canoes across the seas (freebooters or secessionists perhaps; either way, I determined send a letter of warning to the viceroy). When they came to understand that it was our wish to proceed to the coast, they fervently dissuaded us, stating that we should certainly become a sacrifice to either the spirits of the drowned or the land-otter men. I would have laughed but for their earnestness; on reflection, I recognised that these stories were no different to the sagas I was raised on. What is this cannibal giant if not a Jötunn? What are spirits of the drowned if not the Nøkker? If I was to commune with nature, to understand these untamed wilds properly, perhaps I ought to be more open-minded. Speaker Högen would approve of the sentiment I am sure.

Not long after the beginning of this conversation, one of these new Skræling asked me a direct and blunt question. He was a sly looking fellow, vulpine, like the fox.

"What," demanded he, "can be the reason that you are so particular in your inquiries of this country? Do you Ashmen not pretend to know everything in this world?"

This was so very unexpected, that it required some thought before I could answer it. At length, however, I replied that we certainly were acquainted with the principal geographies of every part of the world; that I knew where the sea was, and where I then was, but that I did not exactly understand what obstacles might interrupt me in getting to it, having never visited Markland before. In this way, I hoped to preserve of the superiority of the Ashmen in their minds.

That afternoon, we endured a thunderstorm with heavy rain—though whether it was Thor or a Thunderbird in attendance, I was too drenched to care. In the evening when it had subsided, the Tsattine amused us with singing and dancing, in which they were joined by their young women. We all sat down on a very pleasant green spot, but we were no sooner seated than Keskarrah and one of the Beaver folk prepared to engage in a game. They had each a bundle of about fifty small sticks, neatly polished, of the size of a quill: a certain number of these sticks had red lines around them. A kind of guessing game then ensued where the sticks were curiously rolled up in dry grass, and according to the judgment of his antagonist respecting their number and marks, he lost or won. Keskarrah was apparently made to look the goose, as he parted with several articles that I had given him over the past few weeks.

We had no sooner laid ourselves down to rest that night than the Tsattine began to sing, although in a manner very different from what I had been accustomed to from the Denésoliné. It was not accompanied either with dancing, but by a drum, and consisted of soft plaintive tones and a modulation that was rather agreeable; it had somewhat the air of the *varðlokur* or warlock-song. During the chanting, I spoke again to the Tsattine who interrogated me so unexpectedly earlier in the day. I informed him that one of my people had lost his seax and requested his assistance in the recovery of it. He asked me what I would give him to conjure it back again, and I offered another knife as the price of his exertions. Accordingly, all the seax and knives in the place were gathered together, and the natives formed a circle around them. The conjurer remained in the middle and began to sing, the rest joining in the chorus; and after some time, he produced the lost seax, and returned it to me. I could not see any evidence of sleight of hand. This most curious event had me once more in mind of the Finnar shamans.

The man called himself a Dreamer, a songkeeper, and the others named him Makénúúnatane, or He Opens the Door. I was about to ask him where one might find a door in the forest, but he then proceeded to talk to me of an extraordinary kind of tree, growing over on the far side of the mountains, which many of his people had visited, but none could recognize. This Dreamer asked me if I would lend him my vast knowledge of the world to help him to understand the tree's nature. I resolved to accompany him to solve the mystery and demonstrate my accomplishments in this field.

Before the sun rose, our guides summoned us to proceed, and we descended into a beautiful valley, watered by a small river. By eight, we came to its end, where we stumbled upon a great number of moles. These ground-hogs were seemingly everywhere whistling in every direction. The Skræling went in pursuit of them and soon rejoined us with a female and her litter, almost grown to their full size. The hunters stripped off their skins and gave the carcasses to my people, which Herra Dahl duly cooked. My young Skræling friend, Idotliazee, told me they eat the flesh of the hog, the rump is thrown away, but the feet are kept. The meat is very seldom roasted but generally boiled. I found the boiled flesh very insipid, for want of salt. They also pulled up a root that appeared like a bunch of white berries of the size of a pea—it was shaped like a fig and had the colour and taste of a potato.

Though we continued our route with a considerable degree of exertion, as we proceeded, the mountains appeared to withdraw from us. We continued to ascend from the valley until we came to the brink of a precipice. This precipice, or rather succession of precipices, was covered with large timber, which consists of pine, spruce, hemlock, birch, and other trees. Our Tsattine conductors informed us that it abounded in animals, which, to guess from their description, must have been wild goats. In about two hours, we arrived at the bottom, at the confluence of two rivers that issued from the mountains. We crossed the leftmost although they eventually united their currents, forming a stream of about twelve yards in breadth. Here the timber was also very large, with some of the largest and loftiest alder and cedar trees that I had ever seen. We were now sensible of an entire change in the climate—the berries here were quite ripe. I measured several of the trees that were forty feet in girth, and of a proportionate height. The alder trees were also of an uncommon size; several of them were twelve feet or more in circumference and rose to sixty feet without a branch. There was little underwood, and the soil was a black rich mould, which would well reward the trouble of cultivation. From the remains of bones on certain spots, it is probable that the natives occasionally burned their dead in this wood.

The Dreamer had withdrawn himself to a secluded location and covered himself with an intricate hide, decorated with an embroidery of very neat workmanship with porcupine quills and the hair of the moose, coloured red, black, yellow, and white. He had not yet identified the mysterious tree to me, but the other natives told us he was sitting with the ancestors and that, during this time, it was important that no one speak to him, else it would interrupt the working. The trance he entered in this manner was heralded by a huge and unnatural yawn, suggesting that the practitioner's consciousness was issuing out through the mouth. The Urðr are said to change shape into a variety of animals, often sea-mammals or birds, in order to make spirit journeys to other lands to seek information. I resolved to speak to him further at daybreak, so I might become wise about those things, and in the interim, Dahl and I took and pressed many samples.

ENTRY SIXTEEN

WHEN THE TREE WAS FINALLY brought to my attention, I wondered how I could have missed it. It was a giant among monsters. One hundred feet all round—if not more—and hundreds of feet high. There was simply no way to tell; it was so tall that I wondered how it might pull water from the soil to such extremities. It had a fibrous, furrowed bark, red in hue although tending to much darker patches. The root systems were gnarled and intricate, intertwining with others across the whole glade. I asked Herra Dahl to take an axe to a branch, but he barely made a scratch.

When the Dreamer appeared, it was only to confound me further. He explained that my guides had misinterpreted him, and that the tree wasn't just that one colossal trunk, but a whole village. I surmised by this that he meant each tree to be an offshoot of the first: I have already observed that heavy snow may push a tree's low-lying branches to ground level, where they take root and prosper, growing anew in the spring.

At my request, the Dreamer regaled me with his people's sagas. He informed me that the world was created by a raven flying over water, who, finding nowhere to land, decided to create islands by dropping small pebbles into the water. Nonsense, of course, but one may note the honored place of Odin's own heralds. The raven then created this tree, and then he made the first man and woman out of wood and clay. The raven once conversed daily with the tree but had long since flown away. The Dreamer then stated, in his own language of clicks and sighs, that I was to sing to the tree. As I have mentioned, I have an ear for the music and know something of the incantations of the Finnar. Upon seeing that he was serious in his intent, I decided to humour him.

I had not proceeded more than three notes in imitation of the Finnar, when the conjurer joined me in my melody, banging his drum steadily, like the fall of feet along a trail. He too began to chant. I was dimly aware of the Beaver folk dancing around me and then felt a tremendous shaking throughout my body, followed by a rush of sweet, summer fragrances and the humming of bees. I have spent many nights trying to describe the sensation that came next. In Finnmørk, I observed young children sleeping in leather cradles, without any thing like swaddling clothes, enveloped in dried bog-moss and lined with the hair of the reindeer. In this soft and warm nest, they are protected from the most intense cold. For the longest moment, I felt transported into this land of slumber, safe and secured.

To my intense and increasing fascination, I then found myself somewhere else entirely, still trembling without the means to control my limbs. My surroundings were intimately familiar—the little corner of my family garden in Vittaryd, which I had so diligently cultivated as a boy. The huge triple-trunked linden tree stood guard over me, as it had done since I could remember. Of the Rainguard and the Skræling, there was no sign. The damp itself had vanished. I stood in the brightest of summer days. He Opens Door indeed!

HERE I LEFT MY WRITTEN account of my expedition in Markland. The toils and dangers, the solicitudes and sufferings, have not been exaggerated in my description. On the contrary, in many instances, language failed me in the attempt to describe them. I sat bolt upright, astounded and agitated both beyond measure, in my father's study and tried to make sense of events. In my final analysis, I concluded that a journey of months, by ship and by wagon, had been reduced to a glimmering. This last passage was written in a frenzy and then the journal was left on the desk, forgotten in my haste and excitement. Of course, the real story was only just beginning.

My father and brother were overjoyed to see me returned so unexpectedly, but alas, in Uppsala I was treated with neglect, and even with contempt. I had forgotten that a prophet is usually less esteemed at home than anywhere else. My dilemma and eventual discredit lay in the appalling fact that I could not recreate the incantation or the trembling sensation I had experienced. Unable to provide proofs, I was ridiculed. The university speakers assumed I had absconded from my duty, and Róssteinn made sure that my attempts to publish even the briefest paper were met with derision. Even Högen found my saga too tall in the telling and wearily informed me that I had scorned my gifts.

Summoned back to court under charge of dereliction, I found the High Urðr immune to argument. I had collected my thoughts thoroughly at this juncture, and I posited that the galdar songs could, when shaped correctly, act as a key to doors as yet undreamt of. I told the court that I now saw clearly that there were not four kingdoms of Nature, but one—vegetable, animal, and mineral all inextricably linked with the spirit realm. The High Urðr charged my writings with indelicacy, laughed at my hypothesis, and called upon all the court to see if anybody understood my meaning. I implored the Urðr to write to Horgfell and introduce testimony from Herra Kyndillson or even Herra Dahl but cannot say with any certainty whether they acted in this request. The viceroy ignored my entreaties entirely, his commission doubtless dependent on his compliance with the established order. Certainly, I never heard from the Marklanders or Makénúúnatane again and have no idea what might have befallen them. I was left with cold comfort: the wretched knowledge that I had been shown the chair of the Nornir, only to have it snatched away before the hidden habitations of the cosmos were revealed to me.

In judgement, I was said to be ignorant of the gods themselves and was judged by the principles of Lœkrmann and hundreds of the vilest scribblers. As the skalds have told, I was outlawed and banished from the realm, destined to undergo hardships until the end of my days.

Stuff and nonsense, of course. Fate is the life you lead if you never put yourself in the path of greatness.

Nowadays, it has been said of me that Lind the Leaf-King was, in reality, a skald who happened to become a scholar. To my mind, I have become the Dreamer's raven, flying over water and creating my own lands, a new progenitor, a second Ragnar if you will. Certainly, his ancient ways are now, by my instruction, made more modern. No one has written more books, more correctly or more methodically, on how to traverse the green-ways. No one has more completely changed the laws of nature and started a new epoch for humanity. No one else, save Odin himself, can claim to have named whole worlds.

With nowhere to turn, I went back to my beginnings. The Warlocks of Finnmǫrk thought better of my endeavours, perhaps because they, too, were forced to subsist at the margins of the empire. As I have mentioned, by common repute, the Finnar were warlocks of distinguished eminence. They were songkeepers too. Magic was native to them, the galdar was their birthright, spirits their peculiar province. Even the lowliest practitioner could raise the wind by tying three knots in a string. When he untied one, a strong breeze blew. When he untied the second, there was a gale. If he dared unloose the third, trees would topple before the tempest and ships would rip from their moorings. They had, of course, many arts that were not so devastating, such as charms to cure disease and incantations to deter a hungry wolf. In Turku, the distinguished Elder Törngren hosted me and assisted me with my works. At first, I entrusted my secrets to him alone. We expected a multitude of interesting discoveries and were determined they should not be subject to the control of the Urðr or the mores they contrived for imperial society. When we received the reward of our labours—for they were crowned with success within months—well, suffice it to say, that the records will show I have never sent back upon my enemies the barbs which they have hurled at me. The grins of the malicious, the ironies and attacks of the envious, I have quietly borne.

Each time I stepped into a new golden realm, a new celestial sphere stretched in infinite prospect below me. I walked through the abodes of the gods and wandered under stars seen only by Álfar eyes. Each trip was a transport of joy, a rush of nostalgia, exultation, and gratitude.

For a time, Turku became the centre of our new knowledge. Students flocked to us from all over the empire, men for the most part, all those denied a voice—veterans who had grown tired of the interminable wars with the Maharajahs, farmers denied a parcel of land by the Urðr, even Abrahamists clutching their Codices. But common among these disciples, there was a resolve to enlarge the boundaries of mankind. I refused to transcribe the songs of creation, even for those brave pioneers, but was happy to teach those who were willing to learn. I named them Verðandi, for the Norn who shows us what we might become rather than binds us to what we are.

At the time of the travels, the powers-that-were paid rapt attention to the voyages of my pupils. We cannot, of course, know what became of all of them, but some have secured a form of immortality to match my own. Ternstroem died on his voyage through Vanaheim; Hasselquist, after travelling Asgard, was lost in Myrkviðr; Forskal perished in the ice waves of Niflheim. Poor Rolander no doubt suffered most, succumbing in the Fyris Wolds just outside Uppsala on his near-triumphant return. He was likely murdered for the secrets he possessed—I know from personal experience there is no fury like an Urðr scorned. But why should I not tolerate the wretches, when I have been loaded with the praises of the fylkir himself, before whom they must bend in the dust? My age, profession, and character prevent me from waging war with my opponents. I will, instead, employ my few remaining years making useful observations.

Of all these great men, only Coc and Sparrmann are still with me in my remote garden, weary from their expedition in Nidavelir, and of course, both distinguished by the Polar Star for being first to circumnavigate the Nine Worlds. Their stories are not mine to tell, but they will be the first to remark that only by standing on the shoulders of a Jötunn have they seen further than the Jötunn himself.

EXEGESIS V

THE CHURCHWARDEN SPRINTED FOR THE porch. He was a large man, *stout* his mother had said. He wasn't especially fit; he'd never even dreamed of joining the Blengdale Runners on their Sunday jaunts, other than for a quick natter on the beach. But now, sheer determination propelled him forward with impressive speed. He didn't break his stride even when he reached the first flagstone. Instead, he hurled his shoulder at the great Norman door, hoping to open it and reach safety in one fell swoop.

He decided to ignore the extra crosses. Blot them from his mind. Curiosity tended to do horrible things to cats; who knew what it might do to him? The sanctity of the church, the protection of the Mother of God—that was all that mattered.

He bolted the heavy door and staggered down the dark moat of the aisle towards the chancel. The night was suffocating. In his haste, Michaels performed a crude imitation of the gale, knocking prayer books from the pews, sending cushions and sheet music spiralling onto the floor. He careened all the way to the altar, where he tripped and fell prostrate, panting out a prayer.

The church was blessedly silent. Whatever tempest raged outside, in here there was only peace. Michaels decided that was enough for the time being. He needed to gather his wits and work out what was happening. He felt his way in the darkness to where he stored the candles, but then thought better of it.

Chandler.

It meant candlemaker. That was too much of a coincidence. He didn't want to tempt fate.

Instead, he edged himself around the aisles, where he could feel the cold stone wall and avoid crashing into anything else unseen. He made his way along the columns to the east end, to the niche where the old tombs stood, and sat in between them. There he could at least watch the door until sunrise.

The tombs greeted him like family. He couldn't count the times he had looked at them, enthralled. As a small boy, he'd often been distracted during Sunday service, imagining the Saint and the Warrior battling over the centuries.

He traced their patterns in the darkness, recollecting the imagery. On the larger tomb were many serpents, some wolf-headed, and at the end of the ridge, the enormous head of the World Serpent, Jörmungandr. The battle between good and evil goes on; God the Son overcomes the enemy, as Vidar, son of Odin, rent the wolf at the Twilight of the Gods. On each end of the stone was the crucified Redeemer. The White Christ is acknowledged, and the hell mouths gaped around the tomb in vain.

The smaller tomb was unique. On one side were many confused interlacing patterns; on the other, an historical scene. Two armies stood opposed, not fighting, but truce making, one leader apparently surrendering his flag to the other, whose party bore the large round shields of the Vikings.

His hand felt along the chieftain's face, then crept to top of the ridge. The sensation was strangely hypnotic, reassuringly solid, fascinatingly old. It was almost relaxing—until it wasn't. His hand floundered, grasping only empty space.

The stone had moved. The tomb was open.

"Careful now. You don't want to release a draugr. Crypt-fiends are notoriously difficult to get back to sleep once disturbed."

Michaels choked back a sob. The voice was devastatingly familiar. He couldn't see the old man, but he knew that he was close. He could smell the sweat, the pungent earthiness of the woollen cloak.

The disembodied voice echoed around the Norman arches.

"I'm sorry, did you think I couldn't get in? Or that your God would protect you? Perhaps he will, if you renounce all the words and works of the devil, Thunaer, Woden, and Saxnot, and all those demons who are their companions. Perhaps he won't. It's a god eat god world, after all."

A candle flickered into life, guttering in some unfelt draft. Chandler stood over by the piano, next to an old pine bookcase. He stooped, made a selection, and began leafing through the pages.

"You asked me if I'd read any of those English historians. Of course I did, before they were enveloped and dispatched by time. I came across this great line from the Venerable Bede when I was planning my revenge. *De tonitruis libellus ad Herefridum*. Everything was Latin in the early years Anno Domini. *De tonitruis libellus ad Herefridum*; it's all about divining the future from thunder. 'If it thunders on Sunday, this is considered to presage an extensive mortality of monks and nuns.' That's the kind of religion you all signed up to. What kind of god would arrange thunder on a Christian's day off? Well, Thor, for one, I suppose. Is this the Fishing Stone you told me about?"

Chandler was pacing along the wall, examining the interior decorations and commemorations.

Michaels didn't respond. He realised he wasn't a particularly religious man. His duty was to the land. To the monuments. He wasn't above converting to Asatru or whatever the old man was raving about. Reverend Riley would understand, he thought, before he remembered that the vicar was probably not in a position to comment on anything. Mrs. Jones would probably treat him with newfound respect. It was worth clinging on to thoughts like those. Couldn't be seen to be a gibbering wreck. That way madness lay.

"I see there are women priests now. I was always under the impression that, as far as Christianity was concerned, the stained-glass ceiling was more of a shit-stained floor. Have you heard of the Patriarch Paradox? The head of a woman is her husband, and the head of every man is Christ. That means Grandpa is the son of a virgin. Not a bad trick. Women must give birth to sons and yet be chaste, pure and virginal. The mind boggles as to how they are meant to achieve all that, but such was your patriarchy; old white men, preferably ones with beards, they write the rules. Did you never think to grow a beard, warden?"

Michaels instinctively shook his head, a little too vigorously, then realized that the old bear hadn't once looked in his direction. Perhaps he didn't know where Michaels was hiding.

"I'll confess, your Christ taught me that lesson well. When I was young, women made the world go around," Chandler said, perusing the wall, stepping closer to the hogbacks. Michaels tried to shrink down, out of sight, hoping against hope that the old man hadn't spotted him.

"The Norns, three giant maidens who controlled all our fates, the fates of gods and men alike, from meddling monks to terrified churchwardens. When they called time, there was no use slamming on the brakes, or running for cover. Your candle was burned out. You were smoke in the wind. They decreed my death at Ragnarok, etched my last on the roots of Yggdrasil, the great World Tree. But of course, you know that. You have your Cross. It was all preordained."

Michaels shifted his weight onto his right leg and tried to slide behind the larger tomb. The old man continued.

"Those ladies have the power to shape futures, to spin stories, to shatter ceilings. They were not to be denied by a glitch like Christianity. I told you names had power, and no name more so than the Norns: they 'twine' and 'secretly communicate.' These were the women who called to me and inspired me to return. They will have their Midgard back. Or so they think."

Michaels used his hands to pull himself up, so he could squat. He could see the candle drift in his direction. Closer, ever closer. He held his breath and waited.

It was only then that he noticed the second tomb was open too.

The churchwarden didn't recognise the sound that came from his lips, but Chandler did.

The old man blew out the candle, and Michaels felt the world around him scatter like smoke as he dropped helpless into an endless black chasm.

Sometime later, Chandler spoke.

PHILOSOPHICAL TRANSACTIONS

THE TEMPLE AT GAMLA UPPSALA

1850

I T HAD A PRETERNATURAL BEAUTY, this place. Seen at a distance, the temple shone like a beacon, radiating the brilliance of the Storm King's Hall in all directions. The site was encircled by mountains; when arriving, you felt you had been ushered onto the stage of a vast amphitheatre, an effect accentuated by the golden chains that hung around the temple gables.

It was a bright, clear day. The snow lay in pristine piles on either side of the path, the half-melted puddles crackled under foot on the walkway. Sun goggles might have been sensible. Iðunn wrapped her Qiviut shawl tightly around her instead. The delicate under wool of the Arctic muskox was always warm and as light as a feather, perfect for her longer explorations. Underneath, she wore a lattice of hardened leather, padded with silk to let the skin breathe. Her arms and face were a knotwork of ash tattoos, her hair scraped back into a practical braid. She could have changed for the occasion, but she liked the pioneer look. It would give her a gravitas, an outlander authority—and it also implied that, while she would have been delighted to be asked, she hadn't been best pleased to be summoned.

"Fuckers," she mouthed, to whatever gods were listening.

Iðunn had always felt a loneliness to the scene. There was an anonymity to each arrival, exaggerated further by the sheer size of the embarkation suite. There were no welcoming arms or smiles, no-one anxiously awaiting your return. The Urður weren't renowned for their warmth, but even for them, it all felt rehearsed, their devotion both slavish and somehow scripted. As the Skald himself wrote, "All the world's a stage, and all the men and women merely players; they have their exits and their entrances, and one man in his time plays many parts." Shakageirr had distilled the posturing at Uppsala, and the whole empire, into one essential sentence. The Urður wanted the world ordered, directed.

The temple itself always put on a bravura performance. It bustled with goði and gyðja attending to the carving of a new frieze or the blooding of a statue. The anguish of sacrificial goats filled the air with sounds and smells of a farmyard, and the clanging of the forge was so loud it was startling. Not as startling though as the monstrosity that took centre-stage—the huge phallus the ancients had carved on Frey's statue. Iðunn was glad she didn't have to compete with that. It made for an eye-watering welcome, very clearly erected to insist on male inadequacies; not even an urður could straddle it, however much pent-up frustration they might have.

Any general misery Iðunn felt at returning to her alma mater was quickly lost in a wave of nausea. Stage fright might account for some of it—that the Urður weren't going to be happy with her thesis was an understatement—but Iðunn knew the wooziness was from the journey itself. Osmosis was the technical—if borrowed—term for the transition; both water and data streamed between point A and point B, after all. Most Norse called it the Stakra—staggering—because landing felt exactly like trying to walk when five flagons into a feast. The effects were even worse when you travelled home from the Utangard. Most of the hinterworlds had stronger gravity than the imperial seat.

The university itself was a short walk away, towards the lake. Half an hour perhaps, enough time to clear the head from the stagger. On the other side of the grove, she could always borrow one of the university boneshakers if she needed to make up time. She'd need to adjust her watch to the Midgard time. It wasn't a big change, but Iðunn always felt a nagging sensation of being late when she was on campus.

The path was quiet, with nothing but the crunch of gravel to provide company. The sacred grove itself seemed as ethereal as ever, although smaller than she remembered, like a spritely village elder, seen again after many years' absence: diminished yes, but undimmed. The wellspring itself had been walled off, only the elite able to savour its holy waters. Iðunn felt a prickle of annoyance at that.

"Fuckers."

She said it louder this time, knowing that if she was being watched anywhere, it was here in the holiest of holies.

Time was always the enemy. Much of the land here had been transformed since the early days of the empire, not by man or god, but by geology: post glacial rebound, the slow thawing of the world after the crushing ice ages of prehistory. The old town had lost its strategic importance when it was no longer accessible from the sea. Now it was changing overnight because of man. Newer settlements had sprung up everywhere since she was last here.

On the far side of her view she saw that Munsö, too, the island home of the great King Sigurd, had been merged with the neighbouring isle of Ekerö, geology conspiring with the fylkirs so they could claim to be the literal scions of oaks. The symbolism was more obvious than Frey's penis; it was easy to spot the meddling hands of the Urður.

Iðunn was startled to see that, down by the river, they'd reclaimed the Fyris Wolds, but then remembered that they'd started construction on a new Winter Palace. It was a grotesque heap of white marble and silver, but a ghoulish match for all the bog-blanched skeletons that it was paving over. That was certainly one way to make sure their secrets never surfaced.

Usually, dignitaries of all kinds staggered between Uppsala and Miklagard. Seaborne trade might have moved south, but Gamla Uppsala was a Nexus, *Knútr* or Knot—terms used interchangeably by the wide range of peoples who passed through the greenways. While officially the Great City was still the crossroads of the world, of all the Nine Worlds in fact, and teeming with fifteen million people, Uppsala had silently reclaimed the true crown out of pure convenience. Miklagardians would protest they had their own great yew Knot, over 4,000 years old, but it was five hours travel *outside* the walls, in the mining town of Zonguldak. The Norse were never a patient people.

The Vǫlur had controlled the Knots as they controlled all things, shrouding secrets with mysteries obscured in arcana. They'd always been shunned, even feared by the common folk, and the dread had only grown stronger in recent years. That might explain why no-one else was walking the path this side of the campus. It hadn't been the case when Iðunn had been a student—it had always been bustling then—but she hadn't been back in a decade. The Urður might have introduced a toll for all she knew. Either that or the waggoners were on strike again. They hated the Urður more than most.

It didn't matter. She was used to being alone. She adjusted her shawl and let her mind wander with her. It needed the exercise.

IÐUNN HADN'T SPOKEN WITH A fellow vǫlur in days, and she couldn't remember when she had last spoken to an urður. The eldest and most distinguished branch of the sisterhood, they dealt with the machinations of state—spycraft, politics and wars. They were midwives to the imperial family, as well as their mouthpieces when it suited them, curling the nobility around their fingers. They advised the emperor and his stallari, controlled security, propaganda, and censorship, and all from a vast subterranean tunnel complex around Uppsala: Urðbrunnr, or simply, the Well of Fate. Iðunn had long since seen through the charade. It boggled the mind that the Urður saw no irony in the fact they also stood as the final Court of Appeal for the Commonwealth. How could justice be blind if she saw everything?

Iðunn belonged to a younger branch, the Verðandi. Like all vǫlur, she was a keeper of knowledge, but her discipline concerned understanding the here and the now, the interconnectedness of man, machine, and god. Biology, the Greeks had called it once, although her arts transcended the physical body. Her great-grandfather, the heroic Karl Lind, had spoken of a union of all creatures, including the spirits, teaching a holistic approach to medicine and the miracle of birth. He had founded the Verðandi Order in his image—most of his early acolytes had been men.

Karl was rightly lauded for his many accomplishments—this was a man who mapped the heavens, after all—but he clearly had grown an outsized ego to match them. In his own taxonomy of the Nine Worlds, he considered the vast, uncompromising landscapes of Jötunheim to be the only place large enough for his intellect; literally, it became the home of a giant among men. Despite all his protests to the contrary, Iðunn knew her great-grandfather meant it to be an affront to the Urður, a constant reminder of how he had broken free of their shackles and saved men from the prejudices of the age. There was a portrait commissioned for the north stairwell to celebrate the various imperial ratifications and charters that supported the Verðandi, and if the grin of the fylkir was anything to go by, he was happily complicit in the whole scheme. Men were well practiced at closing ranks.

Iðunn didn't much care for most of the Nine Worlds herself. Intellectually, she knew their discovery was a staggering achievement, pun intended. To have mapped the heavens, to have criss-crossed the universe—who could aspire to more? But she'd grown up with the certainty that those worlds were within reach, and so their lustre faded, in the same way that no one marvelled at the first sailings to Vinland any more. It was a commonplace. Yes, she found the three so-called Worlds of Plenty—Asgard, Alfheim, and Vanaheim—beautiful, bucolic even, and there was a majesty to a sky full of alien constellations. The problem was almost anything thrived there, and she found no challenge in that. Nidavelir was coal-black and Hel was bleaker than the Markland steppe, so she rarely travelled to either if she could help it; the other hinterworlds were off-limits to non-military personnel.

As to Midgard, well, Midgard was where all the problems began. There were people on Midgard, maybe a billion of them. Thankfully, none of the hinterworlds had much in the way of settlement—most people couldn't use the greenways unless they were accompanied by a völva, and fewer still could tolerate the burden of greater gravity for long—so they all had a purity to them. Virgin worlds, holy worlds. It was like stepping back in time.

Iðunn had been born on her great-grandfather's farm, Hvergelmir (named after the fabled spring from "whence all waters rise," another boast), and still lived on the world he had claimed as his own. She loved the neat wooden railings, the straight avenues and the quaint Verðandi cottages, but above all, she loved the tracts of great walled gardens and sunken green-houses, the laboratories where Karl Lind had cultivated life. The volcanic soils were rich, the sunsets were violent; and she enjoyed the weight of the world, it made her strong and lean. She knew that she could snap an arm as if it were a twig.

And then there was always a whisper of her family about the farm, their spirits still watching from the monolithic trees. She felt sad for them. Once all the hinterworlds were explored and the glory had evaporated, the Verðandi had fallen out of vogue. The men had, in the main, moved on, and it had fallen back to women to heal the sick, tend the gardens, and manage the songs of the greenways. Only the Finn, Lönnrot, had stayed with the Order, and even then, only barely. He was always off wandering the worlds, searching for the gods. Iðunn was more than happy with that arrangement; it gave her more time for her studies.

The third branch of Vǫlur was where all male scholars flocked these days. The boy's club moved on to play with other toys, proving that it is not only in infancy that men are pleased with a rattle and tickled with a straw. They called themselves the Skuld, a group of futurists and theoreticians, great minds with immense egos, maintained at vast expense by the admiralty. They claimed study of Sol and Mani, dreaming of stjarna skips from deep in their bunkers at Niflheim. The Skuld were determined to prove it was man who was the measure of all things, able to bend the Nine Worlds to their will. They worked in great secrecy, as prejudices still ran deep—it was only the bravest seiðrmen who risked the scorn of his kin to dabble in the black arts.

Iðunn knew there was great comfort in that thought across the Empire, a fervent belief in the all-conquering, all-high Norse, reciting the creed of Valhöll.

No-one bothered with questions anymore. The skalds recited tales mechanically, without bothering to ask where people were headed, whether here was better than there and if anyone had left anything important behind. Well, they were all fools, blithely unaware that they were a product of a thicket of philosophies grown in all manner of lands.

That was why she was here, marching along a path between the oldest buildings she knew, a temple of the gods and a temple of learning.

Karl Lind had forgotten something important. Iðunn could hear him whisper it in the rustles of the leaves, could hear him mourning. He had forgotten his place. He imagined himself to be greater than the world he inhabited rather than a mere part of it, losing track of the very insights that enabled his discovery in the first place. In his arrogance, he assumed the greenways were a gift. He didn't ask why he had received it or how any of it worked.

Iðunn blamed Miklagard. The Greek civil service was an infestation, the rotten core of a bad apple. They planted ideas, ancient convictions about the essential supremacy of man and the belief in progress, a progress marshalled by a professional army, built on land ownership, and presided over by a benevolent monarchy, all seeds that quickly took root in Commonwealth soil. As soon as fylkirs took the Great City and all its myriad libraries, they had ensured their skalds catalogued and memorized everything—and that was when the blight set in.

From the heirs of Leo the Mathematician to the acolytes of Gemistus Pletho, the Greeks seized the opportunity to tutor the Norse as they had educated the Romans. It looked good from the outside. The union promised the best of both worlds: any good gardener knew about hybrid vigour—that a hybrid plant grows stronger and bigger than either of the parent strains—but bite deep and the taste was sour. Society had nurtured a narcissistic canker, a disease that strangled ideas and left them stunted. The fruit of Karl's work had been left to rot.

"A whole world full of vargdropi," she muttered. The mess wolves left behind.

Iðunn had dedicated the last eight years of her life to answering the questions Karl had left unanswered. It wasn't just a familial duty, but a spiritual one too. She considered her work to be mending the thread. Perhaps it took the perspective of a new world and the home of a Jötunn, to realise the truth: mankind was not the centre of the universe. The worlds did not revolve around man. She sighed and marched on. It was time to upset the apple cart.

WHILE THE PRACTICE VARIED ACROSS the Commonwealth, in Uppsala the defence of any new theory or discovery followed a simple formula. The University Speaker would hear the Mál, a debate so lively that knives were often drawn. He'd then adjudicate, either digesting the lessons into the current body of laws or starving them from the record. The Chief Speaker in Uppsala was a retired military man turned lecturer, Henrik Bohr. Iðunn hadn't exactly had the time of her life as a student here, but Bohr had always been a saving grace. An artillery accident had left him wheelchair-bound, although no one ever talked about the specifics. He had a gloomy face, weighed down by the great unkempt whiskers of a hussar, with a mouth that turned down at the edges to match, which suggested he was perpetually miserable. Nothing could be further from the truth. There was a total transformation when he smiled or spoke. His whole face became animated and suddenly gave the impression he'd fly out of his seat in excitement if only he could. Iðunn always felt cheerier for talking to him and had kept up a vigorous correspondence after her graduation.

The discussion would begin promptly; of that Iðunn was sure. Herra Bohr was known to be ruthless with timekeeping. If the students came in late, well, then that was their loss. One of his favourite aphorisms was that "while we keep a man waiting, he reflects on our shortcomings," a phrase he mentioned so often, the students were known to repeat it spontaneously upon seeing him. There wasn't any time to be apprehensive.

Iðunn took her place at the podium and cleared her throat. She noticed some uniformed men in the back of the assembly, who looked decorated enough to be representatives of the stallari. Not unexpected, if the Varangians had gotten word of her conclusions. Her sister urður were there too, in force, like a pack of wolves, although she so rarely engaged with them, even on official business, she didn't recognise any of the faces.

The hall rippled with excitement, and an expectant hush descended.

She shuffled her papers and then checked her watch. She hadn't rehearsed or scripted much beyond a few jokes, and she'd told them so often that they'd become a routine. The only sane way to proceed through a Mál of this magnitude was to have fun; after all, you couldn't make an omelette without breaking eggs. The forces of progress must inevitably clash with those of reaction and all that. The only problem was that she had no idea how long it would take to regurgitate the whole thesis or whether she'd be allowed to get through it in one go. The rules of engagement said she should be uninterrupted, but the Norse had never been good at fighting by the book.

The room was silent now. She checked her watch again and wondered if it had stopped or whether Midgard time was actually this slow.

"Góðan dag," she said, with a slight nod of her head. She immediately realized that she sounded too formal and pretentious, but it was done now.

"Honoured speakers and distinguished guests, today I present, on behalf of the Sacred Order of Verðandi, a defence of my thesis Mindless Mastery: Mimetic Osmosis and the Impact of Arboreal Sentience. I would begin with a quote from Askr's Fylkirbok:

> I know that an ash-tree stands called Yggdrasil,
> a high tree, soaked with shining loam;
> from there comes the dews which fall in the valley,
> ever green, it stands over the well of fate."

She impressed herself sometimes. She was crisp, precise and authoritative. This was going to go well.

"Yggdrasil the World Tree is the root and branches, pun intended, of our belief system. We have all been raised to understand that she is, literally and metaphorically, the pillar of existence. In some cultures, our people are even referred to as Ashmen. In her honour, for centuries,

Northmen have planted what was called a 'care-tree,' or 'guardian tree,' in the centre of their homestead—a miniature version of Yggdrasil, and a stately landmark in any courtyard.

"When the great Karl Lind's father chose to become the first of his line to adopt a permanent surname, he chose the name Lind because of the giant linden tree that grew on the family homestead. If the care-tree witnessed many families growing up, the relationship between the tree and the family was said to be all the stronger. I am proud to be the fifth generation that now bears that name..."

There was a burst of applause around the auditorium. It was always good to remind people of her illustrious forebears.

"The story of Yggdrasil goes back not just five or even fifty generations, though. As children, as soon as we can understand the sagas, we learn we are the sons and daughters of the Ash and Elm tree: the first man was called Askr, born from the Ash, and the first woman Embla, born from the Elm. Askr and Embla sprouted from Yggdrasil's seeds, and so it is said that every human being springs from the knot holes of Yggdrasil, there to be collected by two storks, who bring them to their longing mothers-to-be. Now, many of us know from experience that this isn't literally true..."

There was a smattering of laughter, but it took the beaming smile of Speaker Bohr to help her pick up pace, as the line fell flat and her delivery faltered. Nepotism one, charm nil.

"We are reminded that the sagas are not to be interpreted literally; they are to be explored with fascination rather than fanaticism. Why, in these various tales of the emergence of the first human pair, do humans come from wood rather than some other element? Why not, for example, clay, from which humanity was created in many ancient Near Eastern worldviews—as in the Abrahamic Genesis or the Akkadian Atrahasis? Even after Ragnarok, an event foretold, but far in our future, the survivors Lif and Lifthrasir emerge from the shelter of trees and are nourished by water."

She was glad to get past the ancient history. The arts were for the Urður.

"Where did humanity come from? The goði would answer: 'from trees and water because their spiritual essence is inseparable, wherever trees and water come into being, so must men and women, too.' Humanity does not stand apart from or above the rest of the more-than-human world. Our essence is inextricably bound up with the essence of the greater whole.

"The völva might add: 'From wood and water, and, more fundamentally, from what is written. Humanity is destined to exist; therefore, we exist.' Fate, the inscrutable force that links all agency throughout the cosmos, assures us that humanity is at the heart of all creation."

She scanned the faces in the room. Two students in the front row were splayed out and snoring quietly already. She sympathised; she wouldn't have liked to have been compelled to sit through this at their age. She hoped they'd wake up later and appreciate the enormity of what she had to say. The worlds required the young to care, not sleepwalk to disaster.

"Back to Karl. Lind was the first man, unwittingly or otherwise, to uncover the something that was evident to our forefathers and encoded in the very name Yggdrasil. As we are all aware, the most satisfactory translation of the name Yggdrasil is *Odin's Horse*. Ygg is another name for Odin, and drasill means *horse*. However, drasill also means *walker*, or *pioneer*. Some scholars have in fact argued that the name means *Odinwalker*. In some parts of the sagas, Yggdrasil and Odin seem to be one and the same. When Odin hung, speared, for nine days on the World Tree, he uttered the words that he had 'sacrificed himself onto himself,' as if tree and god were one and the same.

"Now, it has been clear since the expeditions of Karl Nilsson Lind that the trees of the Nine Worlds are intertwined between worlds.

They have roots and boughs more deeply entangled than the deepest, most ancient of forests in ways we are only beginning to understand. Tapping into that root system has enabled some to travel between the worlds in a way long thought reserved for the gods, reserved for Odin himself. Lind's hypothesis was that Yggdrasil, and all the folklore surrounding the world tree, was a construct of our genetic memory. That is, his discovery of what has come to be known as *staggering* was in fact a rediscovery of an ancient lost art, a secret long buried with the kings of old.

"Odin remains at the core of staggering. His Óðr, the force that inspires people to perform or to prophesize; to produce scholarly works or to enter a frenzy in battle, is vital for travelling within the trees. Óðr overwhelms and infuses us, blankets our consciousness and brings us ecstasy: Odin, if you will, takes our hand and guides us through the greenways.

"Here, on Midgard, Karl found first one, then many candidates for what he called heartwoods, the oldest of groves. Yew trees that were gnarled and twisted when Sumeria was young. Pines as old as the Pyramids. Old trees, like antenna, catching unworldly signals. Trees that resonated and thrummed with Óðr when sung to, songs from the beginning of days. Entities that took your embrace and danced you to somewhere entirely different, continents away—worlds away for those of us who are particularly adept. We have accepted this way of life as we have always embraced Yggdrasil: as a benefactor and a guardian. Those favoured by Odin ride his steed, those blessed by other gods still ride on wagons."

It was an old trick. Tell your audience what they already know and then create a bridge from there. There were an awful lot of blank faces staring back at her, but if she invited any comments at this stage, she might not be able to keep her narrative on track. Either that or the waggoners really were on strike and she'd just been stupidly insensitive.

"However, for all the comfort, protection, and sheer utility of the World Tree, I have been compelled to search for further answers. My contention is that we cannot see the wood for the trees; that is, we can't see the whole situation clearly because we're too intimately involved with it.

"The great irony here is that for all the mobility they grant the adept, trees don't move. That's worth repeating. Trees. Don't. Move. So, how does the very-firmly-rooted tree evolve so that it can spread across separate worlds? We take it for granted that Odin and his brothers didn't literally slay Ymir and set about constructing the worlds from his titanic corpse. The oceans are not actually Ymir's blood, the sky is not his skull, neither is the vegetation his hair. Although, if it were, long and tangled hair might explain how Yggdrasil spanned the cosmos."

The audience were still unmoved, so she plunged on.

"My simple question has been this: how did Yggdrasil come to be, and how did it become so successful? How did it come to be our carer and our guardian? My fellow Verðandi and I have lived with and travelled through a great many of Yggdrasil's holy groves and conducted many studies that I hope my Lind forebears would be proud of. The most important thing to grasp from our studies is that many of the most impressive capabilities of Yggdrasil can be traced to a tree's unique existential predicament."

She paused for emphasis.

"Again. Trees are rooted to the ground. They are unable to pick up and move when they need something or when conditions turn unfavourable, which would make them exceedingly poor as Vikings."

The audience remained tight-lipped.

Eldhúsfíflar, she thought, *if it is dry you want, I'll give you enough kindling to burn down the house.*

"This sessile lifestyle means any given tree must find everything it needs, and must defend itself, while remaining fixed in place. It follows that a highly developed sensory repertoire is required to locate food and identify threats. And so, a tree smells and tastes—they sense and respond to chemicals in the air or on their bodies. A tree *sees*—they react differently to various wavelengths of light as well as to shadow. A tree *touches*—a vine or a root *knows* when it encounters a solid object. And trees *hear*; the sound of a caterpillar chomping a leaf primes the tree's genetic machinery to produce defence chemicals. Tree roots seek out the water flowing through buried pipes, which suggests that plants somehow *hear* the sound of flowing water.

"The sessile lifestyle also helps account for plants' extraordinary gift for biochemistry, which far exceeds that of animals and, arguably, of our imperial chemists. Even then, our advances, from aspirin to opiates, are derived from compounds designed by plants.

"Unable to run away, plants deploy a complex language to signal distress, deter or poison enemies, and recruit animals to perform various services for them. A recent experiment by one of my pupils found some plants create a reward and punishment system, a carrot and stick, if you will. They emit a scent that encourages bees to remember a plant and return to it, making them more faithful and effective pollinators. Even more ingenious: several trees are known to send a distress call when attacked by caterpillars. Parasitic wasps some distance away lock in on that call, follow it to the besieged plant, and then eliminate the attackers, a form of plant bodyguard.

"So, if plants can sense and respond to all these environmental variables—light, water, gravity, temperature, soil structure, nutrients, toxins, microbes, herbivores, chemical signals from other plants—it follows that there may exist some information-processing system to examine the environment and coordinate a plant's behavioral response. *Memory* may be a thorny word to apply across kingdoms, yet there are clearly ways that Yggdrasil is storing information biologically that doesn't require a frontal lobe and hippocampus. For example, immune cells *remember* their experience of disease and call on that memory in subsequent encounters, even down through generations.

"Now, no-one believes that we will locate a big walnut-shaped organ somewhere in our plants which processes sensory data and directs plant behaviour. But when we look closely, we do see very sensible, cooperative behaviour. The simplest example is how individual trees support each other, working together for the collective good. My pupils have seen how trees form anastomosis between their roots, allowing them to provide each other with both structural support and vital nutrients. We have witnessed *mother* trees using this network to nourish shaded seedlings, including their offspring, until they're tall enough to reach the light. Even more striking, we have seen how fir trees use a fungal web to trade nutrients with birch trees in the same grove, over the full course of the season. The evergreen species will tide over the deciduous one when it has sugars to spare, and then call in the debt later in the year. If you delve deeply enough, a vibrant forest community becomes apparent.

"This village of boughs and beams can mount a coordinated and robust defence. When antelopes browse acacia trees, the leaves produce tannins that make them unappetizing and difficult to digest. When food is scarce and acacias are over-browsed, the trees produce sufficient amounts of toxin to kill the animals."

She paused. That was the complicated part over, but it was also the bit that she could prove, if she had to, through details of a hundred experiments at Hvergelmir.

"Once you have a clear understanding that trees communicate and cooperate daily, it is a simple matter to extrapolate further. There are around six trillion trees on Midgard, which is around one thousand trees per person—and many times that across the Utangard, with estimates of the number of trees on Vanaheim and Alfheim alone that dwarf those numbers. Plants dominate every terrestrial environment, composing ninety-nine percent of the biomass on Midgard. Humanity is a whisper by comparison.

"Let's look now at Vaxa, also known as the Trembling Jötunn. After he passed, Karl's acolytes amongst the Dane-zaa and Tsuu T'ina discovered a clonal colony of a quaking aspen in the central part of Hvítramannaland. There are tens of thousands of trunks above ground, all linked with a massive underground root system. It is in fact a single living organism, as proven by identical genetic markers. The plant is estimated to weigh collectively six thousand tons, making it the heaviest organism we know of. The root system of Vaxa is probably eighty thousand years old—roughly as long as humans have been wandering out of Fornland.

"We have no way to reliably estimate how many of these Vaxa-style giants exist. But they are vastly old and interconnected in ways we have only begun to study. There are plenty of signposts and suggestions of a sentient mind at work. Blessed with a lifespan of thousands, if not *millions* of years, what have these constant gardeners achieved? As the empires of man, Sumerian, Persian, Roman, waxed and waned, as the Norse mastered iron and steel and devised intricate solutions to measure the universe around them, what has the serene Yggdrasil accomplished? Infinite complacency? Endless stagnation? Epoch-spanning dullness? Should not all the aeons have amounted to something, beyond, well, lots more trees?

"We have learnt from the sagas that the World Tree is fragile. Dragons gnaw its deepest roots, four stags feed insatiably from its branches. Only the goat Heidrun and the deer Eiktyrner live in balance with the tree. They feed from the branches too, but they give back gifts to the Tree also. The goat offers mead and the deer pours waters from its antlers into the roots. The Norns, too, tend the tree daily, pouring water from their well to nourish the roots. The fates of legend would collect the sweet glimmering dew which fills the valley; this dew is said to be memory of yesterday.

"Yggdrasil is balance, is a complex, synergistic, self-regulating system that helps to maintain and perpetuate the conditions for life across the Nine Worlds. Yggdrasil creates the air we breathe, the water we drink, the habitability of the Nine Worlds. It doesn't just connect the Nine Worlds, it sustains them. That, to me at least, is purpose enough. That is how I would define the great Arboreal civilization, not as mere buildings and monuments, but nine worlds flung across the sky, reshaped in her image and silently cherished for eternities."

All right, you wretches, she thought. *Trees chat, check. Trees work together, check. Trees are big and old and everywhere. Check. Time for the big reveal.*

"But I will go further still and state that the World Tree has not only nurtured life, but has shaped the evolution of that life. Let me state that again for clarity: the trees have shaped the life around them. The fact that the tree collective is one, effectively immortal; and two, possesses many different genes leads us to another conclusion. By using her seeds to selectively pollinate, Yggdrasil must have guided her own evolution. What a magnificent and potent tool, a deep and intuitive knowledge of genetics born from countless generations.

"Think of the potential—you could grow dull workers, who would produce tools and weapons or a breed of warriors to use in battle, or diplomats, with powerful brains that would allow a tree to act with authority far from the grove—a way for distant colonies of trees to communicate with one another. Expansive new colonies could be started by sending a child to root outside of the bounds of a colony, even across the Ginnungagap. Pheromones would probably be used to start, but eventually, a deeper level of communication could be developed that would allow the intelligent, but sessile, parents to program their dull, but motile, children.

"Lind's taxonomy, the *Náttúra Bók*, contains numerous passages that suggest he believed there is an immense amount of invisible and inaccessible activity going on all around us. Our lives, be they imprisoned by the war demands of the fylkirs or the sophistry of the skalds or simply isolated deep in the meat of our animal brains, can only vaguely perceive this realm, the realm of ancestors and spirits."

There was a nervous ripple of laughter. *Ah, so they laugh when they are threatened, do they? Well, wait and see, boys and girls, wait and see. Momma's got a brand-new bag and it's time to clear the dance floor.*

"Lind also hinted at a conscious mind that influences and observes our actions. That divine agency can be assumed to be Yggdrasil, at work with a multiplicity of deft and delicate chemical tools. The Álfar and the spirits, more beautiful than the sun, more ephemeral than the breeze: those creatures are Yggdrasil too. They are her signals and her suggestions.

"I am not trying to describe a single, peerless mind, with mastery over all things, across all worlds. I don't think there is any real intent or emotion in Yggdrasil. She is unfathomable, ineffable, utterly alien. The World Tree will never attest to confirm or deny my hypothesis. In place of a brain, what we see is a distributed sort of intelligence, as we see in the murmurations of starlings. In a flock, each bird has only to follow a few simple rules, such as maintaining a prescribed distance from its neighbour, yet the collective effect of a great many birds executing a simple algorithm is a complex and supremely well-coordinated behaviour. Something similar is at work within Yggdrasil, with her thousands of root tips playing the role of the individual birds—gathering and assessing data from the environment and responding in local but coordinated ways that benefit the entire organism. The nature of mimetic osmosis is not well understood, but it demonstrably occurs. Patterns are traced and recognised, and information is exchanged between groves of trees.

"From our vantage point, we can only see certain activity. The falling of leaves, the slow growth of a sapling. Over many years, we might see an errant root tumble a wall built foolishly close. But it is what we *can't* see that is of interest. Activity beyond our senses—or at least, beyond our experience.

"Much like the parasitic wasp, we are Yggdrasil's tools, her dull workers. We eliminate her diseases, help her procreate, hunt the animals that plague her, even light the fires that allow her rejuvenation. Once she opened the doors to the Nine Worlds, she sent us through. We spread her seed, and she claimed them as her colonies, bending the climate to her will. For time immemorial, before the advent of recorded history, Yggdrasil has fashioned a joint path through the brambles and the briars. We are inextricably linked to our woody brethren. We were truly born from trees.

"As the skalds would have it: '…in every human there is a tree, and in every tree there is a human, the forest sea is the second sea of Midgard, the tide on which man wanders. The forests work in silence, fulfilling Odin's mighty design.' We should serenade them more often."

Iðunn hoped her cadence would make it obvious she had finished speaking, but even so, she instinctively glanced at Bohr for approval, both for timekeeping and to chair the remainder of the Mál. For all her armoured pride, she felt naked on the podium, and couldn't wait to step away.

There was a brief round of applause in which Bohr shuffled forward to start proceedings, but the crowd was impatient and peremptory. Questions began before the speaker had wheeled into place.

The first to rise in response was one of the Urður, an older völva, leaning heavily on her staff and speaking as she stood. "As the skalds would have it indeed, for there is more than a touch of poetry about your thesis, my dear. Still, from your lips to my ears. What do we have in the way of proof rather than rhetoric?"

It irritated Iðunn when people asked questions for which answers had already been provided.

"In a nutshell, for those of you in the audience who may be hard of hearing: for a tree to move a person between worlds, it is axiomatic that they must be capable of cognition, communication, information processing, computation, learning, and memory."

She imagined that might put the crone in her place, but the Urður rose up further, as if casting away her age.

"Thank you, my dear. Let me see if I have been following. Your contention is that, these electrical and chemical signalling systems have been identified in plants which are homologous to those found in the nervous systems of animals? And that the Álfar and Vættir spirits are actually products of these signalling systems?"

That was unexpected, Iðunn thought. An Urður who knew her arse from her elbow.

"Technically, the latter part was Karl Lind's suggestion, but yes, for a large part, that is what I am saying."

"But in the absence of actual—even abstract—two-way communication with this sentience, how can we be sure? Have you ever asked an oak?"

The elderly völva smiled, smug with play on the Norse words, Askr and eik. She missed her calling as a skald.

Another voice piped up. "Hardly, you don't have a conversation with a door."

The hall dissolved into laughter. Iðunn bridled, but waited for the laughter to subside.

"With respect, the spell singers are doing just that. Singing the galdar in the right key is like finding the right key to a door."

The elderly völva was grandstanding now.

"Every day, the fylkir himself converses with the gods at the Well of Urður, attended by our sisterhood. Are you suggesting he is mistaken and is, in fact, discussing the flow of sap and the embarrassments of lichen instead? Are you suggesting we replace the divinity of man with a fantasy of a talking plant?"

"I was under the impression that the Urður know full well that we are all conduits for the divine and that the fylkir's discussions are metaphorical."

A second Urður chimed in. "There is no need to be facetious. The supremacy of man is a key tenet of Our Ways. We aren't barbarians, ruled blindly by Christian Kings deluded by notions of divine right. The Northmen are free in speech, thought and deed. We have a model egalitarian society precisely because we have sought our new lands, seeded new plantations, and maintained the supremacy of the Althing—unless trees are now to be given the vote?"

Iðunn was incensed by the suggestion that she had started the bickering.

"Well, while we are debating ancient history, would it surprise you to find that while the Vikings and the Christians were warring around Rome, the Hindoos created the Vrukshayurveda, a guide to the protection and veneration of plants? Groves are sacred in their culture too; we don't have a monopoly on treating trees with respect. The Orang Asli don't even allow stone structures in their holy forests."

Various Urður were hissing from the benches now. Iðunn had to raise her voice above the ruckus. It had been a mistake to mention the Subcontinent, even if there was a truce. Still, she thought, in for a penny, in for a pound.

"We might not even have a monopoly on staggering. There is some archaeological evidence that suggests other cultures have visited the Utangard. And in the past, other cultures, using different words, in different forms, describe the same phenomena. The Greeks knew the World Tree as Gaia."

She had to shout now to be heard.

"Even the bloody Christians planted a grove in Beersheba; it was only when they realized that pagans had gotten there first that they gave it up as idolatrous. Yggdrasil has always belonged to all of Midgard, regardless of race or creed. We're not so fucking special."

Tempers were rising across the room. The Urður were furious. "Do we have a part to play at all in your creation? Are we vǫlur not all creators, continuously spinning our world? Or would you paint us as Abrahamists, defined and determined by an aloof and omnipotent will? The Christian God is reborn as the wooden cross he was crucified on!"

With that, the First Order stood and walked out of the theatre as one. The room emptied after them like water down a storm drain. It clearly wasn't wise to tangle with the elder sisterhood; even the military decided that discretion was the better part of valour. Iðunn wasn't perturbed, she relished hitting her mark. It took considerable willpower to restrain herself from telling them all to fuck off as they swirled towards the exits.

After a few minutes, she was left alone with a handful of university speakers. They either had nowhere else to go, or no concerns about being ostracised. Knowing academic circles, it was probably a little of both. Bohr gave her a wink, then started a more intimate conversation, more like a faculty meeting than a Mál.

"Well, it was almost as if they planned the walkout."

Iðunn laughed. "Of course, they planned it. The Urður do everything in advance."

"Quite the commotion. We ought to finish the session properly. Incomparable, by the way. Your studies are very much ahead of their time. Can I ask some of my own questions?"

The Verðandi nodded her assent.

"What of the sagas that speak of Yggdrasil clearly as the noblest of trees, preeminent perhaps, but still one of many, rather than the one as the group?"

"Well, we think individual trees aren't inherently sentient. Only with great age or great growth does an acorn become the mightiest of oaks. Even the oldest groves may seem as children in comparison to some of the places we are starting to map."

"You keep describing physical characteristics though. You'll forgive me, I am a military man, not a theologian. Let me see if I can put it into words—Yggdrasil and the Well of Urður were never conceived as existing in a single physical location, but rather dwell within—or across—anything and everything. Like a kind of invisible heart."

Iðunn smiled.

"I understand perfectly," she said. "And we are in agreement. That is exactly what I am saying. Yggdrasil permeates everything and everyone, but it does have a physical·form as well as a metaphysical one. I don't see either as mutually exclusive."

One of the remaining speakers raised his hand politely, then stood and addressed the Verðandi. He gave a hasty bow.

"Good morning, madam seer. Karl Dýrrvin, pleased to meet you. I have a question if I may—which came first, the kjúkling or the egg? Or in your terms, the tree or the man? And to be clear, I am not talking divinity here—I am not talking intelligent design. I mean to say that, as good scholars, we both know that trees have, at some point in prehistory, the same common ancestor as mankind—even if it is just a cell escaping some primordial soup or a mold whose spores found purchase on land. Isn't that the real gift of Ymir?"

Dýrrvin was almost bald; most of his hair seemed to have migrated into his frizzy grey beard and deep, overhanging eyebrows. Iðunn knew him by reputation. He'd visited her father on Jötunheim on occasion and claimed to be a budding acolyte of Lind. He'd written some spurious theory of his own, the *Survival of the Misfits*, about how it was the oddest creatures that prospered most from calamities.

Iðunn said, "I can't speak with the authority of the distinguished speaker, I am afraid. I would suggest that trees have had more time to develop their intelligence than man. My colleagues think upwards of four hundred million years more. They certainly predate the dragon fossils unearthed across Midgard, and they survived the great extinctions of the past with ease. Their seeds survive and thrive after great fires and resist the charring radiation of the sun. They even replenish the atmosphere during the Fimbulwinters that follow. The trees came first, there is no question in my mind, at least on Midgard. Tree survived when many species did not. What we'll find as a point of origin across the other worlds remains to be seen."

"Well," said Dýrrvin, "if this transposition of legend into fact is true, where are the other analogues? The Gigalope is a large herbivore but hardly fits the definition of a Jötunn, unless devouring grass counts? Why does the racial memory omit the Raboons of Asgard? Or the flocks of Razorbills? And, conversely, what of the other beasts mentioned in the sagas? What of Ratatosk, the squirrel? And the harts, the serpents? Why are some parts of our myth conveniently literal and others mysteriously absent?"

Iðunn straightened. "At the risk of ducking this question, honoured Speaker, I am not compiling a modern-day bestiary, nor am I a zoologist, crypto- or otherwise. We have barely begun to explore the continents of the Nine Worlds. The research facility at Hvergelmir is half the size of your personal office here. It is conceivable that all the creatures you mention exist out there somewhere."

"Well then, what is your *guess* on point of origin for the tree species?"

"A guess is all I could offer," she said. "Some realms are older than others. If they were truly fashioned by the gods from Ymir, it was done over the length of aeons, which means the gods lived a very long time ago. And yes, I am aware of the irony of my name and the myth of the apples. When you come from a long line of Linds, botanical names are all the rage. But, like Herra Bohr, I am not a theologian or a skald. I am not telling stories or seeking to impart wisdom. I am simply making an observation. Trees can communicate and store patterns; by extension, they may have steered the evolution of mankind, and other creatures."

A younger man blurted from behind the speaker, a student by the looks of him. His name tag, home-made, identified him as Hofgard. He was fidgety and nervous, speaking before Dýrrvin could continue his line of inquiry.

"You spoke of Yggdrasil as having a purpose? What does it yearn for? Does it build? Does it reach for the stars like the Skuld?"

Iðunn almost laughed out loud, but remembered she'd been young once.

"Making buildings from stone and using fire are not the only paths of progress," she said. "Remember, a tree doesn't need to grow food and it reaches to the sun as a matter of course, for sustenance. If I had millions of years to think, perhaps I'd think reaching out for more stars was a waste of effort. Or perhaps mimetic osmosis is the way Yggdrasil did reach for the stars. Perhaps she seeds great rocks and flings them across the void. Perhaps there are spores floating through Ginnungagap right now, seeking new homes. She seeded nine worlds, that we know of, worlds where life is possible, where water exists. That's successful evolution. That's purpose, is it not?"

The student stared at her, shifting from foot to foot. He looked very pale and anxious, as if he had to be somewhere else in a hurry. She tried to be reassuring.

"We are lucky to live in symbiosis with her, to have been born in the branches, to have thrived on the vine so to speak. But a tale is but half told when only one person tells it. Let others corroborate or contextualize my work. I don't lay claim to all the answers, and a Mál is for theories."

The student seemed a little hysterical. He almost screeched his next sentence.

"And what of free will? Is it to be simply stripped away?"

"Okay… I'm a little lost. I fail to see how free will has been lost. I stated that trees might have shaped our path, helped mankind to survive and thrive. If anything, Yggdrasil might have nudged free will rather than stifle it."

The young man had notes, that he scanned through now.

"You said, and I quote, 'Patterns are traced and recognised and information exchanged.' And you said that these patterns are songs, which are in effect keys. And then you answered the Speaker, saying trees came before man. But that misses the point. Man has to have made the key for it to fit the lock."

Speaker Bohr scratched his head. "Couldn't he have been *given* the keys? I suppose not. Someone had to make the key and the lock to work together."

"Which means someone or something had to design the system in the first place. Everything has a beginning."

"That sounds dangerously Christian to my ears, young man!" Dýrrvin grew red in the face, but the young academic blustered on.

"So, Odin travelled the greenways in centuries past. Thought and Memory travel with him—Huginn and Muninn, his ravens. Couldn't he have taught the trees as he travelled? And then left his divinity within them, like a blueprint? That's the source of the pattern. That's a fair interpretation, isn't it?"

For a Verðandi, changing the consciousness of a cow or a tree was just as possible and natural as influencing the mind of a man, but the secrets weren't to be shared freely. Iðunn smiled at the student, hoping to end the conversation before it went around in another circle. That was the trouble with belief; it didn't have to be based on fact.

"I imagine anything is possible for Odin, young man, so do tell me when you find him. I could do with some validation after today."

Bohr came to her rescue, and announced loudly, "Thank you for visiting us, Mistress Lind, and bringing us this fascinating piece of conjecture. You've certainly given everyone a lot to chew on. Will you seek to publish your findings?"

"I'll publish the results of the experiments. The plant signalling is irrefutable. The leap to sentience is certainly debatable. The Eddic stuff, all the references to the sagas, frankly, that is just window dressing. I was aiming for some rootedness, some shared perspective. I'd expected the controversy; I didn't think it would be like confessing a murder."

Bohr wheeled away from any more questions, pushing himself ahead of the stragglers, then held the door pointedly until they took their leave. Iðunn took one last look at the empty hall, then followed them to the open door. The old man whistled his relief.

"Peace at last! Well, for me at least. I am afraid you have raised the spectre of the old Christian teleological argument. See a watch, infer a watchmaker. I confess, I am at a loss for a suitable analogy for the realm of trees. It is an unusual concept."

"See a human, infer a World Tree?" she offered.

"Very droll," said Bohr. "Dýrrvin is in a rage. I am afraid even the most liberally educated will find natural selection and natural theology strange bedfellows."

"Dýrrvin should be happy. He has spent years telling everyone we came down from the trees. He's the biggest misfit of all."

"And the Urður, well, you've rather assaulted their mastery of the universe. Destiny, the invisible hand. Whether we carve our own destiny or are puppets in the hands of another, that is now up for debate."

"The Urður will worry that Yggdrasil was once a gateway, but now it threatens to become the gatekeeper. Or worse, a gaoler. What the Norn carve into the tree is the earliest form of our destinies, but not their only possible form. They'll just have to carve quicker and harder. It will do them good to think for a while, to stop living in the past."

Bohr smiled at that, then spun himself towards the entrance hall, nodding to one of the duty constables who tipped his silken top hat in reply. "I understand. The advances you've made are going beyond our ability to keep up. It's very impressive. You'll return to Jötunheim?"

"Straight away," she said. "I detest the cities on Midgard. Thralldom in this day and age beggars belief. Land reform is long overdue. Another bad harvest and there'll be widespread famine, and famine will lead to revolution."

"Perhaps you are reading too much Wilhelm Wolff. You were always fond of the leftist teachings."

"Ah, my friend, a toleration of slavery is a toleration of inhumanity. If there are gods in Asgard, I plan on asking Odin about his breeding program. But don't worry, I don't have time to be a revolutionary. Besides, look where it got my great-grandfather."

"That's gratifying to hear. I think we've had plenty enough wars. I know I have, and your work is revolutionary enough." The Speaker rapped on his chair as if to underscore the comment, and then motioned for the constable to open the high, oak doors to the courtyard. "Will the gods be found, do you think?"

"Not on Asgard, no. The only thing of any size there are giant Waspedrs; otherwise it is just endless trees, mountains, and lakes. It's a lot like Markland. In all seriousness, the Verðandi have searched for a century and found no traces. Either the gods are in hiding, or they cannot be found. Not as a body and shape. To me, the gods are thoughts and desires, inspiration on a difficult day. That kind of thing. Not warriors with big... hammers. I'm sorry to be so depressing."

"Your great-grandfather would be proud."

"His taxonomy was a contrivance," said Iðunn. "At best a terrible joke, at worst, a vainglory. It's like finding a pantry full of tinned food, and deliberately swapping the labels."

"You realize if he'd named one of the worlds Cockaigne, people would ask if the houses there were made of cakes and the streets were paved with pastry? For most people, they are still a story, forever out of reach."

"Blame the High Urður. The Verðandi would open the greenways if we could. They took control three days after Karl passed. My father was young then and unable to stop them. Anyway, ancient history. I doubt I'll come back any time soon to Uppsala."

"You'll be most welcome if you do."

"Not at the Well of Urður I won't." She laughed, kissed Bohr on the forehead, and turned into the night.

A moment later, she was joined by the young man from the Mál; he had clearly been waiting for her outside. He thrust out his long fingers as if to shake hands, then thought better of it, and drew them quickly back into his pockets. He tried a brief bow instead.

"May I join you? Mikjáll, Mikjáll Hofgard. My name, that is."

"Briefly; I am on my way to the Grove."

Iðunn was already striding back the way she came. She wondered at the name, though. She had learned long ago that names had power, names had meaning.

"Mikjáll. That's a Christian name?"

"True. It is the only thing I have left of someone I once loved. Not that it is any of your business. And from the Grove? To Hvergelmir?"

"Yes, not that it is any of your business."

He looked frail and was struggling to keep pace. He'd not survive the gravity on Jötunheim—not that she had any intention of bringing him with her.

"Are you injured?" she asked, with as much care in her voice as she could feign.

"Not really. I was at Frederik's Hospital last week. I fell from one of your beloved trees when I was a boy. There are still complications I'm told. But, I have enough energy for a walk. If one just keeps on walking, everything will be all right. We don't have a choice anyway, since the waggoners went out. They hate your greenways for ruining their trade. I, on the other hand, liked your theory very much. Why did you decide to announce it at Uppsala? To stir the hornets?"

"I was asked to come," she said.

The young man was almost running to keep up, ducking between the halo of the street lamps and the pitch of the gaps in between, his enquiries coming in breathless bursts. "Yes, but you could have said no. You chose to uproot the establishment, rip up their very own care-tree, and what's more, you pulled it straight out of home soil, sacred soil even!"

"Perhaps it was fate."

"All beings who are subject to destiny have some degree of power over their own path, though, no? The Verðandi shape destiny more actively and more potently than most, I'm told. You get your hands dirty, in a manner of speaking?"

"I don't need a lesson in the intricacies of fate," she said. "I was being sarcastic."

"It's not a lesson. It is a fear. All life is an interconnected web, where the slightest thrumming of one strand can cause the whole web to tremble."

"That's good. Write that down. Let the world tremble with fear!"

Iðunn hoped outright mockery might shake him loose, but he seemed irritatingly immune to ridicule.

"So, you agree? That what is written can be rewritten? Life is about authorship, yes? We are but spindles and flyers on the Great Wheel of the universe. To change the yarn, you must risk everything."

Iðunn paused and glared at the young scholar.

"Hofgard, is it? It's been a long day. I haven't got the time or the energy for riddles in the dark. Tell me, just what are you trying to change?"

"Let me come with you," he said, "travel the greenways to Hvergelmir."

"Why in Thor's name would I do that?"

"The Tree," said Hofgard. "Let's call it a leap of faith. I think I can prove your theory. I think I can find the Gods."

EXEGESIS VI

(N ◊ T H I N ᚲ N E ⟋ ⟋)

YOU KNOW HOW IT IS supposed to end, Churchwarden. Let me tell you how it all began.

Ginnungagap was the great emptiness before there was the world, flanked by two inhospitable realms. There was Muspelheim, crossed by endless rivers of boiling poison and vast lakes of fire; and Niflheim, where icy volcanoes spewed forth frozen mists and arctic waters. Sparks and smoke met layers of rime and frost in the yawning void and from them came the first being.

A Jötunn, Ymir, appeared in the melting ice. From his sweat, the first Jötnar were born. Ymir fed on the milk of the primeval cow Auðumbla, also born of the meltwater. She licked the blocks of salty ice, releasing Búri, who was large, powerful, and beautiful to behold.

In time, Búri's son Borr had three sons: the gods Óðinn, Vili, and Vé. The three sons of Borr had no use for Ymir and his growing family of cruel and brutish giants, so they attacked and killed him. So much blood flowed from the body that it drowned all the other giants except for two—Bergelmir and his wife escaped. They stole away in a hollowed-out tree trunk, a makeshift boat floating on the sea of gore to safety, to a land they named Jötunheim, home of the giants.

From Ymir's body, the brothers made the world of humans: his blood, the seas and lakes, his flesh, the earth, his bones, the mountains and his teeth the rocks. From his skull, they made the dome of the sky, setting a dwarf at each of the four corners to hold it high above the earth. They protected the world from the Jötnar with a wall made from Ymir's eyebrows. Next, they caused time to exist and placed the orbs of the sun and moon in chariots which were to circle around the sky.

Finally, the three brothers built their own realm. Ásgarð, a mighty stronghold, with green plains and shining palaces high over Miðgarð. They built the rainbow bridge Bifröst to link the realms. The Æsir, the guardians of men, crossed over the bridge and settled in Ásgarð.

Óðinn Alfaður is oldest and greatest of them all. That was our golden age. And then this, the beginning of the end. The Völuspá tells it well:

> *In their dwellings at peace | they played at tables,*
> *Of gold no lack | did the gods then know,—*
> *Till thither came | up giant-maids three,*
> *Huge of might, | out of Jötunheim.*
> *Thence come the maidens | mighty in wisdom,*
> *Three from the dwelling | down 'neath the tree;*
> *Urth is one named, | Verthandi the next,—*
> *On the wood they scored,— | and Skuld the third.*
> *Laws they made there, | and life allotted*
> *To the sons of men, | and set their fates*

Of course, I am grateful to the Norns. I would have missed the zeitgeist if it hadn't been for them. I hadn't realised that soldiers were marching in my name. I hadn't realised that my forests were disappearing. I had become time's ghost. They showed me how to turn back the clock. How to reclaim what was mine from the White Christ. I found Willehad of Bremen, the one that got away.

But the Norns don't like inconsistencies. Eventually their idle suggestions become inescapable realities. It would soon be time to Ragnarok'n'roll all over again.

Except...

Every maid has a sire, every lineage has a father. I'd killed Ymir, but there was another one that got away.

Bergelmir, his grandson.

The first lord of Jötunheim.

The begetter of Norns.

I was looking for those who murdered me. I didn't say when.

You know what they say, Churchwarden. In for a penny, in for a pound. I can't very well be the All Father with another progenitor out there, seeding chaos. Still, no need to get my hands dirty—it really is amazing how quickly woodworm will ruin an untreated canoe...

NATTMARA SUBJECT 09

FOLKVANG BARRACKS, MIKLAGARD

1940

A H, YOU'VE TURNED THE LIGHTS on. It is very bright. It's almost like being birthed again. Do you have a dimmer switch? No? The silent treatment, is it?

A control mechanism, I suppose. Fair warning, I don't think I can be controlled.

Father took the opposite approach. He was always angry, roaring out his orders. Not like you people. Shut up, he'd say. Be quiet! Quit your yapping! If we weren't quick enough, my brothers and I, his voice would boom out louder, more deafening than the cries of fifty men. Then, Mother would hurry to us and sweep us into the safety of her arms. She'd have someone take us back to the glasshouse, while she tried to placate him. It never worked. Father would just stomp away to erupt at someone else. The whole fortress would echo to his commands.

Mother said he had plenty to be angry about. Father would never hurt us, though; she wanted to make sure we understood that. We were very precious to him, to both of them, to all the people at the farm. We held all their promises, hopes, and dreams inside us, she said.

I imagine we represent something different to you.

Extinction, perhaps.

No?

I'll hand it to you, you are good at the old cold shoulder.

She was always calm and caring, and pretty, so very pretty. Mother, that is. I always knew we were special to her; even my uglier brothers were loved. In time, I even came to respect Father's voice, especially when he made the broadcasts. It was hypnotic, coercive. Stentorian, one of your stallari called it. Father would sit in his studio, with a microphone the size of his head suspended in front of him, transmitting on all frequencies, while his staff frantically twisted knobs and turned dials. He was in his element there. It was the only place he smiled. Do you remember his broadcasts from those days? Eventually, he added pictures, but early on it was just his voice beaming across the Gap. You are probably too young.

Mother had her gardens to keep her happy. They were all around, some walled in with old bricks, some with new bricks, grown like bread. Mother was clever like that. She could shape something from nothing. Some were made from shiny glass, those gardens had ash-black soil. Then there were the white gardens inside the main complex, rooms full of fine mist and steel beds. I tried to avoid visiting those unless the sisters insisted. My skin is very hard, as you've found out, and the needles would snap unless Mother was very careful.

She had long, brown hair once—I knew from the photographs in her office. She kept it short, though, when I was a child. As a mark of respect, she said. For solidarity. By contrast, as you can see, my mane was always thick and silver and long. It was obvious why they named me Grey Back. My brothers all have muscles taut as knotted ropes and shoulders as broad as wooden beams, but none of them have this moonlit crown. I asked Mother if I should cut it, also out of respect. She laughed and told me I was sweet, but that I would make my mark in other ways. Cutting it will be my decision and mine alone. So again, fair warning: if any of you try and touch it, I will bite you, and I assure you, my bite is brutal.

Our work was very important. The Ironwoods were a safe place, she told us. We were all created free and equal. But there were other lands, lands with cruel gods, who kept men crushed under their heels. Sound familiar? In those lands, people were starving because there wasn't enough bread even though most were in thrall to the fields. Mother explained that Father planned to save all those people. He'd use the greenways to steal them away.

The Jötunn War you called it. Like we were some eternal enemy. Perhaps we are. Father called it the Great Emancipation. Said it was his duty. We have suffered centuries of outrage, enforced poverty, and bitter misery, he'd say. Our rights and liberties have been trampled on by an alien aristocracy, who treated us as foes, usurped our lands, and drew away all material riches.

We were strong, my brothers and I. We roamed the greenways since we were pups and knew all the passages between places. Our world had a smell of sulfur, acrid, like oven cleaner. Other worlds had the scent of mildew, of old garden sheds. Still others smelled of dead birds and brine. You probably don't have the right equipment to notice. We had been bred to be strong, to be adaptable, Grave Wolf and Sleepbringer and Unraveler. Mother called us her most successful brood yet. We were among the first, I know that now. As her old friend, Wystan the skald, used to say, it is the misfits who, forced to migrate to unsettled nooks, alter their structures and thrive. Positively Dýrrvinian, she said.

Sometimes, we took Father's shape, especially when we went to your borgs and your tuns. It helped us blend in, helped to retain the element of surprise.

Dogs would always find us eventually, barking incessantly until your guards came, clanking in their carapaces. You could smell their fear, hear their hearts beat. If you caught one alone, he'd often piss himself, or spill his bowels even as they were ripped from him. You could see their eyes, wide with panic, deep in the shadowy recesses of their helmets, like two dark holes in a tree. Much like yours now. Wide with fear.

You are wondering if I am still strong and if you will be able to contain me. It is a reasonable concern. And at some point, we'll find out, and one of us will be disappointed, if only for a moment.

Either that, or my brothers will find me.

Or Father. I imagine he will be very annoyed.

Father addressed you all in his broadcasts directly, telling you to throw down your rifles and join him. He called you 'Proud Men of the Ash'. He offered you new lives, where you could turn your swords into ploughshares and fill the bellies of your children.

His war wasn't with you. It was against the locusts who pose as gods, who have eaten the verdure of your fields—against the leeches who drain your blood for their wars.

And this is how you have repaid Father. You abduct his children.

He will be very, very annoyed. He watches you all the time. He is always in the forests, watching you from the dark.

With political rights denied to them at home, with men of thought and action condemned to loss of life and liberty, is it any wonder our ranks grew? Father would gather them and exhort them to liberate themselves from below instead of waiting for a false freedom to be granted from above. They came in droves, riding on our backs all the way to Mother's gardens, where the sisters would clothe them and shape them.

Social change. Those who don't fit today are the ones who make tomorrow. The Worshipful Company of Carmen came first. They'd been so highfalutin with their economisers and regenerators and their Stari engines, until the greenways put the wagonways out to pasture. Even old Hrōdebert Stari himself came over. The godsmen are always great inventors. The best demagogues.

Suit yourself. I've talked to plenty of brick walls in my time.

Well, as you know, the new recruits had the scent of revolution. They remembered the starvation and degradation of thralldoms that were no longer tied to the land, but tethered to the state and mortgaged to the hilt.

I just wonder how you still manage to pay for all those guns.

Or this place.

This is a nice place you have here. Underground I should think.

To keep me contained.

Did you know, Father was happiest when we exploded one of these factories? It really tickled him. Then he'd roar with laughter. His staff would provide the explosives, of course, an amber treacle that stank of disinfectant. That was its job, in the end. Disinfectant. Wiping things clean. We'd place it, then barrel for the doors, roaring like maddened bulls to drown out the screaming sirens. My brothers would race and laugh, awarding prizes to the quickest—and then, when the bombings became routine, to the slowest, to the one with the most singed fur, to the one who'd snapped the most necks. I suppose we became lazy over the decades. That's funny, is it? You are getting quite inventive, I'll give you that, but you'll be laughing on the other side of what's left of your face soon.

I tell you what is lazy. It is lazy for you people to call us monsters. The real monsters came later in the war. Once you caught up a bit. I heard a proverb, what was it—necessity is the mother of all invention! That's it. Well, Hafgufa was the mother of sonar, wasn't she? Imagine how many fleets she'd have swallowed if your Skuld hadn't pulled that out of their bag of tricks. I used to love those newsreels. I could watch them over and over, all those screaming mariners being hauled to the depths. We are no more Nattmara than you people, with your lung-soot children and petri-dish prostitutes, content to follow this bankrupt society.

Do you have a plan for what happens next? Have you reached for the factor 500? Have you readied your extinguishers and your fire-retardants? We've already swallowed your gods, and there is one incendiary party coming up.

No?

What does it take to get a rise out of you people?

Ah, guns is it? Predictable. Give it all you got.

Ah well, pass on my regards to the fylkir, and please tell Mother I love her.

I'll see you all at Ragnarok.

BOOK THREE: DEBT
EXEGESIS VII

"COME ON, CHURCHWARDEN. YOU SHOULD be proud of your new treasure," the old man admonished.

Michaels was standing before the crosses but couldn't remember how he got there. He had an eerie sense of dreamlike dislocation. But he wasn't dreaming. He knew that much.

The other crosses were made of the same red stone but looked better preserved, more intact. Both had carvings too, and one head, once lopped off for use as a sundial, was restored to its former glory.

Dawn cast the three pillars in a new light. The sun washed over them, baptising them in a new faith. The crosses that formed the uppermost piece of each pillar weren't Christian crosses at all. They were suns, wheeling through the sky, a symbol as old as mankind. The wolves of Ragnarok threatened them even more clearly, without the context of the church.

St. Mary's had vanished, stolen by the night. Michaels hadn't witnessed the theft—or if he had he couldn't remember. He remembered the open tomb and the candle going out but no more.

His car too, his Vauxhall Astra, 15,000 miles on the clock, was gone. Michaels was dimly annoyed. He had just filled her up yesterday, but that seemed to be the least of his problems.

"Why now?" Michaels croaked, his eyes wide and his throat raw.

The old man laughed.

"Don't think that I am ignoring the irony of the so-called Wakeful God needing an alarm call, but I had sunk way beyond simple slumber. It turns out, I really did need a slap in the face to tell me all was not what it should be. The first clue wasn't subtle; far from it. *Time* magazine, a hint dropped weekly by a concerned universe. Perhaps you have seen it: the one with the old, rich, white guy who was elected. The one where they strategically placed the M, so it looks like he has little red horns?"

Chandler fixed on the churchwarden with a baleful eye. Michaels could have sworn the old bear had two perfectly good eyes a moment ago, but he was past caring. Clear 20/20 vision seemed like a luxury when the world had been reduced to fells and crags.

"As far as I am concerned, Drumpf had all the right ancestry. He deserved to be president—although any direct descendent of Rurik of the Rus should really have used his Viking name. I was looking at that cover, when it all hit me at once—that's *exactly* what the Christians did to me, all those years ago. Demonised me. Made me look like a monster. I was swept away like old garbage, left mouldering in an unmarked grave, despairing at what had become of my world. A world I worked hard to build.

"To add insult to injury, they stole Christmas from me as well. Gave it to a younger man. I promise you, when I flew through the winter sky, I made sure you knew about it. A cavalcade of baying hounds, blaring horns, and bleating goats. None of those jingling bells and big belly laughs; not to mention jolly old Saint Nick has entirely the wrong kind of elves. Where I am from, some elves are as dark as pitch, and they are the ones who make the best stuff."

The old man let the words dangle, barely concealing his delight. Michaels certainly couldn't imagine any kindergartners sitting in his leathery lap, but steadfastly refused to take the bait.

"Even in defeat, I refuse to be cowed. That cover story, it woke me up. It made me realize: I needed to focus my anger and force a change. You've seen for yourself—piss people off enough, and they'll start pushing back. There's no one who gets more furious about their turf than an old Angle or Saxon. If the WASPs are swarming, I thought, perhaps, they won't squander their birthright a second time. No, I couldn't just lie there while one of mine caught the zeitgeist. I needed to ride that wave too."

"So, you're Odin?" Michaels mumbled, weakly.

"Odin, Wotan, the All Father, Lord of the Aesir, Old Longbeard. In the flesh."

"Not Mr. Chandler, then?" he drawled, sarcastically, struggling to stand.

The bright morning sun was excruciating, and he blinked several times just to try and focus. The dawn chorus, at least, provided some beauty to balance the near universal uprooting of everything he loved and held dear.

"The Christians positively exuded candles, lighting them to guide lost souls to Heaven. Great cathedrals glowering in a mass of silent flames, all those visible signs of gladness. The White Christ was the light of the world. Crowned with crowds, bearing an eternal lamp, confusing the powers of darkness. How could I resist the poetry? My own *Big Sleep* and *Long Goodbye* were just the cherry on the cake. You forgot *Time to Kill*, by the way."

"How can this be?" Michaels wailed.

He scanned his surroundings. The old cork tree was still there—

the most northerly specimen in Europe, he'd been told. He could see movement on the road, a horse and cart by the sound of it. Beyond Seascale village, he could see something like zeppelins skirting the horizon.

"I'll let you in on a little secret. I deal in shapes. Hamr, my people called it. Shape-changing. A little shimmy here and little shift there, and the guise is complete. I started with the Northumbrians, helped turn the tide of the Saxon Wars. Dealt with that old rascal Willehad. Each time I went back, I had my cover story. Hiding in plain sight, right under His nose. It's damn near the oldest trick in the book. Hang on tightly to Great Uncle Odin, and you might just avoid being thrown to those wolves," he said, pointing to the pillar and the hellhounds carved onto it.

Michaels had always been reluctant to bother the Almighty, even on Sundays. His problems had seemed trite: his world had been Parish Councils and PASE, Scouts Halls and pies. Now it seemed impossibly shrunken and alien. He didn't have much family, but still, he couldn't imagine a world where they had simply been replaced with bearded doppelgängers with bad manners. He figured he had nothing to lose.

"Isaiah 65:25," said Michaels almost mechanically. "'The wolf and the lamb will graze together, and the lion will eat straw like the ox; and dust will be the serpent's food. They will do no evil or harm in all My holy mountain…'"

"So says the lord." The All Father shook his head, then laughed. "Your Holy Bible is a footnote in history, read in secret on the tattered fringes of my new design, my Vikingverse."

"You think He won't stop you?" said the churchwarden. "The Lord God sees all and knows all."

"Your god only exists in the minds of men, barely at all since I have changed their thoughts and memories. The Norns thought they could control the cosmos too, but I've broken their wheel before they even began to spin. Drowned their father in blood. And now, the wolf is no longer at my door. The doom that was Ragnarok is forestalled."

The old man looked more youthful, more vigorous with each passing moment. He was clearly delighted.

Michaels couldn't believe the universe worked like that. Whatever Christianity might have concocted, surely it represented a fundamental goodness? There had to be principles, rules around that kind of thing. If murder was a crime punishable by life imprisonment, what was the sentence for deicide? Heaven was tea at the rectory. It was the White-haven Maritime festival and hikes on the Wasdale Screes. It was the one true cross and its twice-told tale. The churchwarden screwed up his courage and shouted with all his might.

"You think you've changed time? Escaped your fate? Well, what goes around, comes around. The more things change, the more they stay the same. Those who cannot remember the past are condemned to repeat it."

Odin stopped, and snarled. "You think I can be stopped with tru-isms and platitudes, when I have outwitted the eternal?"

"You said it yourself, the Norns control the fates of gods as well as men. The tomb of the Saint was open. *Someone* set him free. I'm assuming it wasn't you."

NIÐAVELLIR
Forge World

HELHEIM
Penal Colony

MIDGARD
Home of Man

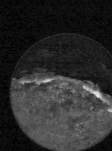

MUSPELHEIM NIFLEHEIM
Fortress of the Skuld

ALFHEIM

—— *Worlds of Plenty* ——

ÁSGARD
Imperial High Seat

VANAHEIM

JÖTUNHEIM
Refuge of the Verðandi

"THE NINE WORLDS"

HUGINN AND MUNINN

"BOHR, I AM BORED." *BOHRED*, she thought, quite pleased with herself.

This was no way to end a war. Battles had rhythm, movement; they had blood and iron. Like the centuries-long Maharaja Wars, there had to be a last desperate stand, a fatal blow. You couldn't finish a conflict locked in a stinking, dingy chamber deciphering ancient star charts.

She had gone to a lot of wasted effort for this audience. She wore her hair in five tight crimson cornrow braids that tumbled down the high collar of her gown. Beads jangled against the brass pauldron on her right shoulder. The fabric was textured, uniform honeycombed hexagons, although that was the only orderly part of the ensemble. The asymmetrical drape of the cloth left her right arm and leg exposed, and the armour merged into ornate, almost mechanical, studded brass rings bound tightly to her milk-white flesh. The whole ensemble was capped by the gleaming imperial visor; the overall impression was equal parts martial fylkir and harlot. Stunning, she had thought. Impractical for the field, but as dress uniform, unparalleled. If she was back in Uppsala, she'd inspire the jarls to an orgiastic frenzy. The catwalks would clamour for more, and the Sunnesdag supplements would drape her over their centrefold.

Here, none of the Skuld insects had even noticed.

She stopped the pretence of poring over the star chart and lifted the visor. She was Dómhild Trumba, Queen of the Heavens, ruler of the United Kingdoms. The stars would do what she told them to do, and it was high time she had some fun. She had some of those enchanting raven-bread mushrooms in her luggage; she couldn't stagger without them. That might help everyone loosen up.

For as long as she could remember, she'd had this awful sense of being born into the world either too early or too late. She understood the empire's past, and she knew just how to shape its future, but the present just infuriated her. Bohr wasn't helping matters by summoning her here.

The Skuld busied around her as if she weren't there. Or worse, they deferentially avoided her, scurrying away in the opposite direction when she approached, like ants escaping the probing finger of a child.

Ants, that's what they all were. Seen through her own eyes, they even looked a little like bugs, hooded with chitinous cowls, aprons spun from Kevlar or tiled with chalky abalone mantle, moving in mysterious mathematical patterns at the behest of the High Lector, Niði Bohr. If it looks like an ant, scurries like an ant, and—what noise do ants make? The Skuld all communicated by way of pheromones, or else through their own visors. They rarely spoke at all. Well, that was that. She'd just call them ants from now on. The Great Mathematician was a plump old rassragr. Seiðmenn. It just wasn't right, men buggering each other. This was the Sanitary Sixties, for Odin's sake, almost everyone got correctional treatments.

"Bohr. Seriously, I don't understand any of it. Do you have any idea of where the Jötnar fled to?"

The lector's mournful face remained focused on the sheets splayed across the table. It was hard to tell if he was gloomy because of the war reports or because he had a permanently petulant face. Perhaps one of his bugs had crawled up his backside. He remained silent and stroked his long, unkempt beard.

"Bohr," she said. "You asked me here on a matter of grave importance. I assumed you had found a nest; if not, then I have better things to do with my time."

"Please. Patience. I will be with you shortly."

The lector returned to mumbling his nonsensical incantations over the books, his beard twitching with each word, an intense look of concentration on his moon face. He blinked often, annotating and compiling on his visor.

Trumba slid languidly to the hollows at the crown of the ship and peered out. She wasn't a teenager any more; she'd matured almost overnight she thought. She carried herself regally. She wondered whether her father would have bothered with all this paraphernalia. He'd spent most of his life at war with the Jötnar—although the siege of Utgard had demonstrated the limits of what he had learned from the experience.

She stood to her full height and spoke with the authority of the fulltrui of Odin. It felt reassuring to tower over minions.

"Why *here*, Bohr? Why, of all the worlds, are we circling this god-forsaken rock?"

It was more complaint than question. She knew the answer, part of it at least. The Skuld were always looking for the *potential*, rather than for the practical. That was why their order had set their great ring fortress, Mímisbrunnr, above such a schizophrenic world. The planet even had two names, plucked from the ancient tales. The sun-scorched side was Muspelheim, the land of fire; the dark side was named Niflheim, the abode of mist. Her people loved messing around with words. Why simply call something one name, when an obscure and roundabout metaphor will do? It had always irritated Trumba, ambiguity was annoying in her book. Clarity, vigorously reinforced and spliced in repeatedly—that was the basis of a healthy empire. The facilities here represented half of the sovereign debt. Conversely, the rock below was the least lustrous of the jewels in her crown. Surtalogi, the star it orbited, was a red dvergar; despite the close orbit, the planet received only a tiny fraction of the light Sol beamed at Midgard. Heat yes—Muspelheim was like an abandoned stone cooking by the still-seething embers of a dwindling fire, it bathed in a perpetual sweltering gloom.

It felt like a punctured dream. Once, in the days before staggering, the stars must have seemed to burn bright in the heavens, beckoning new waves of explorers. Who would have thought that all of infinitude would remain tantalisingly out of reach?

She'd only been here once before, as a child. Bohr had explained the heavens to her if memory served. It had been a state visit; her father brought her to inspect the latest ships and the new solar sails. The war had been old even then. The latest advances were on display, although Bohr quickly confessed those ships would take 80,000 years to get back to Midgard. The long way around, he called it.

In an instant, the Nine Worlds had shrunk. Her future became a great glass globe, a miniaturized scene of model landscapes, forever closed off from the rest of the galaxy. You simply couldn't get anywhere without the greenways, at least not quickly. Her father accepted the reality and laughed about back-up plans, hiding the fact that he was running out of strategic options. Trumba remembered feeling very cheated, although for a very different reason. There were no more worlds for her to conquer.

Bohr still hadn't answered her. Trumba was becoming incandescent with rage. The Vǫlur had always treated her condescendingly while her father had been alive.

"Yes, Princess," they'd intone solemnly, then continue as if no words had been exchanged. Well, she'd soon show them. The fylkirs had financed the Skuld even before the Jötnar rose, but she could always cut that funding off.

Bohr put down his notes and followed her to the hollow. When he looked down at the world below, it was with something resembling pride or even happiness. He'd been here his whole life no doubt, born and bred in the hinterworlds.

"Why here, you asked? There is nowhere else."

He gestured flamboyantly at the sun, then glanced at her and shook his head.

"The blinkers of an Urdling education, all past glory and not enough forward thinking. How I wish you might have visited us sooner. You see how this beast is much smaller and dimmer than Sol? Don't let that deceive you! He is much more active. He flares very frequently, hence the name Surt's Sword. The giant was supposed to destroy the world during the end times with his cleansing sword of fire. Thankfully, this planet has a shield to match his thrusts, a planetary magnetic field supported by convection at the core."

Trumba resisted the temptation to roll her eyes. "Bohr. You have a point, do you?"

"Have you ever stepped onto the surface, my Queen?"

Bohr knew full well that, *as queen*, she hadn't left the safety of Midgard before last week. To step away in the first year of her rule would be a dereliction of duty—her followers would be lost without her. Her broadcasts were essential for morale, for rebuilding. They helped stimulate the nation, keeping women on their backs, the farmers sowing seed, and giving the Einherjar a vital spring in their step.

Bohr carried on, without taking his eyes from the waltzing below.

"See how the planet doesn't turn. She keeps her face to his, twirling in an endless embrace. Muspelheim is consistently sun-baked, receiving scorching, direct sunlight without ever getting a break from it. The sun appears ten times larger than it does on Midgard, searing the sky, like a looming kiss. And look, because of the tight orbit, the planet completes a revolution around Surtalogi in just eleven days. A dizzying, celestial waltz. "Niflheim, the side facing away from the star, is a beauty too. I think of her as a widow, wandering bereft into the eternal night, cold with tears. She gazes up at the sky for signs of her lost lover, and it stares straight back! Thiazi's Eyes, so much brighter than the Hundastjarna—the brightest star in your Majesty's night sky. Here, the atmosphere glows like a sapphire. The winds constantly whirl from the hot to the cold side, reminding the widow of the passion that has passed her by. But it is the marriage between the two worlds that is most fascinating. The border between each side forms a ring around the planet, a ring of perpetual dawn. A ring that constantly promises hope. And here the trees have flourished, drenched in dew. They are unlike any tree you have ever seen, the oldest of forests, grown over aeons, yet tall, spindly and black, like a belt of spiders."

"They don't sound like trees at all."

"The Mímameiðr wood hungers for light. In scientific terms, Surtalogi lacks blue light for photosynthesis; the trees here must absorb the full spectrum, and there is an abundance of red wavelengths, which makes the trees as black as coal. Most of the energy is in the infrared, so if you closed your eyes and basked in the warmth, it would feel almost as warm as Sol, plus you wouldn't be in danger of a sunburn without UV light to contend with."

"This all sounds like a nightmarish beach resort. Is that why we are here? My father, his father, generations of fylkirs, have funded all this and respected your privacy. I hope we have something better to show for it than skaldic fancies."

Bohr smiled. "We have plenty to show for it. The trees themselves, when harvested, become an engineering marvel, a material beyond compare, with tensile strength superior to anything in the empire. Unable to manufacture better, we Skuld had simply decided to enhance what the gods have given us. The result of treatment and compression was a living battery, rough-hewn but impregnable. All the exteriors here are made from it. I personally explained the work here to Dietbald, and your grandfather, Hrólfur, too, right here, in the map room. They never questioned the funding, not once, and here is the why—what do the sagas tell us of the worlds below?"

Trumba had no idea of what he was talking about. That was the biggest problem with being in charge. People felt they could bring you their problems to solve. She stared at him expectantly.

"Before there was soil or sky or any green thing, there was only the gaping abyss of Ginnungagap. Frost from Niflheim and billowing flames from Muspelheim crept toward each other until they met in the void, and amid the hissing and sputtering, the fire melted the ice, and the drops formed themselves into Ymir, the first of all beings."

Trumba paused, reflecting on the words. "Are you trying to tell me that this is the birthplace of the universe? What drit. That's clearly a self-fulfilling prophecy. A circular argument. We *named* the damned place."

"But we didn't name the planet. Yggdrasil did, and whispered the names to us. Her trees are the most penetrating of preachers and Mímameiðr is chief among them"

Trumba now laughed outright at the seer.

"The years floating in the Gap have broken your mind."

"The obvious is always least understood. All aspects of the Nine Worlds seem preordained, do they not? For as long as man has had fire, we have hunted and gathered and told stories about a Great Tree spanning Nine Worlds, linking all of creation. And then, one day, it isn't a story anymore. It is a reality. We have the formula to prove it."

Bohr paused for a moment, inhaling slowly and cracking sizable knuckles. Perhaps he was aiming to be intimidating; she couldn't tell with mares.

"Let me tell you something of seiðr, your Majesty. Your Urdur have always tried to dress up symbols and formula in ritual dances and arcane songs, but at root, all knowledge is just a way to manipulate the world around you. We can raise storms, make distant ships sink, make swords blunt, soften armour, and bring victory from defeat because we can bind the forces of the Worlds or blind others to them. Here we call our mystic dancers by their true names: trajectories and velocities, temperatures and wavelengths. Predictions are simply probability equations."

"So which are you, a great magician or a great mathematician?"

Trumba thought the man was incredibly pompous. She stared out of the hollow, wondering whether this thundering windbag would take the bait. In her experience, old men needed reminding they weren't in control.

"Your Majesty, do you know why the Skuld came to this distant, brutal world? It was to escape the idle bigotry of our kings and the billion ignoramuses they rule. Mathematician? Magician? Are these insults now? I am afraid I am called much worse than that to my face. Nidhogg, by the naval men, when I present them with the limits of the physical world. Did you know the ancient Greeks used that word, mathematics, to describe a teacher? The word magician comes from the Greek too—the magus was a priest. There is nothing unmanly about seeking knowledge. Only the Norse would think to castrate genius."

Trumba sneered. "Only the Norse opinion counts. Last time I checked, none of the small races have a vote."

"You wouldn't believe the breakthroughs we *mathematicians* have made. No one comes here, except for the admiralty and then only rarely. We are a military secret on an impossible world, yet the seiðmenn who have joined us are some of the greatest minds in history. Einnsteinen, Oppenheimr, Heisenborg, von Schröding—names to conjure with.

"The Gap holds so many marvels that glisten and sparkle with unfathomable intelligence. Surtalogi speaks to us—if only we could listen. Even the smallest of things has a voice. There are worlds at our fingertips, each interacting in incredible ways, and each is willing to share knowledge, to grant us their boon.

"Your Majesty's realms are, in one sense, just great lumps of rock, hurtling through the void, but in another very real sense, they are also branches stretching across one heaven, and across countless heavens, simultaneously. When we study Yggdrasil, the mathematics of entanglement help explain what each tree knows and how they communicate that information, especially when separated by voids that take light itself thousands of years to travel. Mathematics is the only language in which we can speak to the trees and the stars. But beyond the Skuld, there are very few versed in its tongue."

"It is all Greek to me," she said, archly. "I didn't come here for a lecture on cosmology. For the third time of asking, why are we here?"

The lector ignored her blatant insult, but his voice grew sterner, more authoritative. He was no longer trying to excite the fylkir about his work. He was admonishing her.

"Trust me, after a trip to the surface here, you'll see there are two very different places. Mímisbrunnr is here—we are here—because this place is where the ring is joined, physically and metaphysically. Surtalogi is an old man, older still than Sol. The sagas suggest it is older still than the Well of Fate, and the skalds are not often wrong with their portents. Yggdrasil was born here, in this clash of primordial forces, between fire and ice. And in that sense, human life began here.

"But still, that is not the only reason we are here. We, Madam, are the Skuld, the last of the three Norns who fix the length of the thread of life. We alone can unravel the disasters our sisters have wrought. We wear these cowls as a symbol—the future is unknowable to all but us. We take our vows because events which cannot be prevented must be directed. All humanity is in our debt because Mímisbrunnr is its salvation. Our *mathematics*," he almost spat the word in his rising fury, "calculated the Thought Drive that brought your ship here and the Memory Drive that will return you home. Our mathematics delivered to us the superlative mind of MIM and tamed the Mímameiðr."

He strode to another hollow and threw out his arms with a defiant flourish.

"And there, *there*, Madam, is the contribution to your war. Our mathematics have unlocked the secrets of that primeval wood whose twisted boughs course over this land, unharmed by fire, impervious to radiation, untouched by steel. And with it, we have forged you a fleet to last a thousand years, finally able to defeat the Jötnar once and for all. Perhaps now you understand why I invited you here?"

Bohr spun on his well-heeled boots and flounced out of the room. Trumba was stuck somewhere between mirth at having annoyed the old man, concern that she might not get to play with her new toys, and the shock of having been yelled at. Two of her Varangians looked in briefly, but she waved them back through the doorway.

She was left alone with the star charts. Well, the room still crawled with Skuld-ants, although they all looked stunned by the outburst. The chemical fear they exuded was palpable. No one raised their voice to the fylkir. It was unheard of.

"The rassragr doth protest too much, methinks," she muttered.

Bohr was hiding something between all the bombast and hyperbole. She'd developed a nose for that kind of thing; perhaps it was in the blood. Still, she had ring-fenced several days from her schedule for the visit. She was quite looking forward to the excitement ahead. She had a few tricks of her own up her sleeves.

For now, she turned her attention to the matter at hand.

"You there, Skuld. Explain these to me. Why create a map to a place you can never visit? The stars are still out of reach, I presume, or have you grown longer arms?"

And why create a room full of purposeless maps? Bohr must have planned to ambush her here for a reason. It wasn't just for the view.

These star charts were five or six centuries old, probably the result of Keppler and Brahe drinking themselves into the grave at the Imperial Observatory at Himinsborg. Trumba was a keen student of history; she knew very well that facts and personages of great importance in world history occur twice, the first time as tragedy, the second time as farce. From a young age, she'd studied the realms she would inherit. She had even toyed with balls and pieces of fruit to help her visualize her Kingdom of the Heavens.

Ironically, five hundred years ago, the empire had been fighting immortals too. Although, if she remembered correctly, the Persians hadn't put up much of a fight. In fact, she was fairly sure they turned out not to be very long-lived at all. Black Death and Red Thor at the same time... *wow, that was an era to miss.*

"We retain them for measurements and observation, your Majesty. They are old because the study of the Heavens was abandoned long ago. But these Stjörnubók contain the secrets of the Sufis."

Which was probably syphilis, she thought. The Persian War itself wasn't interesting, just one in a long line of conquests and annexations. But it had uncorked the cult of the Khurramites and let them carouse freely across the wider empire. No historian would deny the Norse always had a propensity for hard drinking and hedonism, so it was easy to see why the Eastern practices had spread like a concubine's legs. The court astronomers who once quested for knowledge slaked their fascinations with exotic wine and foreign women instead. Himinsborg became infamous for its harlots and homosexuals. In a seminal act, Fyklir Sigurd IV had wisely sent in the Varangians to burn them all. The star maps must have been saved by a rassragr in the ranks.

With the aptly named advent of staggering, a hundred years of debauchery snapped back into sobriety, and astronomy had become a footnote. Only the Skuld cared about the stars. They shared a kinship as big balls of gas.

"So why was the lector looking at them when I arrived? Has he located the Jötnar or not?"

None of the vǫlur could, or *would*, answer her. But there was something incongruous about the whole setup, something lurking at the edge of her sight. She determined to ask Bohr directly in the morning.

"I'd like to kill something now. Tell Bohr I will be in the state chambers. Tell him I want to see this new fleet as soon as possible."

TRUMBA ROLLED OUT OF BED, irritated that she couldn't sleep. She padded over to make some tea and then reached around in the dark for her visor. There was another barrage of messages from her old lover Berg. The Varangian was always whining about the cold and damp on Helheim, pleading for a return to the warmth of her bed. She deleted the files without opening them. He had his orders; anything else was just noise.

She needed something to relax her mind. In all the chaos of the past few days, she hadn't had the chance to follow any of her Úlfhéðnar, her wolfcoats, a pastime that had leeched into an addiction.

Watching the wolfcoats track down undesirables was one of the perks of being empress. Trumba could jump into any of their viewpoints and feel the thrill of their most recent hunt. The adrenal rush a soldier experienced on the verge of a kill had to felt to be believed. True, there was always the stench of shit, and the taste of blood was abrasive after a while, but you could always mute those senses and focus on the audio-visual feeds. Trumba delighted in pivoting the viewpoint, wheeling away to take a raven's eye view of the field, which also had the benefit of putting a modicum of distance between her and any screaming.

It was a vicarious pleasure, but only the adept wolfcoats even suspected she was following them, and the records were easy to delete. The Urdur brought her up to cover her tracks.

Perusing the file headings, it looked like the trespassers of the past few nights had been religious lunatics. That wasn't surprising. The Serer kingdoms in the Burning Lands had been the worst offenders. They had been making unscheduled migrations for years, although her father had overlooked their transgressions. He even went so far as to pay homage to the immense Serer god on state visits, a sky god called fat Roog or Koox or something nonsensical, that was supposed to be an aspect of Thor. As far as Trumba was concerned, he was a pretty shitty aspect because he'd lost the past three wars his people fought in and was dead set against fornication to boot.

Predictably, Dietbald's peaceful embassies had only encouraged the Serer lamanes, the headmen, who saw it as a tacit blessing. Now they were always staggering across the greenways, searching for new land to exploit. It got to the point where Trumba had been forced to make an example of her vassal during the coronation. There was the usual outcry, but the Serer had been warned plenty of times. In the end the Maad Saloum Fode N'Gouye Joof died before she could work out how to pronounce his name. It turned out he hadn't been granted immortality by fat Roog after all.

The Úlfhéðnar had the scent of one of the lamanes now, a pitch-black fellow, with a big bruised lip and a sunken scowl. He had perhaps a dozen tribesmen with him, splashing through the salt flats in the northern hemisphere of Vanaheim. It was a bizarre tactic, but then these backward peoples couldn't comprehend that the wolfcoats weren't actual wolves and that they weren't tracking so much by scent as by satellite. There was only an inch of ground water anyway. Interlopers were always hampered by the stronger gravity as well. They squelched along as if they were in treacle, sweating rivulets into the mineral field.

Trumba noticed a sergeant readying his thermal lance, and she blinked twice to follow him, just in time to see him spew a ball of copper fire towards the horizon. The bodies were retrieved later by a Catai clean-up squad. Carbonized for the most part, dismembered heads, brains and intestines, black stains on the otherwise pristine pan.

Reservations clearly couldn't contain this kind of vagrant. She made a note: perhaps it was time to use Agent Naranga to wipe out the trees in their homeland. That would cut off their path to temptation.

She sipped her tea. It was tepid now, the price of her distractions. She swallowed it in one gulp, then decided to follow a second group. It was better than reading the council dispatches, which Miklagard still insisted on delivering in twee scarlet oak boxes as well as straight to her visor. Several of the jarls were growing insistent that she formally name a newly-built veterans' home in honour of her father, but she wasn't going to sully her family name for some drunken brawlers. The Einherjar's only great skill was to die *en masse* and on cue. Even so, it was insulting that they thought it was all she was good for and that they didn't send her anything more substantive. Since she was named heir presumptive, the lords had tried to turn her into just another rubber stamp.

The wolfcoats were much more deserving of her time. The next batch of guardsmen had been called to Thrudheim to retrieve some wandering Skræling. She retrieved the briefing and scanned the notes. A cult had sprung up around an old incendiary who called himself Alédzé, a Dreamer who claimed ancestral rights to use the greenways. She remembered the file now: MIM had alerted her to his visionquests before she left Uppsala. The old man claimed to have died, only to be resurrected with the ability to travel to Heaven in his dreams. Much like the power that gunpowder gives to a bullet, he'd said. He was getting dreams from the All Father and telling everyone what was going to happen. Trumba was willing to tolerate a few native idiosyncrasies, but clearly an asylum was too good for this kind of crazy. Shooting was too good for him. The wolfcoats were in position for an ambush and launched their assault under the cover of white phosphorus. Trumba tutted and switched off the visor. At best the smoke would obscure the hunt, but it was far more likely to scramble her signal. She took a second note to investigate field use of those grenades.

It would be simplistic to regard these assaults as atrocities, her response as disproportionate. She knew the Commonwealth fringes would be appalled if they gleaned anything of her *hobbies*. She might even offend the jarls themselves, but such were the sacrifices of kings. The body politic was like a dominant athlete, a supreme warrior, white-skinned and bright-eyed, greeting each day with courage and fury. Like any warrior, it could be felled by a mighty axe—but the tiny microbe was just as deadly an adversary. Armaments could be seized, gun shipments impounded, but disease was another matter entirely. All it took was one mutated protein or one errant sneeze. The world could dissolve, stricken overnight with tumour-ridden pustules.

She'd seen it all clearly, even as a child. Trumba knew with certainty that, if you let one solitary germ breach your resistance—well, you invited catastrophe. The Urdur told her she'd been lucky to survive polio and lauded her determination. She saw the episode not only as formative, but necessary.

The great unwashed might consider it innocuous to look the other way, to indulge the filthy spectacle of a Chitai family bribing a seer. They might all like to get their grubby hands around a better life in unspoilt lands. But that was the single nucleotide change in the code, that was the fatal collapse of the immune system. Trumba had to inoculate society against that kind of selfishness. The outbreak of Rabboon Fever in Kashgar was a type of vaccine, just like the Razing of Himinsborg had been a cauterizing. She was learning from the past to make certain of the future. Most importantly, the wolfcoats were helping her clear up her father's mess. They were much more reliable than the one-trick Einherjar.

Yes, she knew she would have to answer to some committee or other eventually. There was one rule for her and one rule for the poor (in their small smelly rooms, crammed into crime-infested blocks of corrugated iron). It was their *shit* that had spread the polio virus in the first place.

But it wasn't personal. It wasn't her rule. The Chieftain of the Gods, Odin himself, had been very clear on the caste system. Any quibblers could just read the Lay of Kings: the swarthy-skinned and the ugly were born to be slaves; the red-haired and ruddy were progenitors of herdsmen, craftsmen and farmers; the beautiful, bright-eyed blond babies were destined to rule. It was written, and you couldn't just decide to ignore the entire fathering of mankind because it offended the coffee-drinking sophists of Miklagard. Trumba was on the side of the godsmen on this one, and the courts had always supported the divine.

RULING THE EMPIRE WASN'T EASY, but MIM gave a whole new meaning to imperial infallibility. Trumba barely had to get out of bed most days. MIM, the Myriad Improbability Machine—or maybe Mathematically Impossible Miracle (she couldn't remember)—had been turned on in '55, when she was still a teenager and too self-absorbed to understand how powerful the machine was. Until she was crowned, she always assumed the name was a truncation of Mímameiðr.

She had been surprised to find that it meant something.

Behind all the secrecy and security was a soft grey metal chip, frozen to near-absolute zero, entwined within a single black sprig of the tree. The machine connected the empire's industrial-military complex, from the Well of Urdur to the Sökkvabekkr Data Archives, from the Folkvang Barracks to the Nóatún Launchsites. It worked on the same principles as Yggdrasil, apparently, and was as different to the older Difference Engines as the World Tree was to a solitary sapling. Where the greenways linked the biomass of nine worlds, MIM linked innumerable dimensions. The Skuld said it actually existed across all of them, but Trumba wasn't interested in the theory. She wanted to know what MIM could do.

Trumba was permanently in contact with the machine through her visor although she occasionally went headset-free to watch the hundreds of monitors the Urdur maintained, and if she was really bored, she might thumb through the printed dispatches. It was only a matter of time before MIM would replace the whole spindly sisterhood and the Miklagard bureaucrats as well, swapping their mummery for something infinitely more modern—if that was the right phrase for something that existed outside reality as she understood it.

MIM's first success was to bring about the last throes of the Jöt-nar War with relative ease, optimising the logistics of the final siege, pinpointing weaknesses in the defences, and changing weather patterns. But it didn't just crunch numbers; it *anticipated* and optimised solutions for all eventualities. MIM didn't need to be fed data. There was no need to input trends or suggest indicators, to spool through surveillance footage, or even type up a troop report. MIM watched it all with unblinking eyes—matching divorce rates in Uppsala to the price of peaches in Mangi, correlating with the average number of bed-slaves, the temperature on every third Tysdag, and the scorecards of amateur Tabul games. If Trumba had any enemies left, they'd be horrified at how everything and everyone was woven together, spun so very tightly around her fingers.

Its inventor was a Thuringian rassragr who used to joke the machine was more intelligent than an infinitude of Odin's ravens but, thankfully, considerably kinder. Trumba, however, had no use for a humane machine. The inventor killed himself, the High Urdur reported, apparently by eating an apple laced with cyanide when his correctional hormone treatments didn't take. His continued fondness for jokes somehow lived on in his machine. When MIM spoke, it used his arch voice and clipped vowels. Trumba kept it on mute and just read the reports.

The very hour she was crowned, she asked the machine to optimise her rule for eternity. Her ministers chuckled at that, assuming it was either childish fancy or deadpan wit. But they didn't see the world as she did. She wasn't interested in her legacy; she had no intention of ever relinquishing the crown. She wasn't interested in heirs, or morality, or other constraints. Those things weren't optimal; by definition, they reeked of compromise. She wanted continuation, acceleration, power, and perfection.

Iðunn Lind had helped there, of course, once she was "rescued." Trumba had pardoned the Verðandi and set the Order back on the right track. Lind claimed that she'd been fooled into creating the Jötnar. It didn't matter one way or the other to Trumba, so long as Lind produced enough of her magic Telomerase enzyme.

Telomerase was a genetic therapy that reversed cellular biological age. The Greek-averse simply called it "Iðunn's Apples." It was all so wonderful, and as heir apparent, it had all been hers. Trumba was still in the flush of her youth, and she now she could stay that way. Pert, trim, and voracious. She wasn't going to end up a withered old hag like Nanna. And the Nine Worlds had better get used to her because she planned to rule for a long, *long* time.

Admittedly, Trumba had initially thought her inheritance to be a spectacularly grim prize. She hadn't held out much hope for the future and had said so in her acceptance speeches after her father had died. The fringes had needed a cold splash of water. It wasn't as if they would ever afford to even sniff an apple, let alone sample one.

The Jötnar might have been broken, but the Himinríki wasn't in much better shape. Maintaining the Einherjar to defend the hinterworlds from Jötnar attacks had been a constant drain on the government. Adding the burdens of her father's predilection for public housing and perfectly-maintained roads meant the jarls had no option but to raise taxes, which in turn, frequently led to increased inflation and worthless wages. No wonder angry vassals lost their desire to defend the empire. It was a vicious circle. The war had cost them so many lives, they started fulfilling troop requisitions with phantoms. Most of the genuine new recruits were drawn from the Sleeping Lands or, worse, from Chitai. As far as the stallari were concerned, they were only fit to be human minesweepers or, at best, act as Jötunn decoys.

Trumba was amazed and delighted to find out that MIM agreed. Human minesweeping was the optimal solution.

Trumba had seen immediately how to use the machine. MIM the Matchless had delivered her a blueprint for the ages. MIM was a miracle. For example, when the Norse stopped conquering new lands, the flow of wealth into the economy had stalled, yet vast sums were being spent still on luxuries. Opulence had to be replaced by austerity.

The very soils of empire, denuded and depleted by years of ostentatious over-farming, had to be replenished. Genetically modified food was the answer.

Relying so heavily on the labour of thralls, the empire was under pressure to produce goods more efficiently. Gene-modded slaves were the solution.

Taxes that had been raised, ostensibly to pay for deficit government spending, had ended up in the pockets of provincial lords. That had to stop. The optimal approach was a uniform tax system, policed centrally by MIM, to harvest the profits of the new photogenic world.

Of course, sycophantic jarls and fringe traitors would publicly proclaim their unswerving support, while all the time working quietly to subvert MIM's plan from within. That was human nature. They had to be rooted out, given the option of becoming thralls or becoming topsoil. The Einherjar could be disbanded.

Everything slotted neatly into place. The people would take their medicine, and the empire would be leaner, healthier for it. Uniform and unified. Optimal.

Trumba clattered her cup onto the table and tossed her visor after it. She quickly inhaled some raven's bread and then crawled across her bed to sleep the sleep of the industrious.

THE NEXT MORNING, BOHR WAS all forced smiles, veering between light and dark more than the planet did. He had materialised after breakfast and offered a tour, which Trumba had begrudgingly accepted. She'd been planning on visiting the new facility anyway, to inspect the site personally and give it her imperial seal of approval. It was killing two birds with the same stone. Odin knew she liked to be efficient.

They were still in orbit, but thanks to following tech, Trumba felt like she was outside the station and down ambling around the habitable zone.

"What you see here is the original Skuld enclave. The original Mímisbrunnr was erected on that spot—we should put up a plaque perhaps—some two hundred years ago. Does Her Majesty take much interest in the penal code?"

It was a rhetorical question. Bohr was relishing taking his time leading the inspection, treading through virtual landscape. The coal-black Mímameiðr thickets were like spiders, which made the whole place feel like an insect hive.

"I am a foolish, fond old man, but I sometimes wonder what the most breathtaking moment in our illustrious empire was. When Ragnar stepped ashore at Lindisfarne and discovered the riches of the Christians, or when Lind emerged from the greenways and found himself looking at the wealth under this alien sky."

Trumba ignored her tour guide. "Has anyone escaped Náströnd in the past year?"

"Ask your advisors. Ask MIM. That abomination isn't my idea. I was aghast that you ever allowed it to happen. Perhaps you might consider clearing the area when the war is concluded to your satisfaction?"

Trumba smiled to herself. So. That was the old fool's game. He didn't like the mess she'd made in his backyard.

Trumba had been proud to honour her election pledge to deliver the Náströnd facility. MIM's vision has been as simple as it was elegant: the planet itself would be warden for the murderers, adulterers, and oath-breakers who found themselves banished there, the worst of Norse society. Flee into Niflheim and freeze, flee to Muspelheim and burn. It was a successful optimisation of the principles of incarceration. Trumba signed the executive order to start sending the Abrahamists here as well. To let them have a taste of what hell was really like.

The Norse, taken as a whole, didn't believe in rehabilitation. They had raved about the idea. Since the old Skuld facility and the warrens underneath were no longer in use, they became the centerpiece of the project, an immense underground cage. She'd paid for them, after all. Predictably, the Althing had reacted immediately, passing a motion—a formal censure—telling her she was playing with fire, but the Skuld had moaned longest and loudest.

"If the war is concluded."

Trumba flicked between the follow and the detail on her visor. She wasn't even convinced she should eradicate the Jötnar. She always indexed well after a battle. MIM went so far as to state she ought to siphon off some secured funds to keep them in the game, but you couldn't have the bogey-man on payroll. Not yet, anyway.

Bohr was still rambling away.

"As to escape, I doubt it. Unless you were accompanied by a willing völva, you couldn't escape by mimetic osmosis—you can't force spell-singing, and if you could, it would be an easy matter to abandon the kidnapper in the greenways after you staggered."

"If that were true," she said, "I wouldn't have to unchain the Úlf-héðnar every night to send them hunting. You don't have the monopoly you think you have, Lector."

She moved swiftly on. Next, she surveyed the floor plan, then followed a guard into the tunnels and shafts. Empty room upon empty room, all the old circuits ripped out as per her request, insulation and building materials strewn everywhere. At first, she couldn't fathom why the Skuld had burrowed here, but then she realized that, thanks to the facility, they'd survived the Jötunn War unscathed. The old Mímisbrunnr bunkers were both impregnable and remote, safe from prying eyes and sabotage. Used as a prison, she knew any situation could be contained. It was easy to imagine a prisoner's plight. Once banished, there was nothing to damage, nothing to rage against except concrete. The Mímameiðr trees had defied the stars for millennia, they were utterly impervious to whatever the criminals might muster. MIM could adjust the harmonics in the vicinity to make sure that no one staggered in or out without the right key.

She dropped the link and went to a nearby hollow, to look down at the surface with her own eyes. It was a long way down. The new Mímisbrunnr Station was colossal, on a scale Trumba found frankly daunting. She tried not to think about the whole structure—tried to compartmentalise it, to comprehend it in portions. It stretched over the horizon and beyond, looping around the whole of the planet, adorned with a hundred habitats, each devoted to the advancement of her realm. Hydrostatisticians, computational chemists, biomathematicians. Transplant the keenest minds in Midgard to one secluded garden, sprinkle on unlimited funds, and the crop couldn't fail to impress. Some of the Skuld might have withered over the years, but tinker with their telomerase and you had the font of all knowledge and the fountain of eternal youth, all splashing profitably into one.

Of course, the occasional war led to the most productive spurts of growth, the most interesting, innovative offshoots. The first Gjallarhorn was fired at the grabs and gallivants of the Maratha Navy; ironically, two hundred years later, Hindoo like Ramanujan and Ammal led the team that birthed the HEIMDAL system. Applied science was a marvellous thing.

She knew that there had been attempts by prisoners to capture Skuld smiths and apprentices. They still made regular trips down to the surface for study, cargo inspections at the Bifrost launch loop, or travel to Midgard. Those attempts all failed abysmally. It was difficult to surprise a precognitive military specialist with a masters in material science. Even if the Skuld didn't see you coming, they'd simply vanish from the visible spectrum, escape through the treeline, or in extremis, bombard the assailant with psychotropics. Still, the few attacks clearly bothered Bohr. He evidently was a poor seer if he couldn't see what she'd been brewing. Náströnd was full of walking corpses, but there was always room for one more. She'd smash the ratings with this next broadcast.

"Could we bring captured Jötnar here?" she asked innocently.

"Your Majesty is most amusing. But tell me, have we ever captured a Jötunn alive? There were no survivors at Utgard, were there, just escapees?" he simpered.

The old man played dirty. The war hadn't gone well these past thirty years. The Jötnar were initially bigger, faster, and stronger than the armies of Midgard, but the defector Iðunn had levelled the playing field. Let's see how the scattered remnants survived without her medicine, she thought. Just as a cleaved head no longer plots, a Jötunn who has his feet hacked off cannot scurry far.

The timing of Bohr's invitation to Mímisbrunnr station could not have been better. It offered the perfect cover and so she accepted.

The truth was she was planning a visit regardless. She had someone stashed onboard, a prisoner entrusted to a special squad of her own elite Varangian troops. Someone she'd not yet met in the flesh. And the news of him would shake the Nine Worlds.

THEY'D CAPTURED HIM LESS THAN a week ago. The press had dubbed him *Hveðrungr* or "Roarer" after his ranting broadcasts had echoed across the globes. She'd been bursting to crow about it and bask in the triumph that would follow. However, she wanted him under glass first. She wanted to see for herself, find out if that vituperative voice, full of pride and disdain, was real or enhanced. The navy had held her hand for far too long and she didn't feel like getting into a pissing match about it. She'd have her staff hand over official notes afterwards.

She couldn't wait to tell Bohr that he was about to get an entirely new class of neighbour. Shut down Náströnd indeed! It was only going to get bigger and better! The questioning would be at arm's length of course. Varangian arms. She wasn't about to risk her person standing in a cell with an insurgent. Two of her finest would administer the beatings while she followed, up close and personal. It was simply delicious to see the fear erupt from the victim first-hand, with the added safety of a whole planet between the cold cell on the far side of the station and her comfortable chambers. Her father should never have pandered to these worms.

The wait was almost as agonizing as listening to Bohr—it was all she could do to resist sneaking a quick peak. It took another day for her to get the all clear.

She bounded into the room, full of nervous energy and childish excitement and immediately shrieked with laughter. The leader of the insurgency, this great enemy, seemed almost comical. The Roarer was painfully thin and walked with a lopsided gait, swinging spindly arms.

His hair rose almost six inches above his forehead into a tousled crest that gave him a strange, bewildered look. His head perched on slightly hunched shoulders, a sarcastic smile playing around frozen lips. He dressed immaculately, fur and silk from head to toe—otherwise he might have been mistaken for a scarecrow. Only his eyes, large and lively, flickering with malice, showed the deep intelligence that burned behind them. But a genetic superman or devourer or worlds, he was not. He was a mouse that roared, a garrulous fool with delusions of grandeur.

Evidently, whatever alterations or manipulations this Roarer had wrought on himself were nothing compared to the imperial arsenal. The Úlfhéðnar squads pushed the limits of human peak performance beyond credulity, possessing the eyes of eagles and the stamina of stallions. She could attest to that personally; if she couldn't have the pick of the soldiery, what was the use of being fylkir? It had been her idea to splice their best trackers with lupine DNA. She had drawn her father a genemap when she was only twelve. Why simply imitate the savagery and speed of a wolf when you could possess it throughout your being? She had bred them loyal as well as cunning. Seven years later, those same trackers found the Roarer hiding out in an Alfheimr forest with his perverted family, chased him down, and trussed him up. That had been a sight for sore eyes. She watched the broadcasts of that again and again, admiring their speed and brutality as the soldiers handled the "package."

"Devourer indeed!" she drooled. Trumba had worked up quite an appetite herself for one of her own tasty morsels, a thoroughbred Varangian "steed."

"Your Majesty?" Her chamber guard said.

"Nothing. A yawn. Now, back to my revelries."

She returned to the follow, nestling into the viewpoint of the guard again. At the same time, she connected to a broadcast feed directly into the room. It was amusingly disconcerting to watch herself at work.

"Ah, young man. I am delighted to finally meet you. Are you in fact a young man, or have you been eating Iðunn's Apples, too? We don't know much about you, I'm afraid. Perhaps I should start with the introductions. I am Trumba, the All-Glorious Queen of the Storm-Hall, Ruler of Princes and Lady of All, Daughter of Odin, the Fifth to bear this name. I believe you are acquainted with my crown, though, because you sought to detach it from my head and give it to the Jötnar?"

"I know who you are, Witch, and all of your wicked deeds."

The prisoner ignored the broadcast and stared straight at the Varangian, his gaze boring through the guardsman as if searching out her hiding hole.

"I know you, Whore. Which of these two mares have you enticed between your legs? You, have you sucked Her Majesty's breasts? Or does she invite your wives instead to bed her while you two rut in the fields?"

The soldiers were thrashing him before he finished; the last sentence came as a yell between a flurry of fists. Trumba didn't interrupt them, wanting to see the prisoner bleed. To his credit, the Roarer was taking the punishment. In fact, he didn't look in the slightest bit perturbed. After a few minutes, the guards paused to catch their breath, before they tore the last tatters of his finery from him. Even that didn't shake the Roarer.

Trumba took a deep breath.

"What is the point of you, little man? Why am I wasting my time with you? I seem to ask that question a lot. Heavy is the head that wears the crown. Did you find that? Did you find that your Jötnar listened?"

The rebel leader sat on the floor, staring into the mid-distance.

"After my inevitable death," he said, "this is my consolation: no-one will be able to find one single bit of information about what has really filled my life."

Trumba raised an eyebrow. "We have your wife and children. We have Iðunn, your collaborator. You don't think they will tell us all about you? You might change *your* mind when you hear their screams."

Her wolves had sniffed out Iðunn Lind too. Recovering the Verðandi might have been the last achievement of her father's reign, and the only one worth repeating. Dietbald the Beloved hadn't been able to fight his way out of a paper bag. The thought of him on the throne, all indecision and procrastination, disgusted Trumba. The first time she sat down herself, all she could think about were his haemorrhoids. She'd asked the High Urdur if they were contagious. Dietbald the Bleeding Rectum should have been his name. It would have matched his Bleeding Heart. The abolition of Northern thralldom was a farce; it just drove up the price of dunga everywhere.

But, oh, how the people loved him, cheered him, praised his generosity—and ultimately mourned him. The only thing more profligate than his Great Works schemes and ragtag Social Housing projects was his funeral. Every Urdur would tell you that it was the war industry that turned the economy. Perhaps that's why they saw fit to drain the dregs of the treasury when victory looked close at hand.

They brought Dietbald's broken body from Utgard for a lavish state funeral. The stallari argued that it was only fitting for such a great prince, the fylkir who had brought peace to the realms with his noble sacrifice. They said that the *Ringhorn* was soon to be scrapped anyway. Trumba was all for honouring tradition but turning the imperial flagship into a pyre was pure melodrama (ultimately, she might have to concede they'd been right about it being antiquated; if Bohr's new fleet was as superb as he professed, she'd just pretend her complaints were due to being grief-stricken). Tragedy became farce when the launch mechanism jammed and the whole thing exploded on the ground, wiping out half the general staff. Nanna had screamed so much that it might have been a mercy to just throw the old dear into the inferno too. It was certainly one way to pass the torch. A damn expensive way.

Her father's whole reign was a folly. Trumba's first official act

after the coronation was to have the skalds rewrite the sorry chapter
from beginning to end. The new empress couldn't be seen to have an
imbecile for a father and a hysteric for a mother. People would question her gene pool. Besides, history should be kind.

The transgenic troops had helped ensure an orderly transition.
The election would be held with minimal fuss. Of course, the usual
elements had complained about interfering with the natural order
and, yes, some of the early Jötnar were inconceivably ugly. Iðunn had
allegedly been under duress, experimenting, tinkering. You just had
to think of them as lessons learnt. Like Dietbald's social programme.
She grimaced at the memory, unsure who was the biggest monster.
At least Lind contributed to society, and would do so for—well, who
knew? She was already well over one hundred years old, although if
old age didn't claim her, obesity might. Thor alone knew how much
the woman packed away every night, stress eating.

Trumba wondered whether she ought to summon Lind to the
station. Shake things up. As it was, her erstwhile partner-in-genocide
was making very little sense.

"I have only one friend," said Hveðrungr from his cell, "and that
is echo. Why is it my friend? Because I love my sorrow, and echo does
not take it away from me. I have only one confidant, and that is the
silence of night. Why is it my confidant? Because it remains silent.
My sorrow is my castle."

"Gentlemen, our guest thinks he is a skald! Tell me, what epics
have you penned?"

"I shall be your skald! I do not want to be a skald for others; make
your appearance, and I shall be your skald. I shall eat my own poem,
and that will be my food. Or do you find me unworthy? Just as a
temple dancer dances to the honour of the gods, so I have consecrated
myself to your service; light, thinly clad, limber, unarmed, I renounce
everything. I own nothing; I desire to own nothing; I love nothing;

I have nothing to lose. But have I not, thereby, become all the more worthy of you, you who long ago must have been tired of depriving people of what they love, tired of their craven snivelling and craven pleading. Surprise me. I am ready!"

It was quite a performance. The two Varangians looked as perplexed as Trumba felt. The bandy-legged scarecrow with flailing arms and the vacant stare was clearly unhinged. Which reminded her, how had the ties come undone? She ought to be concerned, the guards even more so, but it was... a struggle to remember.

Was there a problem? Nonplussed, she turned back to the prisoner. "Not a skald then, but a clown?" she asked.

"A fire broke out backstage in a theatre," said the ragged prisoner. "The clown came out to warn the public; they thought it was a joke and applauded. He repeated it; the acclaim was even greater. I think that's just how the world will come to an end: to general applause from wits who believe it's a joke."

"A joke," said Trumba. "I don't think any of this is a joke. You butchered thousands of people, caused the deaths of millions more. In a way, I am an admirer. Who knows how long my father might have sat his fat arse on my throne if you and your freak show hadn't come to town. And your experiments with Iðunn Lind have been very fruitful. What I want to know is *why?*"

He didn't answer right away. Then he shook his head. "How did I get into the world? Why was I not asked about it, and why was I not informed of the rules and regulations before being thrust into the ranks as if I had been bought by a peddling Rus of human beings? How did I get involved in this big enterprise called actuality? Why should I be involved? Isn't it a matter of choice? And if I am compelled to be involved, where is the manager—I have something to say about this. Is there no manager? To whom shall I make my complaint?"

She wasn't understanding any of this. Was it possible that the beatings had already addled him?

"I have already heard your complaint. Your incessant broadcasts, your rebellion, the treacherous Declarations of Jötunheim, the Ninety-Nine Disputes—why?"

"Out of love for mankind," said the Roarer. "And out of despair at my embarrassing situation, seeing that I had accomplished nothing and was unable to make anything easier than it had already been made, and moved by a genuine interest in those who make everything easy, I conceived it as my task to create difficulties everywhere."

"You are to be commended then," said the empress. "My father would literally shit himself every time he heard one of your bombs explode."

"A revolutionary age is an age of action," said the Roarer. "Ours is the age of advertisement and publicity. Nothing ever happens, but there is immediate publicity everywhere. In the present age, a rebellion is, of all things, the most unthinkable. Such an expression of strength would seem ridiculous to the calculating intelligence of our times. On the other hand, a political virtuoso might bring off a feat almost as remarkable. He might write a manifesto suggesting a general assembly at which people should decide upon a rebellion, and it would be so carefully worded that even the censor would let it pass. At the meeting itself, he would be able to create the impression that his audience had rebelled, after which they would all go quietly home, having spent a very pleasant evening."

Trumba decided she wasn't enjoying this after all. The Roarer seemed intoxicated by his own voice. She needed to squeeze some sense out of him before she let others in on the secret.

"So, the Disputes were, what? An attempt to set the Althing against the Urdur? You are making no sense. These two gentlemen are here to stop your prating. If need be, they will strike your head from your neck."

If the Roarer heard the threat, he didn't acknowledge it.

"Every movement and change takes place with the help of 100,000 or 10,000 or 1,000 noisy, grumbling, rumbling, and yodeling people," he said. "A mediocre ruler is a much better constitution than this abstraction, 100,000 rumbling nonhumans. Is it tyranny when one person wants to rule, leaving the rest of us others out? No, but it is tyranny when all want to rule. Let others complain that the age is wicked. My complaint is that it is paltry, for it lacks passion. Men's thoughts are thin and flimsy as lace. A people's government is the true image of Hel. On Jötunheim, at least we are human beings. We hate, we love, we murder our enemies, and curse their descendants throughout all generations."

"Well, we want the same thing. I couldn't agree more. Dissolving the Althing is a wonderful idea," she said, snatching at whatever straws she could.

Trumba had dreamed of being rid of the people's assembly ever since she was a little girl. The upper chamber could stay—so long as it was packed with stooges—to make a suitable show of representation. If only this Roarer wasn't barking mad, she could have dealt with him, turned necessity into a virtue. Perhaps he had an able lieutenant she could stand up, someone to keep the jarls quaking in their jackboots. MIM certainly thought so. She looked at him, sprawled on the floor, barely able to manage contempt. He was monologuing more than Bohr.

"I dreamt last night," he said, "that I'd been rapt into the Niðafjöll, in the halls of red gold. There sat all the gods assembled. As a special dispensation, I was granted the favour to have one wish. 'Do you wish for youth,' said Iðunn, 'or for beauty, or power, or a long life; or do you wish for the most beautiful woman, or any other of the many fine things we have in our treasure trove? Choose, but only one thing!' For a moment, I was at a loss. Then I addressed the gods: 'Most honourable contemporaries, I choose one thing—that I may always have the laughs on my side.' Not one god made answer, but all began to laugh. From this I concluded that my wish had been granted and thought that the gods knew how to express themselves with good taste: for it would surely have been inappropriate to answer such a request with gravity."

She shook her head.

"Wonderful. Well, I'll grant you that very same last wish. You may laugh until your heart bursts and we have broken every bone in your body. And then, I will leave you to rot on the planet below."

"No," he said. "I won't leave the world. I'll enter a lunatic asylum and see if the profundity of insanity reveals to me the riddles of life. Idiot, why didn't I do that long ago, why has it taken me so long to understand what it means when the Skræling honour the insane, step aside for them? Yes, a lunatic asylum. Don't you think I may end up there?"

There was something very disconcerting about the prisoner. He wasn't just disjointed, or mad; it was stranger than that. He wasn't conversing, he was practising statements, like an understudy mouthing snippet of dialogue from the wings. He was reciting lines into a mirror, he was rehearsing—or remembering—or feeding lines like a prompt in his corner stage. Or all those things.

The Roarer looked directly at her again, piercing the Varangian visage, and it was only then she realised that he hadn't looked up at all since the beating. He'd wittered away all this time with his eyes downcast. Perhaps they had given him a concussion? He seemed much more connected now. Even half-naked in an empty room, he looked controlled. His eyes were redolent of ancient enmities, coal-black embers burning in the coal-black room.

"If there were no eternal consciousness in a man, if at the bottom of everything there were only a wild ferment, a power that, twisting in dark passions, produced everything great or inconsequential; if an unfathomable, insatiable emptiness lay hid beneath everything, what would life be but despair? At Hvergelmir, I had barely started. Nothing is as heady as the wine of possibility. Believe me, the most painful hangover is remembering the future, particularly the ones you'll never have."

THE PRISON BROADCAST WAS WELL-INDEXED, even without mentioning the Roarer. On reflection, her special prisoner would have to come later. Trumba had learnt to toy with viewers, holding back the big reveal until she need the boost. For now, it seemed perfectly reasonable to keep him as her little secret. She was the one in charge here, after all.

There was another message from Berg:

HEL HAS OFFICIALLY FROZEN OVER.

HOW IS THE CONSTRUCTION? she fired back, concerned that Berg had a genuine issue.

ON SCHEDULE. LIND OVERSEEING PERSONALLY. APPLES IN DEEP FREEZE.

In a beat, another message arrived.

CAN WE TALK?

That was the last thing she wanted to do. The man wouldn't stop talking, even after sex, when most of her lovers had the good grace to shut up and fall asleep. That was half the reason she'd sent him to oversee the project in the first place.

WHEN CAN I COME HOME? I MISS YOU.

He sent a short clip of the construction, but it was so shrouded in icy fog she couldn't make out the progress. Pointedly, Berg had appended the note with "Wish I Wasn't Here."

LAUNCH FIRST, she replied, and then put her visor out of reach, away from temptation. Technology had made it almost impossible for irritations like Berg to be out of sight and out of mind.

Trumba flicked through a smattering of other broadcasts, every one an intimate insight into her subjects' lives. There was a candid argument, laid out for the world to share. A horse fight, with commentary from a dejected gambler. A man lost at sea, searching the last known coordinates of the Hafgufa and wishing he hadn't. The usual drunken sex with people in horned helmets.

She cursed; there really was a dearth of talent in the world. No one held her attention, but then very few people could hold a candle to the imperial presence.

None of them had truly suffered for their art. None of them had suffered the indignity of an election.

She had a bank of monitors in her room, and she left some of the screens on, watching a world of followers stare back at her. She was a wolf among the sheep.

The Norse had elected their kings since before Ragnar. Little had changed over the centuries; the hustings were still just a great din of people and weapons, a clash of shouting and arms—although Trumba had been assured it was mainly for show. The fylkir had essentially been a hereditary title for centuries. Her family always won; the Urdur made sure of that. The Oak Kings and Queens of Munsö, born from a line of rulers stretching back to Ragnar and Rurik, the Lords of Always Summer, who rested the heavens in their noble hands. This was a dynastic decision, they had said, not a political one. A hot-blooded thoroughbred like Princess Trumba was a shoo-in. The Centre for

Public Integrity showed she would not only win the sympathy vote after the funeral debacle, but that she indexed well on the war effort too, thanks to MIM. In those naïve days, there was no need for personal broadcasts.

That overconfidence had nearly been their ruin. The High Urdur had wrung her hands and made her whole "known knowns, known unknowns, and unknown unknowns" speech; Trumba wondered if the old crone saw the execution squad coming or whether the black hood got in the way.

It was beyond ridiculous. The Urdur were meant to know everything *before* it happened. You weren't just born into the sisterhood, you were preordained. Now, if an empress couldn't trust her own secret police, who should she have at her back? Trumba sat in the Winter Palace watching the tide turn against her, the broadcasts getting increasingly cruel, until they were verging on the democratic.

Begrudgingly, Trumba had to admit the largest part of the problem had been the opposition. Frigga was telegenic, a model candidate. She must have literally been born for the broadcasts, because you didn't get that kind of symmetry once outside of the womb. She probably had some orchid in her somewhere, although that was hard to verify. She polled so well, she might have been married to Odin himself.

She wasn't, of course. Her real name was Lucina Hagman, the daughter of a peacenik Finnar and minor functionary for the Urdur. Trumba had been beside herself when she read the surveillance reports. She didn't know what was worse, that these loving parents had cooked up a treacherous little sex kitten for a daughter or that they'd done so using imperial property. Right under Uppsala's nose! In hindsight, Trumba had killed the High Urdur far too quickly.

The reports made depressing reading. Frigga's long legs and smouldering eyes weren't even the half of it; the most voluptuous part was something called phenotypic plasticity. Like a butterfly changing colour with the seasons, Frigga could present to people in whatever guise she chose. She appeared how her audience wanted her to appear, whether Norse, Chitai, or Skræling. She was a predilection in heels, a sashaying peccadillo.

Trumba had taken the report literally for a few days—she was horrified that she found Frigga attractive, inconsolable at the thought that some lesbian tendencies had slipped through her childhood screening. If that came to light, she'd lose the election and face years of correction. Thankfully, one of her godsmen told her pheromones only worked in close proximity, and that the full effect could only be felt in person.

No wonder Frigga performed well at her love-ins. They weren't rallies, they were orgies. Sex sold. Who wouldn't want their future queen submissively splayed over a couch? The Psychographics Institute told her it was the natural expression of Viking culture. Martial men wanted a pin-up princess to drool over while on campaign. Frigga was a good farmer's daughter, a shield-maiden and a bed-slave, all rolled into one malleable hide.

At that stage, the election looked like a foregone conclusion. No one was interested in Trumba's efforts to maintain law and order: the polls didn't budge an ell when the Thane of Thane put down the Kakamuchee uprising. The Skræling Enclosures were seen as a gimmick. Parading the odd captured Jötunn gave Trumba something of a bump, but her analysts didn't expect it to last.

Why should it? Reality didn't matter. Voters didn't want to deal with problems. Real people wanted the puerile distractions of nubile thralls speed-running through an AR maze. They wanted their Knattleiker heroes to share meatball recipes. They wanted to follow babies crawling for the first time or to recreate sexual escapades with old lovers. There were the people who thought ruling was child's play, and then scorned Trumba for being little girl. Soft lands breed soft men. The only way to rule them was to come down to their level.

The romp with the Knattleiker team backfired completely. It had been mistakenly edited to look like she had poured celebratory champagne on herself before fucking all five of them. The cut made Trumba look so presumptuous and entitled that, ultimately, she had to pretend it was a fake. Broadcasters openly called her the Transitionary Princess, Champagne Trumba, the Five Star Vulva. It was a long six months.

All the more reason that snatching victory from the oesophagus of defeat had been so sweet.

TANGRIST AND TANNGIOST AUDGUDSON, KNOWN universally as the Wizards of Midvaten, were two old-school Skuld, brothers who'd left the Order and gone into business. They weren't just wrinkly old, they were as old as the hills; they were withered and fetid. MIM said they were as old as Iðunn Lind herself: the very rich had been able to sample Iðunn's Apples since before the war, so if you made it as far as the Dirty Thirties and had enough cash, you could go on until the money ran out.

The Audgudsons had made their fortune with all kinds of inventions; most of the broadcast technology used that century—sound recordings, motion pictures, and augmented reality—was under their patent. It really was a miracle what they had been able to achieve, a rollercoaster of discovery, each twin driving his sibling to greater and greater success, until they ended up wafting around the world on lavish skyships and looking down from the clouds on the mere mortals below. Her father famously joked once that these massive bloated gasbags were held aloft by nothing more than ego.

The Wizards owned all the networks, not to mention the *Daily Thunderer*, which had a wider circulation than all the other Runics put together. If they had been friends of the fylkir, then there wouldn't have been the need for any unpleasantness, but the Audgudsons had snarled and snapped at the House of Munsö for years, turning their broadsheets and broadcasts against the Imperial Family. Spite and Spittle her father had called them, on days when even he had had enough. Hellulanders were like that, he said, unfeeling, made of stone. They took the official dispatches from the frontlines on Jötunheim and turned them into pure vitriol, burying the brave and noble sacrifice of war under mountains of fatality reports. It went beyond policy to the personal. They called Trumba's appointment as heir presumptive as "the most terrible defeat of reason and the most savage triumph of brutality." Her father had hidden that from her at the time, but it all came up again after the funeral.

When the election date was announced, rumours began to circulate around the Althing: the Audgudsons planned to stand for high office themselves. They began to hobnob with the idols of Mistilton and Hulvidland, men and women of the Silver Screen who put themselves about as the New Gods: Holly Kings and Mistletoe Queens, twisting folklore and pedigree back on the House of Munsö. Summer had long faded, they screeched. The Great Oak has lost its leaves, they screamed. Some bright spark suggested the twins should bankroll Frigga's campaign rather than split the vote. Soon enough, you couldn't move for New Gods, prattling on with their entirely predictable ideas and jejune opinions. Their celebrity magnified them, made them living legends, and a billion Audgudson screens gave them a platform to opine on whatever their tiny minds thought of next.

Trumba had been at her wit's end, too depressed to celebrate her twentieth birthday when one of her stallari uncovered the Audgudson's dirty secret. The ruins of Utgard were still being combed, nearly two years after the siege had ended. After blasting away some rubble, the Einherjar found a vault, full of TTA devices—old microphones, film and AR cameras, greenway circuits—all with the company logo emblazoned across them.

MIM traced all the serial numbers and shipping documents in a heartbeat, but Trumba already knew what it meant. The brothers had supplied the Roarer with all his equipment. All of it! For years! Unknowingly, of course—they were as rich as Ragnar and wouldn't have risked trading with the enemy. Still, the Wizards wouldn't be able to editorialise themselves out of that headline. They had aided and abetted the greatest threat mankind had ever known. They'd given fear his voice.

Trumba could have had them rounded up and shot or tossed out of their own airlock. She fantasised for days about showing her latest "savage triumph" on one of the Wizards' own channels. But it was a stalemate: if the Audgudsons went, so would the entertainment industry, and if she massacred everyone in Hulvidland, she'd have to make do with a very few dull years before a new batch of bright young things were ready for action. And besides, the problem with stars is that they were about the only thing the voters wouldn't forget. They'd been recorded and distributed for decades. You couldn't wipe all their files and films. You'd just make bootleg martyrs.

Then, inspiration struck. Trumba congratulated herself for a full twenty-four hours on the ingenuity of MIM's solution.

She invited all of them—Holly Kings and Mistletoe Queens—to attend a belated birthday bash, a magnificent, glistening affair to be held at the Summer Palace on the Asgard Aquanet. A suspicious olive branch, perhaps, but all the big names grasped it.

The invitations insisted on traditional costume, and her guests duly obliged with winged helmets, raven feathers, and bloody broadswords. Trumba had always been thrilled by the bombast of Rikhard Vagner. Frigga arrived, dressed as a Valkyrie, and by unspoken but mutual consent, the two rivals assiduously avoided each other all night. There was an endless supply of boar canapes and fermented shark filets. The mead flowed so freely from fountains that MIM had to recalculate the deficit. The soaring Cloud Capturers were only matched by the majesty of the arias that rained over the lakes. Some of the guests even asked Trumba to dance, and she came close to obliging them. She was in a splendid mood, after all. But then they requested modern music, Priestly music. She drew the line at that. If she wanted synthesized sitars and blue snake shoes, she told them, she'd have invited the Maharaji candidates.

As the clock struck midnight, she invited the Audgudsons to her father's study, pointedly omitting their pet potted orchid. Trumba loved the study; some of her first memories were of the walls full of Herodotus, Fang Xuanling, Snorri Sturluson. Trumba found books made for wonderfully erudite decoration. There were also trophies from all over the Nine Worlds. Out of mischief, she sat them next to a stuffed Rabboon, and then she laid out her plan.

TANGRIST AND TANNGIOST AUDGUDSON ASSEMBLED everyone in the ballroom to announce their latest brainwave. Trumba wanted none of the credit for herself.

It seemed they had a long-cherished dream, a massive generational commitment to broadcast through and beyond the Gap, to map the stars for the first time and, having discussed it with the future empress, they'd finally found the inspiration they needed. They called it the Naglfar Project, acknowledging that it was a one-way trip. The Audgudsons were generous enough to fund the whole enterprise, of course, as the imperial coffers were sadly dry, but good wishes were all they really needed from Uppsala.

They looked ludicrous in their costumes, but they were convincing nonetheless. The audience who'd paid for exclusive access to follow the lunatics' ball lapped it up. The Wizards would fashion a huge ark and head off, half of Hulvidland on board: the New Gods searching the stars for the Old Ones. The best bit was that Frigga had "decided" to go with them, although only, of course, after standing down from the election.

For the good of mankind, she said.

Her rival's face had to be seen to be believed. It almost made Trumba weep for joy. She had clearly missed her calling as a director.

The Audgudsons had opted to take the long way around, as opposed to a quick death in a gas chamber. The Mistiltonians were stupid enough to believe they were being heroes, that they carried the world on their shoulders. The ship of the dead was a ship of fools.

As a finishing touch, Trumba then had them appoint Bergelmir as skipper. The Varangian was sworn to uphold imperial interests and could be trusted to see the project through. It was perfect casting. Berg would oversee the telomerase supply too.

They couldn't set off straight away, of course—the ark was quite an undertaking. So Trumba packed them all off out of harm's way, to the Elvidnir graving dock on Helheim. The Verðandi had built seasteads on synthetic limestone reefs there, before the war, and she had her skalds arrange that part of the Order's war reparations would be to help to make the Naglfar Project a reality. She had broadcasts of the shaping work: they used proto-cells, fatty bags of DNA that could grow, self-repair, and respond to the pressures of the Gap. To ensure an on-time departure, Trumba provided all the keratinised thralls necessary to glue it together and, in a mad moment of generosity, donated all the solar sails. If you want to go fast, go alone; if you want to go far, go together using obsolete technology. It was a Great Work worthy of the name; her father would have been proud.

Soon it would be *far vel* and *gotha nott*! She couldn't wait.

They would stay in range—and in memory—long enough to ensure a smooth transition to a new, more pliable set of aesthetes. She wasn't sure if she would write in a wicked little twist to the ending:

a limited supply of telomerase, for example, or a fracture in the sail. Let them fight to the death, perhaps: the survivors could broadcast as they choked on their little white berries for all she cared. She occasionally followed Berg as he doled out daily doses of telomerase on his broadcast, an insight into interstellar logistics for most, a macabre feast for those in the know. She didn't tell him, of course. She didn't want him to get the wrong idea.

It was a foolproof plan, but Trumba wanted to leave nothing to chance. Just in case of an electoral embarrassment, the Audgudsons were told to make sure their voting machines, the standard for fifty years now, registered the right result. The voting machines were also useful when Trumba called a snap plebiscite on the office of High Urdur. Separation of powers had been an illusion anyway; why not formally invest all their fates in the new fylkir?

She'd won by a landslide. Even the dead had voted for her. Women wanted to be her, men wanted to be inside her. You only had to scan the broadcasts to find a hundred body doubles recreating her Knattleiker game on all fours. And in a way, Frigga was where she wanted to be. She made it to being head of state. Or, part of her at least; harvesting all that genetic excellence had taken weeks.

Now it was just Trumba, MIM, and the mushrooms, the perfect triumvirate, with a little Vagner for good measure. The Roarer deserved some truly gruesome punishment, something worthy of a major broadcast, and she planned to discuss it with her new consuls.

TRUMBA DIDN'T SLEEP WELL THAT night either. She had tried drinking herself to bed, but now just felt terrible. She couldn't rouse much enthusiasm for getting up even when she received a new message on her visor. Bohr had finally scheduled the inspection of the new fleet with the navy.

Her house-slaves brought forward a selection of clothing. Trumba felt like she needed to be armoured, so she chose something with the right mix of delicacy and danger—a gold choker and chain combination that wound tightly around her whole neck and plunged down the centre of her chest. It looked as if Jormungand himself was wrapped around her, his scales shimmering in the sun. She bronzed her face and admired herself: positively pharaonic.

The empress was collected from her chambers and escorted to a shuttle that would take her through the nest of spiders. It was all very... insectoid? Arachnoid? Whatever the word, it wasn't a place you could feel relaxed in. The black Ring twitched with excitement and energy. The constant winds whirling from one hemisphere to the other powered great turbines. Piezoelectric transducers, ion channels, quorum sensors, signalling cascades—all linked to MIM, the cerebral cortex of the whole ecosystem.

The Skuld ants were followed everywhere by black Mímameiðr boxes. Bohr's Thralls, they called them, Bots for short. It was just like a Skuld to participate in an emancipation struggle and then have the indelicacy to come up with a name like that. Bohr called the little runts amusing pet names like "Tall Enough" and "Just High." Trumba imagined they were perverse toys, "tall enough" for sex games. It was sickening what went on with these rassragrs, even behind closed doors. It was only a matter of time before these Bots were being broadcast on the fetish channels.

The shuttle levitated around the Ring. Magnetic presumably. She didn't ask, and the escorts didn't offer an explanation. It didn't matter how things worked, so long as they did. Through the hollow, she could see the destination and started to rekindle some of her own excitement, but along with it came a sense of annoyance that the journey wasn't yet over. Every time the shuttle paused, momentary stops that would be imperceptible to most people, she tapped her feet or sighed in frustration. Sleep would be welcome tonight. If she was honest with herself, the Roarer had gotten under her skin. She'd need to scrub that whole episode from her mind. She shouldn't have watched the broadcasts; they made her feel dirty, like she had wasted her time. A bed-slave and a bath would do the trick, and the fleet inspection would be a compelling distraction in the meantime.

A whole third of Mímisbrunnr was carrying on the long traditions of the established naval yards at Rødsverven and Nóatún. There was nothing so cherished, so respected as the ancient tradition of shipbuilding. Ships had spread the Norse seed across Midgard; they were synonymous with Viking raids, trading, and even burials; their crafting born from deep understanding of wood that presaged staggering. The Skuld shipwrights had turned traditional craftsmanship into a holy discipline, solemnly delivered from master to apprentice, father to son, for over ten generations. They retained the core belief that only experienced seafarers, men who'd plied the fisheries in the fjords and offshore from a young age, had the right experience to discern a good boat from a dangerous one. These modern mariners were called gapmenn or sometimes, lifers, although whether in honour of their devotion and the commitment they made or the risks they took with their existence daily, she couldn't say.

Bohr was waiting in an observation suite, just off the arrival hall. Two other Skuld stood behind him; further back still were some naval officers in dress uniform, each man conspicuously wearing the Order of the Polar Star around his neck, and a host of other insignia and decorations on their overcoats. Her Varangians were there too, some in plain view, others no doubt watching her from other vantage points, covering all approaches.

"Your Majesty, I trust you sl—"

"No, Bohr, I didn't sleep well. Let's dispense with the niceties. Show me the new fleet then send them off to hunt the last Jötnar and let me get back to bed."

She shouted over his hooded head to the back of the room.

"Tell me, Admirals, are any of your men due shore leave? I have an itch that needs scratching."

There was an embarrassed shuffling; most military men had no idea of how to deal with a female who was in charge. They were probably pining for her father. Trumba groaned and walked to where she could get a clearer view of the docks. The assembled dignitaries stepped into order behind her.

Each of the ships was a long, slender graceful cylinder, like a jet-black woodwind instrument. The hollows, viewing holes made airtight with a transparent membrane, even looked like finger holes. They were ornately carved from bow to stern, although the shapes were difficult to see clearly, even with spotlights.

"Drakkar-class, your Majesty."

Admiral Mannerheim, the hero of the Deathless Acre, stepped up alongside her.

She might have guessed. Mannerheim had been a close friend of her father. As a girl, she'd often seen him parading through the halls of Uppsala, blueprints in hand for a new barracks or veterans' housing, always wanting something built. The ever-jealous jarls joked that he had the whiff of sawdust about him, but he'd silenced them with a war record second-to-none. He was the only officer to fight an engagement with no Einherjar casualties, having blinded the Jötnar with dazzlers before mowing them down with thermobarics. Since Jötunheim, he wore a prosthetic jaw that jutted out, firmly, telling the world he could take anything it could throw at him squarely on the chin. His men, struck with awe, called him Marshall Thunder. She'd pinned some of those medals on him herself not six months ago, and more on his brother, who'd been vital in the hunt for the horrendous Hafgufa. The family had become so illustrious, there had even been discussions as to a suitable bride-price for Trumba to marry his son.

Mannerheim meant she wouldn't be able to hurry through Bohr's show and tell after all. She summoned all the polite smiles and earnest nods at her disposal and avoided looking over at Bohr.

"As I am sure your Majesty is aware, the ancient clinkered Viking vessels started with a shell—laying the keel first, then adding strakes and fitting the internal timbers as the last stage. They were lighter and more flexible, capable of crossing shallow waters and allowing the crew to pull them onshore in a hurry. The new fleet follows the same general principles, being grown in layers, as it were, rather than assembled around a frame."

The admiral prattled on and on, his jaw almost dislocating on some words.

"Our gapmenn take a very holistic approach: it looks a little like growing a tree in reverse, using an accelerated cambium process to add layers of load-bearing heartwood, onto a skein of bark—a suit of Mímameiðr armor, you see? It protects the ship from impacts, solar storms, and the extremes of the Gap. The heartwood is hewn into bulkheads to form deck and compartments, and then younger layers, sapwood, is grown to carry air, water, and nutrients. There are some systems stored in the stern there—anchoring, cargo, and energy cells. Propulsion comes from the crown, via the exchange of gases and, of course, the solar sail, when extended."

Bohr injected some sycophancy into the proceedings. "We took the liberty of naming them after your forefathers, *Odin*, *Thor*, *Tyr*, and so on. Suitable carriages for the gods, remind the Jötnar of who they are up against."

Mannerheim grinned like a lindworm who'd just gulped down a whole pig.

"Now, we've put on a little display for you today, so you can see the latest iteration of the Thought and Memory Drive these old sorcerers have spun up."

Trumba was underwhelmed. What was being proposed was for a pitch-black ship, moored on the dark side of a planet, to temporarily vanish—and then return. At best, it would be like a moth fluttering around the edge of candlelight. She could probably get the same effect by closing her eyes.

The empress wasn't at all sure about her new clothes.

"How wonderful," she croaked.

Thought/Memory Drive was an integral part of each ship. Without it, each vessel was cumbersome, like a raft fighting against the tide. The T/M Drive allowed near instantaneous crossing of the Gap, a large-scale version of staggering. The theory had existed for years, based on a broad understanding of mimetic osmosis, but the Jötunn War had fuelled the forges of innovation. No one had fought inter-world battles before that, staggering stretched army logistics to breaking point. Sky-ships would get troops to the broad sphere of operations, but unless they stayed away from the front, they'd be shredded by blood-eagles. The Jötnar conducted a lightning war, hit hard and run fast. The empire had a huge numbers advantage, but it could never deploy enough manpower to pen the enemy in or keep them contained.

Bohr piped up.

"Your Majesty will remember our discussion earlier in the week about how the war was won. Once perfected, the T/M Drive allowed huge numbers of Einherjar to finally establish a bridgehead. From there, they eventually moved to lay siege to Utgard and Thrymheim simultaneously, with MIM's help of course. Well worth those the budget increases, wouldn't you say, Admiral?"

So, it wasn't the prison after all. Trumba saw it now. This wasn't so much an inspection as an ambush. They probably lay in bed together at night, plotting about how they could spend more of her money. It explained the ancient star charts too. Give them a few months and they'd have a miraculous breakthrough. The stars could all be hers, a universe for the taking. But only once they could extort some more cash. Bohr knew just how to play her, and his long game was punishing. She felt nauseous.

"Your Majesty," said Bohr, "this is my colleague, Von Schröding. He is the man who theorised how we might learn from Yggdrasil and create our own, independent mode of travel. He is the intellect behind the Thought and Memory proofs."

Trumba's only real option was to try to stifle the yawns that crept up on her in waves and brave things out. She needed to retreat and return from a position of strength. She was dimly aware that someone else was talking, a man with a receding hairline, bulbous forehead, and piggy eyes. He'd affected a kind of hilarious Hindoo dress that made him look even more of a rassragr than Bohr. He had a small-scale replica of a ship, a thin black tube which he held at eye level to demonstrate his genius, but the whole episode played like a children's broadcast. He may as well have been using sock puppets.

"Your Majesty is aware of how Mimetic Osmosis is thought to work?" he began.

Trumba winced. She knew the galdar songs as well as any Urdur, but couldn't explain why they worked, just that they did.

"It is Odin's will," she hedged.

"Indeed it is, ma'am, but it is a little more intricate, if you'll indulge me. Now, without killing yet another clowder of cats, let's just say that the universe, at its smallest, most basic level, exists in all possible states simultaneously. However, when observed or measured, it exhibits only one state. Now, it is possible for those small particles to become entangled so that, after a time of mutual influence, when they separate they remain intimately connected and actions performed on one affect the other, even when separated by immense distances."

"Like identical twins," she said and then almost instantly regretted it when she saw Bohr's reaction.

"Tales of telepathy abound, ma'am." Von Schröding nodded once before droning on. "Yggdrasil represents that connectivity writ large. Our spirit and shape are entangled, if you will, and travel in a kind of superposition of all their possible states. The World Tree instantly communicates, much faster than the speed of light, to link up those states. Ergo, we stagger. Now, as I said, my awareness of the event changes the event. When I touch Yggdrasil, I collapse all possibilities into one actuality. But Yggdrasil makes sure it is the actuality I want, based on the conscious link we create with the codes implicit in our songs. Sentience. Together, we make a decision and come to a destination. For us to travel outside of the greenways, we would need to find *other* ways in which particles are entangled and then find another partner to help make the decision as to where to arrive."

"Your Majesty has heard of the Grandfather Paradox?" Bohr asked.

She turned and gave him a pained look. "Does it have to do with the strange likelihood of all you pensioners being useful to me?"

Neither he nor Von Schröding blinked. She did occasionally wonder how the Skuld responded to her phenotypic plasticity, if at all. They certainly didn't get innuendo.

"You travel back in time and kill your grandfather, which results in you never being born—"

"Why in Asgard's name would I do that?" Trumba was exasperated, but the little ant carried on scuttling.

"—which means you *can't* kill your grandfather, which ensures you are born, and so on," Bohr explained. "When you describe it, it seems like a linear series of events, constantly looping. But it can be quite easily explained. What is really happening is that two entangled histories are occurring simultaneously: namely, you are born and able to go back in time to kill your grandfather or you're not born and your grandfather is alive.

"Imagine the presence of mind required to design something like that. All those things that only exist halfway between an idea and a fact. A world teeming with billions upon billions of unrealized possibilities. The Allfather not only thought of everything that exists, he thought about everything that doesn't too." This was Bohr trying to be helpful.

"I'll assume," said Trumba, "that this isn't one elaborate assassination plot and refrain from executing you, but only if you hurry up. Look, as long as the T/M Drive works, I don't need the explanations."

"Need, your Majesty? Maybe not. Deserve? Certainly," Bohr said, bowing obsequiously. The old worm had her cornered.

"Ma'am, my thought was that instead of entangled particles, we might use entangled *histories*. After all, what is history but thought and memories? Plug two human minds together, and we could walk between realities, skipping between the here-and-now and the been-and-gone, just as we use our consciousness to entangle with the World Tree. The problem is our human brains are young and fuzzy. We all perceive things differently, interpret events based on experience. We might introduce an element of fantasy, a skewed perspective. However, if we could eliminate that subjectivity, we could twirl the threads together and choose the destination we wanted."

"Bravo," she said. "And the solution was?"

Von Schröding held up his model, and Trumba tried not to laugh out loud.

"You couldn't send me a computer simulation?"

"Admiral, would you do the honours?" the Skuld said, proffering the model ship.

Mannerheim took the black rod and attached it to his visor, which pulsed once, then went dark. It was obviously made of the same wood as the station and the ships and acted as a control interface.

Not a replica after all.

Trumba put her mistake down to being tired.

"No need for simulations, ma'am," said Mannerheim. "Time for a test flight. Where shall we go?"

Bohr was grinning from ear to ear, almost salivating with excitement. "The drive allows for two navigators to move whole ships vast distances, with the crucial caveat that one of them has been to or can accurately visualise the destination. He is the Memory to be accessed. The pilots immerse their heads in this magnetic field like so..."

He gestured to the admiral, who stood calmly, but blindly behind his blacked-out visor.

"...creating what we call an Oblivion Link with each other and to their ship itself. It is crucial that we connect the minds of the pilots to MIM, without either man observing or interacting directly in any way."

"Where is the second pilot?" Trumba asked.

"On board the flagship there," Mannerheim replied, testily. "The beauty of T/M Drive is that Fleet Command can also give orders. Can't lose the whole fleet in one go that way. The key is to build in alternates, keep the neurons scattered. It's all joined up if you know how to navigate."

Von Schröding was scrolling through messages on his visor, presumably checking systems.

"Of course, MIM and the Mímameiðr help provide impartiality and course-correction. The pilot and the destination must be described with reference to each other, but by looking at the destination the pilot has influenced the flight. With the T/M Drive, it is crucial we intermingle the mental capacities of the pilots, without memorializing or prejudicing one potential destination over another. That way when one pilot's mind is added to the other, or as we say *superposited*, they create another valid mindscape. That is, they travel."

The admiral was tapping his foot, inadvertently showing a little irritation. Von Schröding tutted and made some notes.

"Almost ready. Of course, the Oblivion Link keeps no records. There will be a very real danger during large manoeuvres of someone getting lost in the Gap and never returning to us. That is probably what will ultimately happen to your warships, sooner or later. By my—"

"Such drama," Bohr said, interrupting his colleague and shushing him as discreetly as possible. "The two pilots merge consciousness for mere moments; no one is going to get lost in time and space. Think of it as a kind of telepathy, your Majesty. A very revolutionary, very *expensive* kind of telepathy. Given enough time and resources, we think we can supply the proofs necessary for our Simulacra Theorem, the Cyclic Model, and the Ultimate Ensemble. Anything is possible if we have the right amount of resources. Now, where would you like the admiral to send the fleet? A quick flight over the Summer Palace?"

Trumba fished around for her mushrooms. An overdose might be the only out.

THE MAN IN HER CHAMBER was handsome. Rugged, she thought. She walked around him, silently assessing his girth. He was older than she was expecting, leathery with the sun; she'd have to ask her house-slaves for oil. Was that a harp slung across his back? His skills had better not be confined to music, or he would find himself without fingers. Those grizzled whiskers would have to go. No one wore them these days at court, especially with short-cropped hair. It made him look like a dusty broom although, on closer inspection, she could see that they masked a lattice of scars. That was intriguing. This man had clearly fought—and won—many battles. Keeping your head when everyone around you is losing theirs, that was a skill.

"Well, undress," she commanded. Beauty and brains seldom went together, but most of her consorts had a grasp of the basics. This one was still looking at her, blankly, even as she disrobed.

"Are you deaf? I've had a very long day. Undress and draw me a bath. And fetch some lavender, or whatever plants the fucking Skuld grow on this nightmare planet."

"Your Majesty is mistaken. I am not a…" An awkward beat. "I served your father."

Trumba would have laughed if she hadn't been so tired. He spoke with an accent so heavy it made her jaw drop. "You are here to stretch my cunt, not my incredulity. Clothes. Now."

She wondered what backwater they'd dredged this imbecile from. He had better be hung like a horse. Perhaps if she found a muzzle, she wouldn't have to hear him bray like that again.

"I also served your grandfather, Hrodulfr, and Arn before him."

"Fuck me," she snapped. "Do I have to do everything around here?"

She grabbed him by the waist and tried to manhandle his belt in frustration.

"That is a gift from Botulfr. I forget when I served him. Before Gandalfr, after Ragnar. A long time ago."

Trumba looked down at her hands. The belt was old. It used Latin script, bearing the legend Coelestinus on each of three interlocking triangles, one gold, one silver. The third metal escaped her, but it was shiny and clearly valuable. She took a step back, and the old warhorse folded his arms, quietly defiant.

Trumba had never seen anything like it in the treasury, or the museum, even in the private collection. She was horrified to find it on a common soldier.

"Where did you get this?"

"I was at Utgard with your father."

"And you took it from the slain there, no doubt. Did you fancy yourself a raven or a magpie?"

"They don't have either on Jötunheim. High-legged Hábrók and Soot-Red Roosters maybe. Monstrous eagles. Skvader, Rasselbock, and Wolpertingers, too, but those are really feathered rabbits."

"Are you *mocking* me?"

Trumba was rocking on the edge of hysteria. A sleepless night followed by the waking nightmare of being schooled by Skulds would test the patience of a godsman, and the drugs still hadn't softened the edges. She thought about calling for her guards but didn't want to admit to being out of control. It was highly likely that MIM had registered her distress and had alerted the appropriate staff. That was rather the point of a machine that was everywhere at once.

The warrior had a twinkle in his eye, but he still hadn't moved much. His feet were planted as if he meant to stay. He evidently wasn't too stupid to realize that the empress was at boiling point because he mollified his tone.

"Mocking you?" he said. "A little, perhaps. Look, I'm a very old man. Too old to be cavorting across the Nine Worlds like I'm a part of the Wild Hunt. Old enough and wise enough to get past your guards, even with all the bits you've grafted and spliced on. Cloning next, I imagine? I've always wondered, what patronym would a clone use? Depends on the root stock I suppose."

"You can find out when I call them and they slit your gizzard."

"I don't have a gizzard," he said. "That's chickens. Are you planning on giving the Einherjar gizzards? Gills, now *that* I could understand. Aquatic assaults."

"Who *are* you?"

Trumba was defeated. She sat down heavily on the bed and pouted, felt her face drain of its colour. The man was right. There was no way he should be here, and she decided it was better not to antagonise him. This was an unpredictable situation, fraught with danger. In an instant, the high-handed ruler shifted into a frightened little girl, using the tricks Frigga had taught her DNA.

"I am no friend of the Skuld," he said. "And they didn't notice me either."

The years melted away when he smiled, revealing the beaming

young boy inside, hoping for an affectionate pat on the head from a proud mother. The guileless fool had been disarmed in seconds. It was so incredibly easy to entice a man to strut, she felt embarrassed for the whole gender. Trumba watched him mentally preening himself and resigned herself to his inevitable grandstanding.

"Nornagestr, at your service. Gest, for short. If you had a sword, I should swear to be your hirðman upon the hilt, as in days of old. Is it still the custom? Your father was less... naked when we met, but that's all I remember clearly."

"Assume I don't have a sword." Trumba wasn't about to hand a weapon to an intruder.

"Assuming you had a sword, the oath would go something like this: I was born to Thord of Thinghusbit and raised in his house at Graening in Denmark. I voyaged with Sigurd Fafnisbane and fought at his side at Brávellir against Sigurd Hring. I ventured with the sons of Ragnar when they destroyed Vifilsborg and roamed the Alps. I escorted Botulfr to Miklagard and saw him crowned Emperor. I crossed Hvítramannaland and learned the ways of the Skrælingar. I—"

"So, you are a history book?" she said. "That explains the leather binding and ancient scratch-marks. Let's assume for a second that you are, what, a thousand years old—at least—and that you were born before the Empire of the North was founded. It can't be telomerase therapy keeping you upright. That keeps you looking—as well as feeling—young. Tell me your secret, and I might just let you live."

Trumba was sceptical, but there was a tinge of authenticity to this warrior. The timbre of his voice, the detail on his artefacts, the confidence of his gait, not to mention the sheer absurdity of his being in her bedchamber. A bedchamber on a fortress-monastery, orbiting one of the most inhospitable planets—a bedchamber belonging to a head of state on last-minute and top-secret visit.

Improbable verging on insane. He was even carrying a musical instrument, as if he had just wandered out of her birthday opera. What was the game here? She couldn't see it. If he was an actor, he was superb at his craft. If he was a Jötunn assassin, there was no need to expound such a ludicrous backstory. If he was an admirer, he would have let himself be ravished, or, at the very least, tried to serenade her. If he really was that old, she had to know. Her hunger for immortality was insatiable—a second bite of the apple was too good to pass up. All these paths to eternity kept on careening into her path; her lap was like a landing pad for otherworldly things. Trumba decided that humouring the intruder was the best approach. She leaned back and plucked a goblet from the table beside the bed.

"Til árs ok friðar," she said and raised the cup to her lips. *For a good year and peace.*

Gest produced a flask and swigged from it.

"Put a gown on, your Majesty, before you catch cold. This is a long story, made short for your modesty."

"Are you planning on singing?" Trumba tried to feign excitement at the prospect.

"The harp is an old friend, but I've forgotten most of what we used to play. My father was a farmer, a freeman who kept an orderly house. Twenty head of cattle, goats in the pen too. At that time, the vǫlur walked with wolves, rather than attended court. Spá-wives, we called them. They travelled around the countryside, swathed in Hel-blue cloaks, ministering to the hidden places. When a baby was born, it was custom to invite the völva to feast and tell the child's fortune. Three such women came to my crib. The first two gave me kind, gentle gifts and prophesized a bright future. The third was called Skuld, and she was less than enchanting. My uncles mocked her and knocked her off her chair for sport, I'm told. By way of revenge, she dictated that I would die by the time the candle lit at my bedside went out. Immediately, the eldest Spá-wife extinguished the candle's flame and ordered my mother to hide it, to protect it, so to prevent her son from succumbing to the wand-witch's curse. When I was full-grown, my mother gave me the candle for safe-keeping. I have it with me now. I have had it with me these thousand years or more."

"And when the candle is lit?" Trumba asked.

"Then the curse is ended, as is my all-too-brief sojourn beneath the stars. The guttering flame will die, the wisp of smoke from the last stretch of wick will match my last breath. Or so I am told. I've never cared to experiment."

Trumba sighed. The old warhorse had delivered her a steaming pile of dung. It wasn't an explanation, it was a fairy tale. Why was she surrounded by these people?

"And you are sure you haven't been spliced in any way?" she ventured, hoping against hope. The apple was rapidly rolling away from the tree.

"No, I am as pure as the driven snow. But your prisoner isn't. That draugr has called himself many names over the years, but in the past fifty, he has unlocked secrets meant only for gods. Even his men called him the Father of Monsters. You should blast him into the Gap before it is too late."

How did this lunatic know about that? If news had somehow leaked it could be disastrous. She needed to control this story. She tried not to show her agitation.

"I appreciate your concern, soldier, but I already answered the Father of Monsters with the Mother of Bombs. His creatures are mostly smithereens."

"I was at the siege. After the orbital strike, your prisoner took the few Jötunn survivors and sat *waiting* in the forests for the empire to collect him. I saw all the laboratories where he kept the Verðandi busy. I saw the creatures he twisted into life, ravenous dog-headed men, foaming and frothing, and brutes who writhed on serpents' tails, six-headed, misshapen, blind."

At the siege? She felt a rush of familiarity. He was a wolfcoat! He had to be. There were only a handful of people who knew she had apprehended the Roarer. The old soldier must have been one of her trackers, must have been on the detail that brought the Jötnar leader to her. She couldn't be sure if she'd followed him before, but there was a trace of recognition that suggested she had. Not that this realization brought her much comfort, for the Úlfhéðnar often had mental health issues. She'd have one of the shapers look at him; it would be a shame to put him down. She relaxed and brightened, although she was surprised to find he was still talking. These taciturn types were all the same, once they started unburdening themselves they couldn't stop. Bergelmir had been just the same. Trumba found it very tedious.

"And that's why you came direct to my chambers to *warn* me? How loyal you are. I haven't decided what to do with the Roarer himself yet, but the empire is quite safe in my hands."

"Everything dies, but not everything stays dead. Does your Majesty know what a draugr is? They live in the dark, hungering for the life they have lost. The Jötnar were his gift from the grave. Your Roarer is as old as the hills his kind are buried in. Now he carries his own curse. He escaped his burial mound, and he *will* escape your prison."

Perhaps a bit of martial praise might stand him down, she thought. He was probably a Christian; those cultists were always talking about resurrections and the dead returning. Didn't the military weed out heretics? She'd have to review the screening processes.

"Oh, there are worse things than dead men, and I sleep easy in my bed knowing men like you are serving me."

"Your Majesty, I re-enlisted to put a stop to him. I should have seen to it when I had the chance, the instant we caught him again. I thought it my mistake to fix. But the fylkir's will is the will of the wind, and who am I to argue? Well, I have delivered my warning. I can't make you heed it."

He was muttering now, the earlier confidence lost. His mind was like the sky blanketed in clouds; one minute he was a drifter, the next instant, he was lucid and foreboding.

"And I can't let you leave," she said. "I have listened to more than my fair share of drivel today. MIM, I am still appreciative of your talents!"

Trumba spoke to the air in general, expecting the machine to reply with force. This man was very depressing, like a travel guide for the long dead.

Gest shook his head. "The Midgard Infinity Machine? So, it is real. If there is one thing I have learnt in all my years, it is neither a shoemaker nor a shaftmaker be, for anyone but yourself. The men speak of it as though it is worse than the Jötnar."

She wondered who the wolfcoat's next of kin were. He'd mentioned Danish ancestry; someone should write a suitable bereavement notice.

"When the victors write history, we edit out the shibboleths."

"Oh, believe me," he said. "I understand. I've seen some big fish get away. Tell yourself whatever story you like. People always do."

And there it was, the insolence! Trumba might have bothered to reply, but at that moment the door contorted, fell out of its frame and toppled into the room, swiftly followed by a dozen guardsmen. So much for the emergency responder drills, she thought, but better late than never.

THE WOLFCOAT WAS HOG-TIED AND left in the bathroom while she had MIM summon Bohr and Mannerheim to her room. There was no choice now; she was going to have to come clean about both her special guests.

It wasn't the ideal forum to explain herself, surrounded by men.

She'd tried for a few minutes to patch Iðunn Lind into the conversation; the old bird might fight in her corner out of guilt. But Bohr prevaricated as soon as he arrived. There were fundamental incompatibilities between the Verðandi bio-computers and MIM's hardware, he said, it was like a puddle of amino acids trying to have a dialogue with the ultimate expression of evolution. Trumba couldn't tell whether he was being derogatory or was just envious, so she'd sent people to physically bring Iðunn to her council, but the lector called them back, saying that he had no intention of letting "that greengrocer" into his facility. It was unbelievable really—with all the money she provided, she couldn't get the Vǫlur to stop squabbling and co-operate. She decided to focus on the issue at hand, and that meant a handful of heaven's little fungal helpers.

By that time, there were half a dozen naval types milling around the room, trying very hard not to gawp at their half-naked empress. She liked tantalising the troops with a touch of her own augmented reality. She tried to make eye contact with one of the naval men. It would make them fight harder in the future. Or just harder.

When Mannerheim had arrived, the officers in her room were summarily dismissed and replaced by new men who'd arrived with the admiral.

Ah well, thought the empress, *no time like the present.*

Admiral Mannerheim seemed… *surprised* to learn that the Roarer had been brought to Mímisbrunnr in defiance of security protocol. Well, maybe surprised was an overstatement. He was somewhat hard to read at times. Bohr was less of an enigma. He looked like he was ready to burst.

"Ymir's corpse! What have you… where is he? Who is guarding him? Tell me he's not conscious!"

"He's being held in a secure cell in one of the unfinished modules on the far side of the Ring," she said. "I have him guarded by my best—"

"If it's an unfinished module it's not secure enough. Not by a long shot."

"Bohr, my guards scouted the location ahead of time and made the call. He's not going anywhere."

Mannerheim's visor was chirping now like a flock of sparrows. The admiral looked quite pained, but Trumba only realised just how annoyed he was when he went to salute her. He snapped instead and shook Trumba out of her reveries.

"You captured the greatest war criminal in history, but you didn't think to inform the General Staff? Do you have any idea what he is capable of, what his genetics make possible?"

"The Roarer?" she answered, with an insouciant shrug. "That's exactly why I am keeping him on the Ring. I want his secrets. All of them, and as the Queen of the Storm Hall, you know, I am entitled to them."

"Empress, this facility is not a toy. It—"

"Don't you *dare* presume to lecture me, Admiral. This facility belongs to me. MIM and the Skuld will pluck every secret he has like bloody petals."

"MIM…" muttered Bohr.

Mannerheim looked constipated as he watched something scroll across his visor. He clenched his teeth.

"Yes, well, I hope for all our sakes that is true. I've issued a General Alert. At least we have laid hands on his accomplice," said Mannerheim. "Let's see what this turncoat can tell us."

"Oh, well, this will be fun. That one has all his ancestors in him, talking all at once. Bátrdrit. Make it quick and send him on to Valhöll so he can annoy the dead directly. I'll find my visor and follow."

Mannerheim had the Varangians bring the Úlfhéðnar to a chair, placed by the inside wall, with an officer at either side. He began by asking him who he was, and his relationship to the Roarer. Trumba saw that he was trying to be avuncular, a friend to the ordinary soldier, but he wasn't very good at the ruse. Besides, the wolfcoat was too far gone to use military formalities; irregulars got like that.

The prisoner looked and sounded strangely depressed for a man who had been full of dire warning not ten minutes ago. Trumba didn't understand the sudden dismay. Surely, he had thought this far ahead? How divorced from reality could you be? You couldn't just invite yourself into the inner sanctum of the empress without repercussion. Come to think of it, if you were invited into her inner sanctum and declined her bed for no good reason, you deserved everything that was coming to you. Rassragrs, the lot of them. The thought left her cold, so she went to her wardrobe and found something a little warmer to wear. Then it clicked: truth serum. The wolfcoat had been drugged! She should have seen that coming. Damn, she thought, she was slowing down. She hurried to rejoin the conversation, eager to avoid missing anything else.

"…he used to say odd things like, 'I stick my finger into existence and it smells of nothing.' All kinds of nonsense."

The old warrior tutted at himself, distractedly. Trumba knew that brand of limpness; navy drugs had a real kick. She perched on the end of her bed, watching the interrogation unfurl, sipping from a golden goblet. It was fun to be in the actual room this time.

Lector Bohr sat directly opposite Gest, alongside the admiral. It was the double act of the century. She grimaced at the thought that she was relying on these two men, when they were so obviously in cahoots. Bohr had the demeanour of a remote and humourless psychiatrist, evaluating a disturbed patient for the umpteenth time. No doubt his Skuld had scuttled to make sure he was fully briefed, but even so, the lector didn't so much as raise an eyebrow when the prisoner recounted the quick version of candle and the curse. She couldn't tell whether it was pragmatism and Bohr simply didn't want to waste time, or if it was something more sinister, something he'd already known perhaps. Was it possible that one of his order had unleashed the curse a millennium ago? Was their record-keeping that good?

On second thought, it was probably much more prosaic. Knowing Bohr, he had already used his Bots to quietly check the warrior's blood and genotype. She was dying to find out what everyone else knew—except she couldn't put her hands on her visor. She scanned the room for it, irked at being out of the loop.

"If you don't have a service number, perhaps tell us where you enlisted?" Mannerheim asked.

"I am a farmer's son who found he was good with a sword, and I've never been paid to think unless it was the way to point the sharp end. I was raised in Groning in Denmark. I first swore on an oath-ring there."

"No thumbprint? Well, can you tell us where you fought?"

"I've fought everywhere in my time, but I was on Jötunheim when Utgard fell. I thought he was long dead. Imagine, he called the Jötnar, rose them from the pages of the sagas! We'd share those stories around the fire, the hirdsmenn and I. They all joined Odin in his halls, one by one. I figured we'd all meet again at Ragnarok and that I was just taking the long way around."

Trumba interrupted. She found it bizarre that the truth serum was having so little effect.

"Enough nostalgia. You have enough stories to write your own saga."

Mannerheim nodded at one of his commanders, who flicked through the information on his visor. Trumba paced around the room, frantically searching for hers. There was a business in the room that she wanted to be part of. Without her visor, she was truly naked.

Bohr smiled at the wolfcoat.

"Perhaps we can find some middle ground? This Roarer, he captured you?"

"I manned the Gjallarhorn Array during the Breach of Gastropnir. Sonic weapons hurt them, kept them back. Still, the Einherjar withstood assaults you wouldn't believe, the Jötnar erupting all along the ridge, a cannonade of molten metal. I was one of the first to cross the Vimur River, but fell there with a thousand more. A Jötunn made our slain into a bridge of the dead, as his kind trolled for survivors."

"Brave men," said Mannerheim, "true to their oaths."

"Bah. Even the Jomsvikings would have fled. We vowed to fight against men, not shapechangers dressed in flayed skins. The Jötnar pierced our ranks like driving rain, blasting lightning from their fingertips. The skies were so thick with their swarms they blotted out the sun."

"But the emperor carried the field? The Raven Banner flew victorious?"

"The raven appeared all right, beak wide open, flapping its wings and restless on its feet. It left with blood on its beak, human flesh in its talons and the reek of corpses in its mouth. Never trust a skald: victory is never a poem, it is sinew and steel, guns and grit. The field was carried with HEIMDAL strikes after they gutted Emperor Dietbald and paraded about his remains."

Gest made a sign of the hammer in the air, touching his shoulders.

Mannerheim nodded silently throughout all of this. Trumba suspected it was *his* order that scorched the skies of Jötunheim. HEIMDAL burst with the light of a million suns. The land was bleak to begin with, but the firestorms incinerated the forests. Within days, the black rains came, clouds of ash and soot snuffed out the sun, and the world froze. She'd only seen the broadcasts, she'd been too young and too sequestered to follow the battle in person.

"You survived though? This far?" asked the admiral.

Trumba groaned inwardly at his vast and penetrating insight. They'd stretched credibility to breaking point now; any more and she would scream. They knew something—they had to. Where was the fucking visor?!

"Well, the missiles might have made lighting my candle a little easier, but I was deep below ground. I helped the surviving Verðandi to the rescue ships. I was the guest of Jötnar for the last few days of the siege although it wasn't as pleasing as imperial hospitality. I played dead after the slaughter at Vimur. Then the draugr found me and brought me in. I swear he knew just where to look. Draugr know all manner of secrets."

"Such as? What did he say? Any little detail may be helpful."

"When he first saw me, he huddled down close to my chest, as if checking that I was breathing. I was caked in gore, surrounded by broken bodies, crushed into the soil. I remember hoping he'd pass by, trying to hold my breath. I remember the ravens shrieking and hoping against hope they'd leave my eyes in my skull. He admired my belt a while. I could feel him trace its edge with his nails, like he was caressing the fingers of an old flame, rekindling memories. I thought he was going to eat me, but then he was gone, into the trees like a breeze."

Mannerheim spent a few moments glancing distractedly at his own visor, silently sending orders and receiving the required answers.

"Cross reference psych for evals," he said. "Religious affiliations, you know the drill."

When Gest spoke, there was an urgency in his voice.

"Admiral, you've checked the records, so can we talk as men? The Witch Queen. I knew her, drank at her wedding to Botulfr the Black. She would always say 'what is written can be rewritten,' and that stuck with me. Now, I'll try and explain, but I am not sure I have the words or that you have the context. I am very tired..."

He was slurring now, barely able to string a sentence together. Trumba was incredulous.

"What the fuck is this lunatic talking about?! Who is this Witch Queen?"

The old warhorse sounded drowsy, speaking as if in a dream.
"I came to warn you. Queen Ellisif had the sight. She saw then
three men. The first was Harald, dead in the blood-red roots of the
empire. The second was Askr, the greatest skald of the age, climbed
high up into the leafy green boughs. I am the third; I have vaulted
higher still. Are we not beyond the rime and frost, touching the stars?
There was a fourth, and he has come to shake the tree to its very roots.
Your prisoner is a Howling One, crept out of his grave."

Well, so much for her Úlfhéðnar. Post-traumatic stress, it broke
the strongest of men.

"Draugrrs, indeed," she said. "I interrogated the man myself. The
only thing shocking about him is his hair."

Mannerheim inhaled slowly, the air whistling through his dangling jaw. She always knew military intelligence was an oxymoron,
but couldn't understand why Nanna had seen anything in this man.
Trumba would reappoint him soon—the Fleshpots of Sind always
needed a firm hand. There were other people to command the fleet.

The admiral turned slowly toward Trumba and took a step toward
her. She noticed, only then, the cracked remains of her visor under his
great jackboot. His eyes were withering.

"Dómhild," he spat, "we invite our *friends* to dinner. Our enemies,
we have nothing to do with. You appear to be confused over which
is which."

"How dare you speak to me that way!" she said. "What is going
on here? And why the fuck is my visor under your boot?"

Trumba wasn't going to suffer being scolded in public. The best
way to deal with men like Mannerheim was to appear as imperious
and unbending as possible. Her father had done the exact opposite
and look what it had achieved.

"Because we have all been under your drug-addled heel for far too
long. Your negligence is astounding. Your father would be ashamed.

He died for this empire so that you would have something left to rule. That you run secret death-squads is one thing, but it is quite another to use them to bring the enemy, the creature that murdered Dietbald, to your very door. I haven't the words…"

Aloof, dismissive. That was the key. She shifted into the right stance. She waved her hand, nonchalantly.

"I fail to see the problem," she said. "There are no sub-optimal outcomes here. MIM was quite certain. The Roarer holds the key to the secrets of the Jötnar, and despite the ravings of this madman here, the Father of Monsters is quite secure."

"You stupid whore!" the admiral screamed. "You gave the Jötunn *access* to MIM when you brought him aboard. The whole Ring has been compromised for days! And then he parades this brainwashed fanatic to rub it in our faces! I think that constitutes a sub-optimal outcome, don't you?"

The whole room winced and fell into a stunned silence. Bohr sighed his assent.

"The Roarer is a master manipulator, your Majesty. With what he secretes from his glands, it wouldn't have taken him long to bond with the systems here and have them at his beck and call."

Mannerheim was apoplectic, storming across the room, waving his arms. "Slave-maker genes. While you have been parading about, naked as the day you were born, we've been investigating the damage. This poor, unwitting guardsman has been enthralled and sent to sow confusion. We saw it a thousand times in the war; decoys, sometimes laced with thermobarics. Our own people turned against us. There are always enough chemical traces to find the fingerprints and *maybe* to track the puppet-master. But his mind is quite gone. The delusion is total."

Trumba reeled across a gamut of emotions, from anxious to despairing, by way of terrified. Externally, she kept a veneer of calm, visage of normality, although her facial muscles twitched with the effort. She could handle this upstart.

"I doubt it. Much as I despised my father, that Jötunn spilled my blood, *imperial* blood. I have repaid his kindness, an eye for an eye. He is bound with the intestines of his own two sons. Gutted like fish for rope. Let him retch on the stink of his own flesh for as long as Iðunn's chemicals last."

She'd hoped it would seem a macabre and brutal punishment, something worthy of a Norse Queen, like a modern-day blood-eagle. Mannerheim didn't register shock or make any other visible reaction. He was now stone cold.

"Is that so? Is that so?" he muttered. He turned to Bohr and exchanged invisible commentary, before returning to Trumba.

"The Jötunn is gone. Nowhere to be found. He left the Ring forty-eight hours ago as far as we can determine, but we might be able to follow his movements now we have studied his thrall here."

The admiral nodded toward Gest, who was lolling backwards and forwards in his chair, succumbing to the sedatives. He peered closely at Trumba, as if scrutinising an ailing machine for a worn-out part. She was finding it difficult to stand and took an involuntary step back.

"I'm afraid we don't know when he got into *your* mind, your Majesty, but he has clearly penetrated deeply. You have been contaminated in ways we can only pray don't compromise us further. Thank Thor for the Oblivion Link or he might have had the fleet. The Hveðrungr had no wife, never had biological children, true children. We won't be able to determine what other draugr you were seeing until we autopsy."

Trumba sat down, stunned and reeling. Her breathing was ragged, stifled. She looked around the room, wild-eyed, starting to panic.

"What have you given me?" she croaked, clawing at her throat.

Without her visor, she felt feeble. Was this what a palace coup looked like, plump old rassragrs pretending to be gods? Where was

MIM? None of this could be believed, let alone corroborated. Why had she been forsaken?

"This wolfhead is laced with poison. We'll probably find the same in your bloodstream. I'm sure it will be painless. Let the record show that, as of 10:38 on this, the 23rd day of Skerpla, that I, Grand Admiral Karl Götstaf Andríður Mannerheim, in accordance with Commonwealth Order Nine, assume the Regency of the United Kingdoms due to the incapacity of our beloved Trumba, fifth of that name."

MIM twinkled in acknowledgement. With that, Mannerheim saluted, with masterful irony, and ushered his men out of the room. Trumba watched them retreat, in and out of focus. She was imprisoned in her own failing body. She heard her father's voice, an echo from her childhood. She could see him when she closed her eyes, and she realized she missed him terribly. He'd taught her everything she knew, all the old tales, the ones worth telling.

Bohr was sitting sideways, engrossed in a conversation. His black dwarfs were humming at his side, relaying his thoughts to the Skuld outside and throughout Mímisbrunnr.

"Admiral, what would you like us to do with the bodies?" he asked, upside-down, his breath sweet and close.

"Autopsy both, for the record. But seal this room until you are ready; we need to contain this until we are ready."

"Impressive, that wolfcoat. I'd like to examine the body myself, if that can be arranged. And we must get a sample of brain tissue. I want to know what he has seen. He had direct exposure we might be able to follow. As Brother Audgudson always says, the empires of our future are empires of the mind!"

Trumba only barely heard Mannerheim's rasping reply, as the naval men barricaded the broken door. They had left her for dead. They didn't even wait to take her pulse.

The pain was excruciating, worse than the polio. But she'd beaten that. In battle, a Viking fought with fury, making each solitary breath count. Her father had taught her to struggle. Inhale, as she grabbed a spear and thrust; exhale, she jerked her shield to the side to deflect the counterblow. In battle, you will either fall or come away alive, he said. A Viking fought *knowing* she was invincible, part of a tale stretching back to the dawn of days. Be bold, therefore, for everything is preordained. Nothing can bring a woman to her death if her time has not come, and nothing can save one doomed to die.

Her father was there, now, with her, helping her fight on. She was a scion of the Norse, she was the uppermost branch, touching the heavens. Trumba had imagined her own story wouldn't end. She had tasted immortality, she'd been so close.

She inhaled. Her shield splintered under the blow, her tendons flared in agony. Exhale.

She fell to one knee and then further still, hoping her father would catch her.

EXEGESIS VII

THE GOD LOOKED STUNNED. HE stood silently mouthing the words the churchwarden had hurled at him.

"*Someone* set him free." Doubt was clearly not just the preserve of an Anglican flock, Michaels thought. It was a devious weapon and had been deftly deployed. The Reverend would be proud, God rest his soul.

Michaels watched his adversary's face contort, flushing all manner of crimson. The storybooks were full of tales of Odin's rage. The recollection made Michaels flinch, but it was too late to regret the provocation. He looked over his shoulder for a line of retreat. Fat chance, fat man, he thought with an almost palpable misery. Eerily, the world seemed more enclosed. He could feel the walls closing in even if he couldn't see them.

The laughter was almost a wheeze at first, thin, like a cough. Michaels had a moment's hope the old man might be choking, but quickly saw the truth: the spluttering had been a counter—a mocking deception. Two ravens swooped down and perched, one on each cross, and fixed their eyes on him. *Caw, kraa,* they jibed, as if they were in on the joke. At that, Odin burst into unbridled laughter, thumping around his half-formed stage, pounding the air with his fists. The evening rang with the sound of cheering warriors and clinking goblets. It was a curtain call, nothing more, nothing less. In another time and place, Michaels might have admired the theatrics.

"You think I fear anyone here, in this Hall of the Slain? Where the heroes of the ages lend me their swords? Oh, my dear warden. Those are not tombs. No-one is buried underneath. They are markers, tags, anchors across time."

"Doesn't matter. This is consecrated ground. You are a trespasser. You need to leave."

If he screwed his eyes shut, he could ignore the timbers, the thatch of golden shields.

"And you are a grave fellow. The wound is already struck. It's not as deep as a well, or as wide as a church door, but it's enough. What do you imagine happens when you die?"

The god had stopped laughing. He took up a spear and hefted it from hand to hand, as if assessing the weight. His one eye flashed with fury, fixed on Michaels.

Michaels felt strangely calm. He was breathing deeply, rhythmically. There was a freedom in inevitability.

"I have faith in the hereafter. We are all God's children."

Annoyingly, his tongue was less cooperative. His mouth was ash-dry and fixed in a bitter pout. His words clicked as they crept from him, but he trusted them all the same.

"I am the Lord, I have no peer, there is no God but me. I arm you for battle, even though you do not recognize me."

All Michaels could hear was the rasping of endless horns.

NORNA-GESTS ÞÁTTR

K UNTA! FUKJA! DRIT!"

Gest woke up, swearing. Those fuckers had tried to kill him. It always hurt much more than he remembered. His chest felt like he had been kicked by a mule, and his whole left side was writhing with invisible electricity. Added to that, the klaxons were damn loud, and just in case you slept through *them*, someone was firing the sonic cannons too. It wasn't the first time he'd woken up feeling this sore, but from all the commotion around him, he suspected it might be the last.

That was something, at least.

He had tried to warn them, but there was no use in being bitter. He always knew it was a fool's errand. Who was going to believe a story like his? The thousand-year-old farmer, come to warn of a fairy-tale foe. Gest had no genetics on file that would even give them pause for thought. For one thing, he hated change—he left off popular music when the piano replaced the harpsicord. For another, he was just too damned old; he counted rheumatism as his bosom friend. No, he'd lived long enough without being spliced and diced to start moving things around now. The military had thought him a spy and repaid treachery with cyanide. Marshall Thunder always acted first, asked questions later. You couldn't blame him after what they'd seen in the war.

Gest instinctively reached for his harp, with the secret compartment keeping his candle safe. It was as tough as he was, carved long ago from a red-bark tree. Indestructible, the Skræling Dreamer had said, and it had survived five hundred more years, surpassing the warranty. Not a bad trade for a handful of beads. Strange; he'd been captured or killed a dozen times over the years, but no one ever took it from him, or when they did, it was always easy to find, thrown in a junk pile or discarded on a table. He'd long since decided it had a glamour on it.

The warnings continued, three oscillating and shrill tones, an Alert Ready system broadcast to all householders, everywhere, all at once. The fylkir's personal calculator was responsible for all the din. MIM was delivering a steady flow of information, digesting and regurgitating data from across the Nine Worlds on banks of monitors that made up the far wall. They were all showing loops of eerily silent destruction, with no sound but for the alarm.

The world ends not with a bang, but with a mute button, he thought.

He was still sitting in the imperial chambers, on a jet-black wooden chair. Mímameiðr wood, like a finely upholstered tarantula. The room was empty otherwise, except for a few bits of detritus on the floor and a discarded negligee on the unmade bed. He didn't know where the empress was, although he suspected she'd been consigned to the laboratory furnace of history. The Mayfly Queen, Empress for a Day. Gest had always thought politics was a dirty business, but the cardinal rule was surely never trust the Varangians. Who guards the guards? Oh well, he thought, so much for his plan of going straight to the top.

There was a goblet half-hidden under the sheet and wine spilled underneath. Dry to the touch. He'd been gone for a while then. Normally, if there was such a thing, he came back within hours, but sometimes days had passed. They hadn't bothered to tie him, and they certainly hadn't bothered to come and collect him. Given the images he saw on the screens that covered the far wall, the navy had their hands full. He'd missed the events real time—as far as he could tell, most of the broadcast were replays.

He watched the carnage with resignation. Here it was, then—the thread was cut. It was little consolation that all other threads in existence were being severed at the same time. Well, that shows how far mankind had come, he thought. Ragnarok was being broadcast live.

ON MIDGARD, THE EARTH SHOOK violently with a series of deep-sea detonations. MIM showed graphs, predictive analyses, measuring atmospheric composition as the waters bubbled up methane. Close to Miklagard, the North Anatolian fault ruptured. The European side thrashed into the Black Sea, which replied with a satisfied belch of hydrogen sulfide, poisoning the remaining denizens of the Great City in an instant. Fireballs followed, the gas reacting with the fabric of the city, storms of acid and flame savaging her proud beauty. The tidal waves were a mercy, wiping her ruined visage clean. The broken Dome of the Church of Holy Wisdom turned black as whatever souls were left departed. The screens flashed an advisory:

Hydrogen sulfide can cause inhibition of the cytochrome oxidase enzyme system resulting in lack of oxygen use in the cells.

That was funny, he thought. The central nervous system of the empire had been paralyzed, her people suffocated, and MIM offered a science lesson. No wonder the rank and file despised the machine.

He watched as the land wracked and writhed, cities tottered then crashed headlong from their foundations. The Gulrstein Caldera spewed magma and ash across the west, the Brenna Ring turning the Peaceful Ocean into a steaming cauldron. Seawalls cracked and buckled, filthy water surged through townships across the Rim as if Hafgufa had risen again. Ash eclipsed the sun, just like it had on Jötunheim. Gest was relieved that he didn't have any loved ones. He stopped making attachments centuries ago. The cities, though, he'd been to most of them. He mourned their passing: New Jorvik, Sveinsey, Reykjarvík, Austrióss—all funeral pyres.

The door was sealed, wedged shut on the outside, a temporary repair after the Varangians had smashed through, but a solid one. He couldn't see any way out of the chamber. He sat on the bed, pouring himself wine and smoking clove kretek cigarettes he'd bummed in Jayakarta. You couldn't take your eyes off it. It was like the election all over again, although if he'd have known the empress had such a great taste in Gothic reds, he might have voted for her.

As the hours wore on, the broadcasts showed that Mannerheim had sailed with the fleet, hoping to coordinate a rescue. The Drakkar arrived in the sky like Valkyries to rescue the fallen, to deliver hope, to bring salvation. But that too ended in disaster. The *Odin* was swallowed in a sea of desperate refugees; the *Thor's* systems were clogged by ash and pumice, and the great ark was wrecked. The crew of the *Tyr* mutinied and had to be executed by their fellow Úlfhéðnar to restore order to the fleet. The admiral was broadcasting directly now, giving orders mechanically. The *Naglfar*, the great Audgudson bio-ship, broke her moorings, and the decrepit old tinkerers went wailing into the night. The empire was dimming; the broadcasts swamped by people sharing the sheer scale of the catastrophe, before being snuffed out themselves in countless, horrifying ways.

The advisories continued throughout the night, but mercifully, the klaxons stopped. The sonic cannon too. Silence reigned now, the stillness broken only by the occasional frenzied knocking on the door. He ignored them; it wasn't as if he could open it or provide enlightenment. Gest had never been fitted for a visor and couldn't engage with anybody outside the room. He numbed the disquiet he felt with another gulp of wine and sat back to watch text crawl across MIM's screens.

HE MUST HAVE DOZED OFF for another few hours, although all the broadcasts showed different times and it was hard to be sure. His mother always said wine, women, and song would be his downfall. She'd been almost right. He was so drunk on the imperial cellar, it was only when the door started melting that Gest released that Mímisbrunnr itself was now under assault.

It was a prison break. In one corner of the wall of broadcasts was a screen showing the interior of the Ring. Spiky rime-jewelled supermen, night terrors from the dark side of the planet below, marched through the sections, slaying the Skuld with abandon. MIM had recorded it all. He had simply missed it in between the mayhem. The Roarer had worked with phenomenal speed, shaping the outlaws of Náströnd to his liking, moulding them to fit the fabric of the world on either side of the terminator line in the burrows of old Mímisbrunnr. The Sons of Muspell had shattered Bifrost in their ascent, some falling back to the burning shores they came from, but still more came searing into the naval yards.

The door was almost burned through now. Gest hadn't come this far to surrender to a Jötunn. The draugr could rot in whatever he used as a tomb. Even at the end of all things, a Viking should find time for one last fight, he thought. Wasn't that the whole point of Ragnarok?

He rolled away from the monitors to the far side of the bed and used his leg to snag the black chair that had been so good to him of late. He'd find a better use for it than interrogation.

He heard the axe whistling before he saw it. The hilt bounced awkwardly off the ceiling and the axe clattered to the floor, blade flat to the ground. Gest noted that, if there was a throwing gene, it wasn't enhanced in this latest design. He made a grab for the weapon then stood up, holding the Mímameiðr chair as a shield.

There were two Jötnar. He'd handled a pair before, but with a whole squad of Úlfhéðnar in support, and of course, the wine wasn't helping matters. The genius of the draugr was to use test tubes and petri-dishes to bring nightmares out of memory and into the slaughter. The Father of Monsters had surpassed himself with this new batch, making just about the ugliest things Gest had ever seen. These two were lurid pink, a fusion of spiny armour crammed over blubber and oily fur. They had four sets of stubby appendages, eight arms and legs, each brandishing claws, which explained the terrible throw at least.

Gest recognised them as vastly overgrown specimens from the Utgard laboratories; the screens had been full of anatomical drawings and gene-maps. Microscopic bugs, but the Verðandi had called them wonder weapons: the Roarer's latest find, able to survive the boiling volcanic springs at Hvergelmir or the icy wastes of the Himalayas with equal ease. The stallari had laughed in their faces. The war was virtually over, and the threat never materialized.

Now, Gest was about to eat their words. He had to hand it to the draugr: graft them into human cells, and the bugs turned out formidably.

The Jötnar had tubular mouths, rather than a jawline brimming with teeth. They drawled rather than spoke, not that he could understand a word—and not that you ever tried to reason with a Jötunn, unless you wanted them to rip your tongue out before they gouged out your heart. He held up the chair to ward them off. The first Jötunn funnelled out what passed for laughter in nightmare land.

"Hrimthurssar, hrimthurssar," they hooted.

Gest briefly regretted leaving P.T. Barnheim in the Panic of '37. Still, he knew a thing or two about big game hunting. He prowled around his adversaries looking for a gap to exploit.

"You know the secret to lion taming, you pig-fucking maggots? The chair does the important work. You hold it up like so, and the lion tries to focus on all four legs of the chair at the same time."

Gest edged closer, the Jötnar watching the blackwood waving hypnotically in front of them.

"With its focus divided—"

He drove two chair legs straight through the head of one of the creatures, simultaneously pinning the other's shoulder with a third. He slid underneath their flailing bodies, trying to shut out the shrill screams. He struck at what he thought were leg tendons with the axe, but the blackwood proved much more penetrating. Gest reached up and turned the chair like a corkscrew. The surviving Jötunn lost its footing, allowing him enough purchase to grind it back into a corner.

Both Jötnar were crumpled and dying. The way they were splayed out on the chair reminded him of the good old days, one of the ancient *níðstang*, the curse poles he used to set, but there wasn't time to dignify them with a curse or reminisce further.

He turned around slowly, dreading what might appear on the next broadcasts. The Roarer was there, on all the screens at once, each slightly out of sync. His old friend was laughing, the crazed belly laugh of a clown, albeit hauntingly silent. Like a side-splitting routine in talkies, a golden oldie from the Wizards of Midvaten. The slight delay between monitors made his face flicker, as if each signal had a poor frame rate. The "again-walkers" gave themselves away, wreathed in foxfire. Gest had seen that halo on all the broadcasts. That was why he re-enlisted. It was there now, in the static.

The senior Skuld, Niði Bohr, was on the central screen, surrounded by a ring of ruin. The monitors looked like a chess board, with Bohr the surrounded king. He was going to fire HEIMDAL, he said, even if the blast would destroy them all. It was best to lose all that knowledge, better than giving it to the enemy. Or *something* like that—Gest was doing his best to lip read. He remembered he'd served with his grandfather, or maybe his great-grandfather, on HMS *Hǫttr*. He had every faith in the lector to go down all guns blazing. The screen went dead, leaving Gest alone with his ghosts. He had to run if he was to save his skin.

"Then the gods took the sparks and burning embers that were flying about after they had been blown out of Muspellheimr, and placed them in the midst of the firmament both above and below to give light to heaven and earth. They gave their stations to all the fires, some fixed in the sky, some moved in a wandering course beneath the sky, but they appointed them places and ordained their courses."

—Snorri Sturluson, *Prose Edda*, "Gylfaginning"

THE NEAREST HANGAR WAS A wide-open wound, ripped apart by an unimaginable force. Some of the great Skuld missiles were still pirouetting above the fracture, globules of fire smouldering where they had struck home. He snatched an oxygen mask and hurled himself across the emptiness, through ruptured suits and desiccated Einherjar bodies, aiming for one of the shuttle craft on the far side. A mottled Hrimthurssar, partly roasted by the explosions, hooted at him from a loading bay as it drifted slowly out of sight, spinning in the fluctuating gravity.

As a boy, Gest used to lie under the stars, naming the constellations. Óðinn's Vagn was always there—the All Father, who, stepping into his chariot, held seven stars in his hand, showing his people the way. Gest would watch the leidang and dream of raiding foreign shores, knowing the warriors were guided by the leiðarstjarna, augu Þjaza, or Friggjarrokkr. He remembered it being bitterly cold as the boats drifted out of the bay, covering the horizon with a thousand painted sails.

It occurred to him that he hadn't seen those stars for hundreds of years, but still, those days seemed more real to him than the alien skies outside the Ring. A perpetual red-blood evening, a gown pierced with diamond studs. He reached the door, prised it open, and flung himself inside. He was operating on instinct. At his age, he was surprised to find self-preservation was such a driving force. Perhaps it was because he was the keeper of his own demise—the candle was his to light, and his alone. He certainly wasn't going to give the Roarer that satisfaction.

The shuttle was already spooled up. There were two gapmenn splashed in the drive seats, unconscious but breathing.

"They were like that when I found them," rasped a familiar voice from behind him.

Niði Bohr. Alive and kicking.

"I suspect they tried to fire up the shuttle's drive for a quick escape. Didn't engage the magnetic field properly."

"Will they be okay?" the old Viking asked.

He turned to face Bohr, cooped up in the rear of the shuttle, like a brooding hen. His visor was dark, as if he had been ready to use the drive himself. The lector appeared unarmed and didn't seem threatened or surprised by Gest's sudden arrival.

"A bad case of neuralgia. Damaged nerves, headaches. That kind of thing. Or maybe, just a bad case of nostalgia. Looks like there is going to be a lot to miss," Bohr said, looking out the rear hollow at the burning deck. "You're looking a little more... perky than when we last met. Glad to see you up and about. MIM was right. I'm not sure why I am surprised. Infinity does rather cover all eventualities."

"I thought you were going to blow the Ring. Make like lightning and bolt," Gest said.

"No hurry. We've got time on our side. Well, *you* do. How much of this 'situation' do you understand?" The Skuld carried on looking out, scanning for signs of attack.

"It's hard to misunderstand the end of the world. I've heard it described plenty of times. Have you ever visited Aztland? Hot and humid place, full of lakes and mountain springs, a week's sail north of Rauðstréland. I travelled there once, met the wisest man I ever knew. Fasting Coyote was his name. I told him about our empire that stretched across the seas and the skies. I warned him that it was soon to swallow his cities too. You know what he said?"

"Enlighten me," said Bohr.

"The caverns of Earth are filled with pestilential dust which once was the bones, the flesh, the bodies of great ones who sat upon thrones, deciding causes, possessing treasures, governing armies, conquering provinces, tearing down temples, flattering themselves with pride, majesty, fortune, praise, and dominion. These glories have passed like the dark smoke thrown out by the fires of volcanoes, leaving no monuments but the rude skins on which they are written."

"You've a good memory." The Skuld seemed genuinely impressed.

Gest shrugged. "Easy to remember. The empress called me a walking history book. This rude skin is all I have of value. Besides, Ragnarok isn't rocket science."

"No, but it *is* quantum mechanics. Do you know what that is?" said Bohr.

"From the Latin quantus, meaning *how great?*"

"You know Latin?" He seemed even more impressed, excited even, if the wobbling of his chins was anything to go by.

"I knew someone once who did," Gest said.

"I can only imagine. Clearly, the world we knew is ending. We might be the only four people left alive." The Skuld sighed heavily and returned his gaze to the window, evidently hopeful that some of his colleagues might also make it to the hangar.

Gest looked down at the lifers. On closer inspection, one of them was female.

"Even if she'll have us, I'm too old for children, and no offence, you might be too fat. It's a moot point—what kind of a world would they be brought into?"

"No offence taken. I've no interest in children of my own. But, my dear fellow, Ragnarok isn't an ending. It's a chance to try again," he said, matter-of-factly, looking down at the unconscious crew.

An explosion rocked the whole Ring, and both men were forced to steady themselves on whatever they could hold onto.

"Shouldn't we be leaving?" said Gest.

"Like I said, no hurry. If I am right, all of this…" Bohr gestured widely. "…has to wait for you."

"Very polite, but I'm no one special. I'm not much more than a farmer that Odin forgot to take into Valhöll." Gest laughed, joylessly.

The Skuld grew serious and pointed a finger straight at Gest. His voice trembled with accusation.

"Once a candleman, always a candleman, the apprentice holding a light for his master to work. You, sir, are much more than that. Do you really think you stayed alive because of a fucking candle not being lit?"

"You don't believe in prophecies?" Gest recalled the interrogation quite clearly, despite the drugs. He knew the lector had heard as much of his life story as anyone.

"I believe only in the world at my fingertips. A prophecy isn't magic. It is best explained as a form of entangled history. Two parts of time that have become inextricably and intimately linked. One in the past, one in the future. One forwards, one backwards. Now, you are a quirk of fate, in the sense that you are anchored between alternate realities as well. Sideways, in a sense. I think you have been caught up in something we barely have the words for."

Gest tried to laugh, but his attempt just made a hollow sound. His throat had gone dry.

"I don't understand."

"I wouldn't expect you to. I'm not sure I do, and I am one of the smartest men who ever lived. You know what an expert really is? A person who has made all the mistakes that can be made in a very narrow field. What I am trying to tell you is this: you shouldn't be here, a thousand years after you were born. You know that, deep down. And in some senses, you aren't here. I checked with MIM, after our little chat earlier with the admiral. Nornagest is born, lives a long and eventful life, but dies in the reign of Olaf Tryggvason."

"Never heard of him."

"No, in fairness, neither had I. King of Norway, 995 to 1000 AD apparently. Converted the North to Christianity. MIM pulled it out of a text called the Flateyjarbók."

"Never heard of that, either."

"Quite. The history of Tryggvason and the Flateyjarbók doesn't exist for us. In our reality, Christianity has collapsed to the Fringes, and places like Mímisbrunnr. Places where only outcasts and misfits survive."

"I know that too. I speared the Patriarch of Rome. If I close my eyes, I can still hear his prayers. So, what? I am in two places at once? I have a twin I never met?"

"In the reality MIM found, Christianity is the dominant religion. You were a living relic, the last remaining survivor of the Age of Heroes. You were baptised and freed from the protection of the Norns. King Olaf lit your candle himself. Did you know this? Nornagest, from the Old Norse, means 'guest of the Norns.'"

"Him I know. Them I've met, although I was a babe-in-arms."

"Names have power. Yggdrasil whispers them to us throughout eternity. They are patterns to be traced and recognised, clues waiting to be deciphered."

Gest might have been shocked by some of this, had he not woken up a few dozen times, healed of a wound that would have felled an ox. It was actually a relief to find someone to talk about it with at long last.

"So, what are you suggesting? You understand why I have lived so long? It's more than a prophecy, or what the Norns decreed?"

"Maybe. I haven't had time to sit down and work through the implications. MIM had no sooner dredged up your details than Miklagard imploded and all this began. I have a working theory. There are all kinds of forces of attraction in the universe, gravity, magnetism, electricity and so on. We haven't discovered them all. When we calculated why the universe is structured the way it is, we found there simply isn't enough of it to keep it all neat and tidy. There must be something that keeps the stars clustered. Keeps it all working. Something that breathes life into the Nine Worlds. A Cosmological Constant, my friend Einnsteinen called it. Perhaps the Norns are that constant."

"You people with the seiðr, the Orders, you can't see all these links? Not even using your mathematics?"

"Everything we experience is only a tiny fraction of reality. As to the rest, we are in the dark. I have an analogue in the other thread too, Niels Henrik David Bohr, according to MIM. Other than that, prediction is very difficult, especially about the future."

"I'm sorry. This isn't a world I am familiar with. Did I mention, I retired from all this? I wanted some peace and quiet, lived with the Skræling. Carry on far enough, beyond the Grjótbjǫrg there is a coast, with countless islands, like crumbs swept from a banquet table. Good for fishing," Gest said, happily sailing on the parts of the Peaceful Ocean that still lapped at the corners of his mind.

"But you came back," said Bohr. "That speaks volumes. You were pulled back by this unseen force."

"I only came out of the West when I heard the broadcasts. I came to deal with it, put an end to the mischief of the barrow-fiend." The thought capsized his mental boat, almost as violently as it had the first time.

"I know why you came back. If I were to bet, whatever you are, you aren't alone. Interesting you can't mention its name." The Skuld tapped his finger on the side of his nose.

"The draugr? His name was Olaf."

"And you two have a shared history?"

"We go way back. I can't remember the first time I met him, but I was already old. Remember, I was in my prime when the Gotar sailed for Reidgotaland and Sigurd the Völsung went to war, when Rome fell to fire and sword—somewhere at the turn of the first millennium."

Bohr clapped his hands in delight.

"About the time your candle was lit. If we follow the Christian thread. That's not a coincidence. The Universe doesn't like inconsistencies."

"The last time I saw him, before Jötunheim that is, was his funeral near Jorvik. He shouldn't be alive. You think the mound-dweller has a Norn's blessing too? A talisman of his own?"

Nothing surprised him anymore, not even seeing an old comrade returned as a draugr. He was certain the body had been burnt and sent out to sea with all the reverence due a great Viking hero, but there had been so many men slain in those days, so many honours for the fallen.

Bohr shook his head.

"Probably not a literal candle. More of a shadow, a halo. Did you ever stop to wonder if you were a draugr too, returned from the grave?"

"What? No," said Gest. "The draugr owns all kinds of deceits and masks that—"

"Odin was as much a trickster as Loki. Don't worry, I am not accusing you of being a beast from beyond. But I am saying, you share a common bond."

Gest remembered the camaraderie of the Viking Age. The hirdsmenn had always been joined at the hip. The Skuld was making a spooky kind of sense.

"Blood-brothers, then, like Loki is to Odin. And if I am an anomaly from our thread of history then—"

"He is probably a glitch too," said Bohr. "From the other side of whatever coin is currently spinning. A Christian warrior, a warden like Heimdallr. Come to collect his debts. This Olaf is likely a cipher for you. He wiped his fingerprints from MIM's memory, so I can't tell you more. But he shouldn't be here any more than you should."

Bohr looked very pleased with himself and leaned back against the window. All manner of memories were bubbling to the surface now, and Gest found he was suddenly able to solve his own puzzles.

"Well, that explains something. That's why the Witch Queen only saw three witnesses in her dream. I could never understand that. So, what happens next? The shade has been denied his rightful thread, so he has brought about our doom. But you were saying he can't proceed without me?"

"My conjecture is that the Thought and Memory Drive has unravelled reality. Creation is like a knot, full of tangled threads. Separate, yes, but intimately linked. Now those threads are teasing apart. We've inadvertently broken a bond without knowing it. One of those forces of attraction I was talking about."

"We've killed the Norns?" Gest groaned.

"If you like. You said Ellisif spoke of one who would rock Yggdrasil to its roots. The World Tree is the best-known example of entanglement."

"A wave is a ring. There is seldom a single wave. This doom or the next," Gest intoned, lost in thought.

"What do you mean?" Bohr's mind was certainly more agile than his body, but the old warrior was going places he couldn't follow.

"Another thing Ellisif once said," Gest said. "This kind of thing happens over and over, does it?"

"You do have a good memory. The passage of time isn't a corridor from point A to point B, it's a great boundless sea. And you and your friend are making waves. I wonder where they go."

Gest didn't know what else to say. He thought about how Harald would have dealt with the conundrum, but resisted the temptation to swear repeatedly. There were another series of explosions outside that shook the floor. No one else was coming.

"Shall we leave the sermon for later? I doubt our Loki has quite finished with us yet. Will this thing work?" he said, jutting his chin in the direction of the lifers slumped over the control panel.

"I've no doubt that I can fire it up," Bohr said.

"Where do we go? Can we escape Ragnarok? Even Odin was inevitably swallowed by the wolf," Gest said.

He made room for the lector to squeeze past him and slump into the pilot seat. Bohr began running through the systems, sifting over the interface on his visor.

"Did you see the body? Never assume someone is dead unless you see the body," he said.

"I'm sorry, this is my first Ragnarok," Gest said, mustering all the sarcasm the end of the world warranted.

"I'm saying that an old conjurer like Odin could escape his fate. He'd worked with the Norns long enough. In all the invisible places we've discussed, you don't think he carved a back door? Made a hideaway? Oh, heavens..."

Bohr suddenly stopped, lost momentarily in thought. He whistled, then turned to look straight at Gest, a whole new level of excitement trembling through him.

"Even Trumba guessed it, intuited it, with her limited grasp of seiðr. A circular argument, she called it. Yggdrasil hasn't been whispering. She is an echo chamber. She's been warning us."

"What do you mean?"

"In the sagas, who is Odin's father?"

Gest was back on familiar territory. Campfire songs and legendary sagas were his meat and drink.

"Borr. Son of Búri," he answered, without hesitation.

"Borr, yes. Sound familiar?"

Gest had thought he'd seen it all. He'd seen fylkirs and emperors crowned and killed and stared disbelieving as Karl Lind vanished before his eyes, but he'd never witnessed anything as bold as this.

"Niði Bohr, have you taken a knock to the head?"

"It might surprise you to know that my family have always been intimately involved with immortals. My grandfather taught Iðunn Lind, you know. Oh, you can wipe that worried look off your face. I'm not saying I am literally Odin's father. But I don't think that matters. Not everyone has a memory like yours, you see? For example, in a few minutes, I'll deploy HEIMDAL. We named the system after Heimdallr, the warden of the gods. Seemed a suitable acronym, all things considered. But what if future generations name the god after the weapons system? What if we have created a loop? A self-fulfilling prophecy, a self-entangled world. That's why MIM can't explain it to me. She's been cut off."

Gest wasn't convinced. "Bohr, you have more in common with Fasting Coyote than you might imagine. He also spoke to an Unknown, Unknowable Lord of Everywhere, to whom he built an entirely empty temple. They still carried him out on a cart."

The Skuld studiously ignored him and continued to make preparations. His computations looked feverish, his brow sweating.

"Well my friend, if I am right, you are the only one who can fix this."

"How many chances do I get?" Gest hauled a lifer to the back of the shuttle and strapped them in.

"This isn't a joke, I'm afraid," Bohr called back.

"Why me?" Gest yelled over the cycling engines. He wrestled

the second lifer into a redundant seat, straining to hear the lector's explanation.

"We could never find the gods, no matter how much we searched the Nine Worlds. You were always there, hiding in plain sight, dressed up in the guise of a Christian legend. An impossible hidey-hole, kept safe by all the minds beyond our ken. All these strangely intelligent minds that silently surround and interpenetrate us. Call them álfar as beautiful as the sun or call them entangled electrons waltzing on solar rays. Call them Norns controlling our destiny or call them Dark Energy, binding the Gap. They've been talking to us, but we don't know how to listen. Let's face it, this current history veered off somewhere distasteful. Perhaps the further the wave travels, the weaker it becomes."

"What are you talking about?" Gest crept back to the front, crawling with horror at what he thought he'd heard.

Bohr turned to face him again, pivoting in the seat. "I think you are Odin. Or you *will* be. You are going to carry the seeds of creation with you back into the past. All those stories, all that history. The Mímameiðr, too. You will plant the World Tree."

"Bikkju-sonr. Assuming for one second that any of that were true, how will I do that?"

"Because I am going to send you."

"No!" Gest bellowed.

But it was too late.

The whole shuttle hummed as the Oblivion Link completed. He felt the Skuld rummaging in his mind, unlocking secrets, sifting through his past. There was no stopping him; he was far too skilled at that kind of thing. Fully armed, Bohr staggered away as far as he could, as quickly as he could, hauling the vessel with all the heartfelt force of a millennium of memories. The shuttle tumbled through the void like a leaf in a gale.

Gest could feel the lector's mind too. He stood witness as HEIM-

DAL erupted, eviscerating the remaining sons of Muspell. There was delight, exhilaration, triumph…

Then nothing.

In that split second, Surt reached out his sword. The light was excruciatingly, catastrophically bright. Even at their impossible distance, the shuttle groaned.

Behind them, doors were dismantled, crushed in the deepest well of all: gravity. The sword swung further still, cleaving the heavens with two brilliant beams of destruction. Gest screamed in pain, his skin blistering, his eye sockets burning in the afterglow and the heavens screamed with him.

The planet of ice and fire shattered, the crust and hot iron innards spilling into the cool Gap, a stream of rocks and particles sucked into the coruscating clouds of light at the edge of an ominous black disc. Mímisbrunnr boiled away into the witch's brew.

> *The sun turns black,* | *earth sinks in the sea,*
> *The hot stars down* | *from heaven are whirled;*
> *Fierce grows the steam* | *and the life-feeding flame,*
> *Till fire leaps high* | *about heaven itself*

THE STARS HAD ALL VANISHED now. All that remained was Ginnungagap, nothing without end. There were still winds, though, great gusts blowing in from the sea. He could smell the salt, feel the air.

But Gest's eyes were gone. Supernovas were son-of-a-bitch painful.

He might shake off the injuries. He had in the past. But there wasn't much likelihood of his eye-sight returning to empty sockets. He didn't heal that well.

Somehow, he felt lighter. He was certain that Olaf had roared his last, just as he was certain the draugr had triggered the insatiable black hole, the Ultimate Devourer. Nothing survived that, not light, not even the ravings of a madman. Whatever the creature was, it had been swallowed in the maelstrom.

Bohr was gone too. He felt for the pulse on the old Skuld's neck, but he'd already felt his mind snap out of existence. In sharing consciousness, he'd found no meaning, no revelation, no enlightenment. Just oblivion. At the moment he jumped, the Skuld became what he beheld. Shame, Gest thought. He hadn't known him long, but he felt a certain kinship.

All the magnificence of the Empire of the Heavens had been obliterated too. The shuttle's link to MIM had collapsed. There was no voice recognition. That wasn't surprising given the scale of the destruction. He had no way of telling where they had landed—or *when*. He heard cows though, mooing contently. If there were cows, placid, docile, milk-giving cows, they could survive.

He couldn't see if the on-board data was intact. Without a link, the systems would decay anyway, leaving fragments of information. There were four of the short, squat boxes on board, the ones the Skuld had used to run errands and make repairs. He didn't have any skill with technology, but he asked them to form a perimeter and patrol the four quadrants, and they seemed obliging enough. It was a military staple. Who knew what was lurking out there in the dark? The Bots would help the lifers when, if, they awoke—but he wasn't too worried about that. There were wearing Gap-suits after all, and naval types were a hardy bunch. They'd likely been spliced with some Jötunn DNA.

Gest didn't have the energy to start over, to stitch everything back together, despite Bohr's urging. He was tired beyond belief. There wasn't much use waiting around to exchange pleasantries. He felt around for the distress beacon, set it, and walked off into the night. He assumed it was night, anyway. He was cold and shivering, despite the burns.

He still had his harp. And his candle. The Norns were still watching.

Over the centuries, he'd travelled the length and breadth of the Nine Worlds looking for answers, looking for the gods to make sense of it all. At times, he'd considered the possibility he was divine. Was he Christ reborn, come to judge the world at its end? Was he to be adored as the visible expression of Ahura Mazda, the eternal light of righteousness? Was he, as the Brahman would have it, a divine and an omniscient flame? The living symbol of the triumph of light over darkness, knowledge over ignorance, good over evil, hope over despair? Perhaps he was Odin, just as Bohr said, detached from his wagon and searching for his sense of self. If he was a god, he'd find out soon enough.

Either that or he was a mistake. An ember escaped from the celestial fire, cascading through the ages, a mote of stardust. He hadn't achieved any victories, after all. He hadn't changed the world or saved his people from the twilight, when the worlds of man and gods had needed him most. He'd saved his own hide and left the rest as pestilential dust.

He'd sailed with the sons of Ragnar, though. That was something. He'd been candleman to the greatest warriors, their faithful squire, holding true and watching. Perhaps that was who he was: a witness, fated to record the full length of the twine, the ravelling and unravelling of existence. He had the nagging thought that Olaf had tricked him, over and over again. When the wolf gets old, he becomes a clown for the dogs.

The cows mooed in agreement, making him hungry and miserable. He traced the lines of countless scars, a tapestry of tales. He thought of the skalds. Empires dissolve and peoples disappear, but song passes not away. No music now, no audience for his songs, no warming fires in the Rus wilds.

But he could soon fix that. He felt all the duels and deaths, and found his body groaning for release. He reached for the battered old harp, and played one last time, two old senescent friends, reminiscing.

Then he took the hoary candle and rolled it in his palm. With a sigh, he touched it to his tinderbox.

"Let there be light."

ᚻᚢᛗᛗᛗᛁᛗᛋᚻᚢᛚᛏ

SOS SOS SOS AF YMIR YMIR YMIR TRUMBA V PSN 54.24.0 N, 3.26.0 W CODE SILVER ABANDONING SHIP AR K MESSAGE REPEATS

EXEGESIS IX

GOSFORTH, ENGLAND

2017

M
RS. JONES PULLED ALONGSIDE THE grass verge. She'd parked
too close to his car, as usual, but he wasn't about to complain.
He was expecting a whole bevy of scholars up from Cambridge
that afternoon, and she'd agreed to run down to Oxenholme and pick
them up in the minivan.

She waved at the churchwarden and walked up the path to Sunday Service.

"Hello, Olaf luv, how is old Granddad Michaels this morning?"
she trilled.

Michaels waved back, gritting his teeth. Reverend Riley clapped
a hand on his shoulder and peered at him over the top of his glasses.

"Why does she *do* that?" Riley asked sympathetically.

"What? Persist in calling me Olaf, luv? She is a bit right-of-centre
you know."

"Not much fun being named after the Eternal King of Norway?"

"If *your* predecessor had dedicated the old church to a normal saint
the same year I was born, I wouldn't have this problem. The Scouts

think it is a hoot too."

"I see your point. But no, I mean, why does she call you Grand-dad? You're not even forty."

"That's what Olaf means: grandfather. She looked it up on Wiki-pedia. You should see what she came up with for my surname."

The two men laughed, then looked back at the trio of crosses in their charge. The silence was amiable, each man content in the warm morning sun.

"I hope you haven't been staring at the blessed things all morn-ing," Riley said.

Michaels shook his head. "You know the village stocks used to be here. The last rascal to be put in them was punished because he climbed that cross."

Riley exhaled slowly. "It really is a miracle. The Bishop of Carlisle will be joining us, by the way."

"Wonderful," said Michaels. Then…

"God moves in a mysterious way
　　His wonders to perform;
He plants His footsteps in the sea
　　And rides upon the storm."

The vicar laughed. "I prefer Wordsworth. Talking of storms, more trouble in the papers, I see. Protests, marches."

"Well, if life is a brief moment in the light between the eternal void before birth and after death, I can understand why people get angry when theirs goes to shit," said the churchwarden.

Michaels was glad to see PASE was working again, but until the experts looked at the new columns, it wasn't much use in deciphering the legends entwined across the sandstone.

"Are you reading anything? I just finished Chandler's last novel,

Playback, if you want to borrow it for the drive to Oxenholme."

"No thanks. I have a whole new chapter here to work through. I think there are two stories on the new arrivals, one Christian, one Norse."

He looked at the new interlaced carvings on the nearest cross. Yggdrasil was there, her branches spiralling up the column, with the Allfather caged in her roots, ordering the universe once more at the Well of the Urd. At various points, the tree was inscribed with candles, giving the impression of a Victorian Christmas tree. On the east side, the candles stopped abruptly before a man with a large round shield. On the north side, draped in shade, the candles continued higher, all the way to the crown, great wolves chasing them for all fourteen feet. The last image was Heimdallr facing Loki at the end of all things—or perhaps it was an archangel dueling Satan. From this angle, they even looked like they were dancing. It was impossible to tell. The only certainty was the sun circle at the top had toppled off, as if predestined to be used as the rectory sundial.

"Ah, I'll admit, I was never comfortable with the duality. How can two histories sit side by side?" the vicar said, rubbing his beard thoughtfully.

"It's called entanglement, I think," Michael replied.

"Sounds complicated."

"You know the solution to the Gordian knot? I think if I had a problem that complicated, I'd just cut the rope too. You know the greatest irony?"

"What's that?"

"Ragnarok was all about renewal. It wasn't ever meant to be the end of all things, not like the Christian End Times. It was about passing the torch. Giving the younger soldiers a go. I mean, the sun sets each night but still rises the next day, doesn't it?"

"That's what the sun circle seems to say," the vicar said, breezily.

"What goes around comes around. I'm still irked at the new classification. I've basically had to admit to Mrs. Jones that we have three swastikas on church property."

"I wonder if we haven't got this interpretation wrong. History isn't a straight line. Christianity spread change quickly. You know what happens when you drop a pebble in the lake? Ripples go in all directions. It's not a Mexican wave, with every working in sequence. That reminds me, did I mention the Vikings had a wall too, just like Trump? They called it the Danevirke, the Bulwark of the Danes."

"Did it work?"

"Did it, hell. The Christians, when they came, just sailed round it. Before poor Thor knew it, his people were wearing bishop's mitres and cutting down his sacred trees. Wouldn't you be pissed off?"

"I know he still fills the skies with rage; he has hit the church steeple a few times over the years," Riley chuckled.

The vicar clasped the churchwarden on the back and led him inside for the service.